All Kinds of Beauty

by
Marianne Gage

Azalea Art Press
Sonoma | California

ISBN: 978-1-943471-44-7

Cover Design by
Swati Hathi

To my husband Ed

CONTENTS

PART II:
France | 1974-1989

PART III:
San Francisco | The Retrospective
Taos | 1989-1992

All kinds of beauty do not inspire love;
there is a kind which only pleases the sight,
but does not captivate the affections.

— *Miguel de Cervantes "Saavedra"*

PROLOGUE

THE RETROSPECTIVE
SAN FRANCISCO
1989

I'm Natalie Newbury. People call me 'Nat' for short, but I sign my paintings with my full name.

My ex-husband Ben has amazingly crisp good looks. He's gray-haired now, but when he was young he had a shock of slicked-back black hair and an appealing slant to his gray green eyes. When he came into a room, women turned around and gave him a second look, sometimes a third. I always thought it was amazing that he remained faithful to me all those years.

And as it turned out, he hadn't.

As we drove across the Oakland Bay Bridge on the night of my portrait retrospective, I tried not to let Ben know anything was wrong. I had considered going over alone, so he wouldn't be able to tell how upset I was, but I was afraid I might not be able to give my full attention to driving. Besides, the Jaguar Ben had accepted as part of his new job was so comfortable.

No, it was better to bluff it out.

When we'd driven all the way to the tollgate without my responding to any of his remarks about traffic or the weather, he asked if something was bothering me.

"No. Just nervous, I guess."

"Don't worry, darling. This is going to go swimmingly, like your shows always do."

All my best friends are beautiful—all these women whose portraits I've painted, whose stories I am going tell you. It's bizarre, but even though each woman was a prominent part of my life, some of them have never met each other. Most of us lost touch over the fifteen years that Ben and I lived abroad, but I still loved them all, and hoped to see them tonight. Each of them has wonderful features, lovely skin or hair or eyes or bodies, and several have all of the above.

The whole *megillah,* as Nikki Falkenstein Lippman Williams used to say.

Before you jump to any conclusions, let me state that I've never made love to a woman, or wanted to, finding my attraction to the male sex absolutely and enduringly strong. But I like to have good-looking women friends. Maybe it's because I'm an artist. Or maybe it's the other way around. Maybe my admiration for their beauty comes from my love for them.

There are seven women I am going to tell you about: Fia, Hana, Amanda, Rosie, Ranie, Nikki, and Esther. What delicious and painful difficulties they got themselves into! Not Esther, but she's a special case—older than the others. Six of the women had been going through difficult personal situations when I painted them. And yes, it has occurred to me that perhaps they had so many problems *because* they were beautiful.

As for my own looks, I was a beauty queen at the University of New Mexico a million years ago, and I'm still slim and dark-haired, with odd-colored eyes. Ben calls them my 'topaz jewels'. For years I was less interested in my own appearance than I was in my painting. Not that I didn't love gorgeous clothes, didn't strive to look stylish, but the presentation of my subjects on canvas was more important than the way I revealed myself to the world.

In Provence, with Juan, that all changed.

I had intense relationships with these seven women, the kind where you know all about each other, no holds barred. Maybe I loved them *through* their portraits, through the pictures I painted to enshrine them forever. Or did I love them because I, Natalie Newbury, had painted them? Maybe my life has been one long ego trip, to see what loveliness I can find, what splendor and elegance I can discover and transfer to canvas, thus to the world. Maybe I painted only to garner attention for myself.

The question the artist must keep asking herself is *Why do I want to create? Do I paint for the joy of it, or so that others may enjoy my work? Is it for glory, or for money?*

Juan painted because he had that immense measure of talent coursing through him, bursting out in astounding works of art. I remember the day he swore to me that he didn't want adulation and fame. But then when it began to come his way, he didn't renounce it.

Looking back on my life with Ben, I can see a lot of things I did wrong: actions I didn't take, marital duties I didn't perform, plans he wanted to make which I cast aside. All of this may have contributed to his feelings of coming second to my art. But did he have to betray me in such a vile, despicable way? Why couldn't we have talked about our problems? Maybe I would have been able to change.

Ben was a stockbroker. Maybe I should have dropped my career and helped him more with his. Scouted around for clients, pushed my friends to invest through his firm, all that sort of thing.

Maybe I wanted too much to be a good painter, a respected artist. Was my ambition too strong?

Or perhaps it came down to Ben's weaknesses, the enticements he was offered.

I remember that he was always interested in my friends. I needed him to be supportive of my career, but there were times when his interest went too far. I think his feelings were mixed. On the one hand, he would complain about my being too involved in their troubles.

"Nat, when are you going to learn that you can't help these gals with their messed-up marriages?"

Other times he'd say, "Maybe we should help Hana when she moves," or, "We'd better see if Ranie needs anything."

Meeting Ben was the most remarkable thing that ever happened to me. I was raised far away from him, in New Mexico, so it's amazing that we ever met at all.

I lost my parents when I was three. They were coming back from a party late at night, and a truck pulled out from a side road and smashed into their car. They were killed instantly. The only memories

I have are the feel of my father's scratchy cheek and the soft, shadowy image of my mother's face.

There was no question about who would raise me. Aunt Muriel was my father's favorite sister, and my mother was an only child from the East. Grandmother Evans was involved, but I never lived with her, only Mamaw, my pet name for Aunt Muriel.

Mamaw lives in Española, a few miles from Taos, New Mexico. Albuquerque had become too much like a city for her liking, and when she was offered the position of assistant librarian in a smaller town, she jumped at the chance. Not only is she now the town librarian, she's president of the local Robert Browning Poetry Club. They meet once a month at her home, where she serves petit fours and tea laced with sherry.

Early on I had this aptitude for drawing, and all through the years of growing up, I drew and painted. When I was eighteen, I won an art scholarship to the University of New Mexico in Albuquerque. They had an excellent art department, and I spent four years there. When Mamaw offered me a year of graduate study at the school of my choice (Grandmother Evans had died the year before and left a small estate), I applied to the UCLA graduate art department.

I met Ben when I went with a group of college friends to Lake Arrowhead for a winter vacation. Most of them skied, but I didn't—lucky for me! One late afternoon in the lodge, I was reading by the fire when a handsome young man in ski clothes, sunburned and fresh from the slopes, walked over and asked what I was reading. It turned out he was at UCLA too, getting his master's degree in business. Soon after he finished, we married and moved to the San Francisco Bay Area.

Ben's father had died of pneumonia at the young age of fifty-seven; his mother lived in Philadelphia. But Ben didn't like his mother much, and we seldom saw her. He thought she was a selfish, materialistic woman who had driven his father to an early death. After our wedding, which she attended, I tried to unite them several times, and would write her often and send birthday and Christmas gifts. She would write back, lovely, thoughtful notes, which I read aloud to Ben. I always tried to talk up her good qualities: her wonderful taste, her business smarts. Agatha Newbury had succeeded in the stock market even before Ben went into the business. But he always resisted my efforts.

I lost an ovary and suffered damage to my Fallopian tubes from a bike accident when I was thirteen, and this made my chances of motherhood extremely slim. Five years into our marriage, we learned that I had only a fifteen percent chance of conceiving, so we gave up hopes for a family and settled into a happy marriage and our challenging careers.

When Ben and I walked into the gallery, my main aim was to stay in control of my emotions. This show was something I had worked toward for a long time, and nothing, not even Ben's infidelity, was going to ruin it for me.

I felt the piece of paper in the pocket of my silk trousers, worrying it with my fingers, refusing to think about the hateful thing—not on this climactic night of my life, the night of the exhibit that put a shining cap on my career as a portrait artist.

When Oliver Rakestraw, owner of Rakestraw's Gallery in San Francisco, wrote to me in France asking about giving me a retrospective, I accepted immediately. We exchanged a few letters, resolving that we should include only the best of my adult oil and acrylic portraits.

When we'd returned from Europe, I had to decide which portraits to show. Oliver said there was room for around fifty. I knew the ones that were my favorites, the portraits of my seven beautiful friends; besides those, we would hang the boardroom portraits which had been my bread-and-butter, executives in the formal poses of corporate chairmen. I would include paintings commissioned by their adoring wives, too. These private poses of the business leaders were of course more relaxed and casual.

It hadn't been difficult finding fifty pictures; the difficulty was in keeping the number down. I decided not to include my children's portraits; there would be too many—three hundred or more paintings and drawings; the collection would become too unmanageable. Besides, Oliver said, it would make for a stronger, more cohesive show if we limited the works to adult pictures.

Happily, the curator of the gallery at St. Adolphus College in the East Bay said she would give an exhibition of my children's portraits later on in December.

At last I would receive all the tribute I could want for my long decades of work. And since I had decided in France to drop portraiture and concentrate on landscapes and non-objective work, having the two retrospectives would be a graceful way to bow out.

We scheduled the opening for five o'clock, May 17, 1989, at 555 Sutter Street, San Francisco.

The most momentous day of my career.

We arrived early. Ben looked handsome as usual, wearing his navy blue blazer, striped shirt and gray pants.

And the jade green Italian silk scarf.

I hated that scarf.

When we were dressing he had asked me to find the scarf, said he hadn't seen it for ages. I had given it to him years ago, and he wanted to wear it to the show. I pulled out all the drawers of our bureau and did a search, rifling through his underwear, sweaters and assorted items of clothing. The renters had used the bureau while we'd been in Europe, but it again held Ben's things.

I pulled out his tie drawer as far as I could without dumping everything on the floor. No sign of the thing.

Finally! There it was, caught behind the drawer, along with a piece of crumpled paper. I pulled out the scarf, careful not to snag the silk on raw wood.

Curious about the typed note, I smoothed it out and read it.

Ben dearest,

 Where were you last night? I waited an hour, but had to get back. I'll be there next week, though, same time, same place. Can't get enough of you, darling, as I think I've demonstrated. But I won't call you, since you have warned me so many times not to!

 When you said my portrait isn't as beautiful as I am, did you mean it? My darling! But I'm feeling so guilty. Nat and I are close, and I do love her.

 But I love you even more.

—Until next time

It was unsigned.

Ben was in the bathroom, shaving. As I sank down on the side of the bed, I heard the buzz of the electric razor. My blood rushing hot and cold, I stared into space for several minutes.

I realized I had to try to calm down, because this was my big night.

I went to the laundry room and ironed the scarf, then dressed in the outfit I had bought in Provence. I was no longer young, but I wanted to look like a successful artist; I didn't intend to stint on colorful clothes and makeup. My top was a turquoise paisley design with long, loose sleeves, and with it I wore wide-legged, flowing pants. I started making up my face. I wasn't as thin as I had been in Europe after the trauma of my affair with Juan; I had gained back a few pounds. Juan liked my hair short, but now it fell halfway to my shoulders.

Lastly, I wrapped a silk tie-dye scarf around my head. Amazingly, tie-dye was back; in the '60s, we had all worn some version of it. I gave myself a final look in the full-length mirror.

There was nothing more I could do.

Ben hadn't seen the show yet, so as soon as we got to the gallery, he left me and started walking around. Everything was hanging in the big white-walled front gallery with large windows opening onto Sutter, plus a smaller side gallery. I walked to the back showroom, where Oliver and his assistant Jake were busy rearranging the canvases we'd decided not to hang.

Jake was the latest in a long list of Oliver's effete African-American gallery staffers. He was wearing black leather pants and a black ruffled shirt, unbuttoned to the waist. Oliver wore a gray three-piece suit, and looked nervous. I went up to him and nuzzled his cheek, rubbing against him, which he hated. "Darling," I said, "you're wonderful to do this for me. Everything looks luscious!"

"Stop it," he growled. "You know I can't stand overly-demonstrative women."

"But he likes overly-demonstrative *guys* a lot," simpered Jake.

My portraits and landscapes had helped keep Oliver in business for a long time. I was a fairly conservative artist, although 'conservative' or 'traditional' was a better description of my portraits than of my landscapes. Many of the non-objective and abstract-expressionist painters Jake's gallery had handled over the last thirty years had come and gone. Some moved to New York, some stopped painting, or died, and some changed styles so many times their followers couldn't or wouldn't stay with them. From Oliver's stable of artists from the '60s, only Austin Everhardt and I were left. Austin did seascapes and landscapes in oil. With the agility of Poussin or Lorrain and the sensitivity of Corot, he can paint all of it: water, sea foam, rocks, and skies. His paintings sell in the six figures and he lives in Carmel, but has never exhibited there. He says it's too commercial, too tourist-oriented. Austin has been loyal to Oliver for years, as I have, and it has paid off for all three of us. I was sure Austin wouldn't come tonight. We were both jaded from attending openings for one another through the years.

While gathering the paintings, Oliver and I had inquired if my subjects minded that their faces become public. In every case, the women said that if it would help my career, they would be happy to lend the painting.

I floated around admiring my work, while Ben, Oliver, and Jake stood by the drinks table, chatting up the Swedish catering couple. My corporate paintings looked awfully stuffy to me, but I liked the paintings I'd done of the men in casual poses. In these, the men were wearing sport shirts, hunting or fishing jackets, or long-sleeved shirts without ties.

I had done Abner Rankin III in a crimson corduroy shirt, and the painting glowed, and I had painted two versions of Percy Healy, one for his Board of Directors, and one for his wife Irene. The two pictures were hanging side by side, and I thought I had done a good job of contrasting the dynamic, sexy Percy in his two worlds.

But the paintings that dazzled the room were of my seven women friends.

Damn, I thought, standing back at a distance. *Damn, they're good!*

I crossed to the long main wall, where several pictures I barely remembered were hanging. In the center was my portrait of Hana Kelly, a three-quarter-length torso. Hana was standing, tanned and relaxed in her tennis whites, racket held at her side. Her sorrel-brown hair and bangs framed her face like a warrior's helmet. I had always thought of Hana as a female warrior, probably because she and Bruce had fought so much.

What she didn't do to please that guy!

As I stood there, I felt my neck and face flush, and the palms of my hands grow damp. Now I was much more understanding of Hana's old situation with Bruce—it wasn't all that different from Juan and me. I shrugged off all thoughts of my Spanish lover. It was over, a chapter in my life that was closed forever . . . gradually my breathing slowed.

Can't think about Juan. Can't think about Ben and whoever it was, or is.

Next, I came to the portrait of my buddy Fia.

Fia Rossner. A valued client at the gallery, she had delivered her portrait directly to Rakestraw's. It had been on Fia's recommendation years ago that I was invited to show here, and it had been twenty-three years since I'd painted her, ten since we'd seen one another in France.

When Ben had driven out to Los Ranchos to pick up Hana's portrait, Hana related the tragic news about Fia's son Eric; he had died of AIDS. Now Fia stared straight out at me, and straight out at the world. "How do you like me?" she seemed to say. "Don't you think I'm really something?" I was sure she was coming tonight, and I wondered if she would still have the same raven hair and radiant smile. Would she still give off that insouciant air of unlimited confidence? Fia's magnificence had never been a burden; she carried it with flamboyance and flair.

I had done her from the waist up, wearing a black-and-white-striped taffeta Balenciaga ball gown. When I first knew her she was always going to balls, charity events, and openings, and for a while she roped Ben and me into going to them too. It was the most 'social' period of our lives. But I quickly learned that I didn't want to spend my time that way; besides, we couldn't afford it. I'm really not that interested in Society. Except for an occasional small gathering of convivial friends, I'm happiest either painting, reading, or going to movies or the theater.

Ben is more social than I. He belongs to The Trees, a men's society with a clubhouse in San Francisco and a summer encampment, The Trees, on the Russian River. Although women are invited occasionally to the downtown clubhouse and to picnics at The Trees, those of my gender are barred from participating.

Across the room, the portrait of Ranie Sloan compelled me to come closer.

Ranie, another of my beloved friends, had been one of the fixtures of the Bay Area's cultured African-American scene of the '70s. I hadn't read much about her career lately, but I hadn't been around to read about it. In order to locate her—and the portrait—I had called her mother in Oakland. She said Ranie was living in Los Angeles, and that the painting was at her home there.

(I remembered that when she stored the portrait with her mom, she was going East to marry that loathsome Jock Hollenbeck.) Mrs. Sloan said I should talk with Ranie's son Jason, who was living with his grandmother and attending college. He wasn't home, but his grandmother said she would have him call me. Later Jason called and said he was driving down to Los Angeles the following weekend and would personally deliver the portrait to the gallery when he returned.

"Thank you, thank you! Treat it carefully, Jason," I said, "it's one of my best. Have you got a big enough car?"

"Oh yeah, Grandma lets me drive her van." He sounded like a confident, friendly young man.

I sent an announcement to Ranie at the Los Angeles address Jason gave me, but I hadn't heard back. I stepped forward to peer at her image. Surely Ranie would no longer be this breathtaking!

I had painted her full-length. A long dark braid hung over her shoulder covering one breast; her other breast was bare. She was wrapped in a *longyi*, a half-sarong in shades of cinnabar, rose madder and ocher. Just below her navel, her long fingers were holding a large white conch shell. They were the best hands I'd ever done, other than Esther's, and they commanded the viewer's attention almost as much as her round, sepia-nippled breast. Her feet were bare also, only a few elegant toes showing beneath the skirt. The head was turned entirely in profile, the chin slightly lifted, and there was the almost imperceptible play of a smile on her mouth.

I was happy that I'd been able to get hold of this portrait again. It was the jewel of them all.

Next, I walked over to Amanda's portrait.

If someone were to describe this picture, they might say that it was elegant and patrician. I had painted her in a three-quarters view wearing olive-green velvet; her creamy neck and shoulders were set off by the somber sheen of the dress. A mass of red hair was piled high on top of her head, and her eyes, green as bottle glass, gazed away from the viewer. You could sense the shy girl behind the startlingly attractive woman. Amanda had never played up her looks, and I had attempted to show that quality of modest, shy beauty. Her eyelids were slightly lowered, her lips parted. I thought the portrait embodied the quality some women have, of owning and at the same time disavowing their own beauty. Even though I had painted her soon after the Jackie Kennedy era, I had used an Elizabethan embellishment; beneath the milky décolletage I had painstakingly limned an edging of even whiter point d'Angleterre lace.

Poor Amanda! Her first husband had been a rotter who ignored her and made little attempt to help raise their six children. After her divorce she had several affairs; I'd once even suspected Ben of sleeping with her. But Amanda wasn't Ben's type; she wasn't bright enough to interest him. He said as much when I questioned him about a bit of gossip I'd heard.

Getting ready for this show, when I called her daughter Ashley in Mill Valley and said I wanted to borrow the portrait, she told me her mother was living in Yuba City.

"Yuba City!" I exclaimed. "What's she doing up there?"

Ashley said her mom was married to a roofer, and that was where his work was.

A roofer? Not that there's anything wrong with it.

"What happened to her second husband?" This was a man Ben and I had met at a party in Pebble Beach, a wealthy, successful older man. In the late '60s she'd moved East with him, along with three of her younger children.

"Oh, Mom divorced him. She'll tell you all about it." Her tone was matter-of-fact. Ashley had always been Amanda's stable, reliable child.

"I hope she'll come to my opening."

"Oh, I'm sure she will! Can I come too, and bring a friend? I know Mom'll lend you the painting. She was always so fond of you, Mrs. Newbury. I'm going up there this weekend, and I can bring it back."

Backing away from Amanda's image and circling the gallery, I looked at my watch. Ten minutes to five.

I moved on to my last three favorites—Nikki, Rosie, and Esther.

I stopped in front of Nikki's portrait. Delightful, flirtatious, wanton Nikki gazed out of the picture, her face in three-fourths view, posed to show off her aquiline nose and pointed chin. Her dark, crinkly hair floated in a billowing mass around her head; she was wearing a white sweater, which made her hair look even darker.

Here was the ultimate femme fatale. This portrait established Nikkis's title as Sexpot of the Ages. Not that Rosie and Ranie weren't seductive charmers also, but I was pretty sure Rosie's serial affairs had been caused by poor judgment and rotten luck, not by any sexual aggressiveness on her part. Ditto for Ranie. Simply stated, Nikki Lippmann found a man everywhere she looked, or they found her— at parties, the dry-cleaner's, the dentist's, riding academies, courtrooms, law offices, accountant's offices, funerals . . .

Getting in touch with Nikki hadn't been easy. I had called her old number in Southern California, and was told the number was no longer in service. Then I called her sister Ethel in San Francisco, and she said Nikki was divorced and remarried again. Ethel, the opposite of her sister in every way, and an executive in one of their father Abe's many businesses, had never married.

"*Oy—that Nikki!*" she whined. "What a sister I've got!"

"Ain't it the truth," I said. "I met Paul once when I was visiting down there."

"Who's Paul? *Feh!* Never mind."

She gave me Nikki's phone number and address in Palm Springs, but when I called she was never home. I left my number on the machine, but she didn't call back, so I finally wrote her and said I wanted the painting for my show, the gallery would pay for shipping, and would she mind lending it? I said I would give anything if she'd fly up for the big event. I practically begged her to come.

A few days later she called and said they'd been away, but that she was shipping the portrait the next day. She sounded the same as ever, keyed-up, breathless. Her boys were grown and gone from home, she said, both of them working in Los Angeles for Harry Williams, her fourth husband.

"Is that the man I met, the one who took us to the museum party?"

"Yes, but I'm married to a plastic surgeon now, Joel Moorstein."

"Fabulous!" I exclaimed. "I'm sure you haven't aged at all."

She laughed her brittle laugh and said she missed me, and didn't we get up to some mischief, though, in the old days?

"What's this *we* stuff, Kemosabe?"

She asked if Ben and I were still married, and after pausing a moment I said, "Of course."

There was an even longer pause on her end. Nikki couldn't believe any couple could stay together as long as Ben and I have, and I wondered what that meant. She said she'd love to come up for the show, but they'd planned a trip to the Bahamas in May.

"Well, try! It would be wonderful to see you, Nik. I'll send you a mailer."

Now, I touched my fingers to my lips in a small gesture of homage to her, and walked across the room.

Rosie Rinaldi's portrait was the most vibrant of all. Except for the flesh tones and the white of the blouse, it was done entirely in primary colors. A many-hued cloisonné vase containing red calla lilies and blue hydrangeas drew attention to her olive skin and dark hair, and the patterned wallpaper background, derived from Peruvian embroideries, contributed to the glow. Rosie's father was Italian, her mother Mexican, and Rosie had her mother's brown eyes and dark olive skin, and her father's thin, wiry build. I had met Maria and Paolo years ago at their vineyard in St. Helena.

I'd called the Rinaldis to find out about borrowing the painting, having been unable to reach Rosie at her old number in Berkeley. Her mother said she would tell her to call me.

"How are you, Maria?" I asked. "And how is Paolo?"

"Fine. We are getting old, Natalie, but we are fine." Her voice was thin and shrill.

When Rosie finally got in touch, she said she was living in Petaluma. I couldn't contain my shock. I'd heard about the exodus of Bay Area folks to the small northern California towns, but it had been only a couple of years since Rosie visited us in Provence, and she hadn't mentioned that she might move.

"How do you like living in the country?" I asked.

"I love it—it's so different from Berkeley with all its problems."

"Are you still working?"

"Yes, I have my counseling practice, and I travel around and lead seminars."

She said of course I could borrow the portrait; she was sure her parents would be happy to lend it, and to call and tell her mother where it should be sent. There was something about her voice, something different from the old days when we'd been so close. When she'd been in Provence, then too I had noticed a lessening of her former warmth. I tried to tell myself that I shouldn't expect my friends to retain the same fondness for me that I held for them. I still loved them all, but I had been gone for many years.

When I asked, she said she wouldn't be able to come to my opening, since she was scheduled to conduct a seminar on whole body healing at a Sioux reservation in Montana.

Oliver's assistant Jake drove to St. Helena to get the painting, and was of course treated to a five-course luncheon prepared by Maria. Her mother didn't talk about Rosie, he said. I found that amazing. Rosie had always been the center of Maria's life!

I looked at my watch. *Five more minutes.* Five minutes until my career would be subjected to the judgments of San Francisco's elite society, plus all my other friends.

But wait—*what if nobody came?*

I stood in front of Esther's picture for a moment. I had attempted to show the beauty of a woman in late middle age. The canvas was unique among all my portraits—an older woman done in somber tones, with a body that wasn't graceful, or even slim.

I hoped Esther would come tonight, but I doubted she would. She had sounded fragile when I called her in Sutter Creek, her voice trembling and weak, but when I said who I was, she brightened. I told her about the show, and she was excited for me. She said she had a friend who worked at the post office; she would have him wrap and ship the painting.

"Oh Nat, how I've missed you. So many years. Imagine—a retrospective at your young age!"

I realized that if Esther came to my show, I would see an old woman in her eighties.

I had made a circle of the gallery, and as I neared the entrance, I found my self-portrait hanging with my printed biography. I had done my own portrait in France after Juan's and my breakup. It was when Ben was in Paris, and I was alone. Despite my depression, I needed to paint, and one morning when I glimpsed myself in the mirror, I saw a slim, middle-aged woman with some vestiges of beauty left.

Oliver said it was a remarkable portrait. I had captured a wry, solemn expression, the look of a woman who has experienced much of what life can give. The body was slim; the breasts, barely visible through the thin white blouse, were drooping; the hair graying. A gauze sleeve fell back on the arm holding the paintbrush, and the arm was tanned and sinewy, far from youthful.

I had used a contrivance I'd never used before in my portraits. By using two mirrors, I had painted my likeness endlessly. It receded in multiple images, each one reflecting off the last, becoming younger and younger as the figures receded through time. The portrait in the foreground, present-day Natalie, was not flattering, but it was real—the representation of a woman who saw herself truthfully.

Excited voices brought me out of my musings. I pulled myself away, and as I walked a few paces to the front door, I wondered if my old friends had changed. Fifteen years had changed me, so why shouldn't I find them altered too, influenced by time's alternating currents of pleasure and pain, joy and grief?

At the door I glimpsed one of my beloved beauties. *Good!* If she had come, then maybe the others would come too. I realized that I was terribly keyed up. My hands were shaking.

Part One

CALIFORNIA
1960 – 1970

CHAPTER ONE

FIA

Becoming a full-fledged professional artist wasn't easy for me. With rare exceptions, I don't think it's easy for anyone. Inexperience and gullibility play a big part in early failures, and many times I thought of giving up.

Early on—this was in the '60s—I would try to enter shows.

All sorts of stumbling blocks impeded my way. Maybe my frame would come apart on the way to the submissions panel, or I would be accepted, then show up at the opening and find my painting hadn't been hung. I had all the problems transporting paintings that everyone else had, but in the beginning I never painted big, not like my friend Inga, who strapped her 40" x 40" abstract to the top of her Volkswagen bus and started across the bridge to an exhibit—only to have a high wind carry it off into the deep blue bay.

Then there are the unappreciative clients. When I first started to do portraits, the new owner of a house down the street called one day. "I found your phone number on the back of this little girl's portrait. The people who sold the house to us left it in a closet in the basement. Would you like to have it back?"

My friend Sandy Sorenson found one of her paintings hanging over the fireplace at a friend's home, when she knew for a fact she'd sold it to a businessman in San Francisco.

"How did you get this?" she asked.

"Oh, I meant to tell you, that guy Mueller went bankrupt, and I was doing some temp work at his old office and found your painting on the floor of the utility closet. Doesn't it look great hanging there?"

As for agents, finding someone both industrious and ethical to represent you isn't easy. A male artist friend once had a rep who left town with twenty-four paintings and no forwarding address. And years ago, I had a chance meeting with a friend who told me she'd seen three of my landscapes hanging at a local hospital. I hadn't even known they'd sold, and I went to find them, framed and hanging in this most public of places. I called the man representing me, a reputable agent, or so everyone thought, and waited for my check, which finally came. Then I dropped him.

It was only through Fia's knowing Oliver Rakestraw that I finally got ahead of the game.

I've had art stolen, too, ripped off the gallery wall and carried away when nobody was looking. A Berkeley Magical Realist had one of her paintings filched, and later it was found abandoned on the sidewalk a few blocks away. Now *that's* insulting! I've had portraits commissioned and never hung because they weren't flattering enough; in other instances, I've taken the subject's photograph, done the sketches, then had the commission cancelled, no cash exchanging hands. I can't begin to tell you the money I've spent on slides, and the piles of those same slides returned unopened or never returned at all. Letters to galleries go unacknowledged, even with stamped postcards enclosed.

Being a professional artist isn't easy. The only worse careers I can think of are writing poetry or herding sheep.

In 1965, the year I met Fia Rossner, I was thirty and Ben was thirty-two.

I met Fia, Hana, and Amanda within the space of a couple of years. They were my first adult women portraits, the first three of my "beautiful ladies," and each was unique in the way she handled her beauty. Fia welcomed hers and used it to its fullest advantage. Hana was aware of the effect she had on people, but nevertheless was completely natural and unspoiled. Amanda, when I first knew her, seemed actually to want to try to hide her loveliness.

Ben had become involved in fund raising for the Symphony Guild, and one August we went to a benefit at Fia and Arnie Macintosh's Victorian home on Alamo Square in San Francisco. It was a black-tie affair where everyone was young and affluent. I suppose some of our friends think Ben and I are wealthy, but we aren't. You never think of yourself as rich, because there are all these other people around who truly are. When we first started out, my portrait money was extra income that we very much needed.

Ten minutes after we arrived, I tried to blend in by gulping down a highball, smoking a cigarette, and eating a shrimp canapé all at the same time. I managed to spill mayonnaise all over myself. Fia saw it happen. "Come with me, darling; we'll swab you down," she said, flashing her dimples and laughing her chiming laugh. I followed her into the kitchen, where two maids in black-and-white uniforms were shoving trays into the oven.

"You're from the East," I said, noticing the broad a's in her speech. I immediately regretted saying it—how provincial of me! As if I didn't still have my New Mexico twang.

Fia deftly blotted my outfit with club soda. I had just bought it, a black velvet trouser suit and white satin shirt with a black string tie. By the time she was finished, no spots showed, and I wasn't even very damp.

"Yes," she said, "but I've been here for years. Someday I'll learn to speak Californian. You're that attractive Ben's wife, aren't you? Arnie likes him so much."

"Yes."

"You live in the East Bay?"

"The Berkeley hills. I do portraits." I didn't tell her my studio was a small anteroom off the kitchen, and that mostly I drew the neighborhood kids.

"Oh really? I've been wanting to be painted! Will you do me?"

My mouth dropped open, but I recovered quickly. "Of course. I'll send you some pictures, and you can—uh—see what sort of uh— pose you'd like." I had almost blurted out, "You can see if you like

3

my work," but that would have shown a lily-livereed lack of confidence.

There was always something about those parties.

Was it the gin? The scotch? Or the good-looking men and women, and the excitement of going across the bridge to a stylish party? I don't know what triggered it, but Ben and I always made love afterwards. Sometimes we started in the car driving home, or sometimes we slept, then awoke, aroused and responsive to one another.

The night of Fia's party I awakened to find Ben standing over me, nude.

"Come on, darling, let's go outside," he said.

Our patio in back was concealed, with a tall fence and lots of trees. I went with him, throwing off my nightgown as we walked. The night was warm, and the full moon shone down on our bodies as we moved together on the redwood chaise.

His lovemaking was slow, drawn-out, mindful of my response. Afterward we slept for a few minutes, then, rousing ourselves, walked back to the bedroom over damp grass.

Soon after Fia's party, Marian Morse, the wife of one of Ben's business associates, drove me over the Golden Gate Bridge to lunch in Sausalito. As she drove, she filled me in on Fia. "This is Fia's second marriage. Arnie Macintosh is an insurance salesman, but she's kept up her lifestyle with family money and her divorce settlement from Howard."

"Howard who?"

"Her first husband. Howard Shafer."

"Who's Howard Shafer?" I could tell from Marian's pursed mouth that I should know.

"Just a descendant of one of California's railroad barons, that's all! Haven't you heard of the Shafers? Fia's parents were old money on the East Coast. She went to Radcliffe, Howard went to Harvard, and they married after college and lived in San Francisco in a big mansion on Pacific Heights. I thought I saw you there once."

I shook my head.

"Well," she went on, "they had two children, but it all went sour. Howard got more interested in sailing than he was in Fia, and started asking his insurance agent Arnie to escort her to opera and symphony openings. Big mistake! Arnie and Fia divorced their spouses and got married, and she bought that great Victorian they live in. Fia was dropped from the Social Register, but she doesn't give a fig."

Marian said Fia was always the star in local charity fashion shows.

"The two of them have quite a few kids to support. She had two from her first marriage, Arnie had two from his first, and they have two daughters together. But with Shafer money she can afford to put the children in private schools and keep a full-time housekeeper. Not too shabby."

Marian drove up the covered ramp at the Alta Mira, and an attendant took her car. It was a glorious day, and the head waiter seated us outside on the deck, where we could see all of Belvedere, the bay, and San Francisco. There before us were both bridges, the Bay Bridge and the Golden Gate, plus Angel Island and Alcatraz. Tiny white triangles of sailboats—there must have been several hundred—dipped and skimmed about the water, accompanying the long white shapes of commercial tour boats.

I had a Crab Louis and Marian had a Caesar, and we ordered hot popovers, specialties of the house. The popovers and the view were the reasons we kept coming back. And the margaritas.

It was over the second one that Marian said, "Incidentally, those two first kids of Fia's—Shafer's kids? I think Cissy's okay, but Eric's been a problem since he was twelve. I hear he's addicted to the hard stuff. But don't tell anyone I told you."

5

A few weeks after I met her, Fia commissioned her portrait. "I haven't a thing exciting to do this summer, and the men will be at The Trees. Hope you're not too busy to start right away!"

And so it began. Not only was Fia beautiful, she was cooperative, always on time for sessions, with her hair done exactly the same as the last time. When you're working together, it's a boon when the other is in an upbeat mood, and Fia always was. She never complained about the tiny room I painted in, never objected to having to remain absolutely still for extended periods of time, nor did she grumble about the reek of oil paints and painting medium, my special blend of linseed oil, Damar varnish, and turpentine.

Ben said, "This could be the start of something big for you, Nat. Fia Rossner has connections everywhere!"

Fia and Ben are quite a bit alike. Sometimes I thought they would have been a great couple, though perhaps they're too much the same. Both good-looking in the extreme, both socially ambitious. Ben didn't have Fia's gregarious personality, but he enjoyed the company of the beau monde. Once he said to me, "Why don't you join any of the groups Fia belongs to? You could get more portrait commissions that way."

I answered airily, "If I did, I wouldn't have any time to paint."

He never mentioned the subject again.

I only needed ten sittings with Fia. (She left the dress, and I put it on a dressmaker's dummy and worked on it when she wasn't there.)

The painterly, cool gray background I used was a perfect foil for her warm skin tones. I left a lot of paint strokes showing, and used a large brush to blend a light pearl color into a field of darker ash-violet, giving an effect of indoor clouds. Oil is a wonderful medium for this. The dress was off-shoulder, with enormous puffed sleeves. I simulated the gleam of the taffeta with highlights in pale dove-grays and whites, trying to imitate my idol, John Singer Sargent, who was a master of the spear-like brushstroke and the bravura style in portrait painting. He was the artist who said, "A portrait is a painting of someone with a little something wrong about the mouth."

Not a thing was wrong with Fia's half-smiling mouth in my portrait, nor with her merry, slate blue eyes or bouffant-styled hair. I emphasized her bold, self-assured expression, and I thought the big stripes of the fabric expressed the unmistakable flamboyance of her personality. Her hands, folded demurely in her lap, were the only staid and sedate element.

This portrait marked an earthshaking step forward for me. In trying to imitate Sargent, I moved closer to real expertise and to my own brand of showmanship.

Fia was a connector; always enthusiastically promoting her friends to one another. Whether it was someone who needed a car, a place to live, a lawyer, a dishwasher repairman, or a new beau, Fia had someone to fill your needs. It was after painting Fia that I began to get commissions from San Francisco society, and I always knew that my success as a portrait painter was due not just to my talent, but to Fia's generous spirit and far-flung connections.

She never talked about herself. I made an effort to draw her out, to get her to stop talking about parties and social events and charity benefits, because I wanted to know *her*. Gradually, as I shared my background and inner hopes and dreams, mostly about succeeding as an artist, she began to reveal her own history. One day toward the end of the sittings, as she started to change back into her everyday clothes, she finally began to open up. I don't know why she chose that day, but probably it was because I had mentioned losing my parents at such a young age.

"Believe it or not, Nat, my parents put me in a boarding school at the age of six. They wanted to travel during my growing-up years, and they did, all over the world! I would make marvelous scrapbooks from the letters and clippings and picture postcards they sent me, left completely alone over the holidays. Oh, now I remember I wasn't totally alone. Once or twice; there was a pitiful little girl from Seattle, fingernails chewed to the quick. Oh God, the memories!

"That's why family is so important to me. My children have gone to day school, I've never sent them away. They're home with me every night and every weekend. I fought for full custody when Howard and I divorced. It wasn't much of a fight; he didn't want them. And the kids always knew it, too." Her eyes filled with tears.

That was the only time in all the years I've known her that Fia showed real emotion. She grabbed a tissue and dabbed at her cheeks. "A few years ago, do you know what Howard did, after ignoring our children for years? He married a young Swiss woman he met on an airplane, and started a new family! Besides the marriage and three young children he has now, his life is taken up with his sailing. He's always commissioning bigger and bigger sailboats, hiring larger crews, sailing off to Tahiti and Bora Bora free as a bird—isn't it wonderful!" She laughed, an uncharacteristically bitter laugh.

"Does Arnie get along with your older kids?" I asked.

"Arnie is a good stepfather, but he works long hours. He isn't always there when I need him."

We saw the Rossners at more parties, and as the decade wore on, I noticed Arnie was having a hard time controlling his drinking. His words would slur, and he would occasionally lurch about, unsteady on his feet. But he was never a mean drunk.

I had no reason to believe what Marian Morse had told me, that Fia's son Eric was involved in drugs, but I eventually learned it was true. I had a glimpse of him once, when I drove to San Francisco to get the key to their Stinson Beach house. Fia had offered it to us for the Labor Day weekend. A longhaired boy in dirty, frayed blue jeans came to the door first, then Fia appeared.

"Nat—come in! Do you know my son Eric?"

I smiled, and said, "Hi."

"Hel-lo," said Eric, his lids at half-mast. He muttered a question of Fia, something about money, and she frowned and shook her head. He turned on his heel and walked away.

"That's just like you! Tell me one thing one minute and fuck me the next!"

I quickly took the key, gave Fia a hug, and left.

As I drove back onto the Bay Bridge to go home, the sky was dark and looming. Slate clouds drifting rapidly across the sky were lined with flashes of silver. It looked as if our weekend at Stinson Beach would be rainy and cold, but Ben and I loved the beach in any kind of weather.

CHAPTER TWO

HANA

Unlike Fia, Hana Kelly wasn't 'society'. Fia met her because Hana was married to one of the young lawyers in the same firm that arranged for Fia's split from Howard Shafer. They'd run into each other one day when Hana had come over to the city—everyone calls San Francisco the city— and for some reason had dropped in to see Bruce. Fia was leaving after an appointment, and since she was the effervescent, friendly woman she was, struck up an acquaintance with the German girl.

Fia told me later that Bruce Kelly was a divine Irishman, terribly smart, and that he and Hana had a storybook marriage. They lived in suburbia, Los Ranchos, which was east of Oakland out through the Caldecott tunnel.

Later on, Fia's adjective describing the Kelly's marriage as 'storybook' made me wonder. Could she have meant a tale by the Brothers Grimm?

Fia introduced me to Hana at a women's brunch, a benefit for UCSF Hospital which Fia had coerced me into attending. I was impressed, but not just by Hana's looks. Although she was stunning, wearing a cream body suit, taupe wool tunic, and thigh-length suede boots, I was more taken by the force of her personality.

Hana defied the German stereotype. She wasn't blonde. Her brown eyes were set far apart, and her dark brown hair hugged her head, outlining a long neck. Her bangs were straight, ending just a fraction of an inch above her eyebrows.

A small, fleeting smile seemed to convey the message *I'll try you out, but keep your distance.*

When I got to know her better and learned all she'd been through as a child in World War II, I began to understand that smile. But despite her aura of veiled melancholy, she had a great sense of fun. Bruce was an Irish-American, raised in Cleveland, and they met at a bar in Munich when Hana was studying to be a teacher. Bruce had finished two years at Hastings Law School in San Francisco, and was in Germany for further immersion in international law. With their potent personalities, it had to have been a tumultuous first meeting. Not only were they both gorgeous, they were big. Hana was five-eleven and Bruce six-foot-six, and each had that undeniable drawing power for the opposite sex.

The three of us stood in Fia's breakfast room, with its English flowered walls and chintz covered furniture, looking out onto her small garden filled with topiaries and white azaleas. Fia turned to Hana and said, "Darling, you really should let Natalie paint you. She's a marvelous artist!"

I had tried hard to look like an artist that day. I was wearing an oversized white Mexican shirt with black tights, set off by long dangly earrings. No one dressed that way then for ladies' brunches. Hana nodded and smiled, but she didn't say anything about commissioning a painting. Just then someone came up to us chattering about the Watts riots, and we started discussing Rodney King.

We all agreed that the world was getting uglier—uglier, and a whole lot scarier.

Violence was escalating all over the nation, and especially in my backyard.

It was October of 1965, and I had gone to Cody's Books in Berkeley to get a book I'd heard reviewed on KPFA. It was either *A Thousand Days* or *The Making of the President*, I can't remember which. People were still reeling from Kennedy's assassination two years before, and the American public couldn't read enough about that tragic event.

I had no idea that a demonstration against the Vietnam War was scheduled for that day on campus, or that Telegraph Avenue would be the center of the action. I knew that a couple of days ago Joan Baez had sung at a sit-in on the steps of Sproul Hall, and I'd heard vaguely about a teach-in being held on the campus, with thousands of kids in attendance—Norman Mailer, Dr. Spock, Dick Gregory and a lot of other big names speaking against the war. Ken Kesey and his Merry Pranksters went on stage dressed in Day-Glo military garb, and Kesey yelled to the crowd, *"You're not gonna stop this war with this rally . . . Just look at it and turn away and say Fuck It . . ."*

I parked several blocks off Telegraph and locked my car, since I was aware enough to know that Berkeley crawled with hippies who didn't believe in ownership rights. I walked to Telegraph and strolled past head shops, ethnic-clothing shops and health food stores, and was stopped twice by flower children, young girls with long stringy hair and face paint, each of whom handed me a flower and gave me the peace sign. Up and down the street were vendors selling hand-made jewelry, belts, and tie-dyed shirts. Occasionally I saw women dressed like me in sweaters and slacks. No doubt they were faculty, parents of students, or shoppers. But for the most part what I saw were dropouts and stoners.

I paused a few minutes to admire a collection of turquoise rings spread on a blanket on the sidewalk. I glanced to one side, and suddenly realized I was standing next to Hana Kelly. It had been months since we'd met, and she didn't recognize me until I told her who I was.

"Oh, yes! I was going to call you, but I have put your number somewhere wrong! Bruce wants you to do the portrait!" She pronounced it 'poor-trite'.

"Marvelous!" I responded. "When do you want to begin?"

All at once we began to hear the chanting roar of a crowd. A mass meeting had just ended at Sather Gate and was moving its way down the middle of Telegraph. Surging toward us were hundreds of kids in head rags, buffalo jackets with fringe, African tooth-necklaces, beards, long dresses, waist-long hair—more loud, discontented youths than I'd ever seen together before.

They were carrying banners: *VIETNAM—LOVE TO KILL! GOTTA KILL! WANNA KILL!* and *GET US WHITE PIGS OUTTA THERE!*

I pulled Hana into a nearby sari shop, and the frightened owners ran with us to the back of the store. The Indian proprietor, his wife and their two-year-old daughter cowered with Hana and me behind a counter until the noise and tumult abated. It seems hard to believe, but I think we were there for a couple of hours.

I'll never forget the smells: the incense that permeated the shop, and the tear gas.

A car had been stopped and encircled by the mob, and a young man stood atop it with a loudspeaker exhorting the crowd to do anything, take any measures needed, to stop the war. Thanks be to God, finally there were the sounds of police cars and sirens and the stink of tear gas; ambulances started moving in. Amid the shouts and yells and police sirens, we heard screams of pain.

Such noise, such mayhem! These kids were ready to band together to make things right, and in the process, that day a lot of them got their heads bashed in. I didn't understand it. In fact, I hated it, as all my contemporaries did.

In the midst of all the outcry, Hana and I clung together, afraid the eruption would escalate further and the mob would invade the store. At one point, they broke all the windows, but didn't enter the shop. It was hours before we felt safe enough to emerge and find our way to our cars. Even then, walking together, if we saw two or three young people in a group, we crossed the street. We saw blood on the faces and clothing of students, and several policemen limping with injuries.

We had actually been afraid for our lives, and from that day on Hana and I were bound together.

The next day the newspapers reported twenty-six injuries and fourteen arrests.

I had never had a family member interfere as much in the creation of one of my portraits as Bruce Kelly did with Hana's. Except for the time that Blandensen woman tried to get me to add another child to the portrait I'd done of her two older children years before. She actually wanted me to cram her two-year-old in the space between the other two.

"Oh," she said, "and make it look artistic!"

I'm afraid I wasn't too gracious in refusing.

Hana called and said, "Come over this weekend. Bruce can help you choose my outfit in which to paint me."

That was the way she talked. I could listen all day to her tortured grammar.

"*He's* going to choose the outfit?" I asked.

"You will find when you get to know my husband, he is ver-ry interested in everything I do."

I wanted to paint her in the first outfit I'd seen her in at Fia's. I thought it emphasized her woman-warrior appearance, the tunic and tights so reminiscent of Jeanne d'Arc's armor and leggings, and I thought the colors were flattering to her olive skin and shiny sorrel hair. But Bruce didn't want that outfit. Too masculine, he said. He was sending me a subtle message; his money was paying for the portrait, and he would have a lot to say about it. Hana brought out several outfits and held them up to her chin, and Bruce and I commented on each one. It could have been fun, I suppose, but I felt his need to dominate the situation, and it took all my diplomatic skills to disguise my exasperation.

And I possess very few diplomatic skills.

One dress I liked was long, with a halter neckline, and printed with outsize leaves in shades of brown and beige. Bruce preferred a low-cut red evening dress with a big purple flower blossoming in the middle of the bosom. I told him it didn't express Hana to me at all.

He stared at me, obviously annoyed, and left the room. But he came back, and we finally settled on a tennis outfit. On that day at least, he was enthusiastic about Hana's prowess at tennis; she had won the singles tournament at her local tennis club. I had no idea then of his paranoid feelings about her playing. From all the outfits, we agreed on a pleated white skirt and classic white tennis shirt. I was happy about it, because I thought the sports outfit would emphasize her strength and athleticism.

We got started right away. I don't think I've ever laughed so much while I was painting anyone. (Except maybe with Nikki Lippmann a few years later.) Hana and I found a lot of the same things amusing, and her remarks, couched in her bastardized German-American vernacular, always made me giggle. She didn't mind laughing at herself, so that made it a hoot.

One day, arriving late, she strode in saying, "I have got a sticker! I am so mad—he was not nice, he—he—he pushed it on me through my door!"

"What? I don't know what you mean. What's a sticker?"

"*Sticker! Sticker!* Is not that what you say? I was driving on the Fahrbahn coming here—and Natalie, I was not going that fast! "

"Oh, you mean you got a ticket. A speeding ticket?"

"That's what I said!" She put her hands on her hips and shook her head in mock exasperation.

Another time she flew into my studio (still the small room off the kitchen) where I was squeezing out oil paints, and whined, "Oh Natalie, I am *so-o-o-o-o* upset! You won't want to paint me today—I have got a car bunker!"

It took me several moments to realize she meant the tiny raised spot on her cheek, and the word she wanted was "carbuncle."

Eons before other women were doing it, Hana liked to go braless. One day, two months after we'd started, she came in, got dressed in the outfit, and took her pose, obviously simmering about something. I didn't ask what she was angry about; by then I knew there was trouble in the marriage.

Finally, she spoke. "Natalie, I must have to get out of that tennis club where I play. Do you know they are going to make a rule about you must wear a bra—and they are going to put it in the rooster!"

She usually dropped her kids off at school at eight in the morning and got to our house thirty minutes later, when Ben was leaving for work. Those were the days when he went to work late and stayed late. Flanders & Schuman Investments' home base was New York, but the head of the San Francisco office, Sam Schuman, liked to leave at three in the afternoon, and he wanted Ben to be there when he left.

One day Hana brought pastries and shared them with Ben in the kitchen, and after that she and Ben often exchanged sweets and discussed which bakeries were best. Ben brought Hana fresh bagels from Lakeshore Avenue in Oakland, and she brought him desserts from Eclair in Berkeley, which was on Telegraph Avenue near People's Park. She said things had calmed down there, but I told her to be careful, you never knew when another demonstration might break out.

Occasionally she brought us something she'd baked herself. Hana was a marvelous cook.

Ben was crazy about her in a paternal, protective way; he said he'd like to adopt her. He would shout, "Hana, my German love!" and she would reply, "Ben, *mein Liebchen!*"

Ben was Jewish on his mother's side, and loved to bait Hana about the Nazis, but he was the only one who ever could. It wasn't serious baiting, but I remember once he asked her if she still had it in for the Russians, and she crooned, "Only when they don't provide my special vodka."

I remember two incidents of her prickliness about World War II. Once, at a cocktail party at our house, she flared up when someone made a remark about the Master Race, and once when I was making an attempt to learn to play tennis—I gave it up soon as wasted energy—when Hana put a shot over the net like a bullet, I yelled *"Blitzkrieg!"*

She barely spoke to me after the game. She got over it, though, moments later; she wasn't programmed to hold a grudge. She always accepted the banter from Ben for what it was, light teasing about something she couldn't help, and for which she refused to atone.

I had decided to paint Hana without a trace of a smile, because her demeanor seemed at times so very, very sad. As she posed, standing, her gaze was faraway, as if she had drifted off to some other place. At those times, I would move my brush from her face to some other part of the painting; I didn't want to paint that lifeless expression. Or I would say, "Let's take a break," and I would step back to look at the canvas. I kept the room on the cold side to keep down the odor of turpentine, and she would walk around, rubbing her bare arms and legs.

One day, a month after we'd started, Hana revealed herself to me, heart and soul.

I remarked that Ben's office staff had given him a small birthday celebration the day before, and all at once Hana sank down on the wicker armchair in a corner of the room and began to sob her heart out.

"What is it? What's the matter?" I knelt next to her.

"Oh, Natalie, I am so, so unhappy! And when you are telling about Ben at the office, it makes me remember what happened!"

"What?"

"You know I try so hard—*so hard!*—to please Bruce. And just last week, for his birthday I took his whole office a nice lunch. I cooked it, and I took it over there—"

Another round of sobbing. I brought out a box of Kleenex. Now she didn't look like a tall strong Teutonic woman; she looked like a little girl who had skinned her knee. "And everything was so nice! I made Bratwurst and Leberwurst and corned beef sandwiches—to please him, the corned beef, *ja?* And I took them my own *Krautsalat,* which everyone says is so good."

17

"Well, what was wrong with that? Didn't he appreciate it?"

I had a mental picture of the stuffy law firm where Bruce worked. I couldn't imagine them tolerating any break in their schedule.

"No! When he came home that night he said, 'Don't ever do that again!' He said I embarrassed him, and he didn't want me to come over there to bring food or to hang plants like I did—some pretty ferns, just *once* I did that—or to drop in with the kids. When I took them to the ballet last Christmas, I just wanted to show them where their papa works!"

"What you ought to do is stop cooking for him for a while. Then maybe he'd appreciate you."

"*Oo-o-oh,* Natalie, I did that once. I will tell you." She raised her head, more tears streaming down her face. I took a tissue and gently mopped her cheeks. I patted her back for a few minutes, and gradually she grew a little calmer.

"The children were in Ohio at Bruce's folks last summer, and I played a lot of tennis. I was in a tournament in Oakland, and I was home late, three days after one another. There was no dinner, and on the last day, Bruce beat me. He hit me on the legs many times with my racket, and he threw me against a wall. The swelling and bruises were very bad. I had to stay home and—" She stopped. "When I finally after a long time got out of bed—several days, I—I threw away the trophy I won for that tournament, and all the trophies and *Preise* I ever won in the last years—all of them went in the garbage can. And for days and days I didn't go out."

"Did you bring charges?"

"What?"

"Did you call the police and report him?"

"Oh no. The bruises and the pains in my side went away, and my face looked better, and then the children came back, and I told them I fell down playing on the courts. I had to go out once to get food, and I wore dark glasses, but I saw one of the neighbors. I told her this also, that I had fallen on the tennis court."

18

I knew now why she had that detached look, and why she was so unhappy. Bruce, successful in his law career and outwardly an excellent husband and father, was a cowardly, craven wife-beater.

"What do you mean you can't go?" demanded Ben. "We've had these tickets for three months!"

It was Friday night, and we had made plans to go with Fia and Arnie to an early dinner, then *Fiddler on the Roof* at the Curran.

"I'm sorry, but Hana's in a bad way, and I said I'd stay with her. She really needs me! Can't you understand?"

"I understand that you're putting everybody else before me and our marriage, that's what I understand!"

"Darling, I'm sorry, but I do think a friend in need is pretty important. I'm afraid she'll do something to herself, she's so depressed!"

"You've been her ear now for months—her damned crutch! Doesn't she have a shrink she can talk to?" His expression showed a mixture of frustration and guilt; he cared for Hana too.

"She can't afford one! They're expensive, you know that. That scumbag won't give her money for any kind of help."

Ben turned on his heel and left the room. He dressed and went with the Macintoshes to the theater, and I spent two nights and most of the next three days with Hana. Bruce was out of town, but they'd had a rip-roaring fight before he left. It was about money, plus her appeal for more help with the kids. His career had taken over their lives, and this was putting a horrific strain on Hana. I stayed with her and the children, playing Monopoly or watching television while Hana stayed in her room. Gradually she came out of her depression, and I returned home late Sunday afternoon.

To atone for my absence, I made Ben's favorite dinner, Beef Bourguignon, and we opened a bottle of red we'd been saving for a special occasion.

CHAPTER THREE

RANIE

I studied at CCAC off and on for years. Its official name was California College of Arts and Crafts, a campus located at Broadway and College Avenue in Oakland.

The highlight of my time there was in the early '60s, at a six-week summer painting class taught by Henry Koerner. He was visiting from the east, and was famous as a Magic Realist and *Time* cover artist. Born in Vienna, he had immigrated to the United States in 1938 after Hitler came to power, and in 1945 had been shipped to Germany to draw Nazi war criminals in the Nuremberg Trials. When he taught my painting class, he was newly married, so I never got to know him well, but his teaching deepened my understanding of portraiture, and I will forever be grateful.

Let me be clear; I was never part of the hierarchy of well-known Bay Area painters, not even close. The outstanding artists of the time—Diebenkorn, Park, Oliveira, Thiebaud, Bischoff, Louis Siegrist—had all made their mark by the late '70s, and even though some of them had either taught at or attended CCAC, I never met any of them. I was happy to be merely working at my trade, doing portrait commissions and still life paintings.

Possibly my strongest attribute was that I always strove to be better, and continued to take evening life drawing classes at CCAC.

I first met Ranie Sloan in 1967 when she posed for our life class for four weeks that spring. She was an exceptionally disciplined model—young, self-possessed, and with a marvelous head and superb body. She wore a short Afro, and her skin gleamed in the light of the atelier like highly polished mahogany. She held her poses for twenty minutes at a time, while we sketched her in charcoal or Conté crayon.

Periodically she would don a robe and step inside the cubicle provided for models at the back of the room. Ranie rarely showed herself during our breaks, obviously preferring to be alone, but on her last night, as I returned from smoking outside with some of the other students, I heard sounds of sobbing. I walked back and peered inside the tiny room. Ranie was bent over a small radio she'd evidently brought along. Her face was buried in her hands, her shoulders shaking.

I hesitated. Lately my life seemed besieged by unhappy women. Did I really want to hear any more sad stories?

I stepped inside the cubicle. "What is it, kiddo? What's the matter?"

She was unable to speak, but instead pointed to the radio. The announcer was reporting that a group of armed black men had invaded the California State Assembly in Sacramento.

"It's my brother," she managed to say, shaking her head in despair. "He's got hisself in such a mess with the Black Panthers. *They took guns up there today!* An' he got guns all over his room. My mother gonna kill him if he don't get out of that—that club. Or *I'm* goin' to!"

I sat down next to her on the narrow bench.

"First, what's your name? And second, what are the Black Panthers?"

"Huey Newton an' Bobby Seale an' a bunch of black brothers, they good friends of him, but they are *trouble*. I'm so scared Darrell gonna get hisself shot!" She turned, and briefly smiled. "I'm Ranie. My mother named me Urania, but nobody calls me that." More tears welled up and she turned away.

"I'm Nat," I said. "And that's it, young one. No more posing for you tonight. We're gonna go get a cup of coffee at Millie's. Get dressed."

I stood up, picked up her clothes and handed them to her.

"Oh no! I might not get paid if I don't finish!"

"Nonsense. Everyone in the class looks wasted anyway; I never saw such a drag-ass bunch of artists. I'll talk to the instructor, he can tell them to go home."

I went over to Ned and told him about the emotional state of our model. A few minutes later when Ranie and I left, there was no one around, and we got into my old station wagon and drove to Millie's Diner.

That was the beginning of our friendship.

I was attracted to her, I suppose, because she was different from most of my friends, and I think she liked me because I was an artist. She said that very few artists were money-grubbing phonies. Ranie was practical; she had secretarial skills, and by the time I met her, had worked for several business firms in the East Bay. But she didn't like the world of commerce. In that, we were sisters. She was eager to learn so many things, and she was lively as quicksilver. Over the next couple of years we shared lunch dates or went to lectures on art or literature. We were happy with our exchange; she was adding to her learning, and I was beginning to look at the world through a wider window.

Another thing, Ranie was funny. Gradually her sharp wit and warm personality emerged, and we began to enjoy sharing amusing life situations. I loved her voice, like hot cocoa on a cold winter's night, her quick smile, and her ironic take on "white folks." Once, when we'd gone for a picnic at Joaquin Miller Park in Oakland, she started talking about white women and their men. She was wearing shocking pink pedal pushers and a striped tee, and had wound a fuschia-and-black printed scarf around her Afro. She looked amazing, very theatrical.

"You white ladies are one big mystery to me! For instance, how come you all line up at the gym on those bikes and treadmills, workin' yo' buns off to keep in shape? My mom works six days a week cleaning yo' houses, an' *she* don't have no weight problem. And I walk five blocks to my bus to get to work, then from the bus stop I got four more blocks to git to the insurance office. All in all, I walk 'bout two hours a day, an' do you see any fat on me?"

I had met Mrs. Sloan once when I picked Ranie up on 12th Street. I agreed, both Ranie and her mom looked to be in excellent physical shape.

She took a sip of lemonade and went on.

"And the way y'all dress? *You* got a lotta style, Nat, but I see you wearin' the same ol' white T-shirt and jeans most of the time. You can do better'n that, girl. Bring on the colorful tunics, gypsy blouses an' big twirlin' skirts!"

She looked at me, cocking her head to one side.

"I don't want to get too personal, but maybe you could do somethin' different with your hair. I could fix it for you, get you some honkin' jewelry real cheap, dress up your looks. But it isn't you so much, like I said, it's those snobby-nosed, hill-dwellin' society ladies like my Mama works for—their clothes so plain. *Pearls?* They got pearls wrapped 'round their necks like peas in a pod. Why would they want to do that, all of 'em lookin' alike? I see 'em carryin' magazines 'round, *Vogue* an' *Harper's Bazaar*. Why don't they learn nuthin' from those?"

I kept chewing my sandwich and grinning, even though I was in the hot seat. I decided then and there to throw out all my pearls.

"You know, don't you girl, mos' white men like they cars better than their women. I got a white boyfriend, Jamie, in love with his Porsche. When we go out, he ain't showin' *me* off, he showin' off that yellow speed bomb. Then I got another boyfriend, real dark, all he wants to do is talk baseball, football, an' basketball. It's okay, he's a sports announcer. On the days I got a date with him, I buy me a newspaper and throw everything away but the Sports page, then I bone up on all the games goin' on. He's so happy when I do that, I can talk him out of any other thing he might have in mind, which is mostly gettin' into my drawers."

That night, when Ben wanted to know why I was going to bed so early, I said I was worn out from laughing at Ranie.

One day Ben got home early from work and met Ranie. I had invited her in for coffee after we had been to an art lecture. I remember his eyes opened wide at the vision of dark beauty standing at the kitchen counter. Pouring coffee for himself, and assuming that a young black woman from Oakland would be steeped in the Oakland A's and the Raiders, he asked, "What do you think, Ranie? Is Rollie Fingers the best relief pitcher the A's ever had?"

I was amused at how quickly she got him off the subject.

"I'm not too interested in that stuff, Ben. What I like is good TV. Did you by any chance see *The Glass Menagerie* the other night on television? I never saw anything made me cry like that! Shirley Booth, and an actor name of Holbrook. In the play the sister was strange, had all these little glass figurines, but I just loved her."

I told her we had seen the play on stage, and that it was by a playwright named Tennessee Williams.

"Oh yeah, didn't he write *Cat on a Hot Tin Roof?* Saw a re-run of that the other night. Is it just me, or is that Burl Ives a big ol' ham?"

Later I asked Ben's take on Ranie, and he said, "Well, she's gorgeous, and very different from all your other friends. Are you going to do her portrait?"

"I guess I'm interested in her because she is so different. No, I haven't made any plans to paint her. But take my word for it, darling, underneath all that soul sister act is a very sensitive and artistic woman."

So, with this new friendship with an African American woman, did I suddenly become politically active? Did I join community groups, get involved in the racial problems of the world around me? No. I stayed in my own frangible cocoon, clinging to the good life Ben and I had together.

But I began hearing more about the Black Panthers. They were gun-toting and rebellious, and they were always getting arrested and shot by the police. Huey Newton was the center of national attention, and the Panthers were taken up as a liberal cause all across America. After he was charged with murdering a white police officer, more than five thousand blacks gathered to celebrate Huey's birthday at the Oakland Auditorium. And when his trial began, thousands more bearded white liberals, "Honkies for Huey"—plus Asians, Latinos, and blacks, marched outside the courthouse, while twelve Panthers in black leather jackets and black berets stood guard on the courthouse steps. "Free Huey" buttons abounded, and a poster of Huey in a throne-like rattan chair with a spear in one hand, a rifle in the other, became internationally famous.

He was a handsome young man; that had to be part of his appeal. And he swore he didn't kill that policeman.

I phoned Ranie and asked whether she'd gone to any of the "Free Huey" demonstrations.

"Pardon my language," she said, "but I wouldn't be caught dead demonstratin' for that raggedy-ass."

Around the time I met Ranie, I was halfway through painting Hana's portrait. I'd finished laying in the skin tones, warm beiges modulating to light browns, colors which were lovely against her dark hair and the stark white of her tennis clothes. I had done the highlights at forehead, nose and chin, and had succeeded in capturing the flash of her dark eyes. But I was stuck, and was having difficulty with the background. I seldom laid in a background color that was light or dark, almost always went for a medium tone. But this time I had too many color choices. I had tried gray—not just gray, but fourteen different shades of gray. They were all too uninteresting, so I kept trying. Meanwhile, the edges of the figure were getting iron-hard and overworked. The brush strokes were no longer fresh, and the background was beginning to look as if it was on top of Hana, not behind her.

I finally came to a decision. I had to start over on a fresh canvas.

Before I did, however, I determined to achieve the perfect background color, so I continued to experiment. At last I found it, the color Hana had worn when I first met her, a warm taupe. I used a gray-green wash beneath, and on top I scrumbled in texture, using a brush filled with a color I got by mixing raw umber, raw sienna, a touch of Hooker's green, and a blob of titanium white.

I have never used landscape in my backgrounds, as so many of the Renaissance masters did; i.e. the *Mona Lisa*. Only twice have I ever put anything in a background other than pattern or texture. Once, in a portrait of a nursery-owner's wife, I laid in a few trees, and another time, in a small boy's portrait, I painted in the soft outlines of a rocking horse. These portraits were successful, but usually my backgrounds were much simpler.

I started a new painting of Hana, and it went rapidly, looking good each step of the way. I knew I'd done the right thing by starting over.

Weeks went by, and one day Hana brought Bruce to see it. I told her beforehand that she should let him know I wasn't finished, and that his comments should be few and far between. After my experience with his 'helping' choose her outfit, I was worried he might go too far with some criticism or other, my temper would flare, and the whole thing would go bust.

It turned out very differently that day; he was smiling and pleasant.

He said, "Sorry I haven't been able to get over to see the picture before now, but I've been busy with a tax case."

"That's okay," I said.

He walked over to the painting and studied it for a long time. I stayed in back, and Hana stood halfway between, as if she intended to referee in case a fight broke out. He turned to me and said, "You're making a lovely thing here, Natalie!"

I exhaled, and suddenly realized I hadn't been breathing. "I'm so glad you like it."

"I like the colors, the way she's standing—the whole thing is very impressive!"

He threw an arm around my shoulders, and I realized I was getting the full Bruce Kelly charm treatment.

"Isn't Natalie wonderful?" enthused Hana. "I like it so much—but I do not look that *schön* in real life!"

"Nonsense," I said. "I painted it with every bit of skill I possess, but the *schön* is all yours, kiddo."

Now I had an insight into how Hana existed. She was in constant fear of displeasing her sleeping giant.

On one of our last sessions Hana asked, "What is your next picture, Natalie?"

"A couple of children, maybe three or four. Christmas is always a busy time. Presents for grandparents, surprises for Daddy, you know. Nothing big coming up, though, nothing exciting."

"Well, I met someone for you should paint. She is the wife of the surgeon who operated on my knee; it was before I knew you. I had the operation and met her when I was leaving his office. She is beautiful, it would please you to do her. She seems to me though, a little bit somehow—doomed."

Hana pronounced it 'domed'.

"What do you mean, doomed?" I asked, wiping my brush on an oily rag.

"I don't know—she seems *unglücklich—deprimiert*—you know, sad. Her name is Amanda Reichard, and she has *prächtig* red hair. It is her—how do you say it—crowding glory?"

I didn't tell Hana that I often found *her* to be *deprimiert*. Perhaps even doomed.

"What makes her sad?"

"I don't know, but you must see her. I will introduce you to her myself! Will you come to my *Weihnachts* party?"

Two weeks later for the unveiling of her portrait, she and Bruce gave a Christmas party. Bruce's business associates were there, and Hana's tennis friends and their husbands. Hana had decorated their contemporary home in Los Ranchos sumptuously; everywhere you looked were boughs of pine and laurel, festooned with red velvet bows and gold Christmas balls. Austrian straw and wooden toys adorned the entry table and the mantel over the fireplace.

Hana looked radiant in a long burgundy velvet skirt and pink turtleneck, and when Bruce greeted us I was again dazed by his Irish good looks. He wore his hair slightly long (for a lawyer), with the sideburns many men were beginning to favor, and with his black moustache, heavy brows, and colossal height, he commanded the attention of all the women in the room. Even my handsome Ben dimmed a little in his presence.

But the image of this big hulking guy beating up Hana was almost more than I could stand. I had told Ben about Hana's beatings, and I'd had to badger him to get him to attend. In the end he said, "I'll go, for Hana's sake."

My portrait of Hana hung over the fireplace in the place of honor, the center of attention. Everyone seemed to like it, which of course pleased me. The women guests were all a few years younger than I, as was Hana. Most of them were fit, slim tennis players. Surprisingly, most of them were interested in art, or said they were.

There are three standard comments people make to artists. The first is, "How long did it take you to do that?" The second, in the case of portraiture, is "How'd you get it to look just *like* her?" usually followed by, "I can't draw a straight line with a ruler!" To the last remark I'm always tempted to reply, "Unless you're Joseph Albers, it's really not that important," and to the first, "Since birth." I've never had a good answer for the second question, except for one word, 'observation'.

At one point in the evening Bruce raised his glass of wine in my direction and announced, "This artist Natalie knows her business."

You would never know, you could never guess, how despicable he was.

Hana said, "Yes, but Natalie is a slave driver, she worked me so hard! Her studio is freezing cold, and I had to stand there in *gooseskin!*"

She bustled about the room serving eggnog, mulled wine, and countless homemade German goodies. Young Hans in lederhosen and little Molly in a charming dirndl passed trays of food. Hans was seven and looked like Hana, with strong, wide-set shoulders and brown eyes, while four-year-old Molly was the picture of her father, with curly black hair and the brilliant blue eyes of the Old Sod.

I noticed Ben's eyes following the children around the room. In all our years together, he had never spoken about longing to be a father, or of regret about my barren state. But that evening I wondered, *does he feel that he's missing out on something?*

Bruce reached out an arm and stopped his tiny daughter.

"Hey, little one, give me one of those cookies!"

Molly raised the tray, looking up at him with a look of complete adoration. He took a large *Pfeffernusse*, put the whole thing in his mouth, then bent down and kissed her on the cheek. It was a touching scene I would remember with sadness in the months to come.

That evening Hana introduced me to Amanda Reichard and her husband, Dr. Tom Reichard. Amanda truly was a lovely woman, slim and willowy, albeit with a few extra pounds around the abdomen and hips. I'd been turning out children's pastel portraits by the bushelful, so I was primed for an interesting adult to portray.

Emboldened by the success of Hana's picture, I said, "Our hostess thinks it would be a good idea for me to paint you. I agree, you'd make a great subject. Want me to try?"

Ben was standing next to me. She blushed crimson from the throat up, searching his face, then mine. "I don't know why you would want to paint *me*. Besides, I have six children, and hardly any time to call my own. But I'll talk to Tom about it, and thank you." She blushed again.

I looked across the room to where her physician husband stood gesturing with both hands, enjoying the rapt attention of several young women.

I handed Amanda my card. "If you think you'd like to do it, call me."

Money wasn't mentioned, but of course I didn't want to paint her portrait for nothing. That would be stupid.

CHAPTER FOUR

AMANDA

It was around February of 1968—I remember because it was Mamaw's birthday and I had just finished calling her—when my phone rang. I was finally able to afford an extension in the space where I painted, and it had been connected only the day before.

"It's Amanda Reichard—do you remember me? You liked my red hair. I've finally gotten most of my kids into school, and Tom says I can hire Eufie to come every day instead of just twice a week. So, when do you want to start the portrait?"

I said, "Any time! And can you come every other day?"

Instead of starting immediately on the painting, we spent a day shopping in Oakland at I. Magnin's. We chose a beautiful olive-green velvet dress, knee-length, and I kept it in my painting room.

We lived near each other in Berkeley then, which made it convenient. With six children, the youngest only three, Amanda was tired most of the time. She had Eufie, a wonderful middle-aged black woman, but always came to my studio exhausted. The first day she was early, and as I assembled the paints and brushes I wanted to use, she stood to one side, hugging her body. Amanda had a nervous habit of repeatedly pulling her sweater or jacket over her breasts, as if ashamed of them, and instead of looking directly at me, she would drop her gaze, peering from under the mass of red hair. Her shoulders slumped, too, but I decided I would have none of that. When I posed her, slightly turned away from me in a three-quarter view, I lifted her chin and told her to sit with her spine erect.

I arranged her hair at every sitting, while she smoked and we made small talk.

One day, three weeks or so along, she arrived teary and trembling. That was the day she started confiding in me about Tom. By then I had met him a couple or three times, and I knew I didn't like him much. He was so sure of himself, so self-important in manner. In his presence, Amanda seemed to recede into the wall. She said they had met at UC Berkeley, when he was in pre-med and she was majoring in Child Care. They married, and their parents supported them while he attended medical school for a long, drawn-out period. In his final years of study, they started their family.

Later on was when the trouble started. After a few years, Tom's surgical practice began to be very successful, and he started staying away from home more and more. I knew a couple of women in that doctors' circle in Berkeley, and I asked one of them about the Reichards. My friend Claudia O'Neil, whose husband was an internist on the staff at the same hospital as Tom, and whom I knew from UCLA, said Tom engaged in serial affairs. He'd fooled around blatantly in the last four or five years, she said, acting as though he were some sort of god who could do anything, break any rules, and be forgiven.

He wasn't even very careful. At first his dalliances were with his nurses and assistants, but Claudia said lately he'd begun sleeping with women on the Reichards' own social level, women whom Amanda was likely to know.

I started the portrait with my usual method, doing six or seven charcoal drawings from life to get the composition I wanted. Then, having chosen the best pose, I started on the canvas, painting the figure in broad strokes. I used a color I liked for this purpose, a mixture of umber and Hooker's green. I laid in the skin tones of the face, neck, arms and hands in a lighter, flesh-toned oil-and-turpentine wash. I would stand back every few minutes to see if the figure sat on the surface the way I wanted it to, perhaps changing the position of the hands or the tilt of the head. Using cobalt blue, white, and alizarin crimson, I began to work grayed-blues and plum tones into the shadows of the olive-green velvet dress, and to tone faint shades of those same colors onto the shadowed side of the face.

In Amanda's case, I wanted the hair to make its impression on the viewer—the whole mass, shape, and color of it. I didn't start using color in the hair, though, until I had established the other hues.

I was happy with the way the project was going, but one day toward the end of the month Amanda gunned her station wagon up my driveway in the pouring rain, slammed on the brakes, and dashed into my studio. I knew something was wrong from the set of her mouth, but it wasn't until I'd finished arranging her hair and was zipping up the dress that she began to cry. She broke away and began to sob uncontrollably.

First Hana, now Amanda. What was I, some kind of shipwrecked-marriage counselor?

There was nothing to do but lean against the wall and wait. After two or three minutes, she managed to get control. She fished a cigarette out of her purse, and a few seconds later began to unburden herself.

"Nat, I have to talk to *somebody*. I told Tom a few weeks ago he'd have to work at our marriage a lot harder or I was going to leave him. He's broken so many promises—not just to me, but to the kids! He says he'll attend their school events and music recitals, then he doesn't show up! He's been missing a lot of evening meals, always using work—work—that damned *work*!—as an excuse. Of course he always says he's working so hard so we—the kids and I—can live the way we do! The worst time was three days ago, when he promised to take me out on my fortieth birthday, then called from Carmel to say he couldn't make it! Why would he do something like that, call from out of town, unless he wanted to hurt me?"

She coughed, choking as she exhaled. I was going to have to start a new rule, no smoking in my studio. The mixture of tobacco smoke, oil paint, and turpentine was noxious, and Ben had started to complain about the odor permeating the house.

There was no stopping Amanda. She continued to vent her feelings.

"Last night we went to a party at the home of one of Tom's partners, at a big house near the Claremont Hotel. Betsy, my three-year-old, had had diarrhea all day. There was a lot of drinking and chatter, and I left and went up to one of the upstairs bedrooms to get away from the noise. I went into a dark bedroom, thinking maybe if I just sat down and rested awhile, I would be okay. There was a pile of coats on the bed—I thought, but it was Tom—getting a blow job from one of the women guests—the wife of another doctor! That— that woman—that *slut!* Always acting like she's my best friend! I hate them—I hate them both!"

I sat down next to her. "I'm so sorry! What did you do?"

"I stumbled downstairs and asked my friend Mark to take me home. I told him I was sick, which I was! I locked the bedroom door, and the next morning I kicked Tom out of the house. I don't think I can ever face him ever again, I just can't! Natalie, why doesn't he love me?"

There is no answer to a question like that, especially after a revelation of such a betrayal, so I didn't answer. When she'd recovered a bit I said, "Okay, you've cried. But the next step is to get mad and stay mad, and the third step is to do something about it! He can't treat you like this, and he has to find that out!"

She nodded, apparently agreeing with my advice, and, declining to pose, left the house not long after.

I decided I was going to hang out a shingle like Lucy in *Peanuts*, and start charging a nickel an hour for advice.

I didn't hear from Amanda for weeks. Once or twice I called, and Eufie would answer and say, "Sorry, Mrs. Reichard can't come to the phone right now."

For two weeks I twiddled my thumbs. I turned Amanda's portrait to the wall, and started a series of still life drawings in pastel, using objects at hand: pitchers, flowers, fruit, beer mugs, an antelope skull I'd collected from my days in New Mexico. This task was so intriguing that I got carried away and made more than twenty drawings. I had no idea whether I could ever sell them, but the work was an end unto itself, and I felt happy and productive.

Two months later, Amanda phoned and said we could start the sittings again, so we began once more. She made it clear that she didn't want to discuss her personal life, so I didn't ask questions. She had lost weight and looked more beautiful than ever. The main difference was in the contours of her face and upper arms. I outlined her jaw line more precisely, deepened the shadows in her cheeks, nipped in the waistline and slimmed the arms.

Everyone smoked, but Amanda smoked so much I began to consider giving it up. I did make a new rule that we would only smoke in the kitchen or outdoors.

Ben saw Amanda once or twice at our house. Once we had a late afternoon sitting, and he happened to come home from work early. He stuck his head into my studio, and I said, "Of course you remember Amanda, Ben, from Hana's party?"

"Of course!" He told her he thought the portrait was, so far, a tremendous success. "If Nat doesn't set her foot wrong, you're going to have a great picture!"

He smiled and backed out the door.

Later that evening, I asked Ben his impression of Amanda.

"Well, she's beautiful, but maybe just a little dumb and naive." I had told him about Amanda's marital problems. "The guy's a bastard, so why did she go ahead and have six kids with him? Couldn't she have seen this coming?"

I had to admit I'd had the same thought. Inwardly I agreed about Amanda's intelligence, or lack of it. I thought she had a tendency to avoid the true circumstances of her marriage, a refusal to look straight on at her world, at Tom, and maybe even at herself. I didn't think the word 'dumb' described her, though; 'unrealistic' was a better one. But she seemed to be hitting reality now, coming down hard with both feet, and I hoped the landing wouldn't break her into a million pieces.

One day she came to pose and didn't want to leave, begging me to let her spend the night on our couch. There had been another crisis, and she said Eufie was staying with the children. Of course I said yes. She wouldn't go to the guest room; she wanted to stay in the living room with a quilt and pillow. I left her there around ten and went to bed.

Ben had been out late at his club in San Francisco, and stumbled upon her when he turned on the living room lamp. He told me when he asked if she'd like to share a nightcap, she accepted a glass of wine. They chatted for a while, not about her marriage, just light conversation. I expected him to complain about my allowing her to spend the night on our couch, but thankfully he didn't.

A few weeks later I finished the picture. As Amanda sat stoically as I was putting a touch of pale citron highlights on the jade velvet, I thought I had earned the right to ask one question, so I did. "Do you think you're going to stay in the marriage?"

"I think so. We're seeing a marriage counselor."

"You mean Tom is going too?"

"Not much," she said. "He keeps missing appointments."

Two weeks later when the picture was dry enough to travel, she brought Tom over to pick it up.

It was April of 1968, and those were worrisome times. There had been another racial incident with the Black Panthers, when twelve armed policemen invaded a Panther meeting at a church in Oakland. And Martin Luther King had just been assassinated in Memphis.

The day of King's memorial funeral march was the day Amanda and Tom came to get the painting. There'd been a lot of coverage on television, and I'd been watching it all day.

Tom looked handsome in a camel's hair sport jacket, his ruddy complexion contrasting with his blonde-streaked hair. He stood back from the picture for three or four long minutes. Then he looked directly at me and began to praise my talent to the skies.

"You got her, Natalie. *You got her.* Darling, you're gorgeous!" Tom put his arm around Amanda and drew her close, and they exchanged a long kiss. It was obvious that she still loved the guy, and if he didn't love her, he was putting on a very convincing act. He wrote a check and carried the painting out to his Mercedes.

I waved goodbye, wondering if I would ever see Amanda again. Then I went inside and poured myself a large Stoli on the rocks. As I sat alone in front of the television watching King's memorial march, I mourned, tears pouring down my cheeks. There were a lot of skunks in this world, and I could think of two at that moment. The man who assassinated Martin Luther King was one of them.

Rioting began all over the black community in Berkeley, spilling into the white areas, but not into our hills, thank God! Two days after King was killed, Eldridge Cleaver and another Black Panther, Bobby Hutton, were involved in a gun battle with Oakland police, and Hutton was shot dead.

I hadn't heard from Ranie in ages, and I called her to talk about the shocking news, but she didn't answer.

Sometime later that year, I heard a rumor that Amanda had filed for divorce.

I called her two or three times and left a message, waiting for a call back, but none came. I did occasionally hear gossip about her; Claudia O'Neil used to tell me all sorts of tales. I only listened because I was hurt about Amanda's dropping our friendship. At least I thought of it as friendship, but maybe she didn't. I figured that if one woman listens to another woman's sad tales of infidelity, then surely some sort of comradeship is born.

One day, when I was between portrait commissions (which were few and far between in those days), Claudia and I were having a sandwich in a little diner on Shattuck Avenue. She told me that since Amanda's separation from Tom, her children were suffering.

"What do you mean, suffering? Surely you're exaggerating!"

"Well, Amanda has begun doing a lot of stuff outside the home, and her neighbor Sally Ericson told me that if it weren't for Eufie, the whole house would come tumbling down! Sally says the kids' clothes look ragtag, and sometimes they don't even go to school."

"What kind of things is she doing outside the house?"

"She's spreading herself thin working as a volunteer at not just one, but several of the kids' schools—typing, filing, that kind of thing, and she's actually heading the building committee at one of them. Do you know how much time that takes? *With six kids at home?* I saw her one day, all dressed up and looking elegant—you know how gorgeous she is when she fixes herself up. Well, of course you do, you painted her. She was at the gas station dressed to the nines, getting that old station wagon filled up. She said she was on her way to her lawyer's office, and it was only eight o'clock in the morning! Let me assure you, I'm not the only one who thinks Amanda is up to something!"

"I can't imagine Amanda neglecting her kids," I said. "She's a wonderful mother. And Tom treated her so horribly for so long. Why shouldn't she get out of the house and do anything she damn well pleases?"

I thought Claudia went too far in her criticism. She herself was the most provincial of doctors' wives, with a mindset typical of her social circle.

Hana Kelly, too, decided to end her marriage, but during the divorce proceedings, she confided very little in me. I wondered why, but concluded that she'd leaned on me so much in the period leading up to the divorce that now she'd decided to spare me.

But I couldn't leave well enough alone. I began to call and ask how she was doing.

She said everything was fine. The kids were fine, she was fine. She wasn't friendly and warm like the old Hana, and I wondered if our friendship was over. I was sad about it, because I had begun to care about her. But I was never one to pursue a one-sided friendship.

Then, a few months later, she called.

"Things are looking better now, Nat. I am so sorry I wasn't nice on the phone last time. Can we make a date to see each other? I miss you."

Our comradeship began again, and one day as I was driving with her over the Bay Bridge, we got on the subject of Amanda.

"Amanda invited me and my kids to the *Oster* Fest," Hana said. "Where were you?"

"I wasn't invited," I said. "I don't have children, remember? But tell me."

"Well, she had this *Ostereiersuche* for all the kids, and her neighbors and friends, they came too. We colored the eggs, making pretty designs. Then after we colored them, her girl Ashley and her *Sohn* Lucian hid them in back of the house. My Hans found the most eggs and got the prize! Anyway, what I want is to tell you—the portrait you did of her looked *fantastisch!* I wished you could be there to hear all the great things people said about it. And I am so proud of myself, because I was who told you to paint her!"

Quite unexpectedly, I saw Amanda eight months or so after I'd finished her picture. I was on my way to help hang a group show at the San Francisco Women Artists' Cooperative Gallery on Hayes Street. I had been a member of the SFWA for only a couple of years, and on the show committee for a year. After parking on Van Ness, I walked past the Hayes Street Grill, and happened to glance in at a handsome couple sitting at a table in the window.

It was Ben, with Amanda, and they were laughing, looking like the Couple of the Year. I quickly averted my face and hurried on.

I felt as if the bottom had dropped out of my heart.

I spent the next three hours moving like a zombie as I helped hang paintings, letting the other women decide where to hang every entry, which wasn't like me. Another artist asked if something was wrong, but I brushed her off.

That night I couldn't help myself; I told Ben I'd seen them. He was so casual about it, so off-hand, I soon realized there was nothing to it. He said they were discussing Amanda's investments.

"I know her lawyer, Al Stansbury, and Al set up the luncheon."

"But why didn't you mention you were going to have lunch with one of my friends? I should think you would tell me!" While Ben removed his cufflinks and placed them in a tray on his bureau, I stood with my arms folded across my chest

"Darling, it would have made it seem much more important than it was. And it was a very last-minute thing—just business."

How could it have been a last-minute thing if the lawyer had set it up? 'Setting it up' implies planning ahead. But I was silent. I was sure of Ben's love, positive that he would be faithful to me forever. In the months to come, his attentiveness and thoughtfulness were the same as ever, his lovemaking as ardent.

How profoundly the divorce must have upset Amanda, with its attendant financial and custody battles! I decided to forget the whole thing, and threw myself into the current portrait I was working on, girl triplets, an adorable threesome of blonde, curly-haired cherubs.

Soon after that, Ben planned a getaway weekend for us on the Monterey peninsula. Being that close to the sea invariably brought out all our appetites. We dined on the Monterey wharf, where we had a seafood dinner and a bottle of California Chardonnay, and later at the motel, with the sounds of the ocean in our ears, we fell into a vortex of feverish lovemaking.

When I returned home, the triplets portrait completed, I had no commission upcoming, so for my own amusement I began a large pastel drawing of a dozen cinnamon-colored chrysanthemums. I'd stuck them in a white stoneware pitcher and was using gray pastel paper, so the contrast, hot color on a cool background, was quite nice. I had just finished putting my chalks away and was putting fresh water in the pitcher when the phone rang.

CHAPTER FIVE

THE HAIGHT

It was Fia calling to say that her portrait needed a touchup. She said she'd buy me lunch if I'd meet her and take it home to re-varnish. The trunk of her Lincoln Continental was big enough to hold it, she said, and I was to meet her at the latest hot dining spot in the Bay Area, Chez Panisse in Berkeley.

Alice Waters was causing a minor earthquake in gastronomic circles all over the country. She used nothing but fresh ingredients, locally grown, and she and her assistant Jeremiah Tower were becoming food celebrities. Food mavens called their food by a lot of different names, among them "Nouvelle Cuisine" and "New American Cuisine." Eventually, over a period of several years, it was settled; Waters' food was officially named "California Cuisine."

We met in front, then went through the entry and up the stairs. My society friend looked wonderful today in a lavender three-piece shantung suit, a diamond pin adorning one shoulder. She still wore her hair in an outdated bouffant style, but it was right for her. I was in black pants and a turtleneck as usual, but wore my Mexican silver necklace. My hair was long now, and I put it in a braid. I had a few strands of gray, but Fia's hair was as dark as ever.

As soon as we were seated, I told her about my latest job. "Guess who called—Marlo Werner! She wants a portrait."

"You are a wonder, Natalie, you really are!"

"Well, I'm sure you had something to do with it, and I hope you're not going to start asking a percentage! What have you been up to? How's Arnie? Ben said he saw him at the club at some event or other."

Ben's words had been, "Saw Arnie at the club; he's still drinking too much."

"Are you planning your usual trip to the south of France?" I asked.

"Yes, we're renting a place for a month. I can't wait."

We studied the menu, which had been printed that morning. Everything sounded wonderful, and I couldn't decide between grilled quail *à chanterelles* on toast triangles, or artichoke hearts, chicory, and beetroot in vinaigrette.

Fia ordered a bottle of Cabernet Sauvignon, and while the waiter was pouring, she said, "Oh, by the way, Cissy said she saw Ben last Sunday at an outdoor concert at Stern Grove."

"Oh no, couldn't be. Ben was at The Trees, not Stern Grove."

"Oh! I'm glad, because Cissy said he was with a gorgeous redhead, and suddenly I became a little concerned."

Imagine Cissy conjuring up Ben in a public place like that. But it's a well-known fact that college girls have the least credence of any known segment of society. Besides, Ben would never go to one of those crowded outdoor events. He hated people in large numbers, sweaty hordes stumbling over one another—picnicking on the grass, guzzling beer.

"Stop fretting," I said, "everything's fine with Ben and me—couldn't be better. And I don't like gossip, you should know that."

I picked up my wine glass and took a large gulp.

Fia turned her exacting, discriminating gaze at the other patrons, then looked back at me. "Have you seen Hana lately?"

"Once or twice, but not in the last couple of weeks. Why, what's up with her?"

"I was over there a few days ago." Fia fumbled with her napkin for several seconds, shaking it out, folding it, unfolding it, finally laying it in her lap. "And I think your portrait may have been damaged."

"Damaged! How?" I was so upset that I almost stood up in my seat.

"Well, Bruce—you know that big outdoor deck they have— Bruce actually threw it off of there!"

"Why in hell would he do that! I'll murder him!"

"When I got there, they were arguing about the terms of the divorce settlement. It was about everything they'd ever disagreed on, from Day One—you know how marital fights escalate."

"No, I don't. Ben and I never argue," I said, not bragging, but as a simple statement of fact. I'd forgotten about the night I chose to be with Hana instead of going to *Fiddler on the Roof* with the Macintoshes.

She looked at me in disbelief, but went on. "You know their divorce was final last July, don't you?"

"Yes. So why are they still arguing? Why couldn't they let the lawyers settle everything? Oops, I forgot, Bruce is a lawyer. Surely, though, Hana has her own representation."

"As you mentioned, Nat, you don't like gossip. But I'll tell you all of it if you'll let me."

She lit a cigarette, and so did I, and the woman at the next table immediately coughed. Here we were, in the middle of the Gourmet Ghetto, befouling the air of its most prestigious eating establishment. An attractive, smiling woman walked to the window above our table and quietly opened it, and I realized it had to be Alice herself. Smoking hadn't been outlawed in restaurants yet, and Ms. Waters was nothing if not subtle. I put out my cigarette, bracing myself for more bad news about Hana.

"I was picking her up for lunch," Fia went on. "I saw a Jaguar in the driveway and heard Bruce's voice from inside the house, and he sounded really mad. I knew he had hurt her physically in the past, and I wasn't just going to drive away like a milksop! I rang the doorbell, and at long last Hana came to the door. She'd been crying. I asked if she was okay, and before she could tell me to leave, I brushed past her and stepped inside.

"Bruce is acting crazy!" she said, and she was shaking all over. He was standing in front of the fireplace, red in the face, holding some papers at arms' length and brandishing them about. When he saw me, he threw them in every direction, then he started yelling at *me!*"

Fia paused, and took a long drag from her cigarette.

"Well, what happened next?" My friend was yielding to her tendency to over-dramatize everything, dragging it out, when all I wanted to know was whether my portrait had been ruined.

"He yelled something about how he'd lost thousands and thousands of dollars because of the divorce, and he was in a financial hellhole, and now she was trying to get more. Then Hana yelled something back at him. They were facing each other across that big room, and I took my life in my hands and walked into the middle and stood between them.

" 'The kids have to go to the dentist!' Hana yelled, 'and you wanted that they ride horses and play the piano, it was all your idea—and now you want to pay for nothing!' "

Fia's imitation of Hana's speech was spot-on.

"Then Bruce bellowed, 'Why don't *you* earn some money? I've had to sell the boat, and I live in a dump! I sure can't afford to live in a place like this!' and he swept his hand around the room. 'You'll have to sell this house and live somewhere that isn't so goddam comfortable! And how about selling some of this expensive furniture!' "

"Then he turned around, and with a swipe of his fist, knocked everything off the mantel! Remember those little Baccarat animals that Hana had there? I think a couple of them broke. I've never seen a man so convulsed with rage. And believe me, there was a lot of anger in *my* divorce."

Even though I wanted to get to what happened to my painting, I interrupted. "Hana used to say she thought Bruce was using cocaine."

"I'm not sure. Alcohol can make you crazy too." She gazed off toward the middle of the room, and I knew she was thinking of Arnie's drinking or Eric's drug problem, or both. "But he looked quite thin, so it might be drugs. The next thing I knew, he'd snatched the portrait off the wall, opened the glass sliding doors—walked out and heaved it off the deck!"

The waiter came with our salads, and I controlled myself until he walked away. "Was the portrait ruined? She'll have to get a restraining order against that sonofabitch."

"The painting is being restored, she didn't want to tell you about it. And she has a restraining order; I talked to her last week."

It was a tossup as to which I was more upset about, Bruce's treatment of Hana or the portrait.

I tried to enjoy my artichoke hearts, and neither of us spoke for awhile. Looking around while I ate, I removed myself from Hana's troubles by observing the eclectic mixture of characters on view— bearded, long-haired men in sweaters and cordoroys; wealthy women in expensive suits or blazers; professors wearing jackets with suede elbow patches; well-to-do blacks. Attesting to the international flavor of Berkeley, and mixed in with the locals, was an assortment of foreigners: Asians, Egyptians, and Arabs. Three Africans in long robes were seated with two gray-suited businessmen, no doubt important dignitaries being entertained by university bigwigs, and at a nearby table, a conversation was being conducted entirely in French.

We finished our salads and ordered a chocolate torte. By now we were into our second glass of Cabernet and were both a little high.

"Let's drink to staying married," Fia said, holding up her glass and laughing.

"Cheers!"

I reached for my glass, and accidentally knocked it over. Red wine went everywhere, but the bus boy cleaned it up, and we giggled. When we left we were in great spirits. After I transferred Fia's portrait to the back of my station wagon and drove home, I had to take a long nap.

A few weeks later, when I returned the newly-varnished painting, Fia and Arnie were in France, so I left it with the maid.

A few months after Fia returned from Europe, the insidiousness of the drug culture and its pervasiveness in the Bay Area finally hit home. She had invited me over to Belvedere to get my opinion on a few paintings she'd borrowed from Oliver Rakestraw's Gallery. She wanted to buy one or two, and said she needed my advice. I was flattered that she wanted my opinion, since I liked sharing my views on art with anyone and everyone. She fed me a great brunch, lobster bisque.

I had been sorry when she and Arnie sold the Victorian in San Francisco, but she'd fallen in love with Belvedere. Who could blame her; the views were spectacular. Arnie went along with anything Fia wanted; when all was said and done, it was her money.

"Fia, you're the one who's going to live with these works; it should be your choice more than anyone else's," I said.

"But I want to have the right paintings, *quality* paintings. And you can tell me what looks best in my new house!"

She'd brought home some real treasures, a small Bierstadt and two William Keiths, plus three or four plein air California landscapes from the '20s and '30s. I recognized two artists from the Society of Six—a watercolor boat scene by Maurice Logan, and a paint-laden landscape by Louis Siegrist, done in the period before his heavily textured gypsum and sand paintings. We were standing with coffee cups in hand, ready to discuss the works, when the phone rang.

I could tell from Fia's face that it was bad news.

"Is he all right?" she asked. There was a pause. "Come over *now?*" Another pause. "Well, I guess so. Yes, right away. Yes, I know the address." She hung up. Her face was white, and her hands were shaking.

"Bad news about Eric." She sat down hard on the nearest chair. "I have to go. We'll do this another time, Nat. Please forgive me."

"Don't be ridiculous. What's wrong—is he ill?"

"That was his girlfriend. Yes, well, he was ill—drugs again—but I guess he's recovered. I'll see you out." She stood up.

"I'll let myself out. Dear one, I'm so sorry. I hope he'll be okay." I started for the door. "Can you get him into treatment, do you think?" I knew this was crossing the line. Fia was frank and open, except when it came to her own problems.

No answer. Her back was turned, so I again started to leave.

"Nat—wait. Nat, will you go with me? I hate to go there alone, and Arnie would rather I didn't bother him at work."

I had to think about it. Get involved with that creepy kid? I didn't want to.

"Sure, I'll go," I said. "But what about Eric's real father?"

Fia looked at me with eyebrows raised. "Are you kidding? I've never had any help with the kids, other than financial, from Howard Shafer."

"Okay, let's go."

We drove through dense fog over the Golden Gate bridge, then through city streets past Golden Gate park, and finally into the Haight Ashbury district. Fia was silent most of the way, and her hands gripped the wheel as if she were hanging on for dear life.

I was struck by the change in her. No longer was she sparkling and ebullient. She spoke only once, and that was to say, "The sole contact I have with Howard is through his lawyer. Eric and Cissy have no contact with him at all."

"He's an asshole!" I said. "Why can't he give you some help raising his own kids?"

"Because he doesn't want to. You'd be surprised how many women I know who live with the same situation. If it weren't for Arnie, Cissy and Eric wouldn't have a father at all."

The last time I'd seen Arnie he'd looked pretty blitzed, as if fatherhood was the last thing on his mind. I changed the subject, making some remark about the traffic.

It was a cool, gray afternoon, typical of San Francisco summers. The morning fog hadn't cleared yet, and I was glad I was wearing a sweater. We couldn't find parking on Eric's street, so we pulled into the shoddy business district, got out, and locked the car. All around us were boarded-up shops. We passed several stores with tattered psychedelic posters in the front windows advertising the Jefferson Airplane and Family Dog concerts, with BILL GRAHAM PRESENTS in large faded letters. A bookstore, closed for business, had windows boasting copies of *The Tibetan Book of the Dead*.

Two kids were huddled in a blanket together, half sitting, half lying, propped against the door of a grocery—a young boy playing a flute, and a carrot-haired girl. As we passed them, the girl raised her hand and smiled at me, then slowly extended her filthy palm. I turned my head away, and she yelled "Hey!" and held up a crudely printed sign—NEED MONEY FOR MEDICINE.

We passed other signs posted on telephone poles and on the sides of buildings:

MEETING OF ALL ACIDHEADS
POLO FIELD NEXT SUNDAY

SPEED IS GREAT—ACID'S BETTER!

"Isn't this awful?" said Fia. "This is what the Summer of Love led to. That was when Eric moved here, he and thousands of others from all over creation. I've been trying to get him out ever since."

Entering the residential area of the Haight, we heard a loud commotion. Two cops were struggling with a tall man with long, matted hair. He wore a white robe which trailed along the ground, and as they wrestled with him, one of the cops barked, "Come on, Jesus. You been standin' around here botherin' people long enough!"

The young man suddenly stood quite still. He reached out and laid a hand on each of his captors' heads, his voluminous sleeves cascading from dirt-streaked arms.

"Bless you," he said, a saintly smile lighting his face. Then he became agitated once more and began spouting Biblical phrases.

"Judge not, and you will not be judged," he yelled in a rasping, frenzied voice, "Condemn not, and you will not be condemned;

forgive, and you will be forgiven!" He raised both arms and waved them in the direction of Fia and me. "The Son of Man must suffer many things, be rejected by the elders and chief priests and scribes, and be killed, and on the third day be raised!"

The policemen grabbed him, one on either side, but he only shouted louder. "Foxes have holes, and birds of the air have nests; but the Son of Man has nowhere to lay his head!"

As they led him away, I noticed splotches of blood along one side of his robe, and he was limping badly. I wondered if he had been beaten by these young cops. I decided he hadn't, judging from the careful way they were treating him now. But someone had.

"Nat, I'm so sorry to put you through this," said Fia, "but I really need you today."

"Forget it! We're buddies, remember?"

We kept walking, arm in arm, passing one house after another, some in fairly good condition, others falling to pieces.

Finally Fia said, "Here it is."

We went up splintered stairs and entered the front door of a once-elegant three-story house, no doubt built in the 1840s or '50s, now fallen into a state of disrepair that was hard to describe. The delicately carved scrollwork on the portico was stripped bare of paint, and the angled double bay windows were hung with torn paper shades. The marble floor in the vestibule was cracked and stained, and garnet-red embossed wallpaper hung off the walls in long strips. To the right of the entry was a closed door with the sign LANDLORD.

As we started to climb the stairs, I smelled a rank combination of marijuana and urine. A big German shepherd, friendly but frightening, greeted us on the first landing. We continued to trudge upward.

"Sorry again," Fia panted, "We're almost there." We were on the third floor now, and we started down the hall past piles of old blankets and discarded litter. I knew now why Fia dreaded coming here; it was horribly depressing. Graffiti was scrawled on every wall, mostly referring to drugs or activities one could participate in with various body parts.

She stopped at one of the doors and knocked.

"Who is it?" a male voice answered.

"It's your mom."

"Wait a minute!" Eric opened the door and looked out. "We didn't ask you to bring your society friends," he growled. He looked sick, and was very thin and pale. His hair was long, uncombed and unwashed, and he wore a dirty undershirt and torn jeans.

"This is the friend who did my portrait, remember? Natalie! She isn't society, she's an artist. Let us in, please. Francine called, and you must have told her to do so."

"I didn't *tell* her do it, she just did it," he sniped, but he stood aside, and we went in. The room was small, with a fifteen-foot ceiling, and other than the ubiquitous psychedelic posters and candles, was pretty bare. I could smell incense, which was a welcome relief. The floor had no rug, and there was a dirty sink with stained panties draped along the side. A misshapen upholstered chair sat in one corner. We were at the rear of the house, and the window covering here was a ragged curtain made from two or three Indian bedspreads. The Gothic arched window was the handsomest part of the room, but was defaced by its covering. I noticed an expensive-looking electric guitar and large amplifier on the floor next to the chair.

A girl lay on the bed, covered except for her face and arms. She was young and pretty with long blonde hair, but like Eric, her flesh was sickly pale.

"Hello, Francine," said Fia, putting her hand on the girl's shoulder.

"Hi." The girl attempted to prop herself up on one elbow.

"No, don't get up. Are you not feeling well? What is it that you two wanted?"

Fia had reverted to her usual 'take charge' self. I was glad, because I was going to be no help at all; my knees were weak and my stomach queasy from the sounds and sights of the last half-hour. All

I wanted to do was run away from these children and their self-perpetuating problems. I stepped back toward the door and hopefully out of the scene.

"Well, it's like this, Mom," said Eric. He beamed a simpering smile at Fia, changing suddenly from a sniveling, ungrateful boor to a mama's boy, begging for just one more cookie. "We're kinda behind on the rent. I was hoping you could pay it for this month and next."

I wondered if she was going to ask him about his illness or about the drugs.

"Why next month too?"

"Well, you know that gig I was supposed to get, traveling with the Screwed Tubes? Now they tell me they don't need another guitarist—they've got three already!" He plopped down on the bed next to Francine and put his head in his hands. I thought he was about to cry, but when he raised his head his eyes were dry.

"Weren't you going to look for work at that pizza kitchen?" Fia asked. "I told you I know the owner, and he said for you to come in any time and fill out an application."

"I guess I haven't got around to it."

Fia impatiently crossed her arms, purse dangling from her shoulder. Eric dropped his eyes again, and Francine rolled over in bed and moaned, covering her head with the grimy blanket.

"And, uh, mom, there's somethin' else. Francine's pregnant."

"*What?* I knew it! I warned you both! You're not married, you have no money, no job, and now this!"

"But think about it, Mom, you're gonna to be a grandmother!"

I almost laughed out loud at the boy's audacity.

"I thought you'd be—"

"Shut up, I'm thinking," she snapped.

It was quiet for what seemed like several minutes, but was probably only thirty seconds.

Finally, Fia said, "Get up, Francine. Get dressed. You're coming home with me. I mean it, get up. I'll pay your rent for one month, but the condition is that Francine comes with me, now."

And that's what happened. Eric stayed, and Francine struggled into her jeans and came with us, stumbling weakly down the stairs. Fia held onto her arm all the way. On the way out, we stopped at the landlord's room. A seventy-ish black man stood in the doorway, his face sorrowful, while Fia wrote out a check. As we waited, Francine collapsed, sinking down on the bottom stairs. I wondered if she was nauseous with the baby, or if she, too, was on drugs.

Fia had never asked Eric about his drug problem. I suppose it was because she was sick of lecturing him, or maybe it was because she thought Francine had only used it as a ruse to get her over there.

Our visit was capped nicely when one of a group of hippies standing near our car yelled, "What you mothahfuckahs starin' at us for? We ain't no tourist attraction!"

I got home late that day. Unusually, the San Rafael Bridge had been busy with traffic, plus I got lost going through Richmond.

Ben was angry. I didn't blame him; I'd forgotten all about meeting him for drinks and a late lunch in the city with his New York boss, Freddy Flanders, the millionaire Irishman who headed Flanders & Schuman.

Freddy had a knack for investing other people's money. I had met him before and liked him, and he seemed to like me too. He was a much more sophisticated, flamboyant character than Ben's local boss, Sam Schuman. True to his name, Sam did look a bit like a shoe salesman. He wore rumpled suits and last month's haircut, and had a stubby cigar forever stuck in the side of his mouth.

Poor Ben; not only did he have to endure turpentine, oil paints, and cigarette fumes at home, but cigar smoke at work.

Despite his lack of polish, Sam was admired in Bay Area financial circles. He wheeled and dealed in securities and the stock market like an inspired sorcerer, making money hand over fist, year after year. He put most of the money from killings on the market back into his investments, but farsightedly, he put some of it into

California real estate as well. Ben was making a great salary at this time, a spillover from Sam's magic.

Ben confronted me as soon as I walked through the door.

"How many times is this going to happen, Nat? Do you want me to succeed in this job or not? I would think you could take a little responsibility for our financial welfare! Sam was really pissed, and I didn't know where the hell you were, so I had to make up a cockamamie excuse that you had to fly out to New Mexico to see your sick aunt!"

"I'm so sorry, Ben, really I am!"

We were standing in the kitchen. I had tried to explain Fia's plight, and her begging me to go with her to the Haight. He yanked his tie off, and I plopped my purse on the counter, intending to rustle up a quick supper to appease him.

"Would you like a hamburger?" I asked, poking my head in the freezer to see if we had meat and buns.

"I'm not hungry. You missed a great meal. Chateaubriand steaks and lobster." His tone was icy. "What kind of mother is Fia, anyway, and what happened to her son that he's such a flake?"

"Well, I don't see that it's all *her* fault. That Shafer guy hasn't been there at all for his kids, and Arnie doesn't seem to want to be involved. I feel sorry for Fia. Besides Eric's problems, I'm pretty sure Arnie's an alcoholic. You said so yourself."

"I'll be glad when you start feeling sorry for *me*. I'm going to take a shower."

He spent the evening sitting in front of the TV, drinking Scotch.

It was a day or two before we made up, and that was only after I said I was sorry several times and vowed that I would keep track of our own marital concerns and pay less attention to my friends' troubles.

"Next time I'll just say no," I assured him.

Fia called the following week. *"Darling!* I called to tell you we can choose the paintings later on. Oliver told me I can keep all of them for a while, to just take my time. I'll have to put off choosing, though, because right now Francine is staying with me."

Oliver Rakestraw was no fool. Probably Fia would end up buying them all—the Bierstadt, the Keiths, the Logan and the Siegrist. He told her she could have them all for the ridiculous price of $6,800—the Bierstadt accounting for most of the price.

"I've done everything I can to talk Francine into an abortion," Fia went on, "but she's so stubborn! I'm taking her back to Eric in a few days. She's promised to get Eric into drug treatment and to force him to find a job. I think she can do it, too, don't you? This baby seems to have made her more motivated."

Fia's tone was upbeat. I think she really had convinced herself that Eric was going to take a new direction in life.

I didn't answer. I didn't share her optimism, not for one second.

I can't explain the next part of my life. I can't make clear to the reader or even to myself why I behaved the way I behaved. It must be that, unbeknownst to myself, I have a streak of venality within me; that is to say, a low moral compass. Or maybe I've been programmed to follow the dictates of someone with a stronger personality. This infers that I am inherently weak and cowardly. But weak and cowardly are two words I never thought would be used to describe Natalie Newbury.

Or maybe it was simply that I was corrupted by Nikki's money. Whatever it was, I was about to do something that weakened my marriage.

Investments and the stock market were up, and Ben was feeling that finally we were becoming financially secure. The only fly in the ointment was the pressure he was getting from both Sam and the New York office to bring in business. So far he was doing very well, but I could tell he was feeling the strain. One night over dinner, noticing his tired look, I told him he needed to take a week off.

"Couldn't we take a short vacation? Go up to Mendocino or down to Monterey?"

He nearly snapped my head off. "Natalie, don't you know I can't leave, even for a few days? What do you think I do all day over there, cut out paper dolls? I'm busting my balls trying to get people to turn over their money to us instead of some other firm, some other hotshot with a great idea for turning dross into gold."

Ben saw the house pictured in a realty office window that he happened to pass one Saturday after getting a haircut. After he saw it, I knew he wanted to buy it, and when we went to see it together, I fell in love with it too.

We moved to Montclair from Berkeley in May of 1968. Our house was one of the more interesting homes in the Wildwood Gardens neighborhood. It was built of wood and used brick, and it had arched inner doorways and swooping rooflines. The living room was the most dramatic part of the house, with a high vaulted ceiling, and even though it was large, still exuded warmth and friendliness. The fireplace was massive and the floors were Mexican tile, continuing throughout the main floor and up a spiral staircase. We used white sofas and chairs and Oriental rugs throughout, all of which I shopped for carefully and frugally over the next few months.

My spacious studio was separate, and of course that was one of the reasons I'd fallen so hard. It was built for a mother-in-law, also constructed of wood and brick, with immense north windows. The path to the studio went through an overgrown back garden, a sloping mass of azaleas, viburnum and ceanothus. Weed-smothered beds had probably been crowded with flowers in the past. The garden looked as if it would require way too much work, but Ben said he needed the challenge. Later on, he did a lot of landscaping with shade plants, since we had so little bright sun.

We were in our mid-thirties then and shared an indescribable excitement in fixing up the place; planning projects to improve it, choosing paint colors, tile, and bathroom fixtures. I drove around on a flurry of fabric-shopping sprees, and Ben came home every night wanting to make love in a different room. We especially liked the living room at night, with the fireplace roaring like an inferno. Once, during one of our lovemaking sessions, although nearly every light in the house was switched off, someone rang the doorbell. Ben, naked, hid behind a sofa, and I hurriedly dressed and rushed to the door. An elderly woman introduced herself as Mrs. Fitzgerald from three doors away. With the lights off and fireplace blazing, she must have known what we were doing.

"I'm so sorry to interrupt," she said, holding out a chocolate cake. Her use of the word indicated her complete understanding. In a tiny voice she added, "I just wanted to welcome you to the neighborhood . . ."

CHAPTER SIX

NIKKI

Nikki Falkenstein Lippmann and I met in the '60s when sexual mores were beginning to loosen, and thousands of marriages all over America were breaking up. Men were quitting their jobs to pursue long-held, cherished dreams; women were leaving their children to pursue careers or other men. In some divorces, fathers were given custody of the children. The courts, especially in California, were full of these cases.

But Nikki never lost her boys.

I suppose Nikki and her liaisons were no more shocking than what was going on everywhere else in the Bay Area and in the entire country. It was just that she was the first adulteress I ever knew. She was also the most pampered and over-indulged woman I ever met.

Months had passed since we'd moved, and we were beginning to settle in like old-timers. I went to a city council meeting one night in the Montclair town hall, where there was to be a discussion of a new miniature bridge to be built over a big pond in the neighborhood park; the current bridge was rotting away. I knew an architect I thought could do an aesthetically-pleasing design, and I wanted to do him a favor, so I made a pitch for my friend, endured the rest of the evening's boring civic formalities, then left to go home. As I left, a man preceded me down the steps. He had a cloud of silver-blonde hair and a build that made me think of a Greek statue. I was looking him over as a possible model as we headed for the parking lot. (I always used this excuse when ogling a good-looking man.)

Just then a woman drove up in a Mercedes and yelled, "Aaron!"

He folded his long legs into the car, and I got a glimpse of a woman with jet-black hair in the driver's seat. She threw a smug look in my direction that seemed to say *He's all mine, honey.*

When I got home, Ben relayed the message that one of our neighbors had called, wanting me to paint her twins. *Great!* I needed the money to help pay for new dining room furniture.

A few days later, I was shopping at the local drugstore. At my request the owner, Charlie Sprague, had begun saving empty cans, which I needed to mix and store paint. His store had a soda fountain, and as I went in I saw the woman who'd picked up the Adonis in her Mercedes. She was sipping a soft drink and having an animated conversation with the realtor we'd been dealing with, Marty Stubbs. Marty greeted me, then introduced me to Nikki. It turned out she had recently moved into a house near us on Crocker.

"I know that house," I said, "it's only four doors away from us. Come over and visit when you get settled."

"Sure. I could use some help with dry cleaners and food markets, all that kind of thing." She laughed, and I was struck by her dark, mischievous eyes.

"Your husband certainly got into the community spirit quickly, attending one of the town meetings," I said. "Actually, we're new here too."

"Aaron wants to find out everything he can about Montclair; this is the first time he ever owned a house."

She stood up, shook hands with Marty, said she was happy to have met me, and left. She was wearing tight black jeans, and as she walked away, her small rear end undulated in a slow, sensuous motion. Marty watched her all the way out the door.

Nikki and I got to be friends over early morning coffee, meeting a couple of times a week. She was interested in our house, and said that she liked it three times as much as the one they'd just bought. She said if we ever decided to move, she'd like to buy it.

"But we just moved in!"

Nikki was from the wealthy Falkenstein family who at that time owned theaters and department stores all over the Bay Area. Maybe still do, I don't know. She told me she'd been so spoiled as a young girl that when she got home from her first honeymoon (at age seventeen), she waited three days for someone to unpack her suitcases. She had been utterly shocked, she said, when she had to start washing out her own underwear.

She constantly made fun of her own shortcomings, and I told her some of the dumb things I'd done when I was first learning to cook, like the time I tried to brown the bottom of a pie on an electric burner. It was a beautiful pie I had made myself, cherry with a lattice crust, and it was in a Pyrex dish.

We spent a lot of time laughing.

Ben and I got to know Aaron too. The four of us would go to movies, then hang out at Millie's Diner. Although we had little in common with the Lippmanns in any other area, we all loved movies, and there were some great ones in those years. I'll never forget the night we saw *Funny Girl*, because Nikki and Aaron got into a fight immediately afterward in front of the movie house. I think I'd made a remark about being glad Barbra Streisand hadn't had her nose done because it would have ruined her voice, and Aaron said, "Well, I think she should—it's ugly as hell."

"Then I guess you don't like *my* nose!" Nikki snapped.

After that, the spat got more and more vicious, ending with Nikki telling Aaron he was a schmuck.

The fact that Aaron was Nikki's third husband was incredible to me, since she was only thirty-five. She'd been married young, with her parents' permission, to a young Jewish businessman, and right away had two little boys. She was too young to know what she wanted out of life, and became desperately bored and unhappy. The marriage ended when she fell in love with her psychiatrist, who was twenty years older. Nikki told me after they'd been involved for months in an affair (or as Nikki termed it, office-screwing) the doctor came up with a diagnosis for all her problems. He said Nikki fell in love with *him* because she was really in love with *her father*. When she told me that I said, "Did you ever tell your mother what the shrink said, that you were in love with your dad?"

"Yeah. She said fine, she'd make us a picnic lunch."

I was arranging doughnuts on a plate, and I laughed so hard the doughnuts fell off and rolled all around on the floor. We ate them anyway.

So Nikki divorced her husband and married her shrink.

Nikki's dad, Abe Falkenstein, was a short, dark man whom both Nikki and her sister Ethel adored. Ben and I met him at a big holiday party at the Falkenstein home in Pacific Heights. Liked him, hated his cigars. I liked Nikki's mother, too, a round brunette lady with arched eyebrows and the presence of a Russian tsarina. Nikki said her mom spent most of her time shopping.

Now in her third marriage, Nikki was bored again. I remember how she used to fidget and fiddle with her wedding ring. She would take it off, mindlessly turn it around in her hand while carrying on a conversation, then put it back on. I never thought of the connection until years later. Oh, yeah—she was thinking about taking it off for good.

I loved looking at Aaron, but actually he was dull. Once you got over being impressed with his handstands, performed in our living room the first night we had them over, once you'd heard about his car collection, his children by his first marriage, and his belief in certain dietary regimens, there wasn't much left to find out.

"Aaron buys all this stuff at the health food store," Nikki said, "bottles of pills, packets of powders. If you ask me, it's all a bunch of poppycaca." Nikki was uneducated, and she didn't read. She had a patched-together, bizarre vocabulary which got her meaning across but contained words yet to be found in any dictionary.

Since her family was loaded, I felt no shame in suggesting that I do her portrait. She was a great looking girl, so I mentioned it one day when she was visiting my studio. I was working, shading in a background on my pastel of the twins, and I'd thrown an old red, orange and purple paisley shawl against the back of my newly purchased studio couch. Nikki was sitting on it cross-legged, talking while she watched me. She'd loosened her long hair, and it floated around her head in electric waves.

"You look fantastic today, Nikki! You have to let me paint you. For big bucks, of course. And we'll do it with your hair all bushy like this." I stepped over and felt the texture, unable to believe its heavy luxuriance. "I've never painted hair like yours, it'll be a challenge!"

"Omigod, my hair is like Brillo. And on top of everything, I'm getting my father's moustache."

"Nuts to that. It'll be fun, and you'll be gorgeous!"

I got out the scrapbook I kept with photos of all the portraits I had done up to now. She seemed to love them all, especially Fia's, and when she asked how much, I quoted a price of $5000.

She said, without blinking an eye, "I'll give you $7500."

What could I say to that, except, "You won't be sorry. It will be a fabulous picture, I promise!"

Much of Nikki's appeal was her body. She was short, and her neck wasn't very long, but she had nice boobs, a tiny waist with small hips, and dainty arms and hands.

When I finished the twins two weeks later, I started Nikki. I did a dozen or so charcoal sketches first, as usual, and one of them turned out so well that Nikki bought it and took it home. For the oil painting, a 36" x 40" horizontal, I posed her on the couch wearing a scoop-necked white sweater and black pants. We tried several poses with her sitting cross-legged, like she'd been sitting the day I suggested the portrait. But I decided her legs weren't long enough for a graceful pose, so I put her in a long black velvet skirt, with one arm raised and resting on the end cushion, the other arm bent, with her hand in her lap, body turned to the side. The white sweater defined her figure nicely against the colorful paisley. That first day I sketched in the head and body, then laid in a background of shimmering violets and mauves, which echoed the darker purple in the shawl.

On June 5, 1968, I was painting Nikki's hands, always a difficult task. I had the radio on with Mozart playing, and suddenly the music was interrupted and the news came on. Bobby Kennedy had been shot and killed in Los Angeles, where he had just won the Democratic presidential nomination. I think our friendship was cemented forever the day we heard the news. Nikki and I, both of us dyed-in-the-wool Democrats, embraced and sobbed our hearts out.

Just five years after JFK. Just two months after King.

Nikki's portrait was still unfinished when she and Aaron left for Puerto Vallarta. Like Fia and Arnie, they had the money to travel constantly, forever flying away to any place that had "Palm" in the name. Palm Springs, Palm Desert, Palm Beach.

Getting away didn't seem to be a problem; Nikki always seemed to find good sitters for the boys, and of course there was her housekeeper.

When they came back from Mexico after two weeks away, she was so tanned I would have had to change all the color relationships I had so carefully worked out. I said we would have to wait until her tan had faded a little before resuming the sittings. So that's what we did, and I finished the portrait a couple of months later.

Gradually I learned that disturbance loomed in the Lippmann marriage. Evidently things didn't go too well in Mexico. She told me Aaron got sick, and she left him every day to go parasailing or traveling by bus to see the ruins.

I had a feeling Nikki was on her way to another divorce.

Somewhere on the trip she'd met a wealthy businessman, a man I'd read about in *Time* and *Newsweek*; he built gargantuan office complexes and shopping malls. Gerald was Jewish (Nikki usually stayed close to her roots) and soon after her return from Mexico he called and wanted her to meet him for a weekend somewhere. They decided on Los Angeles because he had business there, and for some reason she began a campaign to get me to go with her. "If you go along, Aaron won't suspect a thing," she said. "And you can go to the museums or do anything you want." She said she would pay my plane fare, that all I had to do was fly down and stay in the same hotel.

I must have been nuts, or bored, because I agreed to do it.

It was true that I had been dying to see the new L.A. museums, but I shouldn't have gone. Both she and Gerald were married to other people, and Aaron was a nice guy, although vacuous as a Hollywood starlet.

But it was the '60s; everyone was doing it.

Nikki told Aaron she was taking me along to southern California on a shopping trip for their new house, how she would be using my artistic eye to help her shop for furniture. She told him she absolutely could not pick out a new table or upholstery fabric without my expert help.

We fed the same story to Ben.

By now I had been so corrupted by Nikki that I didn't even cross my fingers behind my back. I mentioned it a few days before we were to leave, while we were in the dining room having coffee after dinner.

Ben might have agreed to my accompanying Nikki except for one thing; he had planned our own trip for that weekend. He'd been talking about investing some of our savings, by now a goodly chunk, in real estate. The stock market had been churning so wildly that even Ben was having second thoughts about Wall Street. Maybe buying property would be smarter, he said.

He wanted me to participate in some of these financial decisions, and he reminded me that I had agreed to accompany him the following weekend to look at properties.

"You're going with me to Tahoe, remember?" He sounded resentful; I knew he was remembering the time I forgot his business luncheon with the brass from New York.

"Yes, I know," I lied. I'd forgotten about this, too.

"I told you about several areas I want to look at up there, and right now is the time to buy. I can't decide on something like that alone, and besides, I don't want to drive up there by myself!"

"But Nikki is such a good customer," I said, adding cream to my coffee. "She bought the charcoal sketch for $200, and I'm getting $7500 for this portrait. So couldn't you go alone? Or maybe we can do it later on!"

"I don't want to do it later on. Our calendars will fill up, you'll get busy with another portrait, and there won't be a time to do it."

He raised his cup and held it there, waiting for me to change my mind.

But I was growing stubborn. It seemed to me he was making a big thing out of very little, and Nikki *needed* me to go with her. I picked up a fork, twirling it in my hand.

Finally he stood up. "All right, Nat, you win. But if I know Nikki, there's some other reason for her to want to go to L.A. without Aaron. Let your conscience be your guide about that."

I sat there, stunned. How could he possibly have known?

Aaron drove us to the airport, and we flew down from Oakland. In the plane, I noticed Nikki had removed her wedding ring.

Gerald Epstein, an unremarkable-looking small man in an expensive suit, met us at the Los Angeles airport in a monstrous limousine. He looked to be around fifty-five or so. Nikki had fallen for her father again.

She introduced us as we approached the limo. "Gerald sweetie, this is Natalie, my artist friend. Remember I told you she was coming along?"

He nodded briefly in my direction, obviously annoyed that I was there at all. Nikki had gone into the quivering shivers as soon as she was in this man's presence, and I wondered what I was missing. I was sure what she liked was the money and power; you could feel it oozing out of him.

It took forever to get to the hotel, and I was silent on the way to Rodeo Drive, except once when I commented on what I thought was a handsome new building. Gerald raised his head from Nikki's neck long enough to say, "You like that pile of junk? It's nothing."

The titan had spoken. I shrank into my corner of the limo. I was extremely uncomfortable while Nikki and this guy slobbered over each other all the way into town, resisting the impulse to shinny over the seat and ride in front with the driver. The chauffeur's eyes met mine in the rear-view mirror. I wondered how many times he'd driven this limo while a similar scenario played out behind him. A kajillion?

We stayed on Rodeo Drive in a small, luxurious hotel, the kind Ben and I could never afford to stay in. I didn't see Nikki much while we were there except for the first night, when she insisted I have dinner with them in the ultra-exclusive hotel restaurant. Gerald was not thrilled to have me there and made it evident, so I kept trotting from the table to the ladies' restroom. It was garish and glittering, drenched in potted orchids, silver-and-gold wallpaper, and gold-plated sink fixtures. It epitomized everything I hated about Los Angeles—so ostentatious and showy.

Besides peeing, I spent my time fluffing up my hair, adding another layer of lipstick, or smoking. Sometimes I riffled through a magazine. I was going broke tipping the maid.

Each time I went back to the table, there were more empty martini glasses, and Nikki and Gerald were drowning more deeply in one another. They hardly ate, but I made up for that. I finished every course, gulping down soup, salad, entrée, and two desserts. You would think I hadn't eaten for a week. I recall smacking my lips over my crème brûlée, causing Gerald to turn his head in annoyance.

They left the table eventually, and Nikki didn't come back to our room until the next morning.

I spent the next day at the new Los Angeles County Museum, LACMA, on Wilshire Boulevard. It was right next to the La Brea Tar Pits, where aeons before the dinosaurs had been trapped in goo. *Talk about contrasting the old with the new!* The art museum was handsome, mammoth in size, and I was thrilled to see a terrific Frans Hals show.

From my point of view, the trip was particularly worthwhile.

Evidently Gerald was nifty in bed, so Nikki said she'd gotten a lot out of our little vacation, too. Unfortunately, I had even become involved in this aspect of our excursion. At the last minute back home, Nikki asked if I'd mind bringing my diaphragm along. Even though she said Aaron claimed that he trusted her like his own mother, he might decide to check to see if her contraption was in its rightful place, tucked away in her nightstand drawer.

This made me wonder how much Aaron trusted his mother.

I said I would have to think it over. Would Ben check to see if my diaphragm was in the bathroom, where I kept it? I used birth control because, even though the doctors said my chances of ever becoming pregnant were minimal, Ben and I had decided that a pregnancy this late in our marriage would be most inconvenient. I decided that he wouldn't check, so I said okay, and packed the thing.

I don't know why Nikki thought my personal equipment would fit her. I was five inches taller than she, and although I was slender, I didn't have her petite build. But that was her problem.

Remembering that Nikki had been so generous concerning the portrait, I even threw in a tube of vaginal jelly.

By Sunday afternoon our baccanalia was nearing its close. Our plane left in an hour and a half, so I packed my overnighter bag, and since I hadn't heard from Nikki, and since I knew Mr. Moneybags planned to leave early that morning, I went down the hall and knocked.

She opened the door wearing a short red satin robe.

"Hi," she said.

"Hi."

"Come in, but I don't feel like talking. We can talk on the plane, 'kay?"

She plopped down on the side of the bed and started pulling on her panty hose. I shouldn't have looked, but there it was. On the bottom sheet of the unmade bed was a small, semi-opaque white puddle.

It seemed she hadn't needed my diaphragm after all.

I sat down slowly in a satin slipper chair, and said, "You look beat."

"Yeah, I am. That furniture shopping, it can really take it out of you."

"Glad I didn't have to do any."

"Tote that bar, lift that bale."

"Get a little drunk—"

"*—and you pay retail.*"

We laughed.

"I'm not kidding, you really look worn down, girl." She had dark circles under her eyes, and moved as if carrying a heavy burden. "But you look happy!" I went on in my most upbeat voice. She didn't, but I wanted to sound encouraging.

"I'm a sap. I'm sap-happy. But I really like the guy. He told me I was beautiful every time he came. Once he even said he loved me! He kind of—well—croaked it."

"Well, just so he didn't *actually* croak," I said. "How old is Gerald, anyway?"

"Old enough to be rich. He's pretty good in bed, don't worry about it. What's the Kamasutra, anyhow?"

"I think it's a whole lot of positions to make love, invented by the Hindus. All I know. There's the Camel, and the Goat, and the Ox . . ."

"I think we did frigging all of 'em last night. When he first said the word Kamasutra I thought he was talking about a hot new car. It was a funny time to bring up cars, I was thinkin', when we were both naked as jaybirds."

"Okay," I said, "but do you want to get dressed now? We're due at the airport in an hour."

On the way to the airport she said, "Hey, Nat, does Ben ever ask you to do kinky things, like wear his underwear, stuff like that?"

"*Unh-uh.* Kinkiest thing we ever do is go outdoors. Oh, I forgot—once we did it in the shower."

"Outdoors! Hey, never done that. But last night I think we covered everything but sodomy and S&N."

"I think you mean S&*M.* Oh, well . . ." I was laughing so hard, the cab driver turned around and looked at us. He was grinning from ear to ear, too, so he must have heard it all.

Aaron met us at the airport, and when I got home Ben had arrived back from Tahoe. He said he hadn't found anything he wanted to buy, but that he'd decided on the areas he liked, and that he was pretty sure I would like it too. He said all the indicators were that now was the time to invest, and that we should do it soon.

I told him we'd had fun in L.A., that Nikki was a barrel of laughs, and with my expert help, she had found a lot of great furniture.

Ben questioned my story about furniture shopping later on.

"What area did you girls shop in?" Luckily I knew enough to say, "Out on Western Avenue; it was great, lots of stores. They had everything she was looking for, big sofas, chests, rugs. I was exhausted!"

I wanted to tell him all about Frans Hals and LACMA, but I couldn't. If that was to be my only punishment, though, I could get through it. It might be a problem for Nikki to show off her non-existent furniture, but I would try to make sure Ben never went over there in the next month or so. By then, surely, she could acquire some stuff from somewhere.

A night or two after we got back, Ben told me that he and Aaron had gone out for hamburgers while Nikki and I were gone. Aaron said he was sure Nikki was fooling around, that there were all the signs. She'd done the same things with him when she was married to the psychiatrist.

"What kind of signs? What did he mean?"

I was still protecting her.

"He said that lately she isn't as interested in sex, and up to now she'd always been really hot. And she hangs up the phone when he comes into the room, or runs out to the store in the evening for bread or milk, whereas she never gave a rat's ass previous to now whether they had food in the house or not. He figured she was calling some guy."

Ben paused and looked me in the eye. "I believe him, Nat. I don't think Nikki should ever get married. She's a man trap!"

I made some comment in defense of Nikki, I don't remember what I said exactly. I was beginning to have doubts about the basis of our friendship, but I stayed loyal.

Following along the same topic, unfaithfulness in marriage, Fia called and told me she'd heard Freddy Flanders had a mistress he kept in San Francisco.

"I know you hate gossip, Nat, *ha ha*, but since he's Ben's boss, I thought you'd be interested. She's a former showgirl from New York, and he moved her out here to Nob Hill so he could visit her when he comes to San Francisco on business, and so his wife will never find out. Has he been coming out to the West Coast a lot?"

"He was here last week."

That night when I told Ben, he scoffed. "God's sakes! Fia and her scandal-mongering! And who cares, anyway?"

"Well, Freddy is married, isn't he? And you were just consigning Nikki to hellfire and damnation for your suspicions about her. Is there any difference?"

Ben hemmed and hawed, then walked outside to get the mail. He didn't answer my question.

But on my own, I decided to cool the friendship a little. Nikki asked me to go to Carmel with her so she could see Gerald again. This time we would be shopping for gourmet kitchen accessories. I said I couldn't, that I'd been asked to jury a show of figure painting at the SFWA Gallery. It was actually scheduled for another weekend, so I was fibbing, but it made a good excuse. And when she tried for another date for the following month, I made up another reason not to do it. I'm sure she finally realized I had decided not to continue aiding and abetting her mischief.

In August, we were invited to an elegant blast at Fia and Arnie's new home in Belvedere. Fia had finished an extensive six months of decorating, and was anxious to show off the place. She sent invitations, but before I had a chance to reply, she called to say we simply had to come; the portrait was in place and looked smashing.

The Bay Area was in the middle of a hot spell, and she said to bring swimsuits; they had a pool.

We drove over the San Rafael Bridge where traffic was always light, and since there didn't seem to be much parking space, Ben parked on a side road and we walked up to the house. It looked gigantic, a three-story contemporary built on stilts and concrete piles. The lot was very steep, but the landscaping—mostly juniper, toyon, and myrtle—camouflaged the abruptness of the rise.

Fia came to the door. "Darlings! So glad you're here! Please come in and find a drink. I have to speak to someone in the kitchen."

She rushed away, looking spectacular in white crepe palazzo pajamas. Live music was playing in the big living room, a small dance band selected from The Tree's big band, and trays of hors d'ouevres and drinks were being passed around by young men in white coats. Ben found someone to discuss the stock market with, so I grabbed a glass of champagne off a tray and stepped in front of the portrait to get a look. It hung on a wall behind a grouping of chairs.

Fia gazed out with all her charm and charisma. The stripes of the gown worked very well, I thought, and added to the drama of the picture. I couldn't help it; I was filled with a rush of pride. No one was standing near; no one saw me smiling at the wall.

I wandered into one of the side rooms, where the music wasn't quite so overwhelming. From there I walked out onto the large deck to join a few other people congregated there. Here, as at the Alta Mira, one could look out on all of San Francisco Bay. We all admired the panoramic view and the array of sailboats on the water, then somehow segued into a discussion of the news from Chicago. Vice President Humphrey had just been nominated for president at the Democratic Convention, and television had shown us the bloody violence inside the hall and out on the streets. Police arresting demonstrators, demonstrators retaliating any way they could.

"It's that nutty Jerry Rubin again—the God-damned draft dodger!"

"And the Yippies!"

"And Abbie Hoffman—who the hell is he anyway?"

"Dunno, but they're sure givin' it to the Democrats," said Arnie, walking over to kiss me on the cheek.

No one wanted to swim except for a few young people. We could see them far below us in the tree-enclosed pool. After an hour or so of sipping and socializing, we lined up for a buffet—filet of beef wrapped in crust, fettucini Alfredo, and baby asparagus. Ben and I found comfortable seats to eat and chat. This was one of Fia's larger parties, "a slate cleaner" as she so charmingly called it, and we didn't expect to dine at table.

I found myself sitting next to Marian Morse on one of two yellow loveseats. We had been eating and chatting for half an hour or so, when Bishop Pike of Grace Cathedral, that bastion of Episcopalianism on Nob Hill, bustled by. Wearing his white collar and purple robes, and with several gold chains swinging low on his chest, he strode purposefully through the room. He looked neither left nor right, as though he were on his way to an important meeting.

"Well! *If I'd known it was a costume party . . . !*" said Marian, and I started to laugh and couldn't stop.

The Bishop was there to officiate at Fia's announcement; her daughter Cissy was to be married to a boy from Santa Barbara. The newly-engaged couple stood in the middle of the room while we all applauded, and the band played a jazz version of the Wedding March. Fia and Arnie's two little daughters, wearing pink-checked dresses with organdy pinafores, hopped about excitedly, but I noticed that Eric and Francine weren't there.

70

Unfortunately, during the long hours of the party, Arnie got sloshed. At the buffet table, he grabbed my arm and, with an abundance of saliva accompanying the question, asked, "Whattya think of her money—spread all over this place?"

I didn't know how to answer, but finally said, "I think it looks wonderful!"

The Lippmann's divorce was finalized a year-and-a-half or so after I finished Nikki's portrait. It was difficult to get together with them as a couple, so mostly I saw Nikki and Ben occasionally saw Aaron. They sold the house, and Nikki and the boys abruptly moved to Los Angeles. She didn't marry Gerald, although I think she would have liked to. She told me he wouldn't leave his wife. Even so, I think she had a few more trysts with him in one location or another around the country. Eventually she married someone in Los Angeles, a fellow I heard owned a string of beauty salons.

Her name was Williams now. Sounded like she was branching out. I wrote her a few letters and mailed them to the only address she gave me, but she never answered.

I was fond of that girl, and I missed her. But my portrait business was beginning to expand, I made other friends, and our friendship went on hold. I wasn't to see Nikki again until five years later, just before Ben and I left America.

CHAPTER SEVEN

O-O-O-OHM-M-M-M-M-M-M

I remember that Ben and I met Rosie at Botts' Ice Cream parlor on College Avenue in Berkeley. We had jaywalked across the street to Botts after seeing *Midnight Cowboy* at the Elmwood Theater. After that traumatic experience, we needed cheering up.

I turned around, my cone laden with double-dip mocha-chocolate-chip, and found Ben talking with a dark-haired woman wearing a hooded sweatshirt and jeans.

"What flavor?" asked the clerk of the woman.

"That looks good!" she said, pointing to my cone. It turned out she'd been to see Hoffman and Voight too. She said she often went to movies by herself because her life was always in a ferment.

"Why is that?" I asked.

I wasn't usually so nosy, but there was something warm and approachable about the woman.

"Oh, you know, long work hours, and little time to do the things I really want to do."

She flashed a grin and said her name was Rosalia Rinaldo, but that we should call her Rosie. We stood outside on the sidewalk licking ice cream in the warm summer night, shooting the breeze like three best friends. She said she lived in part of an old shingle house on Hillegass, a few blocks away.

Ben told her what he did for a living, and Rosie said that she was a family therapist. I said I painted portraits. "I should paint you!"

"Watch out," said Ben, placing a warning hand on her shoulder. "My wife is completely unscrupulous when looking for models. She'll say anything—tell you that you look like no one else on earth—that you must be committed to canvas for all eternity! It's a lot of bullshit, and she isn't even very good."

I gave him a kick in the shins, and he grabbed me from behind, pinning my arms with his, chuckling.

"Stop! You're smearing me with strawberry!" I yelled.

Rosie looked from one of us to the other. "I've been trying to think of something special to get my parents for their fiftieth anniversary. I wonder if a portrait of me would be too—well, egotistical."

"I think it's a wonderful idea!"

I gave her my card, and two weeks later, she called.

I learned Rosie's story gradually over the next months, during our infrequent, short, postponed, interrupted, and widely separated sittings. Her practice was a busy one in those days. It seemed like everyone in the Bay Area was confused; everyone needed help leading their lives. Marriages were breaking up, young people were dropping out and sliding into the drug culture. Overdosing was rampant, and parents were desperately seeking answers for their own or their children's problems.

Once, when she was sitting for me, she was called away by her office. A father had phoned her answering service in a panic and said his son had just broken all the windows in their house on Grizzly Peak—what should they do? She told him to call 911. She told him the attendants would hospitalize his son, and that he was to meet her at her office. She had arrived for the sitting only twenty minutes before, and she was forty minutes late even then.

But I understood the demands of her profession. If I hadn't, I would never have finished the commission.

Despite all the interruptions, the portrait went pretty well. I was inspired by the project, and went to work each time with a heightened sense of anticipation. I posed her in a white blouse with colorful embroidery against the background of a tall cloisonné vase filled with red calla lilies and blue hydrangeas, then put behind that a wall of pattern inspired by a book of Peruvian embroidery I'd found at the library. I had searched all the antique stores in the area to find just the right vase, finally found it in a second-hand store on San Pablo Avenue.

It was difficult for Rosie to sit quietly as I painted. I've never known anyone with so many nervous tics, but maybe her demanding schedule was the reason for all these distracting habits. When she was talking, she would brush her hair back with one hand, press her lips together, moisten her mouth with her tongue. So I made it clear that she shouldn't talk. Still, she would rub her eyes, touch her chin with her forefinger, fiddle with an earring. During all those months, sometimes we would meet for a cup of coffee in Berkeley, and when sitting at a table in conversation, while waiting for an idea to form itself, or for her companion to speak, she would twiddle her pen or beat a spoon lightly on the table. You would think that her friends would shun her, turned off by all this twitchiness, but she was so engaging and attractive, she drew people to her like pins to a magnet, and when she sat down at Peet's, there was always a cluster of humanity around her.

Rosie was able to help people because she had been through so much herself. As a teenager, she had lost her beloved brother. She told me about it when I got to know her better; it was when I confided in her about my parents' death. Buddy was seventeen when he and some friends went on a beer binge. He was riding in the back of the pickup truck with three other boys when the young driver careened off one of the hairpin turns in Napa Valley. Buddy was the only one killed, although another kid was paralyzed for life. Rosie was fifteen when it happened, and she said the trauma of her brother's death had stayed with her ever since. The result was that, very early in life, she decided she wanted to help others. She said she had considered becoming a nurse, but the sight of blood made her nauseous, so she went into the healing of personal relationships instead.

Rosie was forever searching for answers to the mysteries of life. By the time I met her, at one time or another she had been into astrology, Taoism, and the Vedanta Society in Los Angeles with Swami Prabhavananda. In the late '50s she got involved with a Zen Buddhist group centered around the Englishman Alan Watts, the man who popularized Zen. It was new then, and Rosie was just out of college. Watts lived with the colorful Greek artist Jean Varda— Yanko—on Yanko's houseboat near Sausalito. Watts headed the American Academy of Asian Studies, and broadcast on the local public radio station, KQED, with his talks on "Breaching the Gap Between East and West." Rosie, young and impressionable, was enthralled with the sound of his voice, and began a study of Zen. Her parents, simple fruit farmers in the Napa Valley, supported her during this time.

When she went to hear Watts at a seminar, he befriended her, and invited her to a party celebrating Yanko's birthday on the houseboat.

I was so impressed with Rosie's stories from this part of her life, I couldn't stop grilling her for details. I wanted to know all about these wild artists whom I'd heard so much about. Mount Tamalpais was crawling with artists, musicians, yogis, and wizards, and Rosie met them all. She met Siefried Agnesun, Thomas Cohelan and many others, all of them famous now, who hung out on the houseboat.

On the day of the party, the first words Yanko addressed to her were, "Ah yes! My young Aphrodite sprung from the sea—you have finally come to me—me, Poseidon!"

He sat at the head of the scuffed and scraped table where he did all his art work, crowned and robed as the God of the Sea. The table had been transformed into a groaning board of Greek food—pita bread, falafel, moussaka, dolmas, baklava, and more. A great deal of this food was contributed by his "handmaidens," and most of the wine and liquor was brought by his artist friends.

"Have you slept with any of the lecherous rascals assembled here today, my lovely?" he asked Rosie, sweeping the crowded cabin with his hand. "Do not go to bed with any of them—they are libertines, swine! Wait—wait for me!"

"So what did you say to that?" I asked.

"I just laughed, and slurped down my wine. But I tried to keep moving around away from him, although there wasn't much space to move."

When Rosie knew Yanko he was mostly doing small sculpture, collage, and assemblage. He hated museum curators and detested the works they showed, calling their chosen art 'cow-dung' and 'axle-grease paintings'. How I envied her those experiences! Rosie actually owned two of Cohelan's "sand-scribble" paintings and one of Agnesun's big aluminum sculptures.

She didn't succumb to the grizzled old Yanko or to the smooth-talking Watts, but soon moved in with Simon Schwartz, a hippie sculptor who owned a run-down farm near Muir Woods. Her parents became more and more displeased with her way of life, and when she moved in with Schwartz they stopped all support.

She and Simon lived on the southern slope of Mount Tam; Rosie said it looked a lot like the hills of Italy overlooking the lake district where she'd traveled during college. They lived in a shack with no electricity and Simon's studio was a lean-to several hundred yards away from where they slept. At first she was happy, but then the isolation and lack of money began to depress her; her health began to fail. Three years, two abortions, and several bouts of pneumonia later, Rosie moved out. She went home to the Napa Valley and had a long, tearful talk with her parents. They said the only way they would start supporting her again was if she went back to school. So she did, eventually earning a master's in psychology at UC Berkeley.

Rosie maintained that all her years of seeking and questioning enabled her to help her patients more, but I wasn't so sure. Although I envied her the experience of meeting and living with untamed artists, to my way of thinking someone who was disciplined in her personal life could have provided more guidance to troubled patients. But the capriciousness of her former life style made her all the more interesting to me. Unlike most of the people I knew, she was bent on seeking a higher truth.

I finished the portrait, and it was a knockout. Ben said so, and I thought so, too. It took nine months to paint, and I told Rosie I felt as if I had given birth.

This procreative aspect of painting is a phenomenon I've heard about many times from other artists. In my case, the fact that I can never have children probably contributes to the intensity of feeling I associate with painting. In other words, painting takes the place of any maternal yearnings I might have.

Sunday evening Rosie came to pick up her portrait, Ben was home and since it was cocktail time we invited her for a drink. I propped the big canvas against a wall in the living room so we could all admire it together, and Ben stood looking at it for a long time.

"You've outdone yourself, Nat. Magnificent!"

"Oh Nat, I do love it!" Rosie said, handing over a check and hugging me once more.

Ben had made a fireplace fire, and I think it was the first time Ben and Rosie ever really talked. It gave me a good feeling; here were two people I cared deeply about, and it made me happy to see that they responded so positively to one another. While I was in the kitchen arranging clam dip and crackers on a tray, I heard them discussing the People's Park demonstrations in Berkeley.

"What do these goofy dropouts really *want?*" Ben asked.

"They want to have the park for themselves and turn it into a center for hippie culture. They don't want the university or the town taking it over for a parking garage or a soccer field, even though Cal owns the property." I came into the room as Rosie was saying, "So one day *The Berkeley Barb* printed an announcement that everyone should go to the park with flowers and trees to plant, and they took all kinds of shovels and hoses. Hundreds of young people showed up for this combination building project and festival of freedom. I go by there all the time on my way to work, and now the park is filled with these long-haired dropouts, digging away. The kids have a lot of 'happenings'—that's what they call them—where they get stoned and dance nude and sun themselves."

"Has it gotten dangerous, like when Hana and I were caught in that riot on Telegraph Avenue?" I asked.

"Nat, where have you been?" Rosie exclaimed. "Of *course* it's gotten dangerous! Last May, the Berkeley police decided to eject a bunch of them from the park, and the university brought in an eight-foot-high chain-link fence and put it around the place. After that, three thousand protestors met on Sproul Plaza and decided they'd go take it down!"

"Oh, yes, now I remember." I was feeling stupid for not knowing more about these happenings, which were going on practically next door to Montclair.

"We read about it," Ben said. "Didn't a guy get killed by a sheriff?"

I reached for a cracker and dipped it in the clam mixture, and Ben got up to put another log on the fire. The contrast between the luxurious comfort of our home and the subject we were discussing was immense. All those hippies and their degradation—*the stink*—*the dirt!*

"A student on a rooftop died," Rosie said. "And five days later they had another rally. That was when Governor Reagan called in the National Guard, and they dropped tear gas! Don't tell me you didn't hear about that, Natalie!"

Ben said, "Two thousand National Guard troops in Berkeley! Can you believe it?"

"Rosie, I'm worried about you," I said. "How far is your office from all of this?"

"I'm way up on Vine; I'm okay."

Ben went in the kitchen to freshen our drinks, and Rosie's eyes followed him. While we'd been discussing radical students and tear gas, I noticed she'd been casting a covetous eye on my husband. She came right out with it. "Where can I find someone like Ben, Nat? You're so lucky!"

"Dunno, kiddo," I said, "but he's taken. Besides, he's way too tame for you."

In June, she delivered the portrait to her parents in St. Helena for their big anniversary smash. Ben and I were invited, but we couldn't go. It was about that time I got a commission to do the entire Ferguson family.

Four kids, a dog, and a cat.

It was July of 1969 when Rosie asked me to join her for a four-day weekend retreat at Esalen, in Big Sur. As a therapist, and on a personal level as well, she was getting interested in the Human Potential movement. She'd been through everything else, why not that, too? And this time she wanted me to participate in her search.

I decided that maybe I could go. Ben would be away; he usually was gone on weekends in July at The Trees encampment on the Russian River (I called it his grown-up Boy Scout camp). This year, he and a cast of fifty were in one of their splashy club productions, doing spear-carrying walk-ons. Members of The Trees were mostly men in regular walks of life who enjoyed congregating for amateur productions, art shows, and musical concerts. It was a men's club started by artists, writers and poets of the Bay Area way back in the late 1890s, men like Robert Louis Stevenson, who was living here at the time, Ambrose Bierce, and Jack London.

When Rosie kept urging me to go with her, assuring me that it would prime my creative juices, I began to get interested. Gradually I warmed to the prospect of a long, relaxing weekend of outdoor baths and massages, and finally I said I would go.

All I knew about the Esalen Foundation was that it was a consciousness-raising, self-realization, touchy-feely conference center set in the wilderness of Big Sur, an area located a few miles south of Carmel and Monterey. There had been articles about the region in the *Chronicle* for many years. The coast south of Carmel is one of the most remote and romantic regions in the state. Big Sur was known as a wild place, both in topography and lifestyle. In the early to mid-twentieth century, writers and poets like Robinson Jeffers, Henry Miller, Richard Brautigan, Hunter S. Thompson, and Jack Kerouac began to hang out there. Like Miller, some stayed for years.

I don't consider myself an intellectual, and am not a voracious reader, so I wasn't acquainted with the works of any of these men. But I'd heard that Aldous Huxley had helped found the place, and I had read *Brave New World*.

It wasn't as if the Big Sur area was new to me. Ben and I had eaten at Nepenthe, a restaurant set on a hill overlooking the ocean, with hundreds of acres of untamed, dramatic landscape on view. And I had danced with Bill Fassett, Nepenthe's owner, on our honeymoon. The Fassetts were famous for buying title to the land from Orson Welles and Rita Hayworth back in the forties.

Rosie never mentioned the words "encounter group" once, alluding only to long walks and short inspiring seminars. She said the theme of the weekend was to be "Lose Your Mind and Come to Your Senses."

The subject intrigued me because, having had to sacrifice aesthetics so often for the sake of getting a likeness, my style had tightened up. My brush strokes were becoming more restrained, my compositions less imaginative. With a little help, maybe I could get back to being a painter.

Since Rosie was a professional therapist, all I had to do was send off a registration form with her signature as reference, and a check for $750.

Friday, after a long winding drive down the coast on Highway 101, we checked in at the main building, then went to find our accommodations. They were as bare and ascetic as a monk's, merely a small cabin with minimum bathroom facilities. The beds were simple mats on the floor, albeit covered in patchwork throws and furnished with plump cushions.

There were no windows, so in order to soak up our surroundings, we decided to walk around.

The compound was built to hang above the ocean on the side of the cliffs. Big patches of grass, surrounded by craggy rocks, were laid out with paths, and nestled into this setting were a dozen rustic redwood buildings. These bore hardly any ornamentation except for Gods' Eyes hung near the doors. A large main house containing the dining hall and meeting rooms dominated the center of the compound, and fifty or so yards to the north and up a sloping bank was an open, Japanese-style pavilion. The spa area with hot tubs was a little farther north. Rosie said this was where conference participants met to socialize.

Today the Pacific Ocean was a lapis lazuli color, a more intense blue than I'd ever seen it, and all around were the sights and smells of sage, wild thyme, and Indian paintbrush. Hundreds of cormorants and pelicans skimmed low above the water, lending their sweeping grace to the scene. We breathed in as we walked, taking in all the wonderful scents.

No one else seemed to be present, but as we rounded the path to return to the buildings, we came upon a group of nudists. They were seated in a semi-circle facing a leader, also naked, a long-haired man intoning, *"O-O-O-Ohm-m-m-m-m-m-m."*

The group followed, all together, *"O-O-O-Ohm-m-m-m-m-m-m."*

As we passed, I whispered to Rosie "What're they chanting?"

"It's a Zen mantra," she said. "We'll probably do some chanting later on."

"You didn't mention chanting. Do I *have* to chant?"

"You'll feel a lot more comfortable, Nat, if you simply do as the rest of us do. We'll have none of your artistic independence. Just flow with it!"

"Well, okay." I pulled some leaves from a clump of thyme, and inhaled. "But I'm not taking off my clothes." Even though I had spent years at art school in life-drawing classes, and despite the fact that I had done countless nude drawings of both male and female models, revealing my own body was another matter. I attributed it to my strict Methodist upbringing.

Rosie turned to me, her dark eyes crinkling at the corners. "Nat—you're an old lady—who would want to see *you* nude!"

I was only two years older than she, so I made a fist and pounded her upper arm, hard. She started running, and I chased her all the way back to our cabin.

That evening we ate in the dining hall at a long table filled with offbeat, interesting characters, a stimulating change from Montclair's middle-of-the-road WASPS. A couple of seminar leaders were seated with us: a psychiatrist from San Francisco and a yoga instructor from Los Angeles, pleasant men whose conversation was not at all subversive, nor did their talk drip with New Age phraseology. They seemed to find me fascinating because I was an artist. The others at our table were, like me, enrollees for the weekend: a young male theology student from Berkeley's Pacific School of Religion, and two young women from San Francisco State who said they were studying media communication. We were served curried chicken and *tabouli* with all the accompaniments, and there was plenty of red and white wine.

So far, I had seen no sign of drugs. I'd heard that experimental drugs were used here, both natural and chemical: magic mushrooms, LSD, mescalin, and marijuana, plus uppers and downers. It was only a couple of years since Timothy Leary had been dismissed from Harvard for experimenting with LSD on his students. "Turn on, tune in, and drop out," was his message. Except for my experience with Fia when she was dealing with Eric, I was pretty much shielded from the drug culture, and I was positive that Rosie didn't use them. In case I needed some recreation of my own, I had a silver flask of Stoli's tucked inside my traveling bag, plus a bottle in my carryall.

As the meal ended, a man made the announcement that we could sit *zazen* after dinner in one of the small meeting halls. He said it was by no means compulsory, and that Alan Watts would be our leader.

"What's *zazen?*" I whispered to Rosie.

"Zen Buddhist meditation and prayer. Would you like to try it?"

Before Rosie ever mentioned knowing him, I had heard of Alan Watts, so out of curiosity, I went with her to the ceremony. We entered the room, and like those present, knelt on the cushions.

Soon Watts came in, accompanied by two Asian attendants in white kimonos. The three seated themselves in the lotus position on the raised platform, where a small gong and various smoking incense burners were arranged. More young people gathered on the platform. Evidently our meditation was to be enhanced by these musicians, playing a pair of long metal trumpets, a bass drum, and two large cymbals.

Watts was a handsome man, with long hair brushed back from his sallow face, a small gray goatee, and delicate hands with long, tapered fingers. Rosie had said he had quite a history with women.

He gave no indication that he recognized Rosie, even though we were near the front of the room.

"I am going to ask you to follow me closely. Sit cross-legged, or as we sit in the lotus position, kneeling, but sitting back on the heels. It keeps one alert. Sit erect. You will discover that time will disappear."

I tried to imitate my friend's every gesture and posture. I had never seen her so 'at rest' before. She was always moving—talking, driving, smoking. What had happened to all her nervous tics? She knelt, her back perfectly straight, and I did the same.

Watts went on. "You have heard of *zazen*—it comes from Za—Zen—sitting Zen. Thus one clears one's consciousness, seeing the world as it is. Meditation is shutting off chatter that prevents us from seeing things whole. The doctrine of Buddha is that all things flow away. If we try to stop the process, try to resist the flow of life, we make mistakes. Mantras are sacred syllables, repeated audibly or mentally with every exhalation of the breath. We use a mantra to circumvent our awareness of reality—the mind's awareness—by employing sound and vibration to transcend the limits of the intellect." His voice rose on the word 'transcend,' then dropped to a sensually low timbre again.

My body was beginning to wobble, and I forced myself to sit straighter.

The attendant struck the gong. It reverberated loudly through the small room, echoing on and on. Watts began to speak again in his trancelike, mesmerizing voice, interrupted at intervals by the reverberation of the gong.

I was only able to process a few phrases: "Life is ripples in a stream . . . the eternal NOW . . . ocean waves on the shore . . . rushing water, the ripples of streams, whirlpools, leaves. *Be still*—"

The gong crashed—*ZOONG-G-G-G!!*

We chanted. *"O-O-O-Ohm-m-m-m-m-m-m."*

My knees were killing me.

ZOONG-G-G-G!!

"O-O-O-Ohm-m-m-m-m-m-m."

Watts could hold the sound of the *"O-O-O-Oh-m-m-m-m-m-m-m"* long after the rest of us had run out of breath.

Hit by a spasm of pain in my left knee, I shifted my weight on the cushion and looked sideways at Rosie, who was completely and utterly still.

"—words in your head—mere noise—autumn leaves turning—water in a bucket—flow with the stream of life. Trees bend with the wind. Bamboo bends, doesn't fight nature."

ZOONG-G-G-G!!

Now the pain had moved to my lower back, which I was terrified was about to erupt into crippling spasm.

". . . There is no *p-a-a-a-a-st*. There is no *f-u-u-u-ture*. There is only now . . . difference in the water—rolling with the punch—go with the flow—go with the wind—your Karma—away and back are two sides of the same thing. Let it go . . . do not try to conquer the wind. Go *with* the wind."

ZOONG-G-G-G!!

At last it was over. We all walked—or in my case, hobbled—back to our rooms.

Rosie didn't speak. She seemed revitalized, and was wearing an ecstatic expression.

As for me, I had a hefty swig of vodka and spent fifteen minutes massaging my knees.

The next morning as we entered the dining hall for breakfast, Watts rose from a table near the window and walked over to greet Rosie, giving her a kiss on each cheek.

"My dear! How have you been? I haven't seen you for many ages!"

His English accent was more pronounced than in the Zen ceremony; maybe he could Americanize his speech at will. Or maybe I had been so hypnotized by his cadences that I hadn't noticed.

"Alan, this is my friend Natalie. We sat *zazen* with you last night."

"I know, I was aware. Did you find the ceremony enlightening, Natalie?"

He gave me a piercing look, but no chance to answer. "I must finish breakfast. I'm leaving for Japan this afternoon. Are you still counseling our fellow man, Rosie?"

"Yes, I'm still in Berkeley. How's Yanko?"

"He is getting old, as are we all. I don't live on the houseboat anymore. You must come to our tea ceremony in San Francisco some Sunday! I travel a lot now. There is jet lag on my jet lag."

I was still enthralled by his voice, even now it seemed to vibrate inside me. No wonder he was such a success with women.

He was eating with two other men, and as soon as he sat down again they renewed their discussion, heads close together, voices low. Rosie said Watts was often consulted in the administration of Esalen; he had been one of its earliest supporters, she said, along with Huxley.

She spoke in hushed tones, as if we were in the presence of greatness.

That day I began to discover what Esalen was all about. It was about opening oneself to higher experiences, and about exchanging ideas. But it was also about arguments and insults, and occasionally the arguments and insults led to actual blood.

After breakfast on Saturday, two-dozen of us met for a seminar and encounter group in one of the large meeting rooms. I had never heard of an encounter group before. This one was entitled "Negative Results of Repressive Self-Control on Our Positive Energies," and our leader that morning was a middle-aged psychiatrist, Dr. Leggensheim from San Diego. Dr. Leggensheim had a calming voice, a shock of grey-sprinkled black hair, and long arms which he flung about dramatically to illustrate the various points of his topic.

"Nat, you and I should separate," said Rosie. "No clinging!"

I looked around at the other participants. Up to that moment, except for the chanting group I'd seen when we first arrived, I hadn't witnessed any of the nudity that Esalen was notorious for. Now, however, although almost everyone else was clothed, there was a nude girl, a sort of water-nymph-cum-flower child. Rina had hair like wet sea kelp, blonde with a sea-green tinge, as if she had spent all her adult life mucking about in the depths of the ocean. Sitting not far from us, too, was an elderly woman wearing a long skirt and nothing above. Her breasts resembled gigantic, leathery sausages from which the filling had been removed.

There was another older woman in the room, too, much more attractive than the first, and fully clothed. She looked to be in her seventies, with gray hair worn loose and flowing down her back. At first I thought it was too bad she didn't lift it up or pull it back for a more youthful look, but then I decided she had such an interesting face, it didn't matter.

Our leader at the podium struck a spoon on his drinking glass.

"Which is better," Dr. Leggensheim began, "venting our anger and frustration, or sublimating it in other ways?"

His question was followed by a long recitation of illnesses brought on by repression, or, as he called it, plugging up our emotional outlets. Turning anger inward, he said, only ends up damaging our psyches.

86

"But should we turn our anger outward, inflicting it upon others? If we do that all the time, finally there are no 'others' around us to inflict it upon!"

The crowd looked around, chuckling.

"After we play the encounter game this morning," he said, "you will know which way is better. Let us now learn a few useful tools for handling anger. You are going to do an exercise that will relax you," he said, throwing out both hands and pulling them slowly toward his body, as if pulling us in en masse. As he gestured, his eyes closed, then slowly opened again.

"It will compel you to interact in a forceful but positive way, resulting in a freeing of your dormant negative energy. You will learn to handle crises, and how to guide and control other people's emotions. Yes, I said guide and control *other* people's emotions! Even though that sounds manipulative, don't you sometimes wish you could deflect—and thus control—your family's, or your friends', or your co-worker's anger? I am here to teach you how."

The doctor's assistant, a thirtyish woman in horn-rimmed glasses and a brightly-patterned African dress, instructed us to find three other people, form a group, then sit cross-legged on the floor facing the others in a small circle. After introducing ourselves, we were to choose a leader.

I glanced at Rosie, who was a few feet away with her newly formed group. She grinned and made a face like a fierce baboon, mimicking rage. She knew what I was thinking. All of this psychobabble was beginning to get to me, but I bit my lip and soldiered on. I sat facing my co-gameplayers, the nude Rina, the male theology student from Berkeley, and one of the girls from SF State. We chose the theology student, Gary, as leader. He seemed like an intelligent young man, tall and rangy, with large, big-knuckled hands. His hair fell over one eye in an appealing, boyish way.

I was trying hard not to stare at Rina's private parts, and I'm sure Gary was doing the same. We drew our assignments from a small basket and read them aloud. The instructions told us that the three of us were on the verge of being insane—or at the least, eccentric—and Gary's mission was to try to alter our off-beat behavior by peaceful means. Fixing his eyes on the paper he'd been given, he read aloud:

"You—that's me, I guess—you are in a hospital with a broken leg. You are immobilized, but conscious. You find yourself in a ward with three other people, and you're beginning to wonder if it's a psychiatric ward. The others are:

> (1) An old man who constantly jumps out of his bed to leap over and grab your leg, shaking it violently and causing you intense pain. How do you get him to stop?
>
> (2) A younger man who stares at you fixedly, combing his hair over and over with the same repetitive motion. You want to know his story, so that you can help him. How do you get him to open up to you?
>
> (3) A young girl who is blindfolded. You don't know whether she's blind or not—has she had an operation on her eyes? She keeps interrupting your exchanges with the other two in order to ask embarrassing personal questions, which you must answer by telling the truth."

"Wow," I said.

"Sounds like I'm more of a victim than a leader," commented Gary.

We drew slips of paper to see which role we were to play. I drew the role of the crazy hair-comber, Rina drew the blind girl, and the student Rachel got the part of the sadistic old man.

We began to play the encounter game. I had the easiest role; all I had to do was pretend to comb my hair incessantly. Rachel, as the old man, began to shake Gary's leg, presumably the broken, bandaged one. At one point she shook the leg too hard, and he told her to fuck off.

I was shocked at his language. He was a seminary student, after all.

"I'm hurtin' here! Can't you get that through your head?"

"But you look so smug lying there!" Rachel replied. "I'm old and sick, and I can't pay my hospital bill—you have to help me!"

"How the shit can I help you? I've got a broken leg!"

Rina had tied a blue bandanna around her eyes, now she really did look blind. She began to ask Gary a lot of questions, moving close.

"How did you break your leg?"

"I fell off a horse."

"Are you sure you didn't get drunk in a bar and get beat up? You look like a boozer to me." She slapped his leg, guffawing.

Gary was being handled roughly by both girls, and he was either actually angry, or good at playing the game.

Suddenly Rina stepped out of character.

"Why are you studying theology, Gary? Everyone knows people involved in religion are judgmental and obsessed. Alan Watts says religion leads to holy war and inquisitions, never to an enhanced understanding of life!"

Gary snorted. "Watts is the biggest phony who ever landed in California—he keeps running from Episcopalianism to Zen Buddhism to the Human Potential movement, then back again."

Rina grabbed his arm, hissing, "He's wonderful! Shut up!"

He pulled his arm away, yelling, "You're not in the game, Rina— get in the game! And go get dressed. We promise to notice you, even if you put some clothes on."

She ignored him. Still wearing the bandana over her eyes, she began asking personal questions of Rachel and me, which was again breaking the rules. I was beginning to think this girl broke the rules all the time. She said she'd seen me with Rosie, and she asked if Rosie and I were in love with each other. I said no, we're just friends. Then she asked Rachel if a man paid for her to come to Esalen, and was he paying her way to college too. I thought these questions revealed quite a lot about the questioner herself.

Rachel looked as if she'd like to punch Rina in the face, but instead she quietly answered, "Thank you for your interest. I have a full scholarship to State, but actually, yes, my uncle paid for my weekend here."

"I knew it!" Rina snorted, and settled back on her haunches, her small breasts bouncing.

I continued to comb my hair and stare at Gary, and the minutes seemed to stretch into hours; my arms felt as if they were going to fall out of their sockets.

To get us back on track, Gary asked why I was gawking at him. As I started to answer, we heard a loud foofaraw coming from a group across the room. Two bearded, barefoot men, the younger wearing only a Ghandi-type loincloth, were having a heated argument.

"You are not doing any self-actualizing when you make a statement like that!" yelled one.

"Your irrational behavior is educating the rational!" replied the other. "Try to discern where the irrational is!"

"I'm not the irrational one—*you* are, asshole! Move out of your own frigging ego-sphere! Once again, you're enabling your inner child to become a bully!"

Dr. Leggensheim walked over to them and placed his hand on the shoulder of the older man, exclaiming, "Good! Good! Now you are both expressing your anger!"

Wait a minute, I thought, weren't we supposed to learn how *not* to vent our anger on others? Somebody was confused, and it wasn't just me. I glanced toward Rosie, but she wouldn't look in my direction. Suddenly the younger, more agitated of the two men leaned over and bit Dr. Leggensheim in the ankle. Since the doctor was wearing no socks, blood began to run down his leg.

"Okay. Now you'll have to leave, Barry! Out you go."

Next, the men stood up and began to exchange punches.

People started yelling, "Give it to him!" "Cream him!"

This had all the makings of a schoolground fight. The older man picked up Barry the biter and threw him halfway across the room. He landed on top of Rosie, who managed to hold onto him while the others grabbed the other man and tried to calm him down.

Finally Dr. Leggensheim, hopping up and down and holding his ankle in pain, managed to get the two men to the door. Then, just to thoroughly confuse us all, the older fellow, bleeding from a cut above the eye, put his arm around Barry and gave him a lingering kiss on the mouth.

After dinner that evening, Rosie and I strolled in our beach robes across the compound, past the pavilion, and up to the baths. It wasn't dark yet, but the cliff-side trail was rocky, and both of us slipped several times in our sandals. We reached the large deck enclosing three giant redwood hot tubs, doffed our robes, and slipped into the tub on the far side, where there were only a couple of people. Rosie was nude, but I wore my old black one-piece swimsuit. We floated near each other, feeling the warm water pound against us from the vents, our hair loose and flowing.

A few feet away bobbed one of the resident seminar leaders. Rosie whispered that he was a famous personage, noted for his particularly harsh psychological approach. He stared at us, especially at Rosie. Felix Von Papen was muscular, hoary, and old—no work of art. The hair on his back and shoulders was thick and black, contrasting with the polished baldness of his head and the white hair of his beard. Earlier in the day, when I passed one of the meeting rooms, I had heard him sputtering, "You piece of shit—how many times haf I told you, you vill leaf that all behind—you are my disciple now!"

I stepped back and peered inside to see who he was bawling out. A middle-aged woman who looked as if she could be president of the local Ladies' Aid Society was sitting primly on a straight chair across from him, eyes brimming with tears.

Now Von Papen addressed Rosie. "My dear, I have noticed you—both of you lovely ladies—this is your first time to our establishment?"

"Yes, we drove down from Berkeley."

"I haf many associates in Berkeley; they come to Esalen often to speak and to express their theories. All of them are full of elephant-dung. I myself am from Europe, I am sure you hear it in my speech."

"I barely noticed," said Rosie.

"Do not make fun of me, darling. I know all the games to play, and how to play them. I know the male and female merry-go-round—all the hoztilities, all the sex—open—allowed—forbidden—and reprezzed!"

Rosie turned away and began to talk to me about something ordinary, like the next conference she had to attend, and whether to fly or drive.

Eventually, when we bothered to look in his direction, we noticed that Felix's attentions were now devoted to Rina the sea-nymph, who'd floated to his side. It occurred to me that the baths were where she spent most of her time, which would explain her aqueous look.

Felix was stroking her shoulder, and she had her head thrown back, eyes closed, sea-green hair floating in the foam.

The next morning we had a vast menu of activities to choose from. We could do massage therapy, yoga, Sensory Awakening, Zen meditation, or T'ai Chi.

I chose yoga, and Rosie did the Sensory Awakening thing.

I had never studied yoga before, although I'd wanted to for years. The two hours I spent were stenuous but refreshing, and I decided that if I ever had time for it back home, I would enroll in a class. Rosie loved the Sensory Awakening experience. She said that while incense burned, the participants used peacock feathers, cattails, and the leaves of velvet groundsel to touch and stroke each other, all the while listening to a woman recite Alan Ginsberg's poetry. It sounded very pleasant, and maybe I'd missed something. But we told each other that we couldn't pack everything into one weekend, so we'd have to come back next year.

That afternoon we gathered at the outdoor pavilion for our second seminar and encounter group. This was a much larger gathering than Saturday's; there must have been forty or so truth-seekers present. The ocean surf pounded in our ears, and a cool sea breeze wafted over us as we listened to Hilda and Vladimir Houseman, Chicago husband-and-wife psychologists. They lectured on the subject, "The Survival of Humankind: Ego-Gratification or Self-Sacrifice?"

This was the most high-minded of all the groups, since we were venturing into the subject of national issues like flag-waving, isolationism, and xenophobia. The Housemans were talking about individual ego-centeredness and egomania. They said the question was two-pronged: "How do we keep from living entirely for ourselves, and if we don't learn how to broaden our understanding of the world, what kind of earth will we live in a hundred years from now?"

After their talk, we organized in groups of three for another game. This didn't take long; it was a simple matter of asking or being asked, "Want to be in my group?"

"Get out the First Aid kit," I joked in an aside to Rosie, as we shuffled around the floor of the pavilion, selecting and being selected.

"Keep an open mind, please!" she admonished, as if speaking to a naughty child.

I ended up with the older woman with the lovely face and long hair, and a man I hadn't met before. His expression was deeply serious, and a dense black beard covered most of his face. So many beards!

Esther was a social worker from California's Mother Lode country.

She said she came to Esalen every year to get her consciousness raised. She had kind, deep-set eyes, a myriad of laugh wrinkles, and a luminous smile which came and went, depending on the seriousness of the conversation.

Bernie, an instructor in physics at Stanford, told us that he was going through a painful separation from his wife. I was surprised and flattered when the two decided I should be leader. I walked to the platform at the front, where a smiling Hilda Houseman handed me a page of instructions and three paper bags.

Each group was to play a game called "Three Bags Full," in which we had to decide who deserved to get which of three bags: one full of make-believe oranges, one of imaginary jewels, and one of pretend pink Play-Doh. Each player had to make up a reason why he or she deserved to have the bag, then share with the small group. In the second part of the game, we had to stand on the platform and show the paper bag with its imaginary contents to the whole assembly, explaining why we asked for that particular bag. Those who were too shy to go on stage could speak from where they were.

In our little circle, we three spent a few minutes composing our thoughts, then I began. I said I needed the pink Play-Doh because I wanted to make a sculpture. I was an artist, and I had an urgent need to create. I said that I would become ill if I were ever prevented from creating. The Play-Doh was very stimulating to me, I said. I picked up the bag, pulled it into my lap, and peeked inside.

"Oh yes!" I breathed, "this amazing pink goo is just what I've always wanted!"

Rosie would be so pleased to see me now, I thought. She would be thrilled that I was making such a perfect fool of myself.

Bernie went next. He said he wanted the bag of jewels to give to his wife. He held it up, declaring, "I want to adorn my wife with these jewels. I have been horrible to her—I've mistreated her, ignored her—I've even abused her!" All at once he began to sob, and great tears ran down into the curls of his beard. He wiped them away with the back of one hand, holding the bag in the air with the other. Then he became almost biblically eloquent. "I will put diamonds in her navel and her armpits, and topazes on her toes. I'll twine emeralds in her hair," he sobbed—"and around her neck I will wind a necklace of pearls and rubies!"

Esther and I were stunned at this outpouring of male emotion. We reached out and touched him, and Esther began to stroke his back. Gradually he calmed down, occasionally emitting a small sob, like a small child who has been through an emotional upheaval and is winding down for his afternoon nap.

Next, Esther, sitting like a Buddha, held her bag in the air. Her eyes shone with emotion. "Natalie," she said, "I am so glad you wanted the Play-Doh. I'm sure you will make excellent use of it. And I have no need for jewels, so Bernie, I am delighted that you are going to give them to your beloved wife. As for me, I need to have this large bag of oranges. In my neighborhood in Sutter Creek there is a new family with many children, and they have no money. Soon the father will get a job, or they will get assistance from the county, but right now they are starving. I see them outside their flimsy little house, the children so thin, so scrawny, and once I caught the mother going through my garbage can looking for food. So you see, I must have this bag of oranges—I must have it to feed my neighbors!"

She opened her arms wide, and her face, illumined by the ocean's bright reflection, seemed to portray the loving-kindness of a saint.

I was moved by her story, but mostly I was thinking that, someday soon, I had to paint her.

The leaders announced that it was time for us to tell our stories from the platform. Now we began to hear from everyone—fat people, thin people, well spoken and forceful, timid and shy.

A young woman wearing faded, patched jeans and a Fisherman sweater was the first to speak. "I have a nosy neighbor who spies on me, and I want the Play-Doh to fill a hole in my wall."

"Don't laugh, but I want to make a big pink Play-Doh basketball," said an athletic-looking young man, grinning.

From an acne-scarred woman, who spoke in a raw voice, "I need the Play-Doh to pound out my anger, thump it, whack it, just beat it to a pulp—or I swear I'm gonna kill somebody!" She looked as if she could, too.

One woman said she was an immigrant, lost in a foreign land. She wanted the jewels to pay for a trip to Europe to see the family she had abandoned.

A small, middle-aged Asian man said he wanted the jewels for ransom; his child had been kidnapped, and he was in dire need of money. He was afraid his child was going to die!

A red-haired woman with a sad face wanted the oranges to fill a precious blue bowl that her son had sent her from Saigon just before he was killed in the war.

When it was my turn, I went onstage, told my tale of an artist's search for fulfillment, then got off as quickly as I could.

Bernie went on next and told why he needed the jewels to adorn his wife, but he was so nervous that he spoke almost without emotion. Consequently, his tale was not nearly as heartrending as it had been when he told it to Esther and me.

The stories went on and on, with half the speakers talking from the audience, half from the stage. So many stories—of need, of desire, of hate or love.

I was taken aback when Vladimir Houseman said that, for the last phase of the game, we would vote by applause on who had expressed most movingly his or her motive for acquiring the Play-Doh, oranges, or jewels.

Oh no! I thought. This was too much like real life, with each of us vying for applause from our peers. I hated the turn the game was taking; it was turning into some sort of psycho-dramatic Gong Show. Wasn't one of the reasons we came here to get away from competition? Away from self-striving and self-promotion?

But I was curious about how it would turn out. Maybe I would win!

Six at a time, we lined up on the stage, even the shy ones who hadn't been up before, and the person who got the most applause stayed, and the others sat down. In the end, applause was loudest for the Asian man's kidnap story and Esther's hungry children tale. We applauded for the two once more, and Esther won. The pavilion shook with the sound of clapping hands, even a few "Bravos!"'

Victor Houseman spoke one last time.

"As we played the game, what do you think you have learned about how ego-centered we are? What have we learned about ourselves, about our private motivations? And how did we respond to what other people consider our motivations to be? Think about it, how much do we rely on others' opinions for our actions?"

As we walked to the dining room for dinner, Rosie and I discussed the game. I said that I felt that its competitive element was too much like real life; I had hated the part where we had to applaud. "If Esther hadn't been there," I said, "with her warm-hearted, selfless speech, the whole thing would have been a fiasco."

"But Esther was there," said Rosie.

For our final night at the baths, I took along my flask of Stoli's. Might as well get high by my own tried and true method. By now, Rosie and I had our own group, and we floated in the big tub together, conversing among ourselves.

There was Rina (no hoary, horny Felix in sight), the two college girls, Gary, Esther, and Bernic. Barry the biter and his loving combatant with the salt-and-pepper beard joined us, and the Housemans were there too. They turned out to be down-to-earth, regular folks. I especially liked Hilda; she and I got into a lively discussion of Picasso's Blue Period, and she said I must call them if I ever came to Chicago. Rina had told me her life story over lunch, when Rosie went to check with her answering service. Her mother was an actress and had been married five times, and her father, a Hollywood film cutter with a new family of young children, had no interest in a teenaged daughter from an earlier marriage. There were other sad chapters, too, and as she told her woeful story, I couldn't help feeling sorry for the girl.

Tonight I had made the monumental decision to discard my swimsuit. If I hadn't, I'd have been the only frigging one in the place wearing frigging anything.

"When in Rome . . ." Rosie murmured as we disrobed.

I ducked my head underwater, resolving to look upon my nudity as everyone else did theirs, no big deal. Marijuana was passed, and wine flowed. I was surprised when Rosie accepted a joint and took several long pulls, but by now I was way past being shocked at anything.

Someone put on Ravi Shankar, and Rosie and some of the others got out of the tub and began to dance, gliding and leaping about—a writhing, bare-assed group. The music unwound in pulsating rhythms, as the Housemans, Esther, Gary and I watched from a misty haze, content to be observers. We chatted about the news we'd heard on the way here this weekend: ARMSTRONG AND ALDRIN WALK ON THE MOON! As if we might actually see evidence of this historic event, we gazed skyward at the hanging orange orb.

Rosie stayed, but around midnight, Esther and I walked back to the cabins. The moon was still bright, and Esther had a flashlight. Nevertheless, we stumbled a bit in the darkness,

The next morning at breakfast, where everyone looked either hung-over, embarrassed, or pleasantly invigorated, conversation was muted. I think all the others felt as I did, sad that the weekend was over, but relieved to be going. Addresses and phone numbers were exchanged, vows were made about keeping in touch, and a few tears were shed. Rina, surprisingly clothed in a long denim dress, gave me a warm hug, and Esther and I embraced. She was flattered when I said I wanted to paint her.

"No charge, of course."

"Fine, dear. Let's do it at my house up in Sutter Creek. There's an old cabin where you can set up your paints."

"Terrific!"

We put our suitcases and bags of mementos in the car. At the little camp shop, I had bought several God's Eyes to give as Christmas presents.

"I'm so happy for you, Nat!" Rosie breathed as she drove north toward home. "You really seemed to get in touch with your feelings—you seem more fully alive, more awakened! I think you're finally beginning to soar with your own truth."

"You mean I found my own space and grooved with it?"

To negate the sarcasm, I added, "I enjoyed it, darling. I needed loosening up, and I think this weekend might have done the trick." Hung over from too much vodka, sore from the yoga stretching and Zen kneeling, I did feel incredibly loose—or maybe limp would be a better word.

"But as for some of the issues," I said, "I'll never give up my ego; artists have to have tons of the stuff."

She glanced over at me and smiled. "I suppose that's true. The potent drive of genius. Did you bring that up in any of your groups?"

"No. I think that could be another weekend's topic, maybe a whole month's!"

But if the object of that Esalen weekend was to liberate oneself in all ways, I knew I hadn't succeeded. I had certainly not attained the level of freedom that Rosie had, with her pot-smoking and nude dancing. Now she sat at the wheel, head tossed back, hair blowing, looking happy and refreshed.

The end of the '60s arrived.

Despite the carnage of the decade, there was some good news. In August, thousands of young people celebrated at Woodstock, and there was no violence. It was all about sex, drugs, and rock 'n roll—plus a lot of mud.

On the first nationwide Moratorium Day on October 15th, 1969, millions of people all over the United States protested the war in Vietnam. I thought of marching, but I didn't because Ben said he would disown me. But Esther came down from Sutter Creek to attend a protest, and Rosie and Ranie marched in San Francisco. Each reported to me that they had been inspired and energized by the day's fiery speeches and free-wheeling demonstrations.

There was a lot of bad news—the Manson murders in Los Angeles, for instance. I called Nikki, and she said everybody down there was scared out of their wits, worried that some other branch of the Satanic cult was still out there and operating.

The free open-air Rolling Stone concert on December 6th, at the Altamont Speedway outside of Oakland, was a mad, violent end to the decade. Five hundred thousand kids were there! The Stones made a big mistake—they asked the Hell's Angels to act as guards, and paid them with beer. By the time the performers got to the stage, the bikers had gone berserk. They were using billiard cues in an effort to control people, and they stabbed a black kid and bludgeoned him until he died. In the ensuing melee, when a Hell's Angel rode his bike into the crowd near the stage, a girl got her ankle broken. Two other fans were killed when a convertible ran through the crowd, and another fan under the influence of drugs fell into an irrigation canal and drowned.

But the show went on. I would never have read much, or probably cared much, about any of this, but Marian Morse told me her son was almost killed that night. He was close to the stage, but luckily suffered only a broken leg.

Chapter Eight

New Age Cures and Tarot Readings

In the '70s, California was no longer isolated in its excesses. Drugs, loose sexual habits, a rise in divorce, children going bad— these were spreading all over the United States.

An epidemic, like Asian flu.

Mamaw wrote from New Mexico that they'd had a drug bust in Española; a bunch of hippies were operating a drug lab, cooking up LSD, uppers and downers.

Nationwide, the California psychedelic look was having its effect on fashion. *Life* and *Look* both did articles on it, and *Vogue* put out a five-page spread with strung-out looking models wearing tie-dye, feathers and ultra-long straight hair.

In June 1970, the last U.S. troops were withdrawn from Cambodia, and by August, peace was in sight. The stock market rose 130 points in three months, and Ben and I went out to celebrate with Mort McElway, another investment counselor at Flanders & Schuster, and his wife Judy. We had dinner in San Francisco but stayed cautious, eating at an inexpensive place out in the avenues.

Judy and I made a rule; the men were not to discuss business— especially the new pony they were riding, money market funds—or it wouldn't be a celebration at all.

My young friend Ranie Sloan seemed to go from one thing to another. First she got interested in singing and took private lessons, then I ran into her at the art supplies store at CCAC, and she said she'd discovered ceramics. She was still working at the insurance office, but part-time, and going to Laney College, where she was taking acting classes.

"You're sure covering the waterfront!" I remarked.

"I know. I can't decide what I like best. I'll find it, though, Nat, I promise."

I noticed that her speech was improving amazingly, along with her confidence. We talked about having lunch, but we were both very busy then; it didn't happen.

Then in 1971, to my great surprise and pleasure, I saw Ranie acting on stage.

The Black Repertory Group, which I had never heard of, was performing in southwest Berkeley, and getting excellent reviews in the *Chronicle*. That part of town was a high-crime area, and I doubt if Ben and I would have gone on our own. But Rosie, who was dating one of her psychiatry associates, asked us to go with them to see a production of *Raisin in the Sun*. She said she had a friend who had a leading part.

We met her and Rasheed Goodrich at an inexpensive restaurant, then drove separately to the performance. Ben said he didn't want to stay late; he had an appointment the next morning with our accountant. Rasheed was a good-looking African-American. He wore an Afro with a conservative suit and tie, and looked more like a congressman or college president than a psychiatrist. He and Rosie had adjoining offices in a building on Martin Luther King, Jr. Way, and Rosie said he had a thriving practice.

I thought he wasn't as attentive to Rosie as he might have been.

The theater was the size of a neighborhood grocery, which was its former incarnation, and the stage was tiny and without a curtain. We were shown to our seats a few feet from the stage. Rosie pointed to her friend's name on the program, and Urania Sloan's name sprang out at me.

Ranie!

As soon as she came onstage, I didn't look at anyone else. She melted into the part of the medical student Beneatha like butter melts into toast. Her voice was strong, her diction impeccable, with just enough of a trace of the ghetto to convince us of her character's background. I'll never forget the way she delivered the lines to her stage mother: *I'm just tired of hearing about God all the time. What has He got to do with anything? Does he pay tuition?*

She was sensational in the scene where Beneatha dances to Nigerian music in a homemade African costume, chanting:

> *Alundi, aalundi*
> *Alundi alunya*
> *Jop pu a jeepua*
> *Ang gu sooooooo*
>
> *Ai yai yae . . .*
> *Ayehaye—alundi!*

The battles of the black family: their quarrels, problems with money and conflicts with powerful whites, really got to me. When it was over, I sat immobilized, tears streaming down my face, while Ben wiped away my tears with his handkerchief.

There was no backstage, so after taking their bows the actors came down and began mingling with the audience. When Ranie saw me, she yelled "Natalie!" and we exchanged bone-crunching hugs. She embraced Ben and hugged Rosie.

She said to Rosie, "Why didn't I guess you and Nat would be friends, my two favorite people in the world!"

"I had no idea you two knew each other!" said Rosie.

"You were terrific!" I said. "Why didn't you tell me you were in a play?"

"I was waiting to see if we were any good, then I was goin' to call you!"

When Rasheed was introduced to her, even though he had his arm wrapped around Rosie, he managed to lock glances with Ranie.

Ben took Ranie's hands between his and said, "Did Lorraine Hansberry write that part just for you?"

I blurted out, "Is everything okay with your brother, Ranie? I've been wondering all this time." Ranie's smile faded. She swayed on her feet, and I reached out and grabbed her.

"Darrell was killed," she said.

"Oh, I'm so sorry! I didn't know!"

What a fool I was. I had ruined Ranie's star moment, probably ruined her entire evening. She noticed my reaction and grabbed my hand. "It's okay, Nat. The cops were out to get them, even the FBI was hounding them. Mama's still grieving, but I try not to think about it."

The actor who played Joseph Asagai walked over and began talking to Rosie. He had a dazzling smile and wide, athletic shoulders.

Suddenly Rasheed grabbed Ranie around the waist and started whirling her about. They chanted the words while they spun around the room:

Ai yai yae . . .
Ayehaye—alundi!

They danced back, and Ranie, trying to catch her breath, said, "I have to talk to my director. Don't leave, Nat, I want to catch up!" She walked away, orange chiffon scarf floating behind her.

"That girl got just the right amount o' swing to her boogie-woogie," Rasheed murmured, and we all laughed. When she joined us again a few minutes later, he maneuvered her into a corner of the room, and what he was saying must have been amusing, because Ranie threw her head back and roared with laughter.

Ben spent most of his time talking to a couple on the other side of the room, rich Berkeley liberals he knew from some investment dealings he'd had with the university. On the ride home I learned that he'd picked up a new client.

It wasn't until we had turned into our driveway that the thought struck me.

104

Ranie was probably Rosie's patient, consulting with her because of her brother's death. *That* was how they knew one another, but professional ethics prevented Rosie from telling me. Since Rosie had gone through a similar experience, that of losing a brother at a young age, she would be of immense help.

A few days later Rosie and I were sitting in Peet's. None of her usual hangers-on were around, and I asked her, "Is Ranie your patient?"

She poured more cream into her cup and slowly added sugar. Finally, she nodded.

"I can't tell you anything about Ranie's treatment, but I will tell you how Darrell died, then you'll understand what she's been through. It happened last year in Oakland. Darrell and two other Black Panthers shot and wounded two police officers who were after them. I don't know what they had done, but they were hiding out in an open field. Three police cars showed up, and the Panthers threw some small fragmentation bombs at their cars. I guess all hell broke loose, bombs and gunfire all going off at the same time! A cop was killed, and at least three bystanders were injured. Darrell was shot, dying on the spot. The other two tried to run away on foot, but they were caught and charged with assault with intent to murder."

"Oh my God, that must have been awful for Ranie!"

"And Ranie's mother."

Months later, Rosie told me that Rasheed Goodrich had pursued Ranie, and they'd had a brief romance.

I was livid. "Didn't that hurt you? And why would Ranie do that to you!"

I was very protective of Rosie, but I felt that a lot of her troubles with men were her own fault. She made terrible choices, choosing men who were all wrong for her.

But how could I tell her that? She would say they were the only kind she ever met.

"Yes, I was hurt, pretty badly hurt if you want to know, but what could I do about it? Ranie probably feels even worse than I do. He told her that I told him I had someone else, and that the night at her play was just a casual date."

"What are you, some kind of doormat? Where's your fighting spirit?"

"I knew Rasheed would leave me. He has a history of going from white to black to white again."

"But he's a psychiatrist!" I said. "Doesn't he know how to keep his own life on track?"

Rosie looked at me as if I had three heads, and didn't bother to reply.

I never told Ranie that I knew about her affair with Rasheed; there is such a thing as being *too* involved in your friends' lives. Maybe she really wasn't aware of Rosie's attachment to him, or maybe he was so persistent, so dogged in his pursuit, that she couldn't resist him. Whatever the situation, it soon wore itself out. It wasn't long before Rosie told me that Rasheed had a new lady friend, a television anchorwoman on the East Coast. She said he was being true to his pattern. The anchorwoman was white.

A few months after the play closed, Ranie called and said she needed a favor. Since I still felt guilty for mentioning her brother and almost ruining her theatrical debut, I was delighted. That is, until I heard what the favor was.

She started by saying she'd been asked to perform on a larger stage in a more important role. She was so excited she could hardly get the words out. In the last few years the Elmwood Movie Theater in Berkeley had fallen into disuse and disrepair, but now, through a resurgence of interest, it was being transformed for live theater. Michael Liebert, the director of the struggling Berkeley Repertory Company, had asked Ranie to act in a George Bernard Shaw play. African Americans were beginning to be cast in traditionally white roles on Off-Broadway in New York, but no one had yet done it in the Bay Area. I had heard of Liebert, and he had a reputation for doing the unconventional and unsanctioned.

"How wonderful!" I said. "What's the play? *Pygmalion?*"

"*Arms and the Man.* I'm playing Raina. Funny, isn't it, the names are so close. What I wanta know is, Nat, they don't have much money, and they need some talented people to work on sets. I told them about you, and I'm hopin' you'll do it."

"Do what? You want me to help paint sets? I guess so." I was already regretting that I had been so accommodating.

"Well, actually, they need someone to *design* the sets."

That would indeed take a great deal of time, a lot more than merely painting backdrops.

"I've never done anything like that! Let me think about it. I don't do anything but my own art, you know that."

"It has to be strictly volunteer; they haven't got any money," she went on, as if I hadn't spoken. "Could you let me know in the next couple of days? They're anxious to get started, and you'd be great! "

"Flattery will get you almost anything you want, but please give me time to consider this! It would be a giant undertaking."

I thought some more, talked to Ben, and he gave it a thumbs up. So in the end, I decided to do it, for Ranie and for me, too. Except for an occasional child's portrait, I wasn't busy just then, and a change of direction might be revitalizing.

But I had a quid pro quo. I called her and said, "I'll do it, but only on the condition that you sit for a portrait. I'll make it a gift to you, and I'll keep the sketches."

"Sure! We can arrange it later on when I'm through with the play or, you know—like whenever."

No trace of the ghetto in Ranie's speech now; she sounded like everyone else.

Her speech transformation was amazing. Or maybe she'd been laying on the 'colored' talk before, in order to make some sort of social statement. I knew that many black actors could turn ghetto speech on and off, as some British actors can go from lower class Cockney to posh Oxford accents, and from English to American.

After only a day, I began to get cold feet. Why did she ever suggest me for this? It must be that everyone else with the ability and training to do it wanted to be paid.

The first thing I did was check out a lot of books about stage design from the library, and spent two days poring over them. I knew I needed someone who could do the math for all the construction, and I knew that my architect friend who'd remodeled the Japanese bridge was too busy, so I called the architecture department at UC Berkeley. They gave me some names of a few advanced students who might be interested in helping, simply for the experience.

I talked to three of the students on the phone and actually met two, finally selecting Bert Leidecker. Bert was a serious looking young man from Oregon who was highly recommended by the head of the department. He was old for a student, twenty-four, and wore the traditional garb of the campus, T-shirt and jeans. I told him he would work as my assistant, and I made a deal with the business manager of Berkeley Rep for him to be paid a small per diem. I'd agreed to work for nothing, but it wouldn't have been fair to ask Bert to donate his time.

The theater was small, holding only a hundred and fifty people. We worked on the sketches night and day for weeks. Shaw made it simple; three acts, three sets, and had placed the story in exotic Bulgaria. Major Petkoff's garden was fun to design, a two-level set with outdoor steps, minarets and mountains in the distance. We used phony shrubbery, with some real greenery thrown in, and Bert designed an ornately carved garden gate that Michael Liebert was delighted with.

I made sketches for backdrops, and it was fun working out the colors. After two weeks of solid work, after Bert and I had completed the plans, our work wasn't over.

First, we had to scout out all the cheapest sources for materials. We borrowed a van from a cast member and spent days running around picking up lumber, nails, ladders, saws, canvas, paints—the million and one things we needed. A volunteer scenery crew began to put it all together, as Bert and I supervised.

Though shy and quiet, Bert had a dry sense of humor, often making cracks about our co-workers that made me laugh. I think the convivial life that went with the project was his only social outlet during those months. As a graduate student, he had many other responsibilities, and I realize now that I overworked him. But he seemed content to stay at the theater, laboring late into the night. He told me his work at Cal wasn't suffering, and I hoped it was true.

Luckily, Ben jumped into the project too. There was always something he could help with. He would eat at home when he got back from the city, then drive to the theater where I was slaving away—dirty, disheveled and distracted.

Somehow the stimulus of working together in these new surroundings had a beneficial effect on our sex life. We would lie in bed talking about everything—the play, or the scenery, or the people we had met. Then we would make love, long, delicious spaces of time, everything else forgotten.

I thought young Bert would probably get involved with one of the actresses, since he stayed at the theater for so many long hours. He was a good-looking guy, obviously heterosexual, so why not? But I was surprised at his choice, not that he had much to say about it. In the third week of rehearsals, we began to see Bert and the middle-aged actress who played Raina's mother snuggling among the dust bins and half-timbers of the unfinished set. By the time the play opened, Bert was barely functioning, lost in what I'm sure was his first passionate love affair. I was happy for him, but glad the actress hadn't been there in the beginning, when I needed him to make detailed measurements. Now he seemed befuddled, almost spacey.

There were other flirtations going on backstage, too. I suppose that's true of stage productions everywhere, from amateur plays in Podunk, Montana, to million-dollar epics on Broadway. Once, when Bert and I returned from making the rounds of the lumberyards, I came upon Ranie and Ben sharing coffee in the garden set. He was perched on a lawn chair massaging Ranie's bare feet, which were propped on another chair.

"*Hey!*" I said. "You never rub *my* feet!"

"You never sit still long enough, sweetie," was his answer.

We were all pretty sure that Ranie was sleeping with the director, an intense, temperamental New Yorker, Jock Hollenbeck. I thought he was arrogant and rude, and couldn't imagine what she saw in him, but he had her under his spell. She never talked to me about him, and it wasn't any of my business anyway.

One day I witnessed an unpleasant scene between Jock and the actor cast as Captain Bluntschli. Hollenbeck lit into him, reprimanding the actor for his delivery, his voice, his posture, everything he could find. By the time he'd finished, the young man was writhing in agony and almost in tears.

I sensed a sadistic streak in Jock, and wondered how long Ranie's fascination with him would last.

I got the impression Jock regarded my sets as amateurish, which of course they were. *But I was a volunteer!* I waited for some sign of appreciation from him, but it never came. On the other hand, Michael Liebert couldn't have been more gracious. As rehearsals got under way and the sets neared completion, he left for New York to scout a couple of Off-Broadway productions. Before leaving, he came by the theater to give words of encouragement to the cast and crew, and included Bert and me in his praise. I went home flying.

I'm happy to say that our opening night was a triumph, and Ranie scored a huge hit. Not only was she magnificent-looking in the nineteenth-century costumes and furs, but she gave a marvelous performance. Watching her play the part of the proud, aristocratic Raina, you were convinced she was that privileged young woman.

The race thing caused a considerable stir in the press. A black actress playing *Shaw?*

But it turned out to be of great benefit to Ranie. The *Chronicle* did a Sunday magazine article featuring her, and all at once she was a celebrity. Ben and I had stopped attending the play after we'd seen it three or four times, but after the article came out, Ben teased her about becoming famous.

"Can I have your autograph?" he asked, fanning a half-dozen programs in her face. She retaliated by lifting her foot and jabbing it into his backside.

In the fourth month, when attendance began to wane, *Arms and the Man* closed.

It was my first and last experience as a set designer, and I said to Ranie, "You never know what you can do until you have to do it, or, to put it another way, until some pushy broad maneuvers you into doing it!"

"But Nat, you had fun, didn't you?"

"Yes, but I'll never give Jo Mielziner any real competition. Now, when are you going to sit for the portrait?"

"I'm leaving for Tahiti with Jock. He has a friend who works there managin' a hotel. I'm so excited, I've never even been out of California! When I get back I'll call, and we'll do it then."

Weeks passed. I spent time recuperating from my theatrical ordeal, didn't lift a pencil, piece of chalk or brush.

A few days after her return, Ranie called. She said she was pregnant, so I'd better do the portrait before she ballooned up. I tried to sound pleased for her, but I'm afraid I failed.

How could someone as volatile and temperamental as Jock be good for my precious friend?

"How's the father taking it?" I asked.

"He's not as happy about it as I am, 'cause he doesn't know where his next job is comin' from. He's flyin' back to New York, and I'll go back when he finds something."

"Well, let's get started. Come over next Monday morning."

"Okay. Nat, what do you want me to wear? I've brought several sarongs back from Tahiti. I love them!"

"Bring them, sounds good."

She arrived with four sarongs. My favorite was a *longyi*, a half-sarong in a combination of warm colors, dark cinnabar with a patterned border of rose madder and ocher. It practically shouted Gauguin. I held it against her skin and asked, "Do you mind posing topless? Because this is the one I'd like to use."

"I wear it topless for Jock, but for a painting I'm gonna keep forever? I don't know. I thought I'd wear it with a white blouse."

There was a pause while I waited. Finally she said, "Why not! Let's go ahead."

And that's how we did it.

The big conch shell was a lucky addition. She mentioned during the preliminary sketching that she'd brought some interesting things home, a large conch shell and a *tiputa*, a Tahitian poncho. I said I'd love to see them both, and that's how she came to pose holding the shell, and how I got an interesting background. I tacked it up on one wall. The *tiputa's* rectangular design, black ink on bark-cloth, added a lot of pizazz. At this time Ranie had very long hair. I braided it, and we covered one breast with the long braid. Except for the white shell and the black-and-white of the *tiputa,* the entire painting was in earth tones, accented by the reds and pinks of the *longyi.* The color of Ranie's skin against the other shades of ochers, siennas, and reds was surpassingly sensual.

I did several sketches in pastels and Conté crayon, then began. We only did eight or nine sittings, and I managed to finish the painting in a month. Ranie tired easily and felt nauseous a lot of the time, so I kept the *longyi* in my studio and draped it on a tailor's dummy to paint it, as I had done with Fia's Balenciaga and Amanda's green velvet, thus shortening the hours Ranie had to stand. Most of the time she was cheerful and cooperative, with the discipline she had always shown in her days of life modeling classes.

Ranie loved to talk about the baby. She was so excited about it, filled with anticipation. When she spoke of the child, a small secretive smile played on her mouth, and even though I painted her head in profile, I think I managed to capture that expression.

I remember the day we talked about the Vietnam War. Walter Cronkite had interviewed Daniel Ellsberg the night before about his publishing of the Pentagon Papers via the *New York Times*. Ben and I had seen the interview, and so had Ranie.

"I hope wars are over forever by the time my baby grows up! Do you think he'll be brown like me, or pasty white like Jock? I hope it's a girl—no, a boy would be better. If I'm goin' to be an actress, I'll prob'ly be bummin' around my whole life!"

When the painting was finished, we spent a day together looking for a frame in San Francisco. We finally found one at Butterfield & Butterfield, antique gold and five-feet-tall, a delightfully serendipitous find, but high-priced.

Ranie insisted on paying for it. "You're kiddin' me!" she said, "You givin' me this beautiful thing, and you wanta pay for the frame too?"

We compromised by each paying half.

The only thing that marred the day was lunch with Jock, which was Ranie's idea. We met on Chestnut at a little restaurant which specialized in quiche; she said eggs were the only thing she had any appetite for. When we walked in lugging the frame, Jock was sitting in back in a leather-padded booth, smoking. In the first few minutes, Ranie coughed several times, and when he continued to smoke, she said, "Honey, that thing's makin' me sick. Please, could you put it out?"

He did so, but grudgingly.

"Oops, gotta go again! Seems like I'm always havin' to pee!" She left for the bathroom.

Immediately Jock lit up again. Even though I smoked, I didn't join him. I didn't know what to talk about while Ranie was gone, so I didn't try. Instead, I sat studying some of the other patrons. Nearby was a table of young women, all wearing embroidered denim jackets, long denim skirts, and boots. Suddenly boots were hugely in fashion. These women were wearing the kind lumberjacks wear—tall, with laces all the way up.

Jock nudged my elbow, wanting my attention. "I don't know about having this baby, but *she* wants it." He emitted a short, sardonic laugh.

I turned my gaze back to him. "Do you?" I asked.

"Huh?"

"Do *you* want it?" I repeated.

His reply was a long time coming. "Well, I guess so. Can't tell my folks, of course, they're still living in the Mesozoic Era. Can't let them know I'm sleeping with a colored lady."

I stiffened. His remark embarrassed me. Even though I knew he was being frank in an effort to ingratiate himself, he'd chosen the wrong tack.

"They should meet Ranie," I said. "They'll love her, just like everybody does!"

Jock took a long drag, then threw both arms back over the padded seat. In his black turtleneck and tight black pants, his posture was that of an arrogant, sexually available male, but he didn't turn me on at all. I didn't care for his hooded, heavy-lidded expression, nor for his two-day growth of beard. And I still hadn't forgotten his lack of appreciation for my set designs.

When Ranie came back, she was laughing about how difficult it was to pull up her panty hose, and didn't seem to notice the coolness between Jock and me. When she and I did a tug of war over the check, Jock was a non-participant. Ranie won, and I left the tip.

A week later, when she came to the house to pick up the framed picture, she said, "I can't take this with me, so I'm leavin' it with my mother. I'm sure not leavin' it with you—I might never get it outta yo' gluey fingers!"

It was true; I had fallen in love with my beautiful, sensual painting, and was sorry I'd promised it to her. I kept the sketches, of course, framed one and hung it in my studio.

Ranie called before she left and said her mother loved the painting, even though she wished Ranie hadn't posed "bare-ass naked." She had good news; Jock had found work directing a play in Connecticut, and they were planning to get married back there.

After that phone call, I didn't hear from Ranie for years.

Fia always wanted to try someplace new to eat. We hadn't seen each other since we had met for lunch at Chez Panisse, but a few weeks after she returned from Europe, she called.

"Nat, have you been to Green's, the vegetarian restaurant at Fort Mason?"

"Nope."

"I'll meet you there tomorrow; I think you'll like it."

I decided I should dress like an artist, and I knew the ambience at Fort Mason was strictly low-key. I wore my new jeans and a grey cable knit sweater, and arranged my hair on top of my head with a few tortoiseshell combs. I made up my eyes with black eye-liner and gray eyeshadow, and wore pale, pale lipstick. Then I drove across the Bay Bridge to Fort Mason. The old Army port had long ago been demilitarized, and was now a complex of art shops and meeting rooms. The parking lot, which must have covered half an acre, was crowded.

"You look enchanting!" was Fia's greeting. She was wearing a black pantsuit.

Before we were seated, we stood admiring the restaurant's bakery selections. Delicious-smelling varieties of bread containing herbs I'd never even heard of were displayed inside glass shelves. Copies of the *Tassajara Bread Book* were stacked behind the counter, and people were buying them hand over fist.

We were seated at a table where we could gaze out at San Francisco Bay. Large and small ships were anchored just beyond the wooden docks, and through the slowly lifting fog we could see the Golden Gate Bridge.

Fia told me the vegetables for the dishes here were all grown at the Tassajara Zen Monastery in a wilderness area ninety minutes from Monterey.

"Do you know much about the religion?" I asked.

"What religion?"

"Zen Buddhism. My friend Rosalia knows Alan Watt. I mean she really knows him!"

She wrinkled her nose. "I don't know about it, and I'm not planning to find out. I just like the food here."

I told her about my experience at Esalen, and about sitting *zazen* with Watts. "It's calming, but I don't have the knees for it."

Fia laughed, and all the men near our table looked her way.

"Didn't you say you played some weird mind games that weekend?"

"Uh-huh. Met some weird people too. But I enjoyed it. I want you to meet Rosie someday."

Our salads were delicious, three kinds of lettuce and four kinds of vegetables, covered with a delicious dressing, and several kinds of thick, dark breads. We chatted about Ben and Arnie, although Fia dropped the subject of Arnie pretty fast. I sensed there was something she wasn't telling me. Although I wasn't sure I should mention them, I asked about Eric and Francine. Fia said the child was three now, a little girl, and she was crazy about her.

I said, "It hasn't been three years, surely, since I went to see them with you!" Fia broke a piece of bread in small pieces, her expression preoccupied. "Are they still in that old Victorian house?"

"No, they're closer to us now, in Mill Valley."

Changing the subject, she asked if I'd seen Hana, and I said I hadn't talked to her in ages. I told her about painting Ranie. She knew about my young African American friend; I'd talked about her before. I was still excited about the painting.

"And guess what I did at Berkeley Rep!" I started to tell her about my stint as a set designer, but before I could start, Fia interrupted. "The reason you're out of touch with Hana, Nat, is that she's having an affair."

"Good! I hope she's rid of Bruce forever. Who's the man?"

"I'll save that for dessert, darling. Eat your lunch."

Same old Fia, manipulating her news for maximum drama. We sipped our wine and chewed, occasionally being interrupted when Fia hailed a friend across the room, or someone waved to her. This must be the approved lunch hangout for her social set.

We ordered dessert, and I sat back. "I've waited long enough. Tell."

"You're going to love it. Hana is having a hot-and-heavy with her tennis pro!"

"Lamentable, but to be expected. How old is he, twenty-two?"

"Thirty-two. He's Austrian, so you might say that geographically they're well-suited. They like to do it on the tennis court before dark. There are new courts, I guess, and somewhat out-of-the-way."

"Sounds uncomfortable. What about all those fuzzy tennis balls rolling around? And Hana's going to find herself in a mess. She'll be thrown out of the club, and he'll lose his job."

"Well, it's been going on for months now, and no one knows about it."

"Wanta bet? In a small suburban town, believe me, everyone knows."

"She says he's a God, with sexy calves and lovely blonde hair all over his body."

I said that any color hair all over any man's body would not be a turn-on.

Fia giggled and agreed, and we went on to talk of other things. I never got back to my dealings with George Bernard Shaw.

A half-hour later, on our way out, we both bought copies of *The Tassajara Bread Book*.

I only saw Amanda Reichard once during the '70s.

It was at a party in Pebble Beach on the Seventeen-Mile Drive, at the home of Freddy Flanders, who came out to the West Coast every year for the The Trees encampment. Ben felt that socializing with Freddy could be a big help to the firm. Not only did Freddy provide his house on the fourteenth tee of the Pebble Beach golf course, he also provided never-ending drinks and superb food. A jovial Irishman whose face was always red from drink, he was slender and surprisingly graceful. I danced with him once or twice, and was amazed at his skill on the dance floor.

Getting out of the car, I breathed deeply of the ocean breeze. It was August, but we were close to Monterey Bay, and it was never really hot.

I always drank and smoked too much at these parties. I'd finally learned to keep from embarrassing myself, a far cry from the time I walked out on the golf course with a guy from Texas and threw up all over his dinner jacket.

Ben had imbibed too much last year, and danced with Fia on the patio for the longest time. I remember I had felt a little jealous.

As soon as we walked in, Ben was stopped by a bunch of his club cronies. Suddenly I spotted Amanda across the room, and immediately crossed to her. I knew she had gotten a divorce, but we had lost touch.

She was standing by one of the floor-to-ceiling windows holding a glass of champagne, and was wearing a turquoise silk-jersey outfit, tunic and tight pants. One shoulder was bare, and there were scattered bugle beads decorating the bodice and around the hem of the pants. Her lush auburn hair was worn in an asymmetric ponytail. What a transformation from when I'd first known her, when she had seemed ashamed of her body. She'd never been that interested in clothes; with six kids to raise, she didn't have time to be.

We air-kissed and exchanged hugs.

"You look elegant!"

"You're not exactly a rag-bag yourself, Nat."

I was wearing a long black skirt I'd had forever, but I'd opened up a longer slit in the side, and had gone to Saks and splurged on a long-sleeved white crêpe blouse with silver paillettes that weighed a ton.

I saw Amanda's eyes follow Ben as he moved around the room, clapping men on the back, kissing the ladies. Watching her eyes on him triggered the memory of seeing them in the window of the Hayes Street Grill years ago. Ben had convinced me then that it was strictly business, but now I wasn't so sure.

"What have you done to your hair?" she asked. It was looking wild tonight, bushing hugely around my head in a pseudo Afro.

"I decided to get with the '70s, and have it permed."

An older man with gray hair and salt-and-pepper eyebrows was walking toward us.

"I want you to meet my husband." Grant was at least sixty, and Amanda must be around forty-five now, which was quite a difference in age. My eye was caught by the large diamond ring he wore. Amanda was wearing a headlight, too.

"Nat, this is my husband Grant Chaffee. This is Natalie Newbury, dear, the artist who did my portrait." Turning to me she said, "We have it hanging in the living room."

"I think I just met your husband, Ben, isn't it?" said Grant. "Nice to meet you. Dear, would you mind if I joined the fellows? They're talking about the Watergate burglary. Those dumb-asses—excuse me, Natalie—they've been found with a $25,000 cashier's check made out to the Nixon campaign, and they found it in one of the burglar's bank accounts!"

"Go ahead. Nat and I are dying to catch up."

"He seems nice," I said, as he walked away. "But I didn't know you'd remarried!"

"Three years ago. I always meant to call and tell you how much I appreciated the push you gave me to leave Tom. But I was so unhappy, I didn't call anyone!"

More couples drifted into the room, men in tuxedos and their expensively-dressed wives. The room was full of glitter.

"I wasn't sure you wanted to hear any advice," I said, grabbing a flute of champagne from a passing waiter.

"I *needed* to hear it! Tom was awful. Even his parents, who had spoiled him rotten, agreed with me. Imagine fathering six children and never being home to help raise them! Besides his—his infidelity." The last word was almost whispered.

I was wearing high heels with tiny straps. I had barely gotten there, and my feet were already hurting. "I hate standing around at these parties. Let's sit down, shall we?" I led her to a nearby sofa, and we sank back against the cushions.

"I met Grant a couple of years after the divorce. Nat, he's so good to me!"

I glanced across the room to Ben and Grant, who were standing with a group of other men, all no doubt engrossed in the Nixon scandal. Ben looked like a movie star in his tux. After all these years, I still thought he was the best-looking man around. Amanda took out a cigarette and lit it, and I lit one too.

"Grant's older, but he's—well, he's rich. He's got a ball-bearing business in Connecticut, and several plants in New England. But I have to live back there. We're just visiting California now for a few days."

'What about your kids, are they back East too? Did you take Eufie?"

"She didn't want to leave her grandchildren. Ashley, my eldest, is a social worker in Marin County. She finished Cal two years ago, and Lucian is in premed at USC. I'm so proud of them. But Lizzie dropped out of college and went off with her boyfriend to a commune, of all places! She did it right after those kids were killed at Kent State. Why or how that would have affected her so much, I can't imagine. I haven't heard from her for almost a year." Amanda's face clouded, and I became aware of a network of tiny lines in her face. "I don't know if she's safe, or even if she's alive." She took a drag on her cigarette. "But the youngest three are near me. Taylor and Jennifer are in private schools, and Barney's still at home."

Despite her declarations and the appearance of a settled, affluent life, I sensed that Amanda was still unhappy. She had made a good catch, one that would insure her own and her children's economic well- being, but I thought she had made a dreadful mistake.

I wondered if Amanda was truly *'domed,'* as Hana had always said.

A waiter held out a tray and offered us hot crab rolls, and again I glanced around the room. There must be eighty people here, all prosperous-looking, all chatting one another up. The men had brought out cigars, and the women were waving their bare arms about, each trying to be heard above the others. Freddy's wife, our hostess, a platinum blonde and the living handiwork of a skilled plastic surgeon, was surrounded by several younger women. They were all blonde, sleek and glossy.

I wondered what they were talking about. Clothes? Diets? Golf? I was positive it wasn't Betty Friedan, women's lib, or their careers. I was positive none of them even had careers.

"Have you heard from Hana?" Amanda asked.

I told her of my lunch with Fia, that Hana was divorced now, and involved with the tennis pro at her club.

"Oh no!" responded Amanda. "Hana shouldn't be reckless like that, sleeping around just because she's horny. She's got to think of her children. I know a little bit about that!"

I laughed. "How did you ever have time to be horny, raising six kids? I should think you would be too exhausted!"

Then I remembered the rumors.

"You'd be surprised. After the divorce I tried on quite a few men. There was a young lawyer; he must have been all of twenty-three. And there was my kitchen contractor—he was sexy!" She reached for another canapé and chewed, mouth half open, looking off into space with slightly unfocused eyes.

There it was. That dimwitted expression Ben had talked about.

I said, "You know what my aunt and grandmother used to call any woman who had an affair? 'A bold adventuress'." I laughed, remembering Mamaw describing a friend of hers that way, a woman who got divorced in the 1940s and lived with her lover, unmarried, for twenty years.

Amanda continued, "Then there was the headmaster at Taylor's school in Berkeley . . ."

"Wow. Well, I'm glad you had a good time. I have to confess, I saw you and Ben having lunch on Hayes Street once, and I was a little worried."

Amanda had the grace to blush. I waited, stubbing out my cigarette in a crystal ashtray.

"I should have told you I was meeting Ben that time. I think he was afraid you'd want to come along, make it into a social occasion, and I had a lot of big financial decisions to make. Can you forgive me?"

She put her hand on mine. Hers was manicured, with shiny cerise nails.

"Oh, it's long forgotten. Do you want Hana's latest address? She's moved to a different neighborhood. Write down your address, and I'll send you hers. Same town, but Bruce wouldn't let her stay in their house. The one she has now is smaller, with no pool. He knows his way around that ol' boy network of lawyers and judges."

"How involved is she with the tennis pro?"

"Fia told me he got kicked out of his job. Believe it or not, it wasn't because of his affair with Hana, so I don't know if that ever got around or not. He got fired because he seduced one of the teenagers he was giving lessons to. It didn't go over too well out there in the 'burbs, as you can imagine."

"I'd murder anyone who did that to one of my daughters!"

"Who said it was a daughter?"

She raised her hand to her cheek in mock horror. "I forgot—this is California!"

A group of musicians grouped themselves against the windows and began to play. Grant came to sit next to Amanda, and Ben crossed the room and joined us.

Ben took Amanda's hand and kissed it, and his ultra-smooth manner surprised me. He was always surprising me. Maybe that's why I'd stayed in love with him all this time. He perched on the arm of the sofa and draped his arm around my shoulders.

The music lasted for almost an hour. Besides the band, there was a male vocal quartet, and a handsome tenor with a gorgeous voice. The band played a couple of show tunes, then a Jule Styne medley. After that Gogi Elliott, the daughter of the alto sax player, sang, "Where is Love?" from *Oliver*. It was a beautiful moment, and there was no murmur of voices, not even the clinking of a glass.

As we got up to have dinner, I swayed and staggered on my high heels, realizing I'd drunk too much champagne. It wasn't just my wobbling knees that told me I was high, it was also that every comment anyone made sounded so brilliantly funny! I knew my laugh was getting louder and my remarks more unrestrained, but I couldn't stop. I went up to the tenor, threw my arms around him and told him he should sing at the Met, then I approached Freddy's wife, whom I couldn't stand, and in a voice I never used when I was sober, gushed, "Really, Margot, this is the most marvelous party! You've outdone yourself!"

Tables for six were dotted all over the enormous dining room, as well as several adjoining rooms. Ben and I joined four friends for dinner, Abner Rankin III and Sylvia, and Percy and Irene Healy.

On the terrace overlooking the golf course, another eight or ten groups were assembled. Our hosts had gone to a great deal of expense; floor-length glazed-cotton cloths on the tables, fresh roses as centerpieces, white candles in silver candlesticks, and a small printed menu for each guest. We dined on fennel antipasto, steak with bordelaise sauce, corn pudding, cucumbers with dill in sour cream, and *pomodori ripieni alla Romana*. Translated on the menu, this last dish was simply baked tomatoes stuffed with rice. Lemon soufflé followed, and we washed everything down with three kinds of wine, two Californias and one French.

By the time the meal was over, I was satiated and extremely drunk.

I woke up when the men at the table started asking questions about my portraits. Percy, a top executive at Ampex, and Abner, high up at Transamerica, told me they needed their likenesses done for their boardrooms. I looked at Ben. What had he been telling them? Whatever it was, it must have convinced them that I was good, because as we left the table they handed me their business cards.

I put my arm through Ben's as we walked out onto the terrace. I needed air.

"What did you say to them, darling? What a coup, if it happens!"

"I just told them you were painting everyone who's anybody these days."

I grabbed and hugged him. We stayed a little longer, then said our goodbyes and headed for the motel in Carmel. Ben got behind the wheel, and I prayed he was a lot more sober than I.

The next morning we joined the group, whittled down to forty or fifty, for Bloody Marys and brunch at the Del Monte Lodge. I was able to chat with Amanda, but only briefly. She and Grant came by our table to say goodbye on their way to their plane.

"I never got to talk to you, Grant!" I said.

"We'll see you again. Amanda has to come out here all the time to check on her kids, so we just hop on the company jet." He seemed anxious to leave.

Company jet—zounds!

Ben rose from his chair and gave her a brief hug, Amanda and I embraced again, and they left.

Leaving Carmel, we turned onto the open highway and immediately passed a group of hitchhiking, barefoot hippies. As we drove past them, one of the girls, very pregnant, put her thumb out.

"Would you look at that bunch!" I exclaimed. "The worries people have with their kids! Fia's son is a mess, and one of Amanda's daughters has joined a commune!"

"They don't stay long in those places. She'll probably only be there a few months; maybe just went to learn how to grow vegetables. They're all doing it." His tone of cynicism and indifference annoyed me.

"What difference does it make whether they're growing vegetables or banging gongs or peddling on the streets for Mr.

Moon? They're not getting an education, and they're all sexually promiscuous, contracting terrible diseases! And they're having babies left and right, using speed and LSD and cocaine and heroin! Not to mention the Hare Krishnas! You know what? *I'm glad we don't have kids!*"

"Calm down, Nat." He gave me a sidelong glance.

"Well, aren't you glad? I don't want to have to worry night and day like that." I opened the glove compartment, extracted my sunglasses, and banged it shut.

"Yes. Life is much simpler this way."

To my amazement, I began to cry. All those lost young people!

I was sure Ben meant it when he said he was glad we had no children. But I knew we'd missed some worthwhile things too.

Was that why I was crying? I blew my nose, took off my seat belt, and snuggled up close. I licked his ear and put my head on his shoulder, enjoying the feel of his rough sweater on my cheek. He turned and kissed me, and I went to sleep. The next thing I knew, Ben was saying, "We're home. How much did you have to drink, anyway, kiddo? I'll carry in our stuff, and how about you fixing us some coffee and scrambled eggs?"

Rosie Rinaldi and I didn't have much in common. She worked in the healing arts; my vocation was in the creative arts. Although I had gained something from the Esalen experience—after my time there, I think my outlook toward people was less rigid and judgmental—I secretly looked askance at all of her ephemeral, short-term New-Age cures. I didn't notice any loosening in my work until later on, but there was a relaxation of line, a blurring of edges, a willingness to sacrifice detailed depictions of reality to the dynamic— *the sweep*—of the whole painting.

But whether Rosie and I contemplated the world in the same way or not, there was something about our personalities that meshed. We were having coffee at Peet's one day, enjoying a rambling, unfocused conversation, when Rosie began to complain about being overworked. I had noticed lately that she seemed weary. She had dark circles under her eyes, and was developing a bit of a slouch. I had never been able to understand how anyone could carry other people's problems around the way she did, and remain untouched. She made good money, but I couldn't have done it for the highest pay in the world.

"I'd love to get away for a few days," she said. "Why don't you come up to St. Helena with me next time Ben goes out of town? But it'll have to be after the grape harvest." I said I'd love to, then forgot about her invitation. But one day in late October, she called.

Ben was working terribly hard, gone ten hours a day. He was a nervous wreck, and for the first time in our married life, he was rude and brusque with me. One morning over breakfast he told me "strictly hush-hush, don't tell anyone"—that Flanders & Schuman was possibly going to be merged with another investment company. He said he'd be tied up for some time until it got thrashed out.

I got up and poured more coffee. I said I understood.

I didn't, though. I didn't understand why he couldn't confide in me more.

I told him that Rosie had asked me to visit her folks for the weekend, so would he mind if I went?

"I don't know when this is going to get settled. I'm miserable to be around, anyway, so go ahead."

Around four, Rosie came by in her new blue Toyota, and I threw a small bag in the back and jumped in. It took only an hour and a half to get to the wine country. On the way, we talked about a lot of things, and one subject was Ranie. Rosie had heard my blow-by-blow account of designing the stage sets, and she had gone to *Arms and the Man* and brought a couple of friends, going backstage afterward to congratulate our friend.

I tied on a scarf, since she had all the windows open. Even though I wasn't sure Ranie was still going to her for therapy, I expressed my reservations about Ranie's marriage plans. Rosie knew about the expected baby.

126

"Don't worry, Nat. Ranie will be a fabulous mother, and the child will be gorgeous!"

I changed the subject.

"Did I tell you my friend Fia bought this new house in Belvedere? We went to a party there, and it was fabulous!"

I didn't bring up Amanda Reichard's name, even though I was pretty sure Rosie and she knew each other; they both lived in Berkeley, were about the same age, and Rosie had many connections to the medical profession.

Rosie chatted about her parents and her job, and I talked about Hana's divorce and my new pal Nikki, describing the portrait a bit.

"She makes me laugh! I think she's the most irreverent person I've ever met. I would love for you to meet these women. I need to give a luncheon or something, but it seems as if I'm always painting. Maybe we could all go out for pizza someday."

"That's okay, Nat, I think it's wonderful that you're so creative, and that you actually *do* something with your talent! You wouldn't believe all the women who come to me for counseling, dying to express themselves in some way but unable to find the right outlet. They say their lives are so boring!"

There was little evidence of the changing of the seasons in Montclair or Berkeley, but Napa County is more like the East. There had been a cold snap the previous week, and the leaves on the grape vines had turned. Row upon row of orange, red, and gold-leafed vines trailed off in the fields on either side of the road, and the muted gray-green of the hills beyond was dotted with trees of flaming red, chrome yellow, and copper, with majestic Mount St. Helena as backdrop.

As I admired the fall brilliance all around, I found myself repeating the same comments over and over. "Look at those colors! Look at that grove of trees!"

"Aren't they gorgeous?" said Rosie. "The oldest valley oaks date back more than 300 years. They were alive when Indians managed the valley."

We passed the towns of Napa and Yountville and came to St. Helena. We turned off on a narrow road, eventually arriving at the long driveway into the family vineyard.

"How much land do your folks own up here?" I asked.

"Something like two hundred acres. They've acquired it gradually through the years, when somebody adjoining their property wanted to cash out, maybe when it was a bad year for grapes. Or maybe the vines got mildew or black measles, or little-leaf, red spiders, nematode. Rabbits and gophers are always digging up the plantings. There are a million things that can go wrong in a vineyard, and my parents have been through a lot."

We came to the house, a white late Victorian with bay windows. It was a perfect example of that era of architecture, a gable with fish-scale shingles, and a roof topped by a Queen Anne hexagonal spire.

Rosie's father hurried out to greet us. Paolo Rinaldi was a small man in the humble garb of a farmer: striped-ticking overalls and a straw hat. He shouted, "Rosie, angelina!"

Her mother ran out too, and she was even tinier than Paolo.

Rosie exclaimed, "Mama! You look so different!"

Her mother reached up to pat her gray curls, which covered her head like a frizzy little hat. "I gave myself a permanent."

"Papa, Mama, this is Natalie Newbury, the artist who did my portrait. This is my mother Maria, and my dad, Paolo. She can call you by your first names, can't she, folks?"

"Sure! We enjoy the beautiful picture, and we thank you so much!"

"If we can't have Rosie with us, we have the picture," Paolo said, taking my arm.

Maria touched her daughter's cheek with a work-roughened hand. "We're having a party tomorrow night. Everyone loves you, everyone wants to see you!"

Rosie rolled her eyes. "Oh no, I came up here to rest!" Then she grinned and said, "Wait until you see all the food, Nat, you won't believe it. Let's get our bags put away and walk around." She led me through the entry hall and into the living room to the portrait hanging over the sofa.

"I'm trying to get Mama to redecorate; that sofa looks terrible with your painting." It was true, the painting's primary colors clashed with the rusts, olive greens, and ochers in the room.

"Looks fine to me!" I lied.

We went upstairs. All along the stairwell were pictures of Rosie and Buddy. They looked alike, with the dark coloring of their parents, smiling teenagers with arms entwined.

My bedroom was at the end of the hall, a charming nook filled with antiques. I sat in the Victorian rocker for a few minutes, enjoying the view—acres and acres of grape vines.

In the softness of late afternoon, Rosie and I hiked around the property with Paolo. It was obvious that he was proud of the fruits of his labor. Now I knew where Rosie got her charm; there was an endearing warmth about this man. Rosie's mother was prim and self-conscious, as if unsure of her place in the world, but her father was a man who could fit in anywhere. They had owned the vineyard for forty years, although Paolo said he'd started out with walnuts and prunes, not possessing the courage for grapes for many decades. Gradually though, as the Napa Valley became more and more devoted to viticulture, he decided to try it. He started off with one variety of grapes and a few field hands, developing the property over the years into the successful operation it was now: eight varietals (four reds and four whites), a full time manager, an assistant manager, and sixty workers.

"It's a good thing Papa married Mama, because he has to speak Spanish all the time to the workers." said Rosie.

"I speak Mexican more than I speak Italian," he laughed.

"Were you born in Italy?" I asked.

"No, but Mama and Papa only spoke Italian, never Eng-a-lish!"

"I'm going back to visit with Mama, okay?"

Rosie left and went into the house, and Paolo gave me a tour of the underground wine cellar, an enormous structure with row upon row of oak casks. The interior was silent and dark, the workers going about their business with quiet authority. I told Paolo that I knew nothing about winemaking, so he went on at great length, then finished our tour by giving me a taste of a 1954 Zinfandel, pouring some for himself too.

"Do you think Rosie is happy? Her mama, she worries so much about her!"

His expression was sorrowful, questioning.

"I think so. She helps so many people!" That wasn't what he meant, I knew.

He shook his head. "The boy friends—she has so many—but no marriage, no children! We worry alla time!"

I dropped my eyes, helpless to come up with an answer.

"It's okay, Natalie. I am happy she has a friend like you."

For supper we had spaghetti and meatballs, plus lots of *focaccia* and red wine. I stuffed myself, while Maria kept apologizing because there was so little to eat. We turned in early, and I sank into bed, sleepy from all the wine.

The next morning while Maria and Paolo were busy with preparations for the party, Rosie asked, "Nat, you ever been to a fortuneteller?"

Here we go again, I thought, off on one of Rosie's cosmic searches.

"Gosh no, I haven't. It's one of those important rituals I've missed. Do you think it's something I need to experience?"

"You definitely should. I know an excellent one in St. Helena, Madame Lushenka. We could run over there this morning."

"But shouldn't we help with the party preparations?"

"Mama knows just what she wants to do, and she has lots of help."

Madame Lushenka's place was a ten-foot wide shack on Highway 29, nestled between a 7-11 store and a car repair shop. It was painted bright pink, and across it was a sign decorated with stars and crescent moons:

✪✪
MADAME LUSHENKA • FORTUNE-TELLING • PREDICTIONS
TAROT READINGS • PALM-READINGS
✪✪

"Is this going to cost big bucks?" I asked.

"Ten dollars. Can you afford it?"

We went up the ramshackle steps and knocked on the front door; evidently we didn't need an appointment.

"I hope she's stocked up with peacock feathers and leaves of velvet groundsel," I said.

"Come in!" a woman's voice called. Madame Lushenka was nothing like I'd imagined. No turban, no long golden earrings. She was swarthy of skin, however, and her black hair was pulled back and tied with a black scarf. She wore a full flowered skirt and a simple white blouse. No Hungarian gypsy, her accent was Italian-American. She and Rosie greeted each other like old friends.

"Which of you is going first?" she asked, and Rosie pointed to me.

There were two rooms, divided by a long beaded curtain. I walked through it, following the fortune teller. There was a pile of big cards on the table where Madame Lushenka seated herself, but no crystal ball. I sat down across from her, and she took my hand, turned it over, and began to study my palm.

Several seconds went by as she scrutinized my hand from every angle. Finally she looked up and smiled.

"You are very gifted person, yes? Music? Dancing?"

"No."

"You make pottery, dishes?"

"No."

"You are a lady architect."

"Unhh-uh."

"Art! You are an *artist!*"

I laughed. "You have it. Wish I could dance, though. Sounds like more fun than painting."

She grasped my hand more firmly, pulling it closer to her eyes.

"Natalie—that is your name?"

"Yes."

"Natalie, I think you had a grandmother who loved you very much. Is it not so?"

I felt my eyes fill with tears. Oh yes! My grandmother Evans had adored me, and I adored her, had spent half my childhood on her lap. But how silly to cry about it!

"She made you things, and she cooked for you, yes?"

Little dresses, and gingerbread men. My eyes spilled over. She handed me a tissue, looking pleased that she'd scored a bull's-eye.

"Now, Natalie, let us see what the cards say."

Strange as it may seem, up to that point I'd never heard of Tarot cards, with their colorful drawings of characters: The Magician, The High Priestess, The Emperor, The Sun. After shuffling and cutting them into two piles, she dealt them out; three on one side, three on the other, three at the top, and one card in the middle, The Queen of Pentacles.

Three times Madame dealt them out in this fashion, three times she picked them up and studied them, mumbling to herself. Half the time she reversed the cards, turning them in my direction. She seemed to be working in some purposeful fashion, but it was a complete mystery to me. I was determined to be a willing vessel, though, and didn't say a word. The only sounds were her occasional *"H-m-m-m"* and *"Yes-s-s-s!"* On the fourth reading, she turned up a card that said The Lovers, and stopped. The picture was of two naked people with a background of fluffy clouds and a winged figure guarding them.

She looked up at me and then down at the cards; up, then down again.

I sat still. This no longer felt like a silly schoolgirl lark.

"Oh," she said.

"*What?*"

"Your husband—"

"Yes? What about him?" My heart fluttered in my chest like a small bird.

"He is Nick? Frank?"

"No."

Thank God. She was talking about someone else's marriage—it was Nick or Frank's wife who needed to worry! I sank back against the chair.

"Nevertheless, your husband—he loves you very much."

"Oh. *Good!*"

"But there is some—some little bit of disturbance?"

"Not at all."

"Perhaps it is coming later. Never mind."

Madame picked up the cards and shuffled them, then dealt them out, four rows of eight cards each. This promised to be an even more elaborate interpretation than the other; there were so many more cards.

But I had just about had enough. She had flip-flopped from flattery to old memories to bad omens. Where might she go now?

She continued dealing. King of Cups, King of Swords, The Devil. When she came to the next card, she stopped.

It was The Fool, and was turned toward me.

"This is interesting," she intoned. "Yes . . .*yes.*"

I held my breath again. A long period of silence ensued, while Madame Lushenka squinted at me with one eye closed.

"*Well?*" I demanded.

She changed the direction of her gaze, looking off into a corner of the room. Finally she said, "You have recently purchased something, and it does not work right?"

"Uh, yeah. An electric blender. It's a lemon."

"You should return it, and get your money back."

She stood up, smiled, and took my hand and shook it. I fumbled in my bag, took out a ten-dollar bill, and she stuck it down her blouse.

"Please come back soon, Mrs. Natalie, and tell me how your painting is going. I am sure you are a wonderful artist!"

I pushed through the beads, deflated like a party balloon the morning after the party. I was upset, and wondered why I had come. All my enthusiasm for Madame Lushenka's predictions had evaporated.

Tell me I'm gifted, tell me my grandmother loved me, tell me to take the blender back. But don't tell me there's trouble with my marriage!

Rosie could see that something was wrong. "Uh-oh. Well, see you in a little while." She hurried through the curtain.

Thirty minutes later, we were in Rosie's car on our way back to the vineyard.

She turned to me. "What's the matter? What are you so agitated about?"

"You go first. What'd she tell you?"

"Okay. Well, Madame Lushenka is usually half bad news, half good, with something outrageous thrown in. Would that be your estimate?"

"For sure. But what did she tell you, specifically? Nobody said we had to keep this a secret. It's not like the wish you make before you blow out the candles on your birthday cake!"

"Nat, chill out, will you? First, she told me I have a lot of weighty responsibilities. *Absolutely fucking true!* Last week I had two teen-age suicides. But she told me some good news, too; I'm going to be traveling to a far-off country. And one more thing. She said she could see in my palm that my parents have a big garden. As if everyone in the Napa Valley doesn't have a big garden, ranch, or vineyard! But the best thing she foresaw—after divining that I have had tons of difficulties with men—is that I'm going to meet the right man, the perfect man, and very soon!"

Rosie asked what Madame Lushenka had said to me. I was calmer now, and I told Rosie what she'd said about my grandmother, her stumbling guess that I was an artist, and her invaluable advice that I should return the faulty blender. I didn't mention her doubts about my marriage.

That night at the party, Rosie wore a red dress with diagonal stripes of blue. It had a halter neckline that set off her olive skin, and she wore a pair of raffia espadrilles with high platform soles, making her as tall as me.

"You're going to be the center of attention, Rosie. You look wonderful!"

I didn't have any pretty clothes for hot weather. I wore a plain white cotton-knit dress, dressing it up with my turquoise jewelry from Santa Fe, and Rosie plaited my hair in a French braid.

People arrived in droves. Some were dressed to the nines, others wore work shirts and jeans. There must have been forty or so of the locals there, most of them farmers or vintners, along with tradespeople from nearby towns. In abundance and diversity, the food was like nothing I'd ever experienced. Almost everyone arrived carrying a dish.

To say the wine flowed would be an understatement. We started with all of the Rinaldi label whites: Riesling, Chardonnay, Chenin Blanc, and Gewurztraminer. We had the reds with dinner: Cabernet Sauvignon, Pinot Noir, Gamay Beaujolais, and more of the Zinfandel.

There were adorable children of all ages, and I could see how Maria and Paolo must miss having grandchildren. The kids passed around the appetizers—artichoke frittata, prosciutto with melon, guacamole and chips.

Rosie's friends greeted her with kisses, and one curly-haired man asked, "When you gonna get married, Rosie? And why don' you marry me?"

"*Ah-h-h,* Antonio, I will marry you, just as soon as you divorce Anna."

A big-breasted woman hung on Antonio's arm, laughing.

There was a loud mariachi band on the patio. Rosie said the men were all employees of her dad's, that they played at everyone's parties.

As usual, people were interested in me because I was an artist. There were compliments about the portrait, and the usual "Can't draw a straight line—" and "How long did it take you—?" comments.

"What kinda art you paint?" asked short dark Pietro, who was weaving a bit and staring at my boobs. I smiled and moved back half a step.

"Mostly I paint people, but sometimes I paint landscapes."

Pietro moved even closer and put his hand on my waist, giving me a friendly squeeze. "You can paint me, Miss Friend-a-Rosie, or you can come paint my farm. I got a lotta landscape you can paint!"

When he moved away, Paolo came over. "Don't mind Pietro, he always has a little too much *vino*. Once he was leaving a party and he had a bad accident. The cops threw him in jail, and when he woke up they told him he could make one phone call. You know who he called? Chicken Delight!"

One man brought a dog with a red bandanna tied around his neck. He was a friendly, coal-black dog who wagged his tail at everyone, and the man said the dog's name was Norman Mailman. Norman Mailman was busy sniffing all the women's crotches.

"Norman always acts up at these parties," said the man, "but he never does anything I wouldn't like to do." He and the dog moved away.

Maria served dinner buffet style, with everything spread out on the dining room table and sideboard, spilling back into the kitchen. No paper plates here; we used large white dinner plates that could hold gargantuan portions. There were *canelloni* in an enormous serving dish, *gnocchi* in another—*polenta,* mushroom *torta,* asparagus Parmesan, *risotto* with mushrooms, and *ricotta* cheese pie. There were *chiles relleno de picadillo, arroz verde,* and a chicken dish Rosie told me was *pollo a la chilindrón.* The salads and side dishes were endless—

136

Caesar salad, bean salad, fruit salad. For breads we could choose among buttermilk biscuits, tortillas, or more *focaccia*.

"*Mangiano! Mangiano!*" urged Paolo.

For dessert we trooped outside, where dozens of pies, cakes, and other specialties were lined up on picnic tables. Instead of more food, I went to have a cigarette with a group of smokers.

Even though it was late October, the temperature was in the nineties. The night continued warm, and as the sky darkened, the full moon rose in the sky.

Crickets began their throbbing nighttime serenades. This place was a veritable paradise—if only I had insisted that Ben come!

The younger children went to sleep curled up on their mothers' laps, while the grownups clustered in groups, drinking wine and discussing the recent harvest.

The party went on for hours, and at midnight, Rosie was heavily involved in a discussion with a group of old friends. They were all gesturing wildly, and talk was about how the Napa Valley was changing. I heard the phrases 'environmental disaster'—'just like L.A.'—'open space'.

Finally, I went to bed.

The next morning Rosie said she had paperwork to do at home, and I was ready to leave too. I made my thank-yous with a quick pen-and-ink sketch of Maria, and expressed my appreciation to Paolo as best I could.

There were tears when Rosie said goodbye.

"When you coming back?" Maria asked in a mournful voice. Paolo stood in the driveway with his hat pulled over his eyes, hands stuffed in his pockets.

"Soon, Mama, soon!"

"Whew!" breathed Rosie as we drove away. A few minutes later she said, "You can see why I don't come home more often. Too much of everything—too much food, too much wine, and way too much love! Since Buddy died, it's all been coming at me!"

"Lots of people would be happy to have parents who care that much," I said.

She glanced quickly at me. But I hadn't meant to sound self-pitying. In fact, I could sympathize. Love, in some of its forms, can be oppressive.

The drive out of the vineyard was as pleasurable as the drive in had been, but soon we were in heavy traffic. It was heavy and noisy enough to make me see what the old-timers were worried about.

When I got home, the kitchen table was covered with Ben's office papers, but he wasn't there. He returned while I was drinking a glass of water at the kitchen sink; he'd gone out for breakfast. We kissed, and I noticed that he looked thin.

I told him about the Rinaldis' wonderful old house and thriving vineyard, and about the lavish feast they'd put on for us. "You should see Rosie in her own milieu up there, darling, she's adored!"

I left the room to unpack, calling back as I went upstairs, "I may not be hungry for a week, so don't expect me to do much cooking!"

A few days later, Ben and I were having supper in the kitchen when Rosie phoned.

"Nat, how good a friend are you? Good enough to let me take your husband out to lunch, so I can pick his brains about money? My dad has a lousy financial adviser. I don't trust him, and Papa and Mama are doing fantastically well with the winery. I never knew my dad would be such a financial success!"

"Of course you can take him to lunch," I said.

Something made me hesitate, and suddenly I remembered Ben's lunch with Amanda.

I was sure this was different. I put my hand over the receiver.

"Darling, Rosie wants to find out from you about managing her folk's money. She wants to take you out on a date!" I handed him the phone.

She took him to Trader Vic's, and later he told me that during their long lunch, he made many recommendations about tax shelters, etc. Flanders & Schuman was going to be investing a lot of the

Rinaldis' money. Ben was pleased about the commission he'd be making, and Sam Schuman was ecstatic.

"Are Paolo and Maria getting rich?" I asked. Remembering Maria's home permanent and Paolo's bib overalls, I was unable to fathom such a possibility.

"You better believe it!" Ben replied.

While I was with Rosie in Napa, Ben had purchased, sight unseen, a modern condo on the north shore of Lake Tahoe. He heard about it from a friend, who'd been in High Sierra real estate for many years. He told Ben the owner was in hock up to his eyebrows; it was a repossession deal. Ben said the condo had two bedrooms and two baths, and from the upstairs master bedroom, you could sort of see the lake.

"Even if we never go up there, it's a great investment. We can rent it to families for their summer vacations, and in the winter to skiers."

I had come home to a phone message with the offer of a commission to paint a family of teenagers. I don't remember having a comment, even an opinion, about acquiring our new property. I immediately returned the call, anxious to make some money.

Part of Madame Lushenka's predictions for Rosie came true. In December, she temporarily referred her patients to another psychiatrist and flew off to Italy. She said she was going to sightsee until she dropped, and after that she was going to look up her cousins near Ravenna.

I was green with envy, and so was Ben. "You know something about Rosie?" he said. "She goes off in all directions, just like you've always said, but she seems to have an interesting life."

I'd been thinking about Hana, worrying about her, but it was a long time before I did anything to show I was concerned. The economy was good, portrait commissions were coming thick and fast, and Ben and I were always busy. I had an uneasy feeling that I was one of those people others talked about, describing us as happy recluses, concerned only with our particular worlds of bird-watching, stamp-collecting, the study of Russian icons—whatever.

With me it was painting.

Skiing had once been a big part of Ben's life. That was how I'd met him, at Lake Arrowhead when we were both in college. But he wasn't a fanatic about it, and since I refused to learn, he hadn't skied in years. But after buying the condo he told me he was going to go more often, and I'd better get used to the idea.

Fine, I said, how about if we take Hana and her kids up too? I knew she was as proficient at skiing as she was at tennis, and that she couldn't afford it now that she and Bruce had split. Happily, Ben agreed to the plan.

I called her in December. It was many months since my lunch with Fia, when I'd heard of Hana's affair with the tennis pro, but instead of being cool with me for not calling sooner, she was as friendly as ever.

"Oh, Natalie—where have you been? I bet you are painting until your eyes are falling out!"

"Yes, I've been busy. But I've been wondering how *you* are."

"Not good. Bruce has been awful about the divorce! The kids have been my—how do you say it—my saving blessing!"

"I was wondering about something. Ben just invested in a condo at Tahoe Taverns, and I was thinking we could all go up there skiing, kids too, for the New Year's holiday. I don't ski, but I'd love to see you and the children, so what do you think?"

"Oh Nat, that would be marvelous! I accept!"

We picked them up early in the morning. Hans was fourteen now, becoming quite tall, and Molly was eleven, a slim, pretty sprite. They were attractive, well-behaved children. It didn't seem as if the divorce had done them harm. But I was an outsider to their family, and I wouldn't really know.

Halfway up to the Sierras, and in the midst of driving snow, Ben and Hans put on chains. We drove for what seemed like hours more, and arrived at the condo after dark, cold and hungry. We trudged through the snow, carrying boxes of food. I liked the condo, but we didn't really see it until morning, when we went around exclaiming about the airy kitchen, the handsome fireplace, and the 'almost-view' of the lake. I was glad Ben had bought it furnished; the tables and chairs, beds, sofa and dinette set were almost like new.

The next day the weather was clear and sunny, and Ben said he heard on the radio they had fresh powder at Alpine Meadows. I don't know why fresh powder is so great, but Ben seemed thrilled about it. Everyone but me went out the first day, and I lit a fire in the fireplace and made bean soup.

On the second day Molly stayed in with me; she'd sprained her ankle trying to learn to sideslip. Ben said to keep cold packs on it and to keep her leg elevated. She quickly became bored, so we played Slap most of the day, Molly half-reclining on the couch. It wasn't hard losing to the child; she was quick as a fox.

"I usually lose to Hans, but he cheats," she said.

I made buttered popcorn, and the two of us pigged out on that and Diet Cokes.

The others came home exhausted but exhilarated. Ben and Hana had taken turns skiing with Hans, whose level of expertise was just a notch below Ben's. Ben said he didn't try to keep up with Hana, that she went to the top of the mountain and practically flew down.

As we sat around before dinner enjoying martinis, Ben praised her skill.

She said, "Yes, Natalie, but Ben is a wild man out there on the slopes. And so *anmutig!*" We looked blank. "So graceful, *anmutig*, you know! I saw him once going eighty miles an hour! You should see his paralyze jumps! "

Ben reached across the coffee table, patting her on the knee.

"Parallel jumps. Please don't tell Natalie I'm good, she'll never try to learn."

"Don't worry, I'm not going to anyway," I said, passing the pretzels.

My main memory from that weekend was how we all laughed so much. Except for sharing the bathroom, Hans and Molly got along wonderfully for siblings so close in age.

Hana was in fine fettle. She told us that some of the male skiers were 'dare-demons,' that they took incredible risks on the high peaks 'attempting fortune'.

Hana's bloopers, combined with all the gin and wine we drank, kept the fun going. I didn't ask about her love life, nor did I bring up the tennis instructor, and she didn't volunteer anything.

When we left after the long weekend, the skiers were happy and exhilarated, and I was happy and rested. Getting out of the car in front of her house, Hana said she needed to think of a way to thank us. I told her not to be silly, that it was our pleasure having her and the kids as guests. But two days later she turned up with a complete German meal: *sauerbraten* with potato dumplings, stuffed onions , and a gorgeous raspberry *Linzertorte*.

Chapter Nine

Esther

In January of 1973, President Nixon announced a cease-fire in Vietnam, and Ben and I opened a bottle of champagne and drank a toast. In March, the last U.S. troops left South Vietnam. Our troops had been fighting there for ten years, and we still lost the war. But somehow it didn't feel like losing—it felt like *not* losing—not losing any more American lives.

In February, I completed a group portrait: the six O'Brien kids, plus their Golden Retriever, and not one but three Siamese cats. I didn't do much socializing that winter, but I was confident that Fia's relentless party giving, Rosie's counseling career, and Hana's super parenting went on beautifully without me.

After the O'Brien job, I began doing a few corporate portraits that paid very well, which was good for our bank account. Good for my ego, too. For the first time, I was beginning to be known somewhere other than in the East Bay. One commission led to another, and that year I was honored to paint Abner Rankin III, Percy Healy, and three other important corporate bigwigs. They were so important that none of them could take time out to come to Montclair, so Ben and I rented a studio in San Francisco and I moved all my equipment to Bush Street.

I would ride over the bridge with Ben, work all day, and drive home with him during commute hour. Occasionally we would travel on BART, Bay Area Rapid Transit, the newly-completed transportation system running between Oakland and San Francisco. (Amazingly, part of it ran under the bay!) But usually Ben found it more convenient to take the car. Traffic on the bridge was terrible, and on the trip home my arms would ache from painting, my feet swollen from standing all day. Personal grooming was something I didn't bother with, and everything about me smelled like oil paints. Most of the time I was too tired to cook, so we would do take-out.

I was glad when the boardroom portraits were finished because those were extremely stressful months. I hated the commute, and for the first time I realized how much Ben must hate it too.

As I strived to attain a degree of personal gratification from my art, I began to realize that there was something lacking. Even though my clients were pleased and I was more than handsomely paid (I was getting $6000 per portrait), I knew that once again, and invariably, my style had tightened up. My brush strokes had become more meticulous and painstaking; my compositions stilted and predictable.

I needed a different kind of challenge, and began making plans to paint Esther Graham, the older woman I had met at Esalen in 1969. We had already put it off several times because we couldn't get our schedules to jibe. Twice when we planned to get together, I decided to take a portrait commission instead. Esther was retired from her job as a Calaveras County welfare worker but continued to do volunteer social work, so that was a factor as well.

We finally settled on late July. She mentioned again that she had a cabin where I could paint and sleep; the only other bedroom in her house, she said, was too small for me to be comfortable.

I told her I would be coming alone, since Ben would be at his July Trees encampment.

The '60s counterculture had had its effect in many ways, and facial hair was one. Now, in California, stockbrokers, lawyers, even engineers were sprouting facial hair. As if Ben weren't handsome enough already, with his new moustache he looked positively princely. The moustache was medium-sized, not one of those rank bushy things, and grew in very black; the contrast with his graying hair was stunning.

But something was wrong in our relationship. He seemed withdrawn, detached.

The night before I left for Esther's, I donned my newest and sheerest nightie, and dabbed *Rive Gauche* behind my ears and under my breasts. Gliding into bed, I slid my arm over his chest and began to caress him. For the first time ever, he didn't respond. I lay back on my pillow, trying to stifle my hurt feelings.

"What's wrong, darling? Is it something I did?"

He didn't answer. Instead, he reached for a magazine and began reading.

Switching off my nightlight , I finally managed to fall asleep.

The next morning over breakfast I said, "I shouldn't trust you, Ben—gallivanting off to the Russian River, where hundreds of hookers in those nearby towns are waiting to prey upon you upstanding innocent guys."

I was trying to get under his skin, and it worked. He began to splutter and sputter, and I said, "Don't deny it! I've read all that stuff in the *Chronicle* about the goings-on up there!"

"Don't be ridiculous! We're too busy drinking and listening to Henry Kissinger talk about foreign policy! We never leave the gates, and women aren't allowed in, as you know. So go on, Nat, go on up to the Gold Country. Paint your guts out. And have fun with Esther."

We both laughed, and he kissed me on his way out the door.

"Remember, darling, I'm your biggest fan."

The weather warmed rapidly as I drove up Highway 49 through the foothills of the Sierras. This was the part of California that held so much of California's early history, where gold had been discovered and the 49'ers rushed in to make a killing. Greenery changed to dry meadowland as I gained elevation, and the air began to smell deliciously of manzanita and pine tree resin. Clusters of oaks, pines, poplars, and locust trees dotted the hills, and farmhouses began to appear. Grazing black-and-white cattle and ancient red barns, fading to grey, caught my eye as subjects for future paintings.

Having been raised in the Southwest, I'm very much at home in warm weather, so I rolled all the windows down and let the hot wind blow through my hair. I switched on the radio, but instead of music, got the news. The Watergate hearings had begun back in May, and one sinister revelation after another was coming to light. Just yesterday a Nixon aide named Butterfield disclosed that the White House used a taping system in the Oval Office. This momentous event filled five minutes of the news broadcast.

That ought to do it! I thought. But it seemed like Nixon could weasel out of anything.

After two hours of driving past historic Gold Rush towns like Volcano, Jackson and Fiddletown, I arrived at Esther's small clapboard house outside Sutter Creek. She gave me a warm hug, introduced me to Pansy, her ancient Springer Spaniel, and showed me to the cabin. Her gray hair no longer fell long and loose around her shoulders, and at first I was disappointed. Later, though, I decided I liked the way it curled around her head in soft gray ringlets.

Esther didn't mind showing her sagging flesh. Her cut-off jeans and sleeveless shirt gave full view of her wrinkled arms and baggy, furrowed knees. After I stowed my painting gear and suitcase, we wandered around the property, with the dog running ahead. Pansy, furred ears flying, was skilled at fetching sticks for us to throw again and again. And again.

"Talk about perseverance!" I laughed.

"I think that has to be where the word 'dogged' comes from," she said. "I finally got rid of all the slobbery old tennis balls."

Esther's ten acres were covered mostly in locust trees, manzanita, and scrub. I was amazed that she could keep up the property all by herself, although it was clear she didn't work much at 'keeping' it. However, one small garden patch near her front door bloomed with red geraniums and white daisies, and a wooden swing hung from a tree near the front porch.

Esther was divorced, with four grown children. Her sons lived in Southern California, one daughter lived in Connecticut, and her

146

youngest girl was involved with drugs. Esther thought she was living in Modesto. She said the only time she saw any of them was at Christmas, when she went to visit one or the other of the three elder siblings. None of them liked to travel to Sutter Creek.

The cabin where I was to paint and sleep was used for Esther's pottery making, a detail she had tactfully omitted. She had moved her potter's wheel, worktable and bench away from the big window, and shoved them to the other side of the room near the kiln. When I protested that I was displacing her, she said, "Heavens, child, I can go without throwing pots for a few days—gives me a good excuse to loaf!"

I walked over to admire the pottery stored on shelves against the wall, bowls and large pots in an amazing variety of sizes and shapes, with many combinations of glazes. She was far from the amateur she had said she was; her work was clearly of professional quality. Several big earthen pots, with a semi-opaque glaze of blue decorating the rim and running down the sides, were magnificent.

I had brought several bottles of wine, and at supper we celebrated our reunion at her round kitchen table under a charming old Tiffany-style lamp.

"You know, Nat, when I first met you at Esalen, I was so impressed! You were quiet, but I could sense your dedication to your art. You didn't talk about it much, but when you did, I was amazed at how serious you were."

I didn't know how to respond. I looked away, sipping from my wine goblet. Finally I said, "Maybe I would be a better wife if I weren't so ambitious."

"Nonsense! You're fine just the way you are. Keep going; there's no telling how much you'll accomplish!"

The next morning I set up my easel and the collapsible worktable I'd brought and began to lay out charcoal sticks, Conté crayon, fixatif, chamois cloth, and erasers. Conté crayons are an excellent tool for sketching; I favor black and sepia. Along with the French masters (forgive the presumption), I often use them for a finished drawing. I clipped newsprint to my drawing board and made room for the pile of drawing paper I'd brought along.

I had asked Esther to wear a dark, loose-fitting pullover and a long dark skirt, so nothing detracted from the purity of her face. After trying several poses, I ended up positioning her as Picasso had posed Gertrude Stein: hands on knees, shoulders slanted, body leaning forward. I was pleased with my treatment of her hands. Spread on her knees, they were relaxed, strong and powerful.

By the end of the week I had done twelve large drawings. Half of them were good, and three I liked a lot.

I had no compunctions about imitating Picasso. Since I knew my talent was microscopic compared to his, what did it matter? Picasso himself, I once read, had copied the pose from Ingres's portrait of Louis François Bertin, a Parisian from the time of Napoleon. Bertin sat staring out from the canvas, hands on knees, massive in size and bulk. Ingres was a superb draftsman who never veered from a realistic approach, so the two masters' paintings were dissimilar in treatment as well as technique. Depending on which art scholar you want to believe, the sculptural look of the Stein portrait shows the influence of Iberian reliefs, a bust Ingres did of Empress Livia, or a mask-like painting Picasso was doing of an old smuggler around the time he did Stein.

Adjusting to sleeping in the cabin loft wasn't difficult, even though the narrow, primitive ladder was a bit difficult to maneuver. There wasn't a bed or mattress, but Esther had used quilts and blankets for padding. It was so hot that only a sheet was needed for covering. After a couple of days, I even got used to the privy.

My hostess was a basic, down-home cook, and I immediately started gaining weight. A typical menu was roast pork, fresh green beans, baked yams, and biscuits. Most evenings I made her sit in her parlor, which was filled with Gold Country antiques and furniture she called her 'used junk,' while I did the dishes.

I think it was the night the two of us killed half a jug of red wine that Esther told me all about her life. She said she'd tried her best, raising four children alone, but that it hadn't been easy. Ernie had owned a floor tile business, but he had a gambling problem. He started going up to Reno when the children were young, then began going more and more. Not only did he use up all their meager savings, he got involved with a female dealer at one of the casinos.

Sliding a half-empty glass of wine from one hand to another on the table, she said, "I never figured out how Ernie could attract a pretty young woman like that, but a friend of mine saw them together up there, so I finally had to believe it."

They got divorced and she started to work at a local insurance office. She was fifty-two when she went back to college and got her degree; a year later she started working as a social worker for the county.

I hadn't heard from Ben, but that was nothing new when he was at The Trees.

However, the fact that he had been so uncommunicative before I left had me more than a little worried. While drawing Esther one day, I must have looked unhappy, because out of the blue she asked, "Natalie, is everything okay with you and Ben?"

She had never met Ben, but I'd talked about him a lot, and she'd spoken to him once or twice on the phone.

I held the crayon poised in the air for a moment, caught off-guard. After a beat, I said, *"Sure!* Why do you ask?"

"I'm just hoping you two can go on forever! So many folks are breaking up these days, and you seem so right for each other."

"We *are* right for each other. Ben will never leave me, and I'll never let go of him!" I hadn't meant to sound so intense, so I added, "Don't worry your head about it, my friend."

I was planning to give Esther a drawing, or possibly the painting I planned to do at home; I hadn't decided yet which. She said she wanted to pay me in small installments, but I knew I could never accept money because this project had been my idea from the get-go. Besides, the way she coddled and spoiled me made my stay so special.

Not only did she cook all the meals, preparing lunches for me when I sketched outdoors, but she did so many other things: bringing me iced tea at surprising moments, washing my hair in the kitchen sink.

"There's a special way to wash your hair here, Nat. Let me do it for you, and we'll use this rainwater I collected, makes your hair so silky."

It was terrific to feel like a kid again.

I worked on Esther's portrait in the mornings, and in the afternoons, despite the heat, I started sketching the scenery further out on the property. Since I hadn't done any landscapes for ages, I found it stimulating. I drew with pastel crayons on large sheets of white paper clipped to the drawing board, perspiration pouring down my face, arms and legs, with Pansy keeping me company.

By the end of my stay I began to get the hang of it, and the drawings began to pile up. Knowing what to put in and what to leave out, what to emphasize and what to minimize—that was the trick.

I didn't want to take time to do any sightseeing, but Esther said I shouldn't miss Columbia, the gemstone of the Mother Lode towns, so I planned to drive there on the last Saturday of my stay. That was a good day for me to be gone, she said, since Friday afternoon she would be taking temporary custody of not one, but two foster children: a little girl of four, whose parents had been killed in an automobile accident, with no relatives willing to take her; and a girl of thirteen, whose mother was dead and whose father had been put in jail for passing bad checks. The girls were not related, Esther said; they'd never even met. When the young county worker brought them out together on Friday afternoon, Esther and I were in the kitchen. The younger girl resembled a tiny blond angel, but when I met the older girl, Arlene, I wasn't envious of Esther's challenge. She was skinny and sullen, with thin hair hanging in strings, and refused to do anything Esther suggested, like drink lemonade or eat a cookie.

"I want to go home, and if you won't take me, I'll run away. I've done it before and I'll do it again." She delivered this ultimatum with her chin stuck out and her arms held rigidly to her sides.

Esther spoke in a soft voice. "Honey, I'm afraid your home isn't *there* right now. You're going to be staying here for a few weeks."

The child burst into tears and ran outside, slamming the door. Julie, the four-year-old, yelled, "I bring her back!" and started to run out too, but Esther took her arm and said, "Oh no, we're going to pop popcorn for Pansy. Arlene will be back."

Pansy hovered nearby; tongue glistening, tail wagging.

A few minutes later, while Julie was absorbed in watching the popcorn pop, I asked Esther why she hadn't let her go after Arlene.

"I've been through this before. What would have happened is, Arlene would have talked Julie into running away too—then I'd be looking for *two* kids. If she isn't back in the next fifteen minutes, I'll go out in my car and look for her. Do you think you can keep this little one entertained?"

"Of course," I said, wondering why in the world Esther put herself through this.

Arlene came back within ten minutes, still sullen, but a bit less so. Esther handed her a bowl of popcorn, and she took it and plopped down at the table without saying a word. Julie continued to munch from her bowl, occasionally raising big blue eyes to stare at the older girl.

They began to take turns feeding Pansy the white, fluffy kernels. Eventually Esther said, "Why don't you take Pansy and go out and play on the swing? It goes real high!" They ran outside.

Saturday I drove to Columbia and was gone all day. What with sight-seeing and haunting antique shops, I didn't return to Sutter Creek until ten or so that evening. Esther was waiting up, but the girls had gone to bed. Next morning, it seemed that some sort of miracle had occurred. While Esther kneaded biscuit dough, Arlene read Julie the Sunday funnies, her arm wound tight around the younger child. Julie was spellbound, listening as if Arlene's words were pure gold. While the biscuits baked, I handed my friend a gift I'd bought in Columbia, an old brass hurricane lantern wired for electricity.

"You can put it in your bedroom."

When she started to protest, I said, "Do not give me a moment's argument; it is my pleasure!"

The four of us had breakfast; fresh fruit, scrambled eggs, and hot biscuits with home-made strawberry jam.

"Maybe I'll drive up in a few weeks and bring the portrait," I said. "And you've been worried about paying me, but I have a solution. If you'll give me one of your ceramic pieces, I'll call it even. I have a special place picked out at home for one of those pots with the blue glaze."

"Those are already promised and paid for, but I'm planning to start a new series soon. Okay, Nat, it's a deal."

I had already packed, so now I said, "Esther, I don't think you know how much I've enjoyed my time up here! Thank you so much! Girls, be good, and do what Esther tells you. She is one special lady. I wish *I* could live here and be her child." Arlene looked doubtful, but Julie threw her arms around my neck and hugged hard. I don't know why, but my eyes filled with tears. When I drove away, they all waved until I turned onto the main road.

Ben returned from The Trees pretty washed-out looking, but insisting that he'd had a good time, and that it was great seeing his campmates, even though one of his best friends, Jeff Dreyer, hadn't come because he had been diagnosed with Parkinson's disease, and another, Andy someone, had fallen off the camp bus and broken his arm.

We had only that evening to unpack and rest. Monday morning Ben went to work, and I began Esther's portrait. I decided I would do two paintings, one for her and one for myself. In the end, though, I only had time to do one. When I completed it a few weeks later, I was very pleased. It had something that none of the business portraits had—spontaneity, and the paint quality and composition were assured and bold. Most importantly, I had captured some portion of Esther's truth and goodness, the 'earth mother' quality she radiated.

Ben and I began to make love again, not often, and nothing like the past, but at least we were no longer strangers in bed.

He saw the portrait when it was half-finished, and was very encouraging. He said he liked the pose, the somber colors, everything about it. (I didn't tell him I'd cribbed the pose from Picasso.) When it was finished, I invited him out to my studio again, and was thrilled when he said it was the best portrait I'd ever done. He paid me a fantastic compliment. "This, Nat, should be in a museum!"

I threw my arms around him and hugged him so hard he said he couldn't breathe.

I wanted to present it to Esther as soon as it was dry, a couple of weeks at least, and wrote her a note to that effect. She wrote back that she was coming to the Bay Area for a conference in Marin County, a symposium about strengthening the American family, and would pick it up then.

When she came by on her way to the conference, she brought three large pots for me to choose from. I chose my favorite, and when she threw in another for good measure, I didn't protest. While we were loading the painting into her car, I asked if she still had custody of Julie and Arlene. She said she did, and that it was an ongoing challenge. She'd enrolled them in school, where Julie had made a fine adjustment, but the jury was still out on Arlene. She was in junior high, and had difficulty getting along with the other children. Her father was still in jail, and Esther said this weighed heavily on the child. This weekend Esther had put the girls with a big family in Sutter Creek, people the girls knew. The court would be placing both girls for adoption in a few months.

CHAPTER TEN

FRIENDS IN TROUBLE

Seeing Esther and hearing of her challenge with the girls made me think of Rosie, who often counseled children. I realized that I hadn't heard from her since before her trip to Italy. Why was *that*? I called, got her answering machine, and left a message. 'This is Nat, dear one. What are you up to, and why haven't I heard from you? I hope everything is okay —'

The machine cut off. She would call me, I was sure.

But she didn't.

Ben said he had to fly to New York on business for four days.

"But it seems like you just went back there!" I remonstrated. "Why do you have to go again so soon?"

"This is my *business*, remember? The head office is back there, and I just happen to be on the board. I have to go."

I was between projects, and bored. I decided to call Hana.

"Hey, Hana, want to have some fun? I need a change. Ben's going out of town, so let's think of something to do."

"Where is Ben? That darling man! Is he getting any good bagels lately?"

"He's been bagel-less. Right now he's in New York at a meeting."

"Well," she said. "I could look to getting a babysitter. Nice teenage girls are all around here in Los Ranchos, very responsible. Are you thinking out of town?"

"Yeah. The whole world is out there, kiddo!"

"You know, Nat, I am not spending money like I used to. I am on allowance."

It sounded as if she wasn't too enthused about my idea, so I said, "Okay, I'll call again, or ring me if you get a brilliant idea."

Soon after that, she called and said she would love to do it, but she could only be gone one night, as she'd promised to take Hans and his friends bowling Sunday evening.

I had fallen in love with the Gold Country when I'd been at Esther's, but I'd drawn and painted like a slave, only taking one day off to see Columbia. I called the old Hotel Leger in Mokelumne Hill, and they said they had one room left. I booked it, and we left Saturday morning. I told her we needed to get an early start, since it would be so hot on the road. I drove Ben's new red Mustang, and we went through Stockton and Lodi, turning onto Highway 49 near Sutter Creek. It wasn't long before Hana began to talk about her divorce. It had been final for ages. I asked about the tennis pro, mentioning that Fia had told me about him, and that one remark was all it took. She began to tell me all about the affair.

She said she was crazy about Max. He was a lot younger, she said, and the sex was great. The hardest part was keeping it a secret from her kids; she had to meet him when they were in school or at after-school activities.

And there was another big problem.

"You mean what if Bruce finds out?"

"Oh yes, of course! He is *so-o-o* jealous. But not chust that. Max is bisexual."

"Huh?"

"Bisexual. He likes men, too!"

"You mean he likes to go to bed with you, but he still wants to have sex with a man?"

"Nat, where have you been? Even in München years ago, even in Rüdersdorf when I was little, I know what it means!"

"Sorry. I've heard of it, but I guess I'm still shocked."

This was back in the days when most people thought sexual deviation meant getting it on with your car mechanic. Middle-class people, especially women, knew nothing about bisexuality, transsexuality, transvestism, exhibitionism, bondage, or even child pornography.

We didn't even know a heck of a lot about lesbianism. All those things existed, but we hadn't yet brushed up against them.

"I was *erschüttert*—shocked—also. And I—I was hurt! Besides giving his tennis lessons, he is all the time running off to that place in the Castro."

Hana began to cry—great, heaving sobs.

Here we go again.

I needed to get her out of this mood if we were going to enjoy this weekend. I let a few minutes go by before I said anything.

"Wait'll you see this little town we're going to. Mokelumne Hill is so quiet and quaint. Ben and I stayed there five years ago."

The sobbing continued, and I glanced over. At that moment, Hana's beauty had vanished. Her skin was blotchy, her eyes red-rimmed.

Where was the stunning Teutonic warrior-girl I had painted?

"Bruce and I were so happy, Natalie, most of the time. If only he had not been so violent!"

"But he was."

I pounded both hands on the steering wheel, hard, and took a deep breath.

"Hana, have you thought about getting some counseling? I have a friend—"

"I have someone. Bruce doesn't want to pay, but my lawyer says he must."

"Good!" I said.

She blew her nose, sat up straight in the seat, and said, "That is the last time you will see me cry, Nat, and I am so sorry. But believe me, you are lucky to have your wonderful husband."

"Don't apologize. I'm glad you trust me enough to cry on my shoulder."

The road became more winding and narrow as we rose into the foothills. We passed endless bronze markers signifying the discovery and mining of gold back in the 19th century, all surrounded by cows grazing in the fields. As I had done only a few weeks before, we drove through beautiful country laden with pines, poplars, locust trees, and acres and acres of dry grass.

Around two o'clock we stopped for hamburgers at a mom-and-pop diner on the road. Once we passed the big town of Jackson, the temperature escalated. We opened all the windows and Hana took off her shoes, rolled up her pant legs and put her bare feet on the dashboard, and I took the paper cup of ice I'd brought from the diner and poured it down my shirt.

We turned on the radio, and a sports announcer was discussing Billie Jean King's and Bobby Riggs' tennis match. Billie Jean had beat him in straight sets just a couple of days before.

"Did you watch it on television, Nat? I was so excited!"

"Sure, we watched it. As a matter of fact, we were invited to some friends for dinner, and the men bet on her and the women bet on him."

"You mean the men at the party were happy about Billie Jean winning? You are not kidding me?"

Finally we found a music station. We turned it up loud and listened to Carly Simon sing "You're So Vain."

We arrived in Mokelumne Hill, population 550, around three in the afternoon. Hana was delighted with the old stone and brick hotel and our vintage room on the second floor overlooking Main Street. It was as quiet as any small town in the boondocks, no traffic at all, so I was sure facing directly onto the street would be fine.

There was only one bed, but I said not to worry, I would sleep on the sofa.

"Oh, Nat, you will not—we will throw money in the air!" So we tossed for it. She won, and chose the sofa. In the long run, having only one bed in the room was less of a problem than it seemed at the time. Hana walked out on the tiny balcony, raised her arms to the sky and exclaimed, "Nat, you have brought me to heaven!"

"And did I mention the food here is great?"

We showered in the bathroom down the hall, put on makeup, then crossed the street to The Gold Nugget, which had a sign that said: WE SERVE ALMOST ANYONE. There were a half-dozen or so customers in the place, and we staked out a back table and ordered vodka martinis, where we spent a pleasant half-hour. Suddenly, something made the room tremble under our feet, and we heard an approaching roar and sounds of heavy engines.

"What's that? Sounds like a train!" said Hana.

"No, not a train," I responded, as a sense of foreboding settled on my shoulders like a heavy black cloak.

"Whatever it is, it is coming here and landing right outside!"

Five minutes later, six bikers in black leather jackets and chains swaggered in. They were bare-chested, wearing leather vests, and had greasy scarves tied around their heads. They were big, heavily bearded, and mostly ugly.

How was I to know that Mokelumne Hill had turned into a biker's paradise? Immediately the atmosphere in the little saloon changed. Before, a few customers were talking quietly and enjoying their drinks. Now it erupted into chaos. The bikers were loud and obstreperous, soon to become drunk and disorderly. I felt sorry for the bartender, a bald middle-aged man who looked as if he'd been through this before and was hoping to get through it one more time.

Hana and I were the only unescorted women there, so we kept our heads down and our voices quiet. But it wasn't long before they spotted us. After drinking at the bar for fifteen minutes or so, two of them walked back to our table and began to make seductive small talk.

"Hey, babe, come here often?" was the opening witticism, directed at Hana.

They paid no attention to me. I had put on my dark glasses; Ben said they made me look like an undercover fly. I sat in a hunched-over position, so stooped that it was difficult to get my glass to my lips.

The larger one demanded of Hana, "What's a gal like you doin' in this hell-hole?"

He had small rodent eyes and a shoulder-length mass of curly black hair, plus more furry growth on his chest and upper arms. I could smell leather and underarm odor.

"It was not a hell-hole until you *Schlägertypen* have arrived," Hana responded.

Omigod. Did she have any idea who these guys were?

I shrank in my seat, and pulled my shoulders even closer together. I had no idea what *Schlägertypen* meant, but from the sound of the word, I knew it wasn't flattering. Probably they did too.

Her accent and her vocabulary gave them an excuse to stay.

"Aha! *Fräulein*!" shouted one.

"You're a kraut, right?" bellowed the other. "Hey—Eva Braun back here! Miss Katzenjammer!"

At the Katzenjammer remark, Hana stood to her full height of five feet-eleven, plus the three inches of her boots, and put her hands on her hips. Here was no ordinary bar pickup, but a Valkyrie in suede pants and an expensive leather-fringed shirt.

She stared directly into the eyes of the man, and in a low voice said, "Please, you will not bother my friend and me, we are drinking very seriously here."

The men stood there for several long seconds, no doubt trying to decide whether to force themselves on her. Amazingly, they walked away—leathers squeaking, chains jangling, and left us alone.

Hana and I exchanged glances. I lit up a cigarette and exhaled. The easing of tension was palpable in the room.

But there was one young biker sitting at the bar who, when his nose wasn't stuck into beer foam, kept sneaking glances at Hana, and soon I realized she was sneaking looks back. He had long, slicked-back blonde hair, and was strikingly handsome, in a coarse, reptilian sort of way. He had a long nose, black eyebrows above heavy-lidded eyes, and two hard lines of moustache blending downward into a goatee.

Hana and I continued to drink, chomping on tortilla chips the barman brought us, until nine o'clock or so. By then, I was into my fourth martini. I couldn't talk Hana into going back to the hotel dining room for dinner. Finally I staggered into the ladies' room, and when I came out, Hana and the young biker were gone. I poured myself back to the hotel and fell on the canopied bed, barely missing a hurricane lamp. The next morning when I woke up, I was still wearing all my clothes.

Hana returned to the room around eleven that morning, wearing the demeanor of a stray kitten asking to be taken in. I didn't say much, only, "I'm glad you're safe."

I waited for her in the dining room while she bathed and changed her clothes. I sat at a table looking out on the street and the Gold Nugget. There was no sign of the bikers; the street looked as deserted as when we'd first arrived.

I didn't intend to give Hana the third degree; I refused to play housemother.

But there was a certain protocol to follow when you went away with a girlfriend, and I was angry. It was the old rule about always leaving a party with 'the one who brung you'. I felt a bit betrayed, also worried. How could Hana involve herself with this dangerous, untrustworthy biker? There were stories about the Hell's Angels in the newspapers all the time. I didn't know if the five we saw were Hell's Angels, but if they were even remotely connected, it wasn't worth it. The Angels terrorized whole towns, committed vandalism, robbery, assault, even kidnapping.

I knew of a young girl, the daughter of a friend of a friend, whose entire family had been put in jeopardy because she'd gone off with an Angel. After the girl came home, having decided the lifestyle of the bikers was too perilous (she was also recovering from an abortion), four or five of the bikers staked out her house to show their resentment at her departure, and everyone inside the house became a semi-prisoner. The father was afraid to go to work; the mother was afraid to go to the mailbox. They were continually subjected to catcalls and profanity from the bikers, who parked and revved their motors off and on all day. The police were called several times, but by the time they got there, the thugs had roared away. The whole neighborhood was intimidated, and the daughter, emotionally terrorized, was eventually hospitalized with a nervous breakdown.

I was only a few years older than Hana. How could I warn her of the danger without sounding like a mother hen?

She joined me by the window and ordered cereal and toast, and I ordered eggs and ham. Over coffee, I said, "Hana, I'm worried about your—your escapade last night. You *have* heard of the Hell's Angels, haven't you? And you heard what happened at that Rolling Stones concert?"

Hana's jaw hardened, and her eyes narrowed in anger. Then slowly her expression softened. Her face crumpled, and she dropped her coffee cup into the saucer, then leaned back in her chair, grasping the edge of the table.

"Natalie, did I ever tell you about the war? I was so little, but I lived through some terrible things!" She seemed to hesitate, as if not sure she could confide in me, but took a deep breath and went on. "In Germany in 1943 there was suffering and destruction you would never believe—and it was everywhere. But when the Russians came it was even worse! The Russians were coming into Rüdersdorf, and my mother was so frightened! She had heard horrible things about what they were doing to women and children—they killed and they raped! And do you know what she did? She took me to the train yard. She said she was taking me to find my father, who was in hospital somewhere in the south. The war was almost over, but we did not know. We stayed for two days and two nights in the *Güterbahnhof*, hiding at night under the cars that were—how do you say—put off to one side? We hid under them, between them—wherever we could hide— night and day. In daytimes we would look for food, but there was none. Except one day a poor, poor man, he was like us, trying to leave—I think he was a *Fahnenflüchtiger*, a deserter. He said he would find us food. And he stole from somewhere a crust or two of bread, und he gave the bread to us."

After a few seconds of silence she took a long swallow from her coffee cup, looking out the window. She seemed to have completely forgotten any resentment toward me.

Finally I asked, "Did you find your father, Hana?"

She turned her head back, her expression trance-like. She began again.

"Yes. I don't know how, but we found him. I remember I was only three years old and somehow we begged our way onto a train that was going south, begged some rich-looking *Frauen* who could pay enough on the black market to get a ticket out of there. My *Mutter*, I remember she—she held me up to the window as the train was starting, *und* she cried and screamed at them to take pity on us, and one of the women made a soldier to open a door. *Und* they got us on the train while it was moving! I will never forget that woman, or that soldier. I can still see their faces in front of me. They were frightened too!

"My *Mutter* used to ask of people questions. Everyone was looking for someone then; everyone was *auf Flucht*—wandering, you know? I don't remember how long it took, or what town or hospital we found Papa in, I was so little. *Und* then we waited for him to get well, we stayed there. Papa's leg had spoiled—decayed. He lost it to—what is your word?"

"Gangrene."

"*Ja. Brand.* Then the American Red Cross came and helped everyone. They fed us, and found places for us to stay."

She stopped, looked at me and shrugged her shoulders, as if to say *That is my story, and now you should know me better.*

I lit a cigarette and sat back. "Hana, are you trying to tell me that my warnings to you about the biker are unnecessary?"

At her look of bewilderment, I said, "Wasted? Falling on deaf ears? Are you trying to say that the war was awful, and that you're safe now, relatively speaking, with anyone?"

162

"I suppose that is what I am telling you, Natalie. Last night, and with Max—*ach!*—I don't know how to express it, but with men, I am happy for a moment. I am transported, safe. I forget all my worries."

I didn't know what else to say. I knew I should warn her further, but I was afraid of damaging our friendship. How could I criticize her, when the war had had such a lasting effect on her life?

On the drive back to the Bay Area, she said, "You would like Rattler so much, Nat. He is like you, an artist!"

"What kind of artist?"

"It is a business—he airbrushes designs on motorcycles!"

I didn't reply. But I was thinking that, bisexual or not, the tennis pro was a whole lot better than this.

I didn't tell anyone about Hana's fling with the biker except one person, Fia.

And Ben, of course.

My reason for telling Fia was justified: I was worried. We had a long phone call about it, and Fia completely agreed with me. Hana was being reckless.

"That girl! As if she didn't get enough physical abuse from Bruce! Well, I hope she sees the light and gets rid of—what did you say his name was, *Rattler?*"

Both the economy and Ben's mood were bleak. The end of 1973 was the beginning of an economic slump, brought on, he said, by the Yom Kippur war and the oil embargo. The demand for Middle Eastern oil had been increasing throughout the world, while OPEC was growing stronger. Long gas lines were increasingly bothersome, and we read of flareups at the gas pumps.

I actually witnessed one. I had been waiting in line for an hour when two middle-aged men almost came to fisticuffs; one fellow had tried to nose his car in where he shouldn't have, and the other man was having none of it.

For me, 1974 started off with a sense of renewal and excitement.

Since my visit to Esther's in Sutter Creek, and soon after Hana's and my getaway weekend, I had begun doing a lot of outdoor sketching. It wasn't that portraiture had become boring; it was just that it was no longer enough. I found that by drawing outdoors, then translating my sketches into large, full-color paintings, I was expanding my artistic horizons in ways I never expected. Often, these quickly done scenes would stimulate my hand and mind to do a painting, and in the final canvas I would make a valiant attempt to retain the freedom of the sketch. My work was becoming freer, more dependent on color and composition and less on draftsmanship.

At first I did the finished landscapes in watercolor, which I'd rarely used before, but gradually found that acrylic was my medium of choice.

Using my sedan loaded down with all my painting equipment to traipse about had gotten to be a chore, so one day I went out and bought a used Dodge Tradesman van. It had garish, wildly-colored Sci-Fi themes painted on the side panels, and carpeting inside. Ben said it was a disgrace to the neighborhood, but it was big enough to hold all my painting gear and canvases, with room left over. It was a behemoth, but a practical behemoth, and I was never sorry I bought it.

I began to go out alone three times a week, driving to places around the bay. I would be gone all day, returning home exhausted, and with a drawing pad full of ideas. My subjects were trees, hills, skies, seashores, and occasionally boats, bridges and piers.

My bravery in going out alone seemed preposterous to Ben. Even though there wasn't as much crime then, there was enough; we lived in a metropolitan area. Ben didn't like my daring—he called it foolhardiness, and we had a couple of angry scenes about it.

"At least go out with one other person!" he admonished.

I said I didn't want to be bothered with a sketching partner, because then I wouldn't have complete control over where I would sketch, or for how long. I would have to go where the other artist wanted to go at least some of the time, and start and stop when he or she wanted to. I couldn't possibly accomplish as much as I did alone, so I continued to act against Ben's wishes.

I sketched in a lot of bad weather that winter, in rainstorms and wind. I had an old hooded mackintosh that had belonged to my father, and it was warm, especially over a T-shirt and sweater, and I owned both leather and rubber boots, so could choose whichever was most suitable for drizzly days. When there was driving rain or no sun, I stayed home.

Back at my studio, I stretched large canvases, priming them with gesso. Once the canvas was prepared, I lay in a ground of color—usually gray, sometimes gray-green or gray-blue. My other colors worked into these neutrals splendidly. I would pencil in my composition; then with a large brush, daub in the first washes of paint, later over-painting with successive layers of color. Sometimes I used glazes to achieve a nuanced, mystical effect. If I wanted to be more dramatic, I used the technique of impasto, applying thick layers of paint with a palette knife. After each application, I would step back, standing across the room in order to be sure of the effectiveness of the lights and darks. I used tubes of every color I could buy, from cadmium orange to alizarin to cobalt blue, bright grass-green and yellow-green, all around the color wheel. I used earth tones too: raw umber and raw sienna. No black. I wanted to show the viewer an outdoor scene, but at the same time I wanted him or her to experience the sensuality of color.

For seven months I worked, sketching, drawing, and painting. Ben didn't come in my studio during that time. I was alone; working alone, eating alone.

The canvases began to stack up.

On the days I painted indoors, I carried in a tray of food and worked all day, taking time out for a short nap in mid-afternoon. I kept a coffeepot going, and the coffee kept me going. My confidence grew as the paintbrush began to feel like part of my hand.

I had done probably sixty sketches, and now I had fourteen very large paintings.

Toward the end of the sixth month, I began to think the work I had done was very good.

I was out of touch with everyone, even Fia, Hana and Rosie, but one day Sandy Sorenson, a friend from San Francisco Women Artists, phoned and asked if she could drop by. I hemmed and hawed, but finally agreed. This meant I would have to stop work.

I liked Sandy. She had been working at art for a long time, as I had, but when she arrived I didn't invite her out to my studio. We drank coffee in the kitchen, gossiping about mutual artist friends: which sculptor had left his wife, which printmaker had moved in with her new lover, who was selling, who was starving, et cetera. Finally, Sandy brought up the reason she had come. She wanted me to take over a part-time teaching job at CCAC, a position a friend of hers was vacating while he traveled in Europe. While we continued to sip coffee and chat, I mulled it over.

Pouring her a warm-up, I said, "Sandy, I'm flattered, but I don't think I want to teach right now; I'm pretty involved with portraits. And some other things."

"*What* other things?"

"Just, uh—some large landscapes I've been doing."

"Show me!" So I took her out to my studio.

She walked around, studying each canvas. After circling the room twice, she said, "Nat, these are wonderful! You've made a real breakthrough here. They have strength and brilliance—and they're so big! Why don't you exhibit with Joyce, Christine and me? We're planning a landscape show in April at the Art Center in Berkeley, and these semi-abstract pieces would make a wonderful contrast with my realistic stuff. Joyce is showing her landscape monotypes, and Christine is getting together a bunch of her pen-and-ink drawings. She's done some brilliant studies at Yosemite."

"I don't know."

"Come on. *Do it!* We'd love to have you join us. I know the other two would approve; they've always admired your work."

She was very persuasive, so in the end I said yes.

Organizing has never been my thing. Luckily, the other women were willing to take charge, and they took the reins. I still had plenty to do. I had to choose which pictures to show, then have them framed. And I kept painting.

The Art Center was a large facility, so we would each put in a dozen or so works, depending on their size. My pieces were bigger than the other artists'. Some were four feet square, some three by five, so in the end I put in only six paintings. We shared the cost of the full-color announcements, one reproduction per artist. They were expensive, but they looked great.

One Sunday morning in March, as I sat at the kitchen table addressing mailers to everyone I'd ever met and his cousin, I glanced over at Ben, reading the morning paper. He hadn't shaved, and his graying hair was tumbled about in all directions. In the last three or four years, lines had appeared around his eyes, and recently he'd had to start wearing spectacles.

God, I loved this man.

But he'd been so silent in the last few weeks. I hesitated to ask why, but I hoped he'd tell me when he was ready. He would lie in bed, tossing and turning, sometimes jerking in his sleep, crying out. In all the years we'd been together, he'd never done that.

After one of those nights, I said, "Tell me what's wrong, darling, you were so restless in bed!"

He looked up from the Wall Street Journal. "Just the usual sweat. Worries about the firm, I guess."

One morning, as he continued to stare at a page of the paper for a long time, I said, "You're so quiet, Ben. Please tell me if something is bothering you."

He looked up. "I was just thinking, Nat. You and I ought to get away somewhere, away from your painting and my office. Why don't we plan a trip?"

"That would be fantastic! As soon as this show is over. Where do you want to go?"

"Someplace far, far away from here."

I stood up and threw my arms around him. As coffee sloshed and spread all over the table, he laughed, and it was music to my ears. So that was what was wrong—my husband was fed up with all my time and energy going into my art. He wanted me all to himself, or he was bored, or both. I didn't blame him, and completely agreed. We needed a change, and maybe a big one.

Tremendously relieved, I went back to writing addresses.

The Art Center in Berkeley's Live Oak Park is in a magnificent natural setting, a sprawling redwood structure set amidst hundreds of live oaks, not far from the Berkeley Rose Garden and Codornices Creek.

Today the weather was superb, warm and sunny. It was a big day for the four of us, who were all rather new to showing our work in public.

We had hung the show ourselves, with the guidance of the Center's director. Since the facility was community funded, we had to furnish our own flowers, wine, and food. Sandy brought her hot Mexican cheese dip, and Christine prepared a ton of stuffed mushrooms. Joyce donated a large crab mousse, and I carried in a big wooden board laden with wedges of fancy cheeses and a variety of crackers. The long table, off to one side of the great room, was piled high; some of our friends had brought food also.

I was wearing a new burnt orange pantsuit that made me feel vibrant and electric, I'd splurged on a pair of high-heeled brown leather boots that were already beginning to pinch, and I'd had my hair done in a French braid at the hairdresser's.

A big crowd began to show up, allaying our fears that no one would come, and by four o'clock there were probably three hundred people milling about. All ages were represented; children ran in and out. But what was incredible about the afternoon wasn't the setting, the weather, or the food. Good art inspires tremendous respect in Berkeley. (Bad art inspires tremendous respect there too, but that's another tale.) In those years there were probably more creative folks per square inch in Berkeley than there were in San Francisco. People swarmed around our paintings, and instead of talking about the stock market or how Aunt Lulu had ended up in the hospital again, they discussed the art.

A few homeless characters and a sprinkling of young and old hippies, both groups indigenous to the town, crashed the party. They came for the food and drink, but if he saw them going back for seconds, the Center's director, with great agility, managed to block them off from the food table.

Also wandering in and out were the ever-present Berkeley dogs, mostly mongrels.

Many of my friends came. Fia was there with Arnie, and Hana brought Hans and Molly. Hans looked handsome in a white shirt and dark pants, and Molly wore a long patchwork skirt she said her mother had made. While I chatted around the room, Ben schmoozed with Hana, and I heard him ask her if he could show Hans and Molly the old bridge that crossed Codornices Creek.

"Of course!" she said, and the three of them disappeared.

Esther had come all the way from Sutter Creek, and I gave her a huge hug. She was with a social worker friend, Bernice something, who lived in Berkeley, and with whom she was going to spend the night. Bernice was Esther's age, a small bird like woman with grey frizzy bangs and a toothy grin.

Esther was particularly thrilled with one of the large paintings I had done from a sketch near her house.

"That's my rock fence!" she exclaimed. "And that hill, I recognize it!"

Nikki didn't come up from Los Angeles, although I sent her an announcement, and of course Amanda was back east. So was Ranie, I guess. I hadn't heard from her in years. How I missed that girl! Her child must be two or three years old now. I'd meant to call Mrs. Sloan and ask for news, but hadn't. I think I dreaded hearing that things hadn't worked out with Jock.

As the afternoon lengthened and people began to cluster in small groups around the room, I heard fragments of conversation about the Patty Hearst kidnapping. Patty, a student at UC, had been taken from her home on Benvenue only a few weeks before, and it was big news all over the world. The Symbionese Liberation Army had sent 'communiques,' recordings of Patty's voice, and demands that the family spend millions of dollars to provide free food for the poor. The Hearsts had complied with a food giveaway that resulted in near-riots in Oakland, but Patty's whereabouts were still unknown.

"Isn't this Patty Hearst thing awful?" said Fia, when we had a few minutes alone. "I know her parents, and they're devastated!"

"Terrible," I replied. "Seems like bad things are happening all around us. And getting closer all the time."

Fia and Arnie were on their way to a party in Atherton, and I prayed that Fia was driving, because Arnie was drunk. He tried to compliment me on the show, but all he could get out was, "Pictures. Great!" and a little hiccuping snort.

Ignoring him, Fia put her hand on my arm. "Ben is so concerned when you go out alone to sketch." She'd always had a soft spot for Ben.

"I can't worry about Ben worrying. Could I have done all this work if I was scared to go out on my own?"

"Well, I adore your paintings, but be careful!"

It was thrilling for me to see all my friends together. Fia and Hana were ecstatic to see one another, and Hana got to meet Esther. I could tell that she responded to Esther's 'earth mother' persona. It pleased me to see them take so strongly to one another. I walked over as Esther was saying, "Nat told me about your visit to our area. She said you stayed in the old hotel in Mokelumne Hill?"

"Mmm-hmmm." Hana darted a glance at me.

I tried to send a telepathic message. No, I did not tell her you deserted me for a biker viper.

"Next time Nat comes up, Hana, you should come too," said Esther. "And bring your children. Maybe Nat told you, I have a little cabin where you can stay."

Hana's smile lit up. "Don't be surprised if we sometime may do it!"

I asked Esther how her foster girls were, and she said Julie had been adopted, but that Arlene was still living with her, and this weekend was staying with one of Esther's friends. "It's been hard on both the girls, losing one another, but it's for the best," she said.

"Do you think anyone will ever adopt Arlene?"

Esther rolled her eyes. "Arlene and I have had some interesting times. I'll be both happy and miserable if that child ever leaves me."

I moved away to speak to Charlie Sprague, the druggist who saved his coffee cans for me. Every time I saw Charlie he made the same joke, how he shouldn't have encouraged me, because now he'd never be able to afford a painting. Today he repeated the same old bromide to his wife, and I kissed him on the cheek and made a mental note to give him a drawing.

Rosie arrived late. When I'd called to invite her, emphasizing that this was my first art show anywhere, she said she couldn't come, that she was leading a seminar in San Diego all weekend. *But here she was!*

As she came through the door, Ben walked over to welcome her. I remember now that, as they stood together in the late afternoon light, something flashed through my mind. There was an intimacy about the way he removed her jacket and led her into the room.

Rosie had a slight sunburn, and she had put on weight, but it wasn't unattractive.

A pang of jealousy hit me, but I brushed it away. It had been months since I'd seen her. By now, I had expected to see her pictures from Italy, or at the very least, a phone call saying it was time for us to go hang out at Peet's.

She walked over to where I was standing with Sandy and Joyce, and I stepped forward and hugged her. "Why've you been so standoffish, girl? And where'd you get the sunburn?"

"San Diego. The weather down there was fantastic." Gazing about, she said, "You've put together something wonderful here!"

I introduced her to my co-hostesses, and told them, "Rosie is a therapist. But she believes in astrology, Zen Buddhism, fortune tellers, and voodoo—go ahead, ask her about any of 'em!"

"Well, somebody has to have the answers, so I think I'll just keep on looking!"

The women laughed, and Rosie moved away saying, "I want to look at all the work. See you later!"

I saw Bert Leidecker come through the door, and went to greet him. Bert no longer looked like a college kid, but a young man on the way up. He was with a pretty girl, and he introduced us. Audrey was from Alabama, an undergraduate student in architecture.

"I try to make her feel at home," he said, "but she wants to run around barefoot, and she pours syrup on everything. She says the fog makes everything too cold, and there aren't enough fried foods."

"Bert, knock it off," she said. "Natalie, absolutely none of that is true. I've heard wonderful things about you. You and Bert designed sets together for a Shaw play?"

"Uh-huh." I turned around to find Ben; I knew he'd want to see Bert. He and Rosie were walking around the room.

Bert said, "Nat, I never knew you were such a great artist. Maybe someday I'll buy one of your paintings."

"How's your career going?" I asked. "Any new commissions?" He had called months before to tell me he was going to work for an architectural firm in the city.

"Last week they gave me a warehouse to do."

"Great—next it'll be a new City Hall!"

I spied Oliver Rakestraw across the room and hurried over, pleased that he'd come all the way across the bay. I was even more pleased when he pointed to three of my paintings nearby and said, "If you don't sell those, I'd like to have them for my gallery."

"You've got 'em! And thank you!"

My cheeks burned as I looked around again for Ben. I couldn't wait to tell him.

There was more good news. I sold a painting to the Clorox Corporation. Clorox, with its base located in Oakland, had its own art consultant, and he was here. We had a short discussion, and he arranged to buy my painting of the wharf in Benicia. I had put steep prices on my paintings, so selling one was intoxicating. This, following right after Oliver's invitation, got me jazzed, and I flew around the place, mingling with one and all. I found Ben talking to Esther, and whispered my big news to them.

People were beginning to leave, and by six-thirty no one was there but the artists and our husbands and boyfriends. We divvied up the remaining food and flowers, Sandy locked up, and we left. I was sorry I hadn't planned an afterglow supper at our house, and since nobody else had had the energy to plan one, either, we all ended up at Larry Blake's Rathskeller on Telegraph Avenue.

Back home, even with all the wine and beer I'd ingested, I still felt wide awake. The show had been a tremendous success, both personally and as a group effort, and everyone had had a good time. I was sorry that, once again, some of my women friends had missed meeting each other. Rosie got there too late to meet Fia, and I'd neglected to introduce Fia to Esther. Hana left before Rosie arrived, and I was sorry, because I'd always wanted them to get acquainted. Maybe another time. Maybe someday I would have that party I always meant to have, where they'd all meet and come to adore one another the way I adored them.

As we got ready for bed, I asked Ben if he'd had a good time.

"Of course, Nat, it was your time to shine, and it went great."

"Wasn't it nice that Esther came all that way? But I wish Nikki and Ranie had been there."

"You can't expect everyone to come." He walked into the bathroom and began squeezing toothpaste onto his toothbrush.

I stood in the door. "Well, at least Rosie was there, and I didn't expect her. She looked terrific, don't you think?" The water was running, and he was vigorously brushing his teeth. He didn't answer.

A few days later I put four of the big paintings in my van. I took the first one to Clorox, then drove across the bridge to Rakestraw's Gallery to deliver the other three. Later that day at home, I found enough empty space on the living room walls to hang the two framed canvases that were left.

The next day I went back to sketching outdoors.

It was a couple of months after the Berkeley show. I'd been out drawing all day, and I came home and went to bed early. Ben cleaned up the supper dishes, then came upstairs to say he was going out to meet with our accountant. He said this was the only time the man could meet because his schedule was so full, with everyone trying to get his return filed by the mandatory date.

"Okay," I said. I didn't ask questions. I could have asked, since Ben was in the finance business, why he couldn't have taken care of our taxes a lot earlier. But handling our money was his department.

I was sound asleep when the bedside phone rang. Forgetting that Ben had gone out, I let it ring seven or eight times. Finally the noise overcame my slumber, and I reached for the phone, glancing at the clock.

"Mrs. Newbury?" a male voice said.

This could only be bad news. A call from a stranger after ten o'clock is always bad news.

"Yes?"

"This is the police department in San Francisco, and we have a friend of yours with us who's kind of bad off."

Omigod!

"Yes, Officer. Who is it?" My voice shook as I dragged myself to a sitting position.

"Wait a minute. I'll put her on."

I waited for an interminable period of time. But somehow I knew.

"Natalie?"

"Yes."

"Nat, it's Hana. I'm—I'm hurt." Her voice was almost a whisper. "He threw me off. I want you to take care of my kids."

"How bad are you hurt, darling? Are you at the hospital?"

"I don't know—" Her voice faded away.

The officer came on again. "Ma'am, I let her talk to you because she was so worried about her children, but she has to be treated now."

"How bad is she?"

"Contusions all over, and she's got a broken leg, but her head injury isn't serious."

"Tell her I'll go to her house and take charge. Tell her not to worry for one second! What hospital?"

"S.F. General. It's on Potrero, at 23rd. The guy threw her off his motorcycle out on the Great Highway, out near the ocean. It probably would be good if you or someone close to her could come over and check her out real soon. I'm Officer Delaney, and you can reach me at this number."

"Wait a minute, I'll get a pencil." I wrote down the number. "Tell Hana I'm driving out to her house right now, and I'll come over to see her tomorrow, okay? Tell her not to worry about a thing!"

I got dressed. *Why wasn't Ben home!* I left him a message, and drove east through the Caldecott tunnel to Los Ranchos. When I arrived around eleven or so, the babysitter wasn't concerned about Hana's still being gone. I explained that she had been in an automobile accident and wouldn't be coming home tonight, and that I was a good friend.

"I'll stay," I said. "How much do I owe you?"

"Uh, well . . ." The woman looked unsure about leaving me in charge.

"I did that portrait above the fireplace, that's how I got to know the family." I pointed, pasting on a reassuring smile. The woman looked from me to the portrait and back again.

"Well, you look like a nice person, but I wish she had called me," said the woman.

I paid her and got her phone number in case I needed her again, and she left.

I didn't look in on Molly and Hans, afraid I might wake them. I took off my shoes and got into Hana's bed with all my clothes on. When I woke early the next morning, I went in the kitchen and put out all the cereal boxes and bowls. A half-hour later, Hans came into the kitchen. He was in pajamas, and his hair was a mess. He looked at me blankly as I tried to explain the situation.

He had a lot of questions. "Where is she? Is she hurt bad? Is our car wrecked? When can we see her?"

Molly came in, also in pjs. "Is Mama okay? Why didn't she call us?" I told them their mother had been in an automobile accident, that she was recovering, and that she would be gone for a few days. I made as many oblique explanations as I could, and said that their mother's orders had been explicit; they were not to miss a single minute of school. Hans cooperated, but not without open resentment. I didn't blame him; his mother was hurt, and I wouldn't tell him much about it or offer to take him to see her. When he left for the bus he slammed the door, hard.

Molly was difficult in a different way. "I don't know what to wear," she whined. "Mama always helps me choose." She burst into tears.

I thought her behavior immature for a thirteen-year-old, but I said, in the most matter-of-fact, serene voice I could command, "Let's go in your room and have a peek in your closet." I told her I liked the pink sweatshirt with the picture of David Cassidy, and she said she always wore it with a denim skirt. We found the skirt, and after she brushed her teeth and combed her hair, she ran for the bus.

I didn't remember about lunches. Later, when it did occur to me, I figured the kids could cope with that on their own.

At last I had time to call Ben.

"Nat, are you okay? I know how these things upset you. All your note said was Hana'd been in an accident and you were going out to her house."

I told him everything the policeman had said. "The kids are cooperating. Hans had a million questions, but I think I calmed him down. I'm about to drive over to the hospital."

"I wish I could take you, but the way things are at the office—"

"Don't worry. But could you give me directions?"

Twenty minutes later I was on the bridge.

Hana was on the fourth floor, in a ward with two other women. She looked terrible. Her head was heavily bandaged, and her leg was immobilized in a cast suspended a few inches above the bed. I could hardly bear to look at her. Her face was bruised and scratched, and the scrapes looked deep; no doubt they would take a long time to heal. Black, irregular stains colored the skin under her eyes and over her cheekbones. She must have hit the pavement very hard.

"How are my kids?" Her voice was almost inaudible.

"They're fine. I told them you'd been in an automobile accident, and that you'd be gone for a few days. I calmed them down pretty well, I think. Hans was very cooperative, and Molly wore her David Cassidy sweatshirt to school."

She turned her head and gave me a weak smile. "She is a funny one, so unsure." Her eyes filled with tears, and she said, "I know I am stupid to go with Rattler. I know you think it."

"Never mind. All you have to do is get well."

"I just said to him—take me back to my car, then he got so mad, and you know what he did, Natalie?" Her voice caught, and more tears spilled out. "He shoved me off the motorcycle out there on the highway! If it had not been for some people who found me, I would be out there still!"

"*Shh-shh,*" I cautioned. "You mustn't think about it. Just lie there and be quiet; I'm going to sit with you for a while." I stayed for two hours, and most of the time she slept. Once she woke and in a faint voice said, "You were right, Natalie. They are all *Ganoven!* I don't want my children to see me like this. Why did I do it?"

She dropped off to sleep again. When the nurse came in, I said I had to go. "Can you tell her I'll be back tomorrow?"

I didn't know any of Hana's tennis friends, but I had a feeling she wouldn't want them to know. She didn't have a single relative in the Bay Area, and all of Bruce's family was back in Ohio. Back home, in desperation I decided to call Fia.

"Oh no! We were right, but I wish we hadn't been. Poor thing! I'll go see her and take some flowers."

Somewhere in the depths of my subconscious, I had been hatching a plan. I don't know when it first occurred to me, but I think it was on the bridge, returning to Los Ranchos the second day. That morning, I happened to glance at the kids' school calendar. Summer vacation was only three days away.

I made a long-distance call, and *presto!* my idea became a reality.

The next day I presented it to Hana as a fait accompli, and she was too weak to argue. I said that tomorrow when she was released I was taking her home with me, where I would nurse her until she was better, and that Ben was driving Hans and Molly up to Esther's home in Sutter Creek.

"You remember Esther, my friend the potter? You met her at my landscape show." Hana nodded. I kept talking, selling the idea. "She's a born grandma and caretaker. She has a foster child, a girl, living with her right now. It's summer vacation, so your kids won't miss any school, and they'll have a great time. I told them Esther will take them horseback riding and on picnics, and now they can't wait to leave!"

I was lying. Hans had put up a huge fuss. He wanted to stay home and hang out with his friends, all of whom had just acquired their driver's licenses. He gave me a rotten time about it.

I said, "Now look here, Hans. I am doing what is best for you in the circumstances. Your mother is recovering, but she needs peace and quiet, and you are going to cooperate with me and Ben!"

Throwing in Ben's name helped a lot. The boy continued to look a bit sullen, but he didn't put up any further resistance. All Molly said was, "Can I take a friend?" and when I said no, that there was a young girl living with Esther she could make friends with, she didn't argue.

I drove back to San Francisco to the hospital. Hana still looked awful, her face lumpy and swollen, her complexion now showing lighter shades of purple and green.

"And I am going to your house?"

"Yes. Ben will take the kids up there Friday, and I'll come here and get you Saturday morning."

"Thank you, Natalie, thank you! The only thing now I am concerned with is Bruce should not to know about any of this. He will try to get custody!"

"He never will know, unless he makes contact with the kids. And he hasn't called once since I've been there."

"Thanks be to Gott!"

"Now, you just worry about your recovery."

Hana was a cooperative patient, so grateful for everything I did that caring for her was a pleasure. Since there was no way she could get upstairs, I rented a hospital bed, and Ben found a place for it in the living room. She still needed pain-killers, and I did my best to keep her medication on schedule. Meals were not a problem. I know a lot of ways to make soup, and I made chicken soup, bean soup, tomato soup, asparagus soup, pasta with sausage soup—you name it.

After Ben got back from Sutter Creek, we retrieved Hana's Audi from the Safeway parking lot on College where she'd met Rattler that night. Ben said he was astonished that it hadn't been towed or stripped. Ben drove it to her house while I followed, parked it in her garage, and we drove home.

When the week was over, I got her settled back into her own home, stopping on the way for groceries. By then she could walk with crutches, and her face looked a thousand times better. As I helped her through the living room on the way to her bedroom, I pointed to the portrait.

"Looks good! Fia told me about Bruce throwing it off the deck. I'm glad to see you got it cleaned up."

"Oh, Fia did it. I could not afford it—the other frame was ruined! See? It's a different frame. And one corner of the painting was smashed a little bit, too. Bruce was an animal that day!"

Poor Hana. To be treated so badly by *two* men!

I got her settled and left, so I wasn't there when she welcomed her kids home.

Ben said it was wonderful to see the happiness and love between the three of them. He said Hans was muscular and tanned, as if the week had agreed with him, and that he was a lot more civil on the ride home than he'd been on the way up. They had gone on picnics, and explored the Gold Country towns. The boy was full of information about rowdy Forty-Niners and the way justice was carried out in "Hangtown."

Ben said Molly returned laden with several wrapped packages, but all she would say was that they were for her mother.

I don't know what story Hana made up for her kids about the accident. I presume she stuck with our original version, that it was a car wreck. But they would soon discover that Hana's car didn't bear a single scratch, and I was glad I didn't have to help explain that.

I called Esther, and she said one of the surprising things about the week was how Hans and Arlene had taken to one another. They had gone horseback riding several times; Arlene, now fourteen, had shown Hans most of the riding trails around the area. Esther said she'd never seen Arlene so cooperative and sweet—and it lasted for a whole week!

I thought that any friendship between Hans and Arlene could only be a positive thing. At fourteen, it was unlikely that Arlene was sexually active, and Hans was much too immature for anything like that. But I didn't mention these unsupervised horseback rides to Hana. Molly was afraid of horses, so Esther taught her how to throw pots, and how to glaze and fire them. Molly made several lovely bowls, and those were what she'd wrapped to bring home to Hana.

Esther got a three-page letter from Hana, thanking her for all she'd done. Hana wrote Ben and me, too, ending with, "Our thanksgivings go to you from the bottoms of our hearts. Molly, Hans and Hana."

I called her sometime after that, and was surprised when a man answered. He explained that he was the police officer who had rescued her, and was there checking on how she was getting along. Hana came on the phone, sounding almost like her old self.

"This man Bill Delaney is wonderful, Nat, he is today doing our grocery shopping. Can you believe it?"

After Nixon was forced to turn over the tapes, the American public found out there was an eighteen-and-a-half-minute gap in one Nixon-Haldeman conversation. Nixon said in a news conference, "I am not a crook," but nobody believed him.

In July of 1974, impeachment hearings began, covered on television. Ben would start watching the news—usually Tom Brokaw or Dan Rather as soon as he got home, and would watch everything he could find on the subject until he went to bed.

I was disgusted by all the filthy politics, so instead I concentrated on filthy international espionage by reading *Tinker, Tailor, Soldier, Spy.*

On August 8 Nixon resigned, and he and Pat left, winging their way to Southern California.

Besides the mess in Washington, Ben's job was uppermost in his mind. He was moody, had begun to smoke, and was losing weight. I knew things weren't going well, but he still refused to confide in me.

He had been a prince in helping me deal with Hana's problems, so I didn't want to push him.

One Sunday over scrambled eggs, he loosened up a bit and told me he was depressed because his firm had been affected by all the scandal attached to the Washington mess. We were in the middle of a bear market, he said.

"And that's bad? What's a bear market?" I broke a piece of toast in half and slathered it with strawberry jam. "I can't believe that's all that's bothering you!"

"Natalie, how long have we been married? You should know some of this stuff by now! A bear market is a market in which the prices of securities are falling, and everyone who might invest is thinking pessimistically. Pessimism grows when investors start anticipating losses, so then selling begins, and it just keeps going! A 45% loss on the Dow Jones Industrial Average—the worst since the Great Depression—is bad news, awful news! Our firm would be the first to admit that things are not going well—for us, or for the people who rely on us for advice!"

Searching his face, which was marked with gloom and anxiety, I had no comforting words. All I could do was reach across and grasp his hand.

'Too much responsibility' and 'rat race' were phrases that Ben dropped into daily conversation, and we began to get more serious about travel plans. Our thinking was fuzzy and unfocused, but we totally agreed on our destination: France.

But when would we go? How much should we cut our ties here in the Bay Area? Should we sell the house? The cars? What would I do with my artwork?

It was all too much to think about. We set aside a Saturday morning to get our passports renewed, new pictures taken and so forth, and one day I made an excursion into the basement to check on our suitcases. I found that not only were they covered in cobwebs, they were out-of-date. We needed new luggage.

When Nikki called a few days later, the bad news about the stock market and thoughts of escaping by travel abroad suddenly left my mind.

"Nat! How are you, sweetie? And how's that handsome hunk you live with? Give him a sloppy kiss for me, tongue and all!"

"Nikki darling, how are you? Who are you married to now? I don't know anything about you—I don't even know where you live!"

"His name is Harry, Harry Williams, and he's terrific. We live in Bel Air. He's a laid back kind of guy, which is just what I need—well, you know that! But here's what I called about. You have to come down here! I've been working on the board of the museum for about two years now, and—"

"What museum?"

"The Los Angeles County Museum of Art, you know, LACMA."

"What? When did you get to be so artsy and cultural! Wow, on the board! I'm impressed!"

"Shut up. Here's what I want to tell you. They're gonna have this huge restrospective of women artists from way, way back. I'm reading here: *Women Artists, 1550-1950*. Back before the Renaissance, I think—somethin' like that. Here's what the flyer says: '*The work will cover four centuries, and has been in the planning for four years*'. You gotta come, Nat, this show was made for you!"

"You'd have to tie me down to keep me from coming!"

"You two will stay with us, and we'll all go to the big wing ding opening. It'll be *mechaiyeh!*"

"When is it?" I said. "I'll talk to Ben."

That evening I told Ben about Nikki's invitation. We were sitting on the patio, drinking martinis and admiring a bed of white impatiens he'd planted the previous weekend.

Pouring seconds from the cocktail shaker into my glass, Ben said, "Unfortunately, Nat, I can't go. I have this new investor. He's acting coy, and I have to play him like a fish on the line. And I've got several other pending deals."

His voice sort of trailed away on the last sentence. I said, "I thought you said we're in the middle of a bear market, and nobody is buying stocks."

"Yes, but you know how important new customers are right now. I'm sorry, but that's the way it is."

I couldn't argue; this was Ben's livelihood. *Our* livelihood. I had no illusions that my art career could support the life style we enjoyed.

He settled back in his lawn chair. "And there's another reason that I need to stay home. I have to do over the kitchen cabinets. I can save several thousand bucks if I do it myself." When we'd moved in, we had determined that the kitchen was where we had to spend serious money. The floor wasn't too bad, but we'd had to buy all new appliances, which strained our budget. The cabinets were old, streaked, and slightly warped, and even by stretching, we had no fund of extra cash to replace them.

Ben dipped a cracker in onion dip and sipped his drink.

"It'll be a big job, but if we plan to sell the house, or even if we don't, I need to work on the cabinets. Go ahead and go to Los Angeles, darling, enjoy yourself!"

I'd been to LACMA before to see the Frans Hals exhibit when Nikki had the tryst with Gerald Epstein, but I'd never been to a big museum opening like this. I wasn't active at any of the museums in San Francisco or Oakland; it took too much time away from painting.

Nikki met me at LAX in her black Jaguar XKE and sped us out of there like she was competing at Le Mans. We exchanged remarks about how great each of us still looked and, gripping the grab handle, I said, "I'm so glad you told me about this show, and I'm thrilled to get to go to the opening!"

"I know you're someone who can appreciate it, Nat, but I wish Ben could've come!"

"He's absolutely determined to get these new cabinets installed and stained, and would you believe we're saving thousands of dollars?

We had to buy a new refrigerator, disposal, ovens, everything. You'll have to fly up with Harry and get a taste of my new culinary talents."

I'd been making an effort to learn a few Italian and French dishes. My only problem was that I hated following recipes to the letter, and by indulging myself in too much artistic freedom, I often ruined things. Our new gas range was installed, and the evening before I had made *fettuccine alla Norcina*. It turned out great, and Ben said I was getting to be a very good cook.

"Will it be awkward, my being a single woman?" I asked, as we alternately sped and slowed along the jammed Los Angeles freeway. "Is it a sit-down dinner?"

"No, just a cocktail party for the people who are donors or on the board, and I'm both. It's been a lot of fun, plus a hell of a lot of work. I go to about five meetings a week!"

Nikki appeared to be happy and content, a rare thing when I'd known her in the past. Maybe she'd finally found her niche.

We drove up to their gabled mansion in a ritzy neighborhood, parked in the garage, and Nikki carried in my bag.

I liked Harry immediately. He was middle-aged, heavy in the middle, and balding. He was also successful, with a dozen or so beauty salons scattered over the L.A. area. Amazingly, he wasn't Jewish. He said he was from Kansas, and that his parents had been ranchers. It was obvious that he lived to cater to Nikki's every whim, jumping up every time she raised a finger or cocked an eyebrow.

I couldn't stop admiring their kitchen: teak cabinets that went on forever, and counters of Italian tile. Above the butcher-block divider hung a massive iron rack hung with battered antique copper pans. The cathedral ceiling had huge skylights on either side of massive beams. I had only seen kitchens like this in magazines.

Friday was their cook's night off, and Harry cooked for us, his apron proclaiming him MASTER CHEF OF BEL AIR. We were having *canneloni di melanzane*. Before we ate, Nikki and I sat perched on kitchen stools, drinking red wine and watching Harry sauté eggplant and garlic, his face and bald head shiny with perspiration.

While he stuffed canneloni with the eggplant mixture and arranged it in an oblong dish, he talked about their cook.

"Gussie's a real character, but it's her daughter takes the cake. The daughter gets married, and Gussie invites us to the wedding. It's a nice wedding at their church—Church of the Nazarene, or Assembly of God, one o' those. They have the reception at Gussie's house down in Inglewood, and d'you know what that halfwit girl does right after the wedding? There's a carnival in town, and this kooky girl wants to go to the carnival—*on her wedding day!* The groom doesn't want to go, so the bride throws off her wedding dress and leaves it on the floor for Gussie to pick up, and she takes off with a girlfriend—and they go to the carnival! Didja ever hear anything like it?"

"No," I said, "I confess I haven't. How old is the daughter?"

"Eighteen."

"I think that explains it," said Nikki. She was sitting with her legs crossed, swinging one foot in the air. Taking off her rings, putting them on again.

"I guess Southern California's capacity to shelter fruits and nuts just never stops," I said, reaching for a Kalamata olive. I was an avid reader of Herb Caen's column in the *Chronicle*, and his columns often included jabs at Los Angeles. Sometimes he recommended dividing the state in half.

"Whaddya mean, *Southern* California?" Harry was sprinkling grated Romano cheese over the cannelloni. "We took on some of your folks last May, when the cops shot up their house down here in South Central and killed six of your Symbionese Liberation Army scum!"

"Oops! You're right—we have more than our share of radicals and crackpots up north. Forgive me!"

Nikki's sons, now handsome, dark-haired teenagers, came in to tell us they were meeting friends for pizza.

"You remember Natalie, boys! She did my portrait, remember?"

They politely acknowledged me, shaking hands and nodding their heads.

"Why are you leaving, guys?" I asked. "You can get great Italian food here!"

"Dad doesn't put pepperoni on top," said the older boy, and they left.

"They're good-looking boys, Nikki."

She smiled. "Yeah. They're nice too. Harry, when's the chow gonna be ready? You got Nat and me drooling all over ourselves!"

For the big gala the next evening, we dressed in our best. I wore what I'd worn to the Pebble Beach party, my long black skirt and white crêpe blouse with silver paillettes. I'd had my hair done at Nikki's salon, and the girl had put my long hair in an updo, ingeniously weaving in a half-dozen silver-and-white rosettes I'd brought along. They were my one extravagance for the trip.

Nikki's comment to me was generous. "Nat, you're a *Yefayfiyeh!*" She translated: Yiddish for 'a woman of great beauty'.

But it was Nikki who was the vision, her black mane of hair fluffed, curled and falling to her shoulders. She was poured into a red strapless evening gown with a high waistline. The skirt had a two-foot-long slit in front, and was bias-cut and clinging. She looked like a modern-day combination of Jezebel and Empress Josephine.

"I can't compete with you gals, but have you seen one of these?" said Harry, slowly opening his tux coat to display a maroon cummerbund stretched over his swollen middle.

While waiting for the limo to arrive, we chatted in the living room. It was filled with expensive antiques, and I wondered if Nikki had shopped for them alone or with a friend. I smiled, remembering our mischievous conniving about shopping for furniture together, when actually Nikki was cavorting in bed with Gerald Epstein.

I enjoyed looking at my portrait of Nikki. It was hanging over the marble fireplace, and to my eye, her white sweater and jet-black ringlets still looked breathtaking against the paisley shawl. In the

187

painting her hair was styled much as it was tonight. I was glad Nikki hadn't had her nose done; she still had the same distinctively Semitic profile.

She said, "Every time I get ready for one of these big whoop-de-doos, I start out all calm, cool and collective—then just before I go into the room, I'm sweatin'."

"You don't look the least bit nervous," I said.

"You look like the coolest little girlie on the block!" and Harry gave her a hug.

She wouldn't allow us to have a drink. "We'll be standing for hours sipping wine, and I don't want you two getting snockered on me. I got a reputation to uphold, remember?"

We piled into the back of the limousine and drove to the museum on Wilshire, then went up the steps and entered an immense reception area. Tall orchids and ferns in magnificent oriental jardinières were dotted around the area, and there must have been a half-dozen bars to accommodate the crowd, which soon became a moving, surging mass of posh, well-dressed bodies. The paintings were in galleries adjoining the reception hall, and we could take our drinks and wander off to see them any time we chose to do so.

Hardly anyone did. I got the impression that the women were there to show off their clothes, and the men were there to show off their women.

Nikki introduced me to so many people that my brain circuits began to overload, and after an hour of making the same inane remarks and hearing the same mindless responses, I needed to go to a quiet place. I strolled to a far side of the room to chat with two soberly dressed folks, a couple who turned out to be husband and wife curators at the museum. He was assistant curator in Chinese painting, and she worked at curating contemporary ceramics. We got into a discussion about two California artists, Wayne Thiebaud and Richard Diebenkorn, and I was impressed to hear that they owned a small Diebenkorn.

Nikki and Harry had split up, I noticed. Harry was standing near one of the bars, talking with a white-haired woman, and across the room, Nikki was simultaneously tossing her head, flinging her hands about, and gyrating her hips. She was the center of a group who were laughing at something she was saying, no doubt something outrageously bawdy.

Later, when Nikki, Harry and I went out to dinner, we were joined by two other couples and a single man. I hadn't obeyed Nikki's warning, and had drunk way too much wine. The restaurant was elegant, but the only thing that kept me awake was watching Nikki flirt with Paul Perata, a record producer who was seated next to her. He had curly hair that came to a low point on his forehead, full purplish lips, and the profile of a dissolute Roman statesman. He looked middle-aged and well-to-do. Here was another Abe Falkenstein, only Italian.

I could tell when Nikki was in heat—she would squirm in her chair, wriggling like an eel. And she was doing it now. Harry seemed oblivious to it all. He was talking about the impeachment hearings against Nixon, and I'm sure he didn't notice when Nikki's hand slid under the table.

Before I flew down, I had asked Nikki if we could go back to the exhibition the day after the gala, so I could get a good look at the paintings. Even though I had never been to a museum opening, I'd been to enough gallery previews to know they're purely social, and you can't see the art with any degree of discernment or pleasure. She promised that not only would she take me back, she'd get me into the place two hours before the Sunday crowd showed up. It would no doubt be a massive throng, since this was a highly publicized show.

The next morning after breakfast, she drove us there in her Jaguar. We started through the galleries, and I was studying a still life by Clara Peeters when I heard Nikki suck in her breath.

Paul Perata was walking toward us.

"Look, Nat, here's Paul!"

He barely nodded to me as they walked away, their heads together, his arm around her waist. Same old Nikki after all.

I saw the show alone, but that was the way I preferred to do it anyhow.

In the next three hours I devoured it all, more than 150 works collected from museums all over the world. The show was arranged chronologically, and I carried the catalog with me and perused it as I went along, alternately studying the paintings and reading the text.

Passari, in the introduction to his biography of Caternia de' Ginnasi of mid-seventeeth century Rome, said:

> *Women have never been lacking in intellect, and it is well known that when they are instructed in some subject, they are capable of mastering what they are taught. Nevertheless it is true that the Lord did not endow them properly with the faculty of judgment, and this he did in order to keep them restrained within the boundaries of obedience to men, to establish men as supreme and superior, so that with this lack, women would be more docile, more amenable to suggestion.*

There you have it, man's summary of women's inferiority. Never had I read such bigoted sexist dogma!

I passed the small portraits and still lifes of the 15th century, and quickly moved on to works by 16th- and 17th-century women.

Artemisia Gentileschi's paintings were artfully composed and anatomically superb. Her expertise could be no doubt be credited to her father, a painter and follower of Caravaggio, who trained her, then hired a teacher to give her lessons in perspective. Perhaps her father should have used more discretion in his choice of instructors. Agostino Tassi had already been convicted of murdering his wife, the catalog said, and he raped Artemisia. Her painting *Judith and*

Maidservant with the Head of Holofernes, done in 1620, was more than six feet high, the figures more than life-size.

I moved on to the exquisite still-lifes of Giovanna Garzoni, whose *Dish of Broad Beans* had an intangible quality that could be the result of her medium, watercolor on parchment. More of her small still lifes were grouped nearby, and all of them were gorgeous. Louise Moillon, who was French, had painted *Basket of Apricots* realistically enough to make your mouth water.

Rachel Ruysch's *Still Life with Flowers and Plums* was breathtaking. With her husband, she had joined the Hague Painter's Guild in 1701. She gave birth to ten children, and still achieved an international reputation in her lifetime.

I couldn't help wondering if she'd had day care.

I vowed to tackle still life again, and soon; I had done that series of drawings when Amanda's portrait sittings got interrupted, but I needed to try again—get more serious about it.

Finally I came to a painter I had actually heard of, Vigée-Lebrun, although I must confess I had never known Vigée-Lebrun was a woman. Now I learned that she was the most celebrated woman artist of her time, famous before she was seventeen as a painter of Parisian aristocracy, and employed by Marie Antoinette by the time she was twenty-five. In *Portrait of the Marquise de Jaucourt*, on loan from the Metropolitan Museum of Art, the marquise wears a white dress and a big hat with blue-gray ribbons that match her voluminous sash. Even though the portrait is of a seated woman, the picture conveyed liveliness and movement. Not easy to do!

Portrait of a Negress, by Marie Guillemime Benoist, a student of Vigée-Lebrun and Jacques Louis David, was on loan from the Louvre. One breast is bared (just as I had painted Ranie), and the lower body is wrapped in a white body-cloth. The elegant head is set off by a wrapped white headdress. At the peak of her career, Benoist was deprived of exhibiting because her husband held a high government post. She wrote to him— *"so much study, so many efforts, a life of hard work . . . don't let's talk about it anymore or the wound will open up once more."*

I walked over to examine a sprightly painting of a little boy, again done in 1800, which evidently had been a memorable year for art. It was by Jeanne Ledoux, and was borrowed from the Baltimore Museum of Art. The boy is clothed in the apparel of the aristocracy, but his expression of innocence poised on mischief is the universal one belonging to small boys.

Ledoux was a genius. Why could *I* never achieve such an expression on the little boys I have done! I could make them appear innocent or mischievous, but never both at the same time.

At last, an American! Sarah Miriam Peale's *A Slice of Watermelon* was charming, but it was the only one of her paintings shown, so I found it difficult to assess her talent. Sarah was from the famous family of American painters; her cousin was Rembrandt Peale. She was a landmark figure, the first professional woman artist in America, and supported herself by the sale of her art for sixty years.

I was becoming more and more inspired by these women as I moved along. I was insatiable, devouring everything. I wanted to go slowly, but kept speeding up, anxious to see it all, nervous that I wouldn't have time to take it all in.

I entered the next gallery.

Now we were back in France again. Rosa Bonheur's colossal work *Gathering for the Hunt* demonstrated her facility in the depiction of animals; in this case, horses and dogs. She was the first woman artist to receive the coveted cross of the French Legion of Honor, and Empress Eugénie conferred it on her personally in 1865. Always dressed as a man to avoid harassment by male workers, she went regularly to slaughterhouses, horse fairs, and cattle markets to draw.

Great guts, Rosa, and great glory!

In the past I had seen works of most of the other women artists in the show—Frida Kahlo, Berthe Morisot, and others. There was Mary Cassatt, whose virtuoso portraits of children had been my inspiration for years, and my eyes filled with tears as I gazed at Käthe

Kollwitz's *Self-Portrait*. Not only did she have to live under the Nazis and was unable to exhibit under them, she lost both her husband and grandson in World War II. In this magnificent charcoal drawing, an aging woman looks directly at the viewer, all her years of sadness and sorrow there for us to see.

Having been raised in New Mexico, I was already steeped in Georgia O'Keeffe, but I found myself inspired again by her painting *Ranchos Church, Taos, New Mexico*. Every southwestern artist who ever lived has painted it, and years ago, I too tried my hand. One of O'Keeffe's stark pelvis-bone paintings was hanging, but sadly, none of her large flower paintings had found their way to this show.

There were some fine impressionistic landscapes by Berthe Morisot, *Paris Seen from the Trocadero* and *Girl in a Boat with Geese*, but except for some of the backgrounds in the Renaissance paintings and in Rosa Bonheur's animal pictures, there weren't many realistic landscapes. Of course O'Keeffe painted the outdoors, but her approach was abstract.

Since the show only went up to 1950, there weren't many non-objective works, but here was Sonia Delauney's *The Flamenco Singer*. Despite its title, it was abstract, done in 1916. Circular rhythms of vibrating color swirled about on the canvas, causing in the viewer an almost physical response. The impetus for the painting, I read, was flamenco. The paint *"becomes a visual equivalent for the sensual movements—whirling, stretching and clapping—"*

By the time Nikki picked me up, looking guiltily tousled, I was simultaneously dead on my feet and floating above the ground, buoyed by a feeling of elation and vitality I hadn't experienced for a long long while.

Nikki drove me to the airport Monday morning. I thanked her profusely for the museum party, the chance to see all the mind-blowing art, and her and Harry's free-flowing hospitality. I had had a terrific time, and I tried to convey that to her.

After that, I was quiet as we drove along. Nikki didn't talk much either.

I was worried about her. Another divorce, another marriage or love affair that would leave her life in shambles!

How would her boys react? They must be getting weary of their mother's inconstancy, and how could she hurt a nice man like Harry, who adored her and would do anything for her?

Nikki read my mind. "I know you think I'm on dangerous ground, but Nat, I'm crazy about Paul. He's exciting, he's smart and funny—he's with it, you know? And he isn't married."

I turned to look at her. I knew the answer, but I asked it anyway. "Have you already started with him? And why aren't you wearing your wedding ring?"

It was impossible to read her expression behind her enormous dark glasses.

"Question Number One, the answer is yes," she said. "And for question Number Two, it's being cleaned."

"So anything I say can't make any difference."

I gave her a look I knew she could feel, then stared straight ahead again. We were silent for the rest of the drive. When she parked in front of the terminal, I got my bag out of the trunk, and she left the driver's seat and came over to the sidewalk, where we kissed and embraced.

"Come up and see us," I said. "We may be going abroad, though. I wish you nothing but happiness, you—you *stupnagel!*" I opened the glass door and walked into the terminal.

Ben had taken Monday morning off to meet me at the airport. He greeted me with a hard hug and a kiss. On the drive home, I told him about my glittering weekend and the inspiration I'd received from the show. Naturally I didn't tell him about Nikki's latest fling. He had always said she was a man trap; this would be more proof.

At home, I was surprised to see he hadn't made more progress with the cabinets; they were still unstained, but he said it had taken all weekend just to get the hinges on right.

I had been back a week when Ben sat me down on the sofa, then dropped down beside me. He seemed upset.

"I wanted to wait until after your Berkeley show to tell you this," he said. "I didn't want to—to ruin everything. Then Hana's accident happened, and after that your trip to L.A.—but it's time for you to know."

There had been very few times in our marriage when Ben had stammered and stumbled like this. In fact, I couldn't remember it ever happening.

"Remember the last time I went to New York? I think you and Hana went up to the Gold Country."

I nodded, bracing myself. This was going to be something really bad, worse than just a bear market.

"The reason I had to go back was to testify in front of the Securities and Exchange Commission." He paused to let this sink in.

"What?"

"I had to testify before the SEC."

Now it all came out. Ben's hoarse voice went on and on, overflowing with all the problems he had kept from me. Sam Schuman had been indicted by the federal government for mismanagement of funds; in point of fact, for taking a bribe from a Los Angeles bank to help launder drug money. The bank had diverted enormous sums to Flanders & Schuman to invest. Ben said the amount was preposterous, something like two million dollars. He said that luckily he had all kinds of papers to prove that he, Ben, had known nothing about it, plus Sam Schuman's testimony that Ben and Mort McElway and two other employees, investment brokers like Ben, had no knowledge of Sam's chicanery.

Of course Sam's word was worth nothing by then, but the paper trail would prove Ben's and the four other associates' innocence. The SEC had spent months investigating every possible twist and turn, and Ben and the others had been completely cleared.

"How could you keep this from me?" I whined, feeling betrayed. I also felt incredibly stupid for remaining in the dark about something that was such an important part of our lives.

Incredibly stupid, and somehow incredibly betrayed.

"Why didn't I read about any of this in the papers? Ben, *talk to me!*"

"You never read the business section, and our transgressions never made the front page, for some reason. And I guess none of your friends told you." He shook his head. "Didn't they even hint? Fia, for instance? I never knew there were so many corporate lawyers in San Francisco, or that they charged so goddamn much." He made an effort to smile, but failed in his attempt. I put my arms around him and held him close, wretched and despairing because he hadn't told me before. I needed to cry, but I held back my tears. Tears were something Ben didn't need right now.

He told me he was losing his job, and Sam Schuman was probably going to go to prison. The San Francisco branch of the firm was being closed down, perhaps to be reopened some time in the future. For now, though, it was kaput. The only good news was that the New York office would pay Ben's legal bills; we would not be liable. A good thing, he said; his costs alone came to sixty thousand dollars.

"Has Freddy mentioned that you could possibly go to New York to work?"

"No."

That one word sounded so sad. It made me angry, too.

"Good! I would *hate* living in New York!" With that, I managed to get a smile out of him. "Oh Ben, how could you carry this around by yourself? Why didn't you tell me? You must have been meeting with lawyers for months!"

"I didn't want to worry you. And I kept thinking Sam would get off, that we all would." He stood and began to pace around the room.

"I didn't want to involve you until I had to. You wouldn't have been able to sleep, and it would have taken your mind off your show."

"Now really, darling! You know my career is secondary to our marriage. Don't you realize that?" There was a period of quiet; the clock in the hallway chimed the hour. He didn't answer, but continued to pace about the room. I couldn't think of anything further to say, and sat frozen in place.

Finally, he sat down and took my hand. In a dry, measured tone he said, "I've been thinking, Nat. We have quite a lot in our savings account. Let's take it all, sell the cars and the condo, and go to Europe like we were planning, but let's stay there. We can live much more cheaply, and we can rent out this house for a fairly healthy price."

"I don't want to rent my house out—to anybody. What about my studio, what about our clothes, all our nice things? No, absolutely not!"

But that's what we did. Through Marty Stubbs, we leased the house to a young doctor. Ben hired a firm to finish the kitchen cabinets. They turned out very nicely, though it was another headache before we left. We sold the cars, practically giving away the van, and rented a safe deposit box. We found a storage unit for our Oriental rugs, and I took down all the art, storing everything in my studio. I locked it up tight and put the key in the safe deposit box, along with our silver and Ben's papers. There was no sense in attempting to sell our securities, so Ben held on to them.

Fia gave us a lovely going-away party.

On September 9, 1974, Ford pardoned Nixon. Along with the nation, Ben and I watched his speech on television. Feeling betrayed, along with most of the public, we couldn't wait to leave the American political scene behind. We left for Europe the next day, but I had no idea when we left that we'd be gone so long. And I had no inkling that, when we returned fifteen years later, our lives would be so utterly and irrevocably changed.

Part Two

FRANCE

1974 – 1989

Chapter Eleven

Paris
Saint Montraix
Provence

Ben and I found a tiny cheap hotel on the Left Bank—cheap for the 6th arrondissement—and spent most of our days eating and drinking coffee at the local cafés and bistros. We sat outside in good weather, inside if it was rainy or cold, sipping café au lait and reading American and English newspapers. We dawdled about the neighborhood, browsing in used bookstores and shops filled with interesting, offbeat objects. We went to all the tourist sights we'd always wanted to see: Notre Dame, the Ile de la Cité, the Arc de Triomphe, Place de la Concorde, Montmartre. We strolled along the Seine and sipped liqueurs at sidewalk cafés near the Place de l'Opera.

But we had to conserve money, so we found an apartment nearby and began to do some of our own cooking. Not a lot; the cafés were so incredibly cheap.

Although Ben and I enjoyed playing tourist, soon we needed to find something useful to do. I began to study Cubism and, reliving my excitement from the LACMA show, I found exhibits of my favorite women artists from the past, and went alone or with Ben to all of them. The works of Mary Cassatt and Berthe Morisot were often exhibited along with other Impressionists and Post-impressionists: Degas, Manet, Vuillard, Toulouse-Lautrec. There was a mammoth show of Rosa Bonheur's paintings at the Grand Palais, and a few months after we arrived, there was a group show of early Italian women artists.

This show provoked and moved me as nothing else had. These women had struggled against terrific odds to create beautiful paintings, and now, centuries later, we were here honoring their talent and hard work.

On the night of April 30, 1975, the last American troops departed Saigon, ending the United States presence in Vietnam. Luckily, we had our new English friends, Pamela and Claude Milford, to celebrate with. Claude was slightly pudgy and more than slightly balding, but he had a teddy-bear quality that made him attractive to women. Pamela, with her flawless skin and soft gray eyes, had the most agreeable disposition of any woman I've ever known. The contrast between her tranquility and Claude's jovial, devil-take-all attitude made them amusing companions. As a huge plus, Claude knew how to flatter. That night, when I appeared wearing a new outfit—I'd splurged on a chartreuse jumpsuit and matching suede jacket—Claude looked me up and down and said, "Well, duck, you're certainly up to the knocker today!" I decided to take it as a compliment.

Ben was forty-one now, and I was thirty-nine; the Milfords were ten years younger. Claude worked as a salesman in Paris for British Motors.

Aux Charpentiers was our favorite café, outfitted with checked tablecloths, fresh flowers, and lumpy candles, and the four of us went there at least twice a week. The place had long ago been headquarters for the Carpenters' Guild, and the walls were covered with fly-specked, sepia photographs of the original members.

We weren't the only Americans there that night, and toasts to the end of the war, in French and English, were long and emotional. Champagne flowed, cheers rang out, and loud American singing filled the restaurant.

Claude and Pamela loved to joke and have fun, and Ben and I welcomed the chance to speak English, but there was a mountain of difference between our language and theirs. Claude liked to say,

"Giving English to the Americans is like giving sex to small children; they know it's important, but they don't know what to do with it." Our conversations were fraught with missed connections. One evening at our apartment, after Ben had shown Pamela how he'd rigged up extra storage for our mountain of luggage, she trilled, "Aren't *you* the clever Dick!" We explained to her the unfortunate connotation of that phrase just now, and she blushed and said, 'Oh yes, that business of Watergate! Did I drop a clanger?"

I think Ben and I realized that short periods of separation would keep our marriage running smoothly, so while I made solo trips to the Louvre and other museums and galleries, Ben took a course in French. When he wasn't studying the language, he took photographs all over Paris with his new Nikon. With some trepidation, I enrolled at the Académie Julien, only a few steps off the Boulevard Saint-Germain, and began to study painting and drawing with Professeur Moutet, a renowned teacher there. The Academy, founded as an alternative to the Ecole des Beaux Arts, housed studios that had been attended since the latter part of the 19th century by Bonnard, Vuillard, Valloton and, according to neighborhood legend, Rouault, Matisse, and Derain. I absolutely loved dropping these names in the presence of Ben and the Milfords.

It was about this time that the new Pompidou Center, a huge former railway station, converted into a huge art gallery, opened. It was controversial, with all those exposed pipes and tubes, but the *art!* The Milfords and Ben and I traveled there on the Metro one Saturday, but the crowds were too oppressive, so I went back several times on my own.

It was then that my path and Juan's began to converge, changing the course of my marriage—and my life.

Occasionally there were shows in the adjoining gallery of the Academy. When I first enrolled, there was a retrospective show of former students and teachers going back over a period of thirty years. Among the works were many academic-type paintings, but there was also a lot of recent abstract art. I remember being especially impressed by the work of Juan Bautista del Mazo. His name not only sounded Spanish, but his work showed the authority and potency of Picasso, with strong shapes and powerful colors. Besides the paintings, he was showing a group of assemblages: corrugated cardboard and Styrofoam glued onto various backings, usually painted canvas or Masonite.

I had no idea that one day I would have an intimate relationship with those paintings and assemblages.

I learned so much during that time! I had other teachers, but Professeur Moutet's influence stayed with me more than any of the others. His emphasis in the painting classes was on brushwork and mixing color; in the drawing classes he stressed composition and draftsmanship.

While my knowledge and experience broadened, Ben stayed busy and happy with his own pursuits. I remember that once he spent an entire week photographing Montmartre. The results were fantastic; I told him he should think about going professional, but he scoffed at the idea.

We continued to spend a lot of time with the Milfords, and Claude often spoke of his stressful job at British Motors.

"He'll never set the Thames on fire!" he confided once, speaking of a fellow-worker who had just botched a fleet sale of Jaguars.

"Don't you mean 'set the Seine on fire'?" queried Ben.

Not at all. Claude said his phrase carried nostalgic connotations from his youth, when his father used to say it about him.

Once he complained over dinner about the very unsatisfactory "screw" he was getting. Ben and I stopped eating our *rôti de veau* and glanced sympathetically at Pamela, wondering why she would stand for such verbal abuse.

She saw our look and chortled, "Oh no, chums—he means his *salary!*"

"And the benefits are bugger-all," added Claude.

Throwing out American slang in retaliation, Ben said, "Your salary beats our monthly allotment all hollow. It's a whacking amount compared to what Nat and I live on."

"Well, any time you want to go to work, mate," said Claude, swilling his Bordeaux, "come to my office and I'll introduce you to the guv'nor. He'd love to get his hands on someone like you, someone long-headed who speaks French. It'd be meat and drink to him!"

The gist seemed to be that Ben could have a job at British Motors anytime he wanted.

"No, thanks," Ben replied. "I'm not all that conversant in French, and Nat and I are very happy this way, with her studying all the time and me doing diddly-squat."

We all had a giggle at the jargon game the boys had invented, and went back to eating our cherry flan.

Politically, Paris was anything but a calm outpost. There were peace demonstrations here, too, and students rioted about any number of issues, from A to Z. Enormous troubles in Lebanon began while we lived there. Skirmishes began between Palestinian guerrillas and a right-wing Christian party, and a year later, two hundred and sixty-three Americans and Lebanese nationals had to be evacuated from Beirut. In 1977 the United States ambassador to Lebanon and the U.S. economic counselor were kidnapped by PLFP, the Popular Front for the Liberation of Palestine. Later they were shot to death.

There was anti-American sentiment all over the world, and Ben and I encountered some of it from the occasional Frenchman—or woman. Once, in a department store in Paris where I'd gone to buy hosiery, my American accent gave me away, and I was rudely shoved away from the counter by two angry-looking women. I gave up any idea of shopping, and went to sit alone at a sidewalk cafe, smoking a cigarette until I could stop shaking.

Violence and terrorism were escalating. About the time we met Pamela and Claude, the IRA bombed two crowded pubs in London and exploded a bomb at Harrod's. Claude saw no virtue in the IRA's motives or methods, and he had some choice remarks to make.

As to American, specifically Bay Area revolutionary movements, the Symbionese Liberation Army was in the news again when Patti Hearst was found in September of 1975. *Le Monde* said that when she was arrested she gave the clenched-fist salute, and while being booked, when asked her occupation, she replied, "Urban guerrilla."

Ben and I hunkered down, pulled in our heads like turtles, and enjoyed our lives as non-involved expatriates.

Gradually, we began to explore the world outside Paris. We took a few train trips to Versailles, Fontainebleau, and Chantilly, and afterward Ben decided he wanted to buy a car. Renting a car in France was terribly exorbitant compared to buying one, so Ben bought a darling little blue Renault, and when my classes weren't in session we began to go on excursions into the French countryside. We started with Normandy, staying a night near Mont St. Michel. We visited the landing beaches and the D-Day museum on the seafront at Arromanches, and walked through the American cemetery overlooking Omaha Beach. That was where we experienced, besides our pain at the tragedy of war, our first bout of homesickness.

I wanted to visit Flaubert territory, so we stayed for five nights in the inn mentioned in *Madame Bovary*. It was in Pont-Audemer, the Auberge du Vieux Puits—the Inn of the Old Wells—half-timbered, picture-book pretty. It had a fine restaurant with antique lanterns and thick, whitewashed stone walls. We ordered a bottle of twelve-year-old Calvados and sat soaking up the ambiance of the room. The waiters were not too attentive, and each course was more succulent than the last. We ate *bouillabaisse du pêcheur*, a wonderful onion flan, braised duck in wine, and a pine nut meringue—*gâteau soufflé aux pignons*—that was other-worldly.

Seldom did we indulge ourselves like this. On our first morning I lay stretching in the big feather bed, wallowing in the sure knowledge that our lovemaking the night before had rivaled anything Emma Bovary ever experienced with Rodolphe or Léon. My body had never felt so cherished.

Was it France? The landscape of Normandy? The Calvados? Now, as I lay luxuriating in bed, Ben had gone to order a case of the stuff.

After living in Paris and making side trips around its environs for almost four years, we decided it was time for a change, and moved to the country. By then my museum-trotting mania had been somewhat assuaged, and I was tired of going to classes. On one of our numerous motor jaunts we had fallen in love with Saint Montraix, a village fifty miles southwest of Paris, and Fortune smiled when we found an old stone house there. All around were countless red-tiled roofs, an ancient Romanesque church, and fields of poppies mixed with purple loosestrife. Cows and sheep grazed in grassy fields, and an old mill sat on the banks of a slow-moving river. It had a beautiful old town square, and enough population to support several businesses: a bakery, an inn and café, a real estate office, and a fish market. Even more excited than when we had first left for France, we took out a year's lease and began to set up housekeeping.

Buying bed linens and pots and pans in rural France—also screwdrivers, hammers, and plumbing supplies—was quite an experience. We couldn't have gotten through it, nor could we have managed the occasional household repairs we had to make, without Ben's newly acquired language skills. French shopkeepers are patient for only a limited time if you don't make an attempt to speak their native tongue. By now I had picked up a few rudimentary phrases, which I'm afraid I tended to overuse. They were: *Chic alors!* (Great!) *Comment allez-vous?* (How are you?) *Eh bien!* (Oh well!) and *Je ne comprends pas* (I don't understand). These seemed to come in handy on many occasions. I also tended to say *bien sûr!* (of course!) while nodding as if in agreement. Once in Paris, Ben estimated that I paid $40 for a small bright-green cotton bath rug, and he told me to stop nodding so much. But that was in Paris, where tourists, especially Americans, were fair game. In the countryside we were almost always dealt with honestly.

The house in Saint Montraix was rather dark and cold inside, but I vowed to warm it up with paintings and a few cheap Moroccan rugs. It had brand new shutters on the windows, an expansive fieldstone fireplace, old beams transversing a high ceiling, and a few pieces of rustic furniture. The kitchen was equipped with ancient appliances, a pine table and four chairs. Its saving grace was the wonderful view of hills covered with grape vines and olive trees. The bedroom, with its double bed and scratched armoire, echoed the bare-bones bathroom, which had a toilet, no sink, and a pockmarked bathtub with creaking brass faucets. I put down the green bath rug, and Ben stuck a potted red geranium on the windowsill.

One of the reasons we chose the house was that it had a shed in back where I could set up shop. (I immediately ordered an easel from an art store in Paris.) The shed had good-sized windows on the north side, and was large, twenty by thirty feet. It reminded me of Esther's little cabin in Sutter Creek, and as I settled in I thought fondly of my friend so far away.

The shed had evidently been a blacksmith's smithy, and was equipped with a forge and anvil. I never lit a fire in the forge, though I was tempted to on some of the coldest winter days. We moved out many of the heavy, crude pieces of iron lying around, but didn't try to move the anvil. I stacked some crayons and brushes on top, and it stayed where it was.

Gradually I began to learn to cook in the French way. Wednesday was market day in the village, and Ben and I would set out after breakfast armed with baskets and string bags, park on a side street, and make our way over the cobblestones to the main square, where everything was displayed on extra-long tables. We could select from a profusion of fruits and vegetables, flowers, herbs, cheeses and olives, spices and *charcuterie*. We usually had a choice of twenty different lettuces for our salads, and a selection of many logs or rounds of cheese, and would return home laden with delicious provisions. Ben enjoyed chatting in his new-found language with the food provenders, and even did a bit of haggling. They always ended up laughing, and I would join in, so the whole experience was light-hearted and pleasant. Even though we were not in Provence (yet), I was struck by the Cézanne-like ambience. Groups of men played cards wearing clothing and hats identical to the men in his *Card Players* series, and the countrywomen wore simple peasant clothes, no doubt like their grandmothers had worn a hundred years ago.

Two months after we'd settled in, we invited Claude and Pamela to drive down from Paris, the first of their many visits.

"So good of you to ask us!" Pamela would say, and they would arrive with wine, flowers, and periodicals we couldn't get in Saint Montraix. The weekend would be filled with wine, cooking, and laughter. We talked about everything—the latest art shows in Paris, political events in France and the rest of the world. I remember we were all horrified when the tragic oil spill occurred off the Brittany coast in 1978. Later the same year, the Milfords brought us news that a wing of the Versailles Palace had been hit by a bomb planted by terrorists. Three rooms containing artwork from the time of Napoleon were destroyed. Paintings were ripped to shreds; experts said they would take years to be repaired. Several groups claimed responsibility.

The news wasn't good back home, either. In October, the Dow-Jones had its worst week in history, down fifty-nine points. Ben got a letter from Mort McElway, who told a lot of horror stories about Wall Street, and said he was thinking of getting out of the investments business. Although the stock market crash affected our finances a bit, Ben and I felt secure in our small provincial world.

When the Milfords visited, Claude was full of mock complaints about their sleeping arrangements. We had to put them up in a small anteroom off the hall. Their room got no heat in winter and was stifling in summer, and there was only a cheap mattress and box spring on the floor, with no bed frame.

"Dear, dear Natalie," said Claude after his first night, "the rates here are so reasonable we really shouldn't complain, but there are beastly lumps in your mattress which approach the size of cricket balls!"

"Nat's going to buy a new bed for you soon, but she's waiting until she finds something whimsical and exotic," said Ben.

"Darling, you seemed to be awfully turned on by that mattress last night," joshed Pamela. "Just ignore him, Natalie, he slept like a baby."

"I don't know what you mean by 'turned on,'" Claude retorted, "I was studying the papers in my briefcase until you so rudely snapped off the light and attacked me."

I laughed and gave him a big bowl of café au lait to shut him up.

Ben and I would tell stories about village life, like the gossip about the fishmonger's ex-wife who poisoned the fishmonger's beloved dachshund. The fishmonger then revealed to the village, in great detail and over a period of several months, various rumors about his ex-wife—that she had slept with the fourteen-year-old son of the mayor, that she was a devotee of the Marquis de Sade, and that "she" was really a "he."

Ben explained that they were just a couple of gays who loved riling up the town.

I gave some thought to painting Pamela. She wasn't beautiful, but with her patrician, willowy looks I thought she would make a lovely portrait. But there was always a time problem; instead of staying to be painted, she preferred to go back to Paris with Claude, and when they were visiting, the four of us had such fun rattling around the countryside that there was no time for painting.

Pamela was the most uncomplaining of souls and always wore a cheery smile, so just to get a laugh Claude would bewail her disposition.

210

"Wife's pretty narky today," he would say, and if she protested about his atrocious driving, he would yell, "Downright stroppy!"

We began to strike up acquaintances with some of our neighbors and a few of the shopkeepers, but the postmistress Clotilde and her husband François, the town realtor, became our only real friends.

Soon after we moved there I began again to paint landscapes, going out on sketching jaunts as I had in California. There was less need for Ben to worry, since there was almost no crime in the area. I did make a concession; I found an interesting companion, an older Belgian painter, to accompany me. Or, I should say, I accompanied him. Jean-Jacques Remouillon had lived in the village for decades and knew all the best views for miles around. He was a man of seventy-five or so with a gray forked beard, mischievous smile, and ragtag, paint-spattered clothing. He spoke a little English, which was a blessing. We packed lunches and would go out two or three days a week.

I soon learned I couldn't share wine at lunch with Jean-Jacques. His tolerance was unlimited, and he could keep working for hours after drinking several glasses.

"Natalie!" he would exclaim. *"Nous avons beaucoup de vin!"*

"Je ne peux pas. Je veux sortir maison une dormir," I would reply, and would go take a nap in the car. I finally decided to renounce all daytime spirits.

Occasionally, when I tired of painting landscapes, I indulged my urge to do still life. Not even the still life paintings of the Dutch and Italian women at the LACMA show had inspired me as much as Cézanne's masterly still lifes at the museums of Paris.

I began to set up studies of fruit, vegetables, flowers, and the occasional pitcher or vase, buying produce on market day and spending hours painting it. Using oils, which could be worked and reworked for days, I painted until the fruit rotted and the flowers drooped, which was pretty quickly. Also, inspired by the cheap bright-patterned fabrics at the local *boutique de coton*, I bought a few yards to spread under the fruits and vegetables, and began to incorporate designs stimulated by the decorative iron gratings and railings I had found inside the shed. Influenced by Art Nouveau, my spiralling curves and scrolls wound in intricate serpentine patterns.

I was having a ball.

We got a Christmas letter from Rosie in 1978, and were staggered by her lengthy catalogue of bad news. I told Ben it was the most cheerless Christmas card I'd ever read. In November, someone named Dan White had shot the mayor of San Francisco. Of course we'd heard about it already, it was in all the Paris newspapers, but Rosie told us more; she wrote that Supervisor Dianne Feinstein had taken over Moscone's job. Also, Rosie had been doing many hours of pro bono work related to the Jim Jones-People's Temple mass suicides in Guyana. The cult was based in the Bay Area; many of the victims were from Oakland. More than nine hundred people died from drinking poisoned Kool-Aid!

"You can imagine the devastation of the families that are left," she wrote. "I've been helping them as much as I can."

Rosie included news about herself. Besides her work for the Kool-Aid victims' families, she'd been volunteering at a day care center in Berkeley. I didn't understand what she meant, nor did Ben. Was she counseling the children, or taking care of them? My heart went out to my compassionate friend. Not only was she burdened with the heavy load of her own patients, now she was taking on victims' families and small children.

It wasn't long after the letter from Rosie that Ben said he needed to go home to check on our house. He flew back in January, 1979.

While he was staying in San Francisco, he called Mort McElway, now working for a CPA firm in Oakland, and Mort told Ben that Sam Schuman didn't have to go to prison after all. He had to pay a mammoth fine, but managed to escape jail. But, Mort said, the old man's health was gone, his wife had divorced him, and he was completely broke.

While painting one day, pleased with having made such a serendipitous find as the iron fragments, and enchanted with the vivid colors of my current piece—green artichokes paired with lemons and rich purple eggplants, I began to think about how chance had ruled my life. If it hadn't been for Sam Schuman's dishonesty, we wouldn't be living in France. We had made the discovery—the serendipitous, unforeseen discovery—that since the firm had failed, we were free to go to Europe.

All sheer happenstance!

But what accident of fate had caused Sam to take a bribe from a crooked Los Angeles banker? What was it in Sam that had failed? Where, in his childhood or teen years, had his moral compass taken a wrong turn?

I thought of the lovely friends I'd left behind, and rejoiced in the occasions when luck or happenstance had brought us together. There had been that first encounter with Rosie when we'd accidentally bumped into her at Bott's Ice Cream parlor, and the student riot in Berkeley, when I'd cemented my friendship with Hana. And the night I'd befriended Ranie, which I would have never done if she hadn't been worried about her brother's involvement in the Black Panthers.

Nikki and I had been neighbors, and friendships between neighbors can be lucky or unlucky. Ours had been one of the lucky ones.

And how about meeting Esther? Who would ever have guessed that I would encounter a woman of such warmth and humanity in the wilds of Big Sur?

I had ample time for philosophizing as I worked alone in my shed—missing Ben and painting peaches from every angle known to God.

When Ben returned, he told me our house was weathering the rental storms very well. Marty Stubbs retired in the late '70s, but his son took over the firm, and we always had excellent tenants. We were getting $900 a month in rent, and this helped to finance our stay abroad.

Ben seemed happy to be back, but I sensed there was something that was different about him—a lessening of interest in our little village, and an unmistakable muting of sexual passion. It was very much like the period before we left Montclair, when he had been as cool and unresponsive as he was now.

Was it something that happened in California? Was he worried about something, other than the old troubles at the firm?

"Darling, please tell me if something is bothering you," I pleaded. "What is it? Money? Do you want me to stop painting so we can travel more? You seem—"

I couldn't finish. I couldn't say the words, *You act as if you don't love me anymore.*

"No, Nat, I'm very happy here," he said. "You have to keep painting. I don't have enough to do, but it's my own fault. I'll find something."

By the time we had lived in Saint Montraix for eight or nine months, the postmistress Clotilde and I were good friends. She and François invited us into their home, and we entertained them as well. She was a fortyish, buxom woman, capable to the extreme, with darting hands and a jutting chin. François' most outstanding physical characteristic was his blue-black curly hair, which sprouted from his head, upper lip and the backs of his hands. His voice was loud and blustering, dominating every room, and he had one of those excitable dispositions usually found in rug salesmen. At first Ben wasn't sure he liked him.

The way it happened was this. One day Clotilde told me over lunch in the local café that the night before, François had come home ranting and raving. His number one assistant in the realty office, a woman, was getting married and moving to Nantes. François was frantic; he needed someone to man the phones, show houses, and deliver keys for rentals in the area, while he carried on the business of the company.

Eh bien! I mentioned that Ben needed something to do, François asked if he would help out, and a friendship was born. Ben worked only part-time at first, but François began more and more to depend upon him.

"I didn't come to Europe to work at real estate," Ben complained, although I could tell the work made him feel useful, and of course François paid him. After a while, François hired another woman from Rambouillet, and Ben eased out, but he still filled in occasionally when he was needed.

One night, early in our friendship, the four of us were gathered around the fireplace in the local inn, and in casual conversation Francois discovered that Ben skied. "You must come to Chamonix with me!" he shouted, while everyone looked in our direction.

"Ah non!" broke in Clotilde. "That will be the end of our little gatherings, Natalie—they will be off skiing!" And she was right. In the eight years we lived in Saint Montraix, Ben and Francois must have gone skiing in the French Alps at least twenty times.

I only went once. Ben said I must go on the aerial tramway to see the Mer de Glace, so the four of us went to Chamonix for the Christmas holidays. The glacier was an impressive sight, huge expanses of snow like nothing I'd ever seen. We went up, up, up—changing aerial cars three times, each one smaller and more freezing than the last, ascending to twelve thousand feet at the Aiguille du Midi before dropping down on the Italian side. It was enough to make your heart plummet through your boots, and that one round trip was enough for me.

The best part was the brandy waiting for us when we returned.

We stayed in an inexpensive pension, but I remember that Clotilde and I had lunch on the terrace of one of the luxurious hotels, gazing out at the soaring Alpine peaks around us. The men had gone to check on the tramway's time of departure, and I became aware all at once of the other skiers. Pretty young women were everywhere—

Austrian, German, French, Swiss—decked out in fashionable ski sweaters and tight stretch pants.

"Do you ever wonder if Francois—?" I began, but Clotilde didn't let me finish.

"Oui, Natalie, of course I wonder. But he always comes back, sometimes happy and refreshed, bragging about this peak or that mountain he has conquered on his little boards. Sometimes he is miserable, with sore muscles, once or twice a broken leg, and always cursing the cost of the sport. But women—they are not a problem."

We heard from Fia in June, who told us there was another major oil shortage in the U.S., and that everyone spent all their time in gas lines. She said tempers were short. "Aren't you the clever ones, tucked away over there in France!" she wrote.

Back in the U.S., Ronald Reagan won the presidential election, and Jimmy Carter went back to Georgia. I wasn't a Reaganite, so I wasn't happy about the turn politics was taking at home. I couldn't forget the tear gas he'd used in Berkeley in the '60s.

Ben began to worry and fret over the news; he said he couldn't help it. All the troubles in Iran; the Shah hounded out of his country; the Ayatollah Khomeini, a horrible old man with a long white beard, taking over. Kuwait, Beirut, Tehran, Islamabad, Libya, Baghdad—these were the hot spots. Embassies bombed, terrorists running amok, and always, innocent people killed. Iranian militants seized the U.S. embassy in Tehran and took ninety hostages, sixty-five of them Americans. They weren't released, despite President Carter's best efforts, until the day Reagan was inaugurated. After that Beirut heated up again, and Reagan sent the Marines over to try to keep the peace.

Some of this hit home with us in Saint Montraix, when Clotilde heard from her brother in Marseilles. A suicide truck bomb in Beirut killed two hundred and forty-one U.S. Marines and Navy personnel, and in a separate attack, fifty-eight French soldiers were killed.

Clotilde's nephew was one of them. He was only twenty-one, and his wife had just had a beautiful baby girl.

216

I kept plugging away at the still lifes, and one day when Clotilde saw my paintings, she said the town should give a show of my work. She called the exhibition *L'Americaine et Les Pêches*. We advertised it in the region's one newspaper, and Ben created a handsome poster that we hung in the town café. The mayor said that, if I wished, I could use as my showplace a derelict civic building situated in the center of the village square. I went to inspect it and decided it would do quite well.

When Pamela and Claude came down from Paris, it pleased me that they came a day early to help me hang the paintings.

"I say, Natalie, these paintings are clinking," Claude said, holding one of the studies at arm's length while he gave it a lengthy perusal.

"What the heck does *that* mean?" I asked. "You mean because of all the ironwork?"

"I mean these are damn good, my dear!"

Ben was high on a ladder hammering nails as Pamela handed him the paintings; we were hanging some high up on a second row above the others, since there was only one decent wall to use. I stood back a little way, giving instructions. "No, a little to the right. No, a little to the left."

"How much dropsy did you use on the town fathers to get them to let you do this, Nat?" asked Claude.

"Huh?" I feigned ignorance, but I knew what he meant.

"How much did you have to bribe the mayor?"

"Just the slightest hint that I might give him a painting," I replied.

"*I knew it!*" he said, always overjoyed to find evidence of French greed.

"Don't give the mayor that one," said Pamela, pointing to the painting Ben was hanging, an arrangement of peaches, pears, and chrysanthemums spread on a multi-colored paisley cloth. "We're buying it."

"Pamela—how sweet of you! I'll give you a good deal."

I was getting nervous about the time. It was getting dark outside. *"Vite, alors. Il est tard!"*

"Toujours pressée, Nat—*toujours pressée*. Relax!" said Ben. There was an edge to his voice, and I wondered if Claude and Pamela noticed. He had been quiet the whole time we were hanging the show, and as usual, I didn't know why. He'd become much more reticent lately, and in reaction to his coolness, I literally drank in Claude's friendly remarks.

By nine o'clock we were finished, and everything looked pretty good. I thanked my crew with a home-cooked meal, and invited Clotilde and François to join us. We had fresh perch I'd bought that day at the fishmonger's. Clotilde said the fishmonger and his "wife" were together again, and had a new dachshund.

We finished the meal with peaches in heavy cream.

"I say, these peaches taste a bit of oil paints," said Claude.

"Belt up, Claude," said Pamela.

With that, François began telling ribald stories about English clients he'd worked with through the years, and we finished the evening in gales of laughter.

The next day my painting companion Jean-Jacques offered to pour the wine, and I accepted, knowing Ben would be glad to relinquish the duty. But I worried a little; Jean-Jacques had a heavy pouring hand, and we'd only bought four-dozen bottles of the local vintage. When the whole town turned out, I caught his eye and, squeezing my fingers and thumb together, tried to send him a message not to fill the glasses so full.

"Nous avons beaucoup de vin!" he yelled across the room.

A big crowd of jovial, wine-drinking locals turned out, but besides Jean-Jacques, the only people I knew were Clotilde, François and a few other merchants and neighbors. The fishmonger came with his wife, a tall man wearing a ruffled blouse, short taffeta skirt, and heavy makeup.

Just as at my show in Berkeley years ago, there were many youngsters, which lent a festive air to the occasion. Since neither Pamela nor I had children, we enjoyed watching some of the younger moppets dash about. Ben took a shine to one curly-haired boy who looked to be about seven, the son of the gas station owner. He was a sweet child, wearing corduroy knee pants, white shirt and black string tie, and was the proud owner of a blue top. He took Ben outside to the courtyard and taught him the intricacies of wrapping the top with cord and spinning it on the courtyard stones

I didn't sell anything, except to Pamela, nor did I expect to. I gave a small painting to the mayor and a pastel drawing to Clotilde, and a week later Ben and I took down the canvases and delivered them back to my shed.

In all those years, though Ben made several trips to San Francisco, I only went back three times, each time to see Mamaw. She greeted me on each occasion like a long-lost daughter, which I suppose I was. I flew back to see her two years after we moved to France and twice later on. In '82, it was because she had come down with pneumonia. I thought I might combine New Mexico with a trip to California, but after spending two weeks nursing my beloved aunt back to health, I changed my mind. I had learned that Fia would be in Mexico and Rosie would be at a conference in Atlanta, so decided to forget it. Besides, I was anxious to get back to Ben.

Our peaceful life in Saint Montraix continued, but in Paris there was unrest as always. Pamela and Claude kept us aware of events. There had been a spate of anti-Semitic incidents, and terrorists bombed a Paris synagogue, killing four and injuring ten. A group called the European Nationalist Fascists took credit for the bombing. A hundred thousand Parisians marched to protest this outrage, claiming that President Valéry Giscard d'Estaing had not done enough to stop anti-Semitic violence. The papers were full of it, Pamela said. Citizens wrote letters to the newspapers saying they were reminded of World War II, when the government looked the other way as French Jews were deported to Hitler's Germany. I didn't know whether Pamela and Claude knew that Ben's heritage was Jewish; we'd never discussed it with them. I seldom thought about it, and I don't think he did. He wasn't religious any more than I was, so it never came up. Sometimes, though, when these anti-Semitic issues were raised, I wondered if Ben felt uneasy.

I didn't hear much from my friends back home, and I'm afraid I didn't write them much either. Fia and Arnie planned to visit us twice, but something happened each time to foil their plans. Once, when we were living in Paris, Fia called and said they were coming over for a short stay, but Ben and I both came down with flu and couldn't see them. And when we were first living in Saint Montraix they planned to come, but Fia wrote at the last minute that Arnie had to dry out at a place for alcoholics in Sonoma County. She was more candid about Arnie's drinking problem in her letters than she'd ever been in person. Now she would write things like, "Arnie's just the same; he's never seen a highball he doesn't love," or "I don't go places with Arnie anymore. He spends most of his time at the club, and comes home potted." Later, things got better, and she wrote, "Arnie's boss's warnings have helped; he's been sober for three months."

She finally came alone in the early '80s. It was to have been a visit from both of them, but near the time of their planned departure, Arnie's daughter by his first marriage was in an accident, so he couldn't leave.

Fia said that her mother had come to live with them. This was the woman who'd ignored her daughter while she was growing up, preferring to travel the world instead. Now she intended to live the rest of her days dependent on Fia. The amazing thing was that Fia showed no resentment at this; she evidently felt there was nothing paradoxical in it. "I've got a marvelous Swedish woman to watch her while I'm in France," she said.

When she finally arrived she looked terrific—a few more wrinkles around her eyes, a few more pounds on her hips, but nonetheless, terrific. Her hair was going a little gray (as was mine) but was arranged as always in a bouffant hairdo. I never saw Fia with messy hair. She was still my lovely friend, with the same indomitable strength and 'chin-up' attitude, and the same musical laugh.

She couldn't believe how fluent I was in French. "I'm so jealous, darling! The only way to really speak the language is to live here, and you've done it!"

"Oh no," I protested. "I'm nothing like Ben."

We took her to the village café, and another night we had Clotilde and François over to meet her, and had a jolly time. I cooked *Côtes d'Agneau Provençales*, and Clotilde brought a beautiful *tarte aux abricots*. Fia was at the top of her form, flirting outrageously with the men and telling tales about San Francisco socialites. She said one elderly dowager, an arbiter of San Francisco society for fifty years, had died and left everything to her young gay male companion. He had lived with the old lady for only the last two months of her life. A sizable inheritance it was, too, something like two million dollars. The family was contesting the will.

As always after visits from friends, when Fia left, Ben and I were exhausted. We needed peace and quiet, so I holed up with a book of short stories, and Ben settled down to read a French investment magazine he subscribed to.

Not long after that Ben said he had to go to California again for more government hearings about Sam Schuster and the firm.

"But surely that's all settled by now!" I protested.

"The lawyers say they have to ask me more questions about the bank in Los Angeles. As if I haven't answered everything already! But if it will help Sam, I'll go."

I drove him to the airport in Nice, not without some feeling of resentment.

He'd been gone six days, and I was painting in my shed, listening to the news on the radio, when I heard there'd been an earthquake in California. I remember I stood stock-still, holding my brush in midair until the report was over—then realized I hadn't been breathing. The quake was in Coalinga, in southern California. Even though it was the state's strongest shake in twelve years, no lives were reported lost. Amazing, how news like that can fill one with apprehension. I went in the house and brewed myself a cup of strong tea.

Ben flew back safe and sound a few days later, but it seemed that after each of his visits to America, his coolness toward me increased.

On June 6th, 1984, there was a forty-year commemoration of D-Day, and President Reagan came to Normandy and took part in the solemn celebrations. The next day as I sat reading the newspaper, following the descriptions of the ceremonies and looking at pictures of the endless graves near the beach, my eyes filled with tears. But I wasn't crying for all the dead soldiers, I was crying for my marriage. For me, Normandy had always conjured up the time when we'd first come to France and Ben and I had shared that marvelous night of love at the Auberge du Vieux Puits.

Increasingly, nights like that were no longer part of our marriage.

After eight years in our little village, Ben told me he was bored, and that it was time to give up our lease and move on. We had made a few car trips south to Provence during those years, and he wanted to see if we could find a place there. Since I loved that part of France, I didn't argue.

I packed up most of my paintings and sent them home to Rakestraw's Gallery, telling Oliver to sell some if he could, and store the rest. I let him know we could use the money. I kept three landscapes and a half-dozen still lifes I couldn't bear to part with. My easel was too large to pack into our small car, so I gave it to Jean-Paul. Ben and I rolled up the Moroccan rugs, packed the hanging geranium and a few other things, and said farewell to our neighbors. Then we drove to the village's main street, parked, and went in to say goodbye to Clotilde and François.

Clotilde kissed us on both cheeks, visibly sad that we were leaving, and François took back the key to our house and said he hoped we would meet again.

"*J'espère qu' on se reverra un jour!*" he said. "*Bonne chance!*"

"*Bien, merci, au revoir,*" said Ben.

I couldn't say anything, not even goodbye, because my throat was clogged with eight years of memories.

Chapter Twelve

Juan Bautista Del Mazo

Although Provence and the Côte d'Azur were heady and intoxicating for the next three years, it was much stormier than the twelve years we spent in Paris and Saint Montraix. This could have been due to the mistral, the gale from the north that blew for days at a time through that part of France, or it could have been Ben's gradual withdrawal from our marriage.

Or it could have been my affair with Juan.

Around those years was gathered a mist of sadness, sadness deepened by the knowledge that I had yielded to the temptation I found at my feet.

Ben said that if we were going to stay in France, it was time to put down some roots, and I agreed. We stayed at an inn in Vence while we looked at property, driving out every day in one direction or another. We were hopeful to begin with, then always disappointed. Much of Provence was originally farmland, and each acreage had its own *mas*, or farmhouse. Many of these were now being bought and restored by people with money—some from abroad, some from other parts of France and Europe.

I learned that the word *mas* derives from the Latin word *mansun*, meaning 'something that endures'. This carried a jarring connotation for me later on.

After ten days of looking, miracle of miracles, we found a seventeenth century Provençal stone *mas* outside a lovely town called Montcerny. It was forty kilometres from Vence, and sat between the hills backing the Côte d'Azur and the higher foothills of the Maritime

224

Alps. The farmhouse was in need of much repair, but since the price was so minimal, I urged Ben to buy it. He said if we did we'd have to sell the condo at Tahoe, so he thought about it for a day or so, then called the realty company in Nevada. The realtor said there would be no problem with selling, and he wired us a week later that the condo had sold for $42,500. Since we managed to get the *mas* for $24,000 American, we were thrilled. Ben immediately called our accountant and had him invest some of the money, but not all. He knew we would be needing cash for remodeling.

I never thought I would live in such a paradise in my lifetime, and every morning when I awoke I thanked whatever gods there were for helping us find it. We were surrounded by rolling pasture, short dry grass, lavender, and sunflowers. The skies were blue, with curved, arching white clouds, one layer upon another reaching *up, up, up* to the heavens.

The village consisted of small shops and businesses, much like Saint Montraix. But now, although we were on an extended plain, there were high mountains behind us. Before us stretched orchards of olive trees and scattered rows of cypress and pine. Besides the beauty of the landscape, at every turn were the remains of Roman civilization: ancient battlements, towers, and gateways.

The *mas* had several outbuildings, and one was large enough to make a fine studio. In addition, behind the main house was a large paved enclosure, uneven and cracked to be sure, but with a curved archway leading to a neglected garden. I was enthralled with this courtyard. It contained several old cracked urns filled to overflowing with weeds; a rickety table and benches; and a lush fig tree with leaves as big as baseball gloves. The courtyard was shady in summer but warmed by the sun in winter.

There was a lot to do. We knocked down a wall to create a big living room; that took several months. We painted the stone walls white—I did most of the painting, leaving the beams dark. The tile floors had to be repaired, but were in remarkably good shape. We hired workmen for a lot of these tasks (when we could find someone to work, which wasn't often), and Ben worked alongside the men. Much of the time he struggled alone.

Ben finished my studio around November of our first year; it had been a six-month project, and I was thrilled. It was 18-feet square, and resembled my Montclair space, with one wall devoted to storage for paintings, another wall taken up with cabinets. I had done a lot of shopping at flea markets and second-hand stores, and when I finally found what I wanted, had the cabinets delivered by a guy with a delivery truck whom I'd met accidentally at a flea market. The cabinets were oak, and not the most beautiful oak, but they were serviceable. I had a large table built by the cabinet maker we'd used for the bathrooms. He was expensive, but since I had been so frugal with the cabinets, I thought I was entitled to indulge myself.

I sanded and painted all the shutters, those that could be salvaged, using the blue I saw everywhere on shutters and doors, a stock color already mixed in the paint stores. This was the famous Provençal blue that was supposed to keep away flies. I had some left over, so I used it on the old cart sitting in the courtyard, then planted the cart with flowers. Ben put in a vegetable garden, and hedges of privet and boxwood. He also planted jasmine and orange trees.

Much of our remodeling was finished in the first year, in contrast to what we'd heard about repairing and rebuilding in Provence. This was mostly due to Ben's willingness to do the work himself, his expertise with hammers and saws, and his knack for learning new skills. My long hours of painting walls and shutters speeded things up as well.

We were settled in now, and began to love the place.

For months, Ben had been reserved in his relations with me. Not only did we never make love, but even in day-to-day living he was cool, occasionally not speaking for hours at a time. One night, as he lay turned away from me in bed, I put my arms around him and caressed his neck with my lips, and I put my hand under his open pajama top and stroked his chest. I had often done these things as a preliminary to making love. He pretended to be asleep, but I could tell from his breathing that he was not. Finally I turned away.

It was true that Ben became more difficult in those years. Not abusive, never. Not even disagreeable, nor grumbling. But there were times when he would be unapproachable, distant. *What had happened to make him this way?* I didn't know, and couldn't guess. By their glances, the men I had met so far in France told me that I was still attractive. But there seemed no doubt of it: Ben was tiring of me, *had* tired of me. The only time we talked was when he wanted to discuss something about the remodeling of the *mas*.

Many, many times I would escape into my art. I had painted all through our happy days, and now I painted through these long joyless ones, when Ben's money concerns or other worries seemed to dominate his moods. Sometimes, all through his remote silence, I painted for nine or ten hours a day.

I'd never even come close to having an extramarital affair before, but now I stumbled into it. Fia once referred to an affair as 'stubbing one's toe' and that is a good description of what I did.

No, let me correct that. It was more like walking into an airplane propeller.

In a piece of great good luck, I made a new friend, an artist. Sylvie Montreau was French, and a sculptor of tremendous skill. She did huge nonobjective works of welded metal, and she was sophisticated and worldly in the Gallic way. Our farmhouses were not far apart, and we could walk back and forth to each other on the tree-lined road whenever we wanted to share coffee and the news of the day. She was around my age, slender and blonde, and would have been quite attractive had it not been for her pockmarked complexion.

Sylvie's abstract metal sculptures were massive, some of them ten feet tall. Besides her finely tuned aesthetic sense, they required an informed knowledge of welding techniques and a lot of muscle, and she told me she'd acquired both over a twenty-year period of hard work and trial and error.

"I saw your work at a gallery in Paris once, Sylvie," I said when I first visited her. "I was so impressed, and now I am even more dazzled!"

"Tu vois bien!" she exclaimed. "Not everything comes out so well."

She pointed to a tall heap of bent pipes and metal fragments piled outside in the yard.

By now I felt completely cut off from my California friends. Hana kept promising to come, but it seemed that something always intervened: a visit from relative, an illness of one of the children. Even though she made two trips to Germany during the time we were in France, she had so many relatives to see in her hometown, there was no time left for Ben and me.

It bothered me that Rosie hadn't kept in closer contact. I knew she was busy, but it still hurt. Friends don't act like that; they don't stop writing or calling for no reason. I heard occasionally from Hana and Fia, and I got regular letters from Mamaw and Esther. Nikki, Ranie and Amanda, as far as I was concerned, had dropped off the face of the earth.

I mentioned my hurt feelings about Rosie to Ben one day.

"It ticks me off that Rosie doesn't write or call," I said.

He'd been looking at some rough building plans he'd drawn. He looked up.

"Nat, let's face it, not all your friends are going to come through for you. You expect too much, and remember, we're the ones who moved away. Everyone else writes, so try to be satisfied with that."

"No, everyone else doesn't write! But Rosie is—special, and I'm hurt. So sue me!"

Then, only a few weeks after my diatribe, Rosie wrote and said she'd like to visit us in our new abode. I was thrilled, and Ben was excited too. You would think she was visiting us for a month, from the supply of gourmet delicacies we stockpiled. We hadn't had time to remodel the kitchen, but I scrubbed the cabinets, cleaned the primitive light fixture that hung by a chain from the ceiling, and used elbow grease and sandpaper on the wooden counters.

Ben went to pick her up at the train station in Vence while I finished cleaning and putting flowers in her room. When they drove into the gravel driveway, I ran out of the house, and we embraced and kissed. She was full of glowing comments about the house, the grounds, and the scent of lavender that pervaded the air. Despite her bright clothing and heavy makeup, Rosie looked worn out. She said she'd had delays on the flight, and that had made everything more difficult.

I prepared *blanc de poulet aux aubergines,* chicken with eggplant, for her first night, and we all got drunk on wine and reminiscing.

"Remember Felix Von Papen at Esalen, how overbearing he was?" asked Rosie.

"Remember Rina, the nude sea nymph?" I rejoined. We laughed together as Ben refilled our glasses.

I asked her if she was still volunteering at the nursery school.

She looked blank. *"What?* Oh, no, that was years ago."

For some reason she continued looking at me, licking her lips while touching the yellow moonstones in her necklace.

The next day we drove her all around the village and into the hills, and she couldn't have been more enthusiastic.

"However did you find this place!" she asked.

I showed her my latest work, all the still lifes and landscapes from Saint Montraix, and she said, "Your work is more impressive than ever, Nat. France has been good for you!" I was to remember her praise in the months to come; it meant a lot to me.

She admired Ben's handiwork too. He showed her all the work he'd done, inside the house and out, and she was amazed.

It was her second afternoon with us when I came upon her sitting alone in the courtyard. I was carrying a big tray of crackers and *cassis* and, unaware of my approach, she sat with one hand rubbing the other, her face wearing a forlorn expression. It reminded me of

Hana's face years ago, when she had worn such a look of wretchedness that I had to move my brush away.

"What is it, sweetie? You look as though you'd lost your best friend—and I thought *I* was your best friend."

She jumped, and took in a sharp breath. "I was worrying about how much work I have to do when I get home, and thinking what an ideal situation you two have here. Why can't I just stay?"

"What about Madame Lushenka's prediction? What about that perfect man you were supposed to meet?" I sat down and put my hand over hers.

"Madame Lushenka is an old fraud! The cops closed her down a couple of years ago. She was found guilty of extortion—one of her rich clients testified against her."

I got up later than usual on the third morning of Rosie's visit, having been inspired to work on a canvas until the wee hours the night before. I'd been spending so much time painting shutters, my creative life had suffered.

Ben and Rosie were in the kitchen, sipping coffee and studying some papers. Their heads were close together, and Ben had a pen in one hand. They looked up, expressions of shared guilt writ plain on their faces.

"What're you two doing, reading dirty literature together? Unexpurgated Henry Miller?" I was trying to make light of it, but I felt left out.

Ben laughed. Stretching his arms over his head, he exclaimed, "Not at all, darling!" He was wearing a white T-shirt, and when he stretched, his tanned, tight-muscled arms looked unbelievably sexy to me. Probably they did to Rosie too.

"Well then, what are you up to?" I insisted. "You both look so shamefaced."

Rosie's eyes were somber, hooded. "Ben and I were just—I was just—"

Ben rose, snatching up the papers and moving away from the table.

"Rosie was showing me one of her case files. Very interesting."

Standing near the stove while pouring coffee, I asked, "Isn't that unethical? And when did Ben get to be such an authority on psychiatry?"

"I'm really having problems with this one," she said. "This is a situation where—" She stopped. After a long moment, during which we all seemed poised on the edge of a precipice, she breathed a long sigh, an exhalation that sounded like a kind of surrender. I stood waiting. I couldn't imagine what Rosie was going to say next. Was she about to make some sort of admission?

Ben wasn't, I knew. His face was closed, his expression severe.

All at once Rosie smiled. She said, "Nat, could we go to the village bakery and pick up another of those pastries, like the one you served yesterday morning? I'm dying for more. We don't have anything like them at home. My treat!"

I realized that I was being ungracious. Questioning them, pinning them down. This was my beloved friend from the States, and she was leaving tomorrow.

I tried to match her grin. "Sure. Just let me climb into my jeans. And Ben, were you going to fix those roof tiles today? Sorry to nag, darling, but they have to be tended to. Sylvie tells me the rainy season could start anytime."

Rosie and I spent the day together, and Ben worked on the roof. The next morning he drove her to the airport in Nice, and I got back to painting shutters.

Ben and I agreed that Rosie's visit had been successful. We had dredged up some great old memories, and the three of us had had some good laughs. Other than that odd moment when I'd found them in the kitchen with their heads together, the time with our old Berkeley buddy had been delightful.

"Rosie looks better than ever, don't you think?" I said.

"Yeah, she looks good, but she seems a little strung out. It would be good if she could stop working, then maybe she could get rid of those frown lines around her eyes."

It was true, she had seemed tired. And a bit unhappy. I didn't mention the time in the courtyard when, unaware of my presence, she'd looked so miserable and forlorn.

One evening, as we sat after dinner sipping brandy, I tried to penetrate Ben's silence. I had prepared a good meal, not easy in our bare-bones kitchen, and he'd praised my cooking, as always. Then he opened a *Popular Mechanics* magazine he subscribed to and became engrossed in an article on plumbing.

I put my hand on his and said, "Ben, we need to talk."

He looked up, surprised. He didn't close the magazine.

"What's wrong with us?" I asked. "We both love this house, but we don't act as if we love *each other.*"

He got up. "Natalie, I'm tired. I'm going to bed." He walked out of the room.

The next morning, intent on making my dissatisfaction known, I went to where he was pounding nails into loose floorboards. He wouldn't walk out this time, surely.

"Ben, I insist, we have to talk."

A long moment went by. Finally, he put down his hammer and squatted on the floor, looking up at me while balancing himself with one hand.

I asked, "Have you ever wondered if we might need marriage counseling? I know it sounds like a waste of time, and a few years ago I would have laughed at the idea. I don't know who we would see around here, but don't they have that sort of person in France? Maybe in Vence. There *is* something wrong, isn't there? You haven't made love to me, you don't even talk to me. Is it that I'm getting old, or you're getting old? But we're just starting our fifties! Or have you found someone else?"

I walked away a few steps, shaky and trembling.

"Natalie, I swear, you pick the worst times to have these discussions."

"When do you *want* to talk, then? In bed you turn away, and over meals you read household repair magazines. So when do you want to talk?"

"I don't." He crouched there, gazing up at me, narrowing his eyes.

I left the room with a parting remark. "All right. If this is what you call a marriage, I guess I can last it out if you can!"

I didn't want him to see me cry, so I went to my studio. Finally I calmed down enough to work. I took out a brush and began painting gesso on a bare canvas.

In the spring of '87 I went to the states to see Mamaw. I missed her, so I went over and stayed for a week. I never could talk her into visiting us in France, but she always seemed delighted with my visits to her. We enjoyed going over old photo albums and reminiscing about the days of my youth in Albuquerque. She still loved her library job, and I returned to France at ease with how contented she was with her life. There was only one uncomfortable moment when she asked, "Natalie, how are you and Ben doing? Everything okay?" I had known the question was coming, but when she asked, I wasn't ready. I hesitated way too long in answering, and she gave me a sharp look. "Well? What is it, Nat, what's wrong? You two not so good these days?"

"We're fine. It's just that—" I turned away. "I don't think he has enough to do." This was a lie, and she knew it. For days I'd been telling her how hard Ben was working on the farmhouse.

"Well, of course he doesn't have enough to do!" she said. "No man should be without a real job, and you'd better hightail it back over there and tell him to get one. How long are you two going to stay away, anyhow? Is that what you meant to do when you went to Europe, become exiles?"

I didn't answer. I picked up a book I'd bought the day before and stuck my nose inside *The Prince of Tides*.

Two years after we moved to Montcerny, I met Juan. He had been away all that time, either living in Paris or traveling in Europe, Japan or the United States. He was just then coming into international prominence; museums were buying his assemblages, and he had been accompanying his work to various galleries and museums all around the world.

Juan Bautista del Mazo was of Spanish extraction, but had lived in France for most of his adult years. He was in his teens when his parents moved to le Muy, near Montcerny, to set up a ceramics business. His father was Spanish, his mother French, and she had wanted to return to her relatives in that part of Provence. Juan Bautista, or Juan, as everyone called him, trained at the Académie Julien in Paris, which was where I first came across his work, then went for more practical training at a design school in England. He began work at a film studio in Paris, did film posters for a few years, then began to design billboards, stage backdrops, anything he could to scrape together a living. He and his wife lived in Paris during that time. They divorced, and he moved to the hills above Montcerny, and it was there that I met him. He was in his middle forties, the cynosure of a small circle of painters and sculptors.

It seemed that Juan and I always ended up in the same place. If I went to Vence to get art supplies, he was there. If I went to sketch in the countryside or at the seashore, he was there. Several times he, Ben and I met at get-togethers at other artists' studios, or saw one another at the homes of local art patrons. Artists' studios in the area were almost always primitive, but Juan's was not. He lived in a centuries-old converted stone sheepfold clinging to a hill high above the town, and had converted it into a combination living quarters and modern, high-ceilinged studio.

I had been warned by a couple of women, Sylvie and a local gallery owner, that he could be terribly moody and withdrawn, but the first time Ben and I visited him in his studio, he was the friendliest person we'd met so far. He invited us there when I ran into him at the art supply store.

On a very warm day, we drove up the winding road past rolling pastures, olive groves, and clumps of wild lavender and rosemary. When we arrived, Juan rushed to pour glasses of pastis, then linked arms with us and walked us around his property. He was wearing a white, short-sleeved shirt with an open collar and khaki shorts. I wore capris and a straw hat, and Ben was wearing cut-off jeans and a T-shirt.

I had never seen such a marvelous workplace. It was equipped with pulleys for his large paintings, so they could be let down and pulled up, and it was crammed with every material and type of paint or glue known to man. His works were fascinating amalgams of all these things, with an emphasis on texture as much as color. Glue pots, paint tubes, cardboard, sandpaper, wooden shingles—everything one could use to make an interesting assemblage was there. He liked iridescent, sparkling and mirrored surfaces, also soft or prickly textures, scrollwork, arabesques, foil, beads, jewels—anything that was, in his words, "pleasantly disturbing or appealingly provocative."

Juan spoke English with a half-Spanish, half-French accent. He had a low, almost guttural voice that set off a strange visceral reaction inside me.

"You have been living in France for some time?" he inquired.

Ben said, "Yes, we've been here for more than a decade, but only recently moved south."

"You will like it here; the weather is the best in France, except when the mistral blows. And we have all the greats nearby; their work is spread all over the Côte d'Azur."

"Yes!" I enthused. "We've seen Picasso's paintings at the Grimaldi castle, and Dufy and Leger and Matisse. Matisse is in—indescribable!"

My breath was coming unevenly, and I was stammering. I stopped trying to talk and took a big gulp of the *pastis*.

Something about Juan unnerved as well as awed me. He seemed so accomplished, so driven, so much the consummate artist. He was uncommonly good-looking, with a dark, drooping moustache, collar-length black hair and very dark skin. He was two inches shorter than Ben, but his shoulders were broader.

"Have you been to Chagall's museum yet, in Nice? And you must see the Villa Ephrussi at Cap-Ferrat, toward Monte Carlo—it has many paintings you should view."

"That's next," said Ben. "But we've been avoiding Nice; it seems so big and noisy, and that's not why we came to this area. *Qui en voudrait!*"

"*Ah, voilà*—but it has its own charming out-of-the-way spots; you mustn't disregard it entirely."

"Is it true there are some Rauschenbergs and Stellas there?" I asked.

"Yes, at the museum. You must go."

We left after two hours, saying we would have him to our *mas* soon.

The next time we saw Juan was at Sylvie's home; it was a small party, only artists and their spouses or significant others were invited. Surprisingly, on that day Juan was reserved, even standoffish, and it was as if we had never met. He had a glass of wine, talked briefly to Ben and some of the other men out on the terrace, and left soon afterward.

Not long after that, Ben and I gave a party for all the artists we had gotten to know, including Juan. We showed them around our property, and they were full of admiring remarks. I gave Ben full credit, confessing that all I had done was paint a few walls and shutters. We served aperitifs and wine, and I prepared some light dishes: *tapenade* made with anchovies, Greek olives, and tuna fish; fennel *antipasto* that everyone raved over; several three-cheese (*Gruyère*, *Pont l'Evêque*, and cottage cheese) tarts. After the party warmed up, most of the artists drifted into my studio, where I showed them my work. I didn't have a lot to display, since I'd sent so many paintings to Oliver, but I had some things I'd saved from Saint Montraix, plus the sketches I'd done here. Sylvie liked my still lifes, but she was the only one who commented on them. The landscapes got the most attention.

Sylvie took me aside and whispered, "Natalie, I'm so glad you had this party, so the others can see how you are—*tres ingénieuse.*"

When everyone else had left the room, Juan spoke to me. "Very interesting. You have been working at landscape for some time?"

"Yes. Mostly portraits before that. But now I like landscape. I love just taking off with an idea."

"These have much abstraction. I like them."

That voice, that deep-throated voice, saying words I loved to hear.

"From you, Juan, I find that to be the ultimate compliment."

"Mais non! I am a mere *voyageur,* trying to find my way."

We went back to the main room, and his hand was on my elbow. I was wearing low sandals, but still I stumbled.

It was summer, the middle of July. Ben told me he thought he should go home to check on our house, and added that he'd like to drop in for a weekend at The Trees to see his old buddies. I started to insist again that I'd like to go along. I missed my friends, and I, too, would have liked a glimpse of our home and San Francisco. But he said we couldn't afford for both of us to go; wouldn't I rather stay and spend all that airline money on paints and canvas? He reminded me, in a clipped, unemotional voice, that we ate well and had a comfortable house here in Provence, and that my painting supplies and our repairs on the *mas* amounted to a lot of money each month. He said if I wanted to continue to live in Europe, we had to conserve. I was pulled both ways; on the one hand I wanted to go, on the other hand I wanted to stay and paint.

I drove him to the airport at Nice for his flight to Paris and the U.S., and gave him a long goodbye kiss. He hugged me very hard, and as he turned to go, looked back with an indefinable expression of sadness. I remember thinking there was more to his look than the mere regret at parting.

I always worried when Ben flew anywhere, and I had good reason. Five Americans had been killed recently during a terrorist attack at a Rome airport, and in April, 1986, terrorist bombs had killed a lot of people, including four Americans, aboard a TWA jet going from Rome to Athens. Our British friend Claude Milford had been working in Rome then, setting up a British Motors dealership. And there was the time back in 1985 when hijackers took a TWA plane from Athens to Beirut to Algiers—and back again to Beirut! Fia wrote that journalists in America had had a field day with that story.

But I put my worries aside, and began to paint in a fury. I had many new landscape sketches to work from and was anxious to start.

I wanted to begin using a palette of browns and umbers. *Quel horreur!* Now that I had moved to the brightest, sunniest spot in France, where there were some of the strongest colors on the planet, I decided to descend into a dark, monochromatic world. This had to be a mark of sheer contrariness.

Or did it signal my sadness and personal desolation?

I covered six large canvases with backgrounds in grays, tans, and taupes, and began to draw on them the compositions my sketches suggested. By now, as a result of Professeur Moutet's demanding training, not to mention all the sketching I'd done in Saint Montraix, I was drawing more skillfully than ever. This made for an ease in composing that I had never experienced before.

I worked for five days, barely stopping to eat and sleep. Occasionally I would go outside to the garden to breathe fresh air, also because Ben had instructed me to keep his vegetables watered. It had been unbearably hot, and I was afraid I'd waited too long to water his tomatoes. But I gave everything a good soaking, and the next day the plants were fine.

That first weekend without Ben, Sylvie Montreau had her showing of sculpture in Villefranche-sur-Mer. For the show, her bronzes and other works had to be collected from all over France, those she'd sold to private collectors, and others from the Galerie la Hune on the Rue de l'Abbaye in Paris, where I'd first seen her work. She said that even though the gallery was paying half, the freightage was costing her a fortune. But she didn't care—she wanted people to see everything *tout ensemble*.

Sylvie was single, with no man in sight, but I sensed that she had been romantically involved with some of the local artists, Juan among them. I never inquired about her love life, and she didn't talk about it; she was a private person, like me. The only time she made a comment about Juan was one day when I was enthusing over his recent sale of a large assemblage, one of his "Troubadours and Magicians" series, to the Michelin Corporation. Someone had told me he'd sold it for five million francs, the equivalent of around $75,000.

While I was going on about this, she walked over to me, touched me on the arm, and said, "Natalie, Juan is a gorgeous, talented man. *Mais quelle gueule d'amour.* Be careful."

My mouth fell open. "Sylvie! *Tu ne comprends pas!* There are three reasons why I wouldn't get involved with Juan. One, I'm a married woman; two, I don't need another moody man in my life; and three, I'm old!"

"My friend, he *likes* them married. He also likes women of a certain age. And you are very attractive."

I felt something move in my belly. I took a deep breath, and paused to consider what she was saying. It was true, I had fallen a little in love with him.

"Don't worry," I said. "Ben is coming back next week, and I won't have time to entertain girlish fantasies!"

She looked hard at me, and I realized I'd admitted my feelings.

But Ben didn't come back when he said he would. He called and said that our latest tenants were insisting on a new roof before they moved in, and he needed to supervise. "We could get rooked for thousands of dollars by these guys if I don't watch them every second," he said. "I know you'll agree." I didn't argue; the phone connection was terrible. But I wondered why he couldn't let Randy Stubbs supervise the new roof; their firm had always taken care of these things. I resigned myself to another few weeks of loneliness.

It was Sylvie's show and our old Renault that contrived my destiny. We had held on to that car way too long, trying to save money. It was seventy kilometres to Villefranche. I knew the car wasn't operating all that well, so I started out in the early afternoon. The car chugged and trembled, and when I tried to accelerate, it was slow to respond. The trip consisted of a few smooth patches, but mostly I found myself jerking and lurching along the road.

"*Je t'en prie!* Just get me there!" I yelled.

We finally made it, and I found a gas station where I had the mechanic check the engine. I think he said everything seemed fine, but I wasn't exactly sure what he did say.

"*Eh bien. Je n'y comprends rien!*" I told him, which I probably shouldn't have.

He filled the tank, and I paid him what seemed a tremendous sum, then made my way to the main square of the town. The show was to begin at five o'clock, and by some miracle I had time to kill. I spent some time roaming among the shops, buying a few things I'd been needing: an egg whisk, a new can opener. It was one of those airless, steamy days that hits the Côte d'Azur in mid-summer, and I was glad I wore my coolest outfit, a gauzy flowered skirt, sheer white blouse, and leather sandals. I was wearing my hair long then. I still had forty-five minutes, so on an impulse I stepped into a little salon on a hilly side street and had my long mane cut off. The young girl possessed great skill, because with only a few snips of her scissors and a shampoo I suddenly looked *à la mode*—as she so nicely put it. It felt wonderful not to have the heavy mop of hair on my neck.

I had forgotten to ask Sylvie directions to her gallery, so I inquired of the hairdresser. She told me the Art Moderne du Port was on the harbor, which seemed obvious when I thought about it. I chugged my way down the steep cobbled streets to the waterfront. I parked and went up several flights of stairs, stepping into a vast space filled with Sylvie's work.

The crowd was the biggest I'd seen yet at any Provençal artist's opening, and by now I'd been to quite a few. I wandered among the chattering throng, looking at Sylvie's remarkable creations. After a half-hour, and barely able to glimpse Sylvie across the crowded room, I needed to get some air. People were smoking outside on a long white balcony. I stepped out, and before me was the Mediterranean, three times bluer than the sky's ultra cerulean. The port was occupied by several huge freighters, which dwarfed the many small fishing boats. From here, I could see the 16th-century fortress that was one of Villefranche's tourist attractions. All in all, this was one of the most breathtaking views I'd seen yet in France.

Juan was there with another man. He waited a minute or two, then left his friend and walked over to me. Standing very close, he said, *"Comment vas-tu*, Natalie. I like your hair. Would you like a cigarette? Where's Ben?"

"Merci. No, I quit a long time ago. Ben's in California, watching workmen put a new roof on our house."

"Will it take long?"

"I don't know."

"What do you think of Sylvie's pieces?"

"I think they're magnificent."

"Yes, they are very strong." I think he was about to say "for a woman," but thanks be to God, he didn't.

Flustered, I turned back toward the gallery. "I'm going to find some bread and cheese," I said. "My car's on the fritz, so I drove here early, and I forgot to eat."

He put his hand on my arm. "Don't go."

Shivers ran up and down the arm he was touching. My knees felt weak.

"I will take you home," he said. "Don't try to go on that long journey again in a car that is—how are you saying it? On the fritz?"

He threw his head back and laughed. His throat was very tanned, and I couldn't take my eyes off its taut muscles. His teeth were whiter than milk.

"All right," I said in a shaky voice. "But let's not leave together."

"Why not?"

"I'll tell you later."

"All right. My Peugeot is a block to the north. Can you find it?"

"Yes."

He left soon after that, and I went to congratulate Sylvie on her magnificent show. She looked at me in a questioning way, saying only, "I'm glad you could come." I went down the stairs and walked north up the hill, already wet between the legs. Before he started the car, we embraced for the first time. It was at once amazing and marvelous that this man who could have anyone would want me. His kisses were urgent, and they toppled me. I fell back against the car seat, and if he had wanted, he could have taken me then.

"We'll go to my house," he said, "I will feed you there."

He drove very fast, and as soon as we reached his house, we hurried into the cover of his four walls and threw off our clothes.

Darkness had fallen, and I wanted darkness inside the bedroom. I was no longer young, and was not proud of my body. But I wanted to see him, so I relented. He switched on the small lamp by his bed, and we looked at each other as we made love, gazing into each other's eyes, kissing and tonguing each other. He said I was beautiful, so who was I to argue? I knew that even though my breasts sagged, when they were excited they were firm and full. And I had not had children, so my stomach was flat.

Juan looked so different from Ben. He was more compact, more sinewy. I had always loved Ben's slim build, but now found that Juan's stocky, muscular physique was excitingly different. He was a deep nut-brown color all over, and his skin glistened with perspiration, giving him an animality that excited me. As we made love his eyes were half-closed, his mouth open, wet with my mouth's fluids. I had forgotten the feel of a moustache, and had to get used to the way it felt on my skin. His face wore the look of a mindless beast, but I was not repulsed by his dull, empty visage; I adored it. It showed that I was able to vanquish every part of his consciousness, all his awareness of reality—able to overcome him with voluptuous pleasure.

I, too, forgot time and the world. We went on until I couldn't hold back, and he cried out and came inside me, accompanying me in my spasms.

There is no use in saying I shouldn't have gone with Juan. There is no use apologizing, to myself or to anyone else.

Did I deserve to have Juan in my life? For a long time, my husband had ignored me in the bedroom, so how could I be blamed? Maybe the affair was destined—fortune's lot. Hadn't the card of the Fool been pointing straight at me at Madame Lushenka's?

Maybe, if I hadn't continued to see Juan for the three weeks Ben was away, continued to enjoy his body so completely, drinking in the way it looked, the way it smelled, enjoying his caresses that went on so endlessly . . . if we had made love only once, would I have been forgiven by the gods? If I had only used some restraint, some vestige of self-control, would I deserve to be forgiven?

But I didn't.

After that night we made love everywhere. His studio, my studio, his living room, my living room. His bedroom, but never Ben's and my bedroom; at least I was discreet in that regard. I was happy to have Juan violate the inner sanctum of my workplace, where we found my small couch adequate for our purpose. I loved having him there. Somehow it signified a deeper intimacy, a melding of our artistic temperaments.

When we were in my studio, every comment he made seemed weighted. When he made the smallest remark about my materials, my sketches, the beginnings of my earth paintings, which he thought held promise—I reveled in his words.

As for Juan's sheepfold, it seemed incredibly exotic to me—a mixture of ruggedness and elegance, like him, with its stone walls and antique oil lamps. (In his studio, of course, he had installed track lighting.) In the living area, large suede sofas faced one another in front of the stone fireplace, and colorful Algerian rugs lay at all angles. Juan said that long ago, sheep were herded here to spend the night while the shepherd dozed near the hearth. When entering or leaving, I always had to touch the sheepfold's lucky stone outside the door. It was polished and smooth, worn by the touch of hundreds of shepherds through hundreds, perhaps thousands, of years.

I asked Juan what kind of luck it would bring and he said, *"Bonheur,* Natalie, *happiness!"*

From his stone terrace, the panoramic view of the Côte d'Azur and the Mediterranean was another breathtaking vision, where I could breathe in the scents of many herbs. I stayed out on the terrace a lot, sunbathing in the nude. Sometimes Juan worked, and sometimes he joined me to soak up the sun.

At my *mas,* Juan liked to make love in the courtyard. It seemed incredible to me that Ben and I never had. We pulled outdoor cushions off their frames and shoved them under the shade of the fig tree, rousing ourselves through those long summer afternoons only to bring food and drink from the kitchen. We drank iced tea, which Juan had never appreciated before, vodka-and-tonics with fresh lemon plucked from one of our trees, *cassis* or *pastis,* and the occasional *croissant* or sandwich. I was always ravenously hungry.

Keeping up with Juan's sexual energy drained me, but in the most blissful way. Never had I felt such abundance, such ample fullness. I was saturated with love, filled with carnal desire at all times of the day and night. I couldn't bear for him to leave my side. Once, when he left me in his house and drove to the village to get his weekly packet of mail, I thought I would not be able to live until he returned. It was only half an hour's separation, maybe less, but I paced fretfully about on the terrace and back and forth inside the house. When I heard him in the driveway, I met his car, and when he got out, I wrapped my legs around him and tore off my blouse so he could begin kissing my breasts.

One morning, as we lay in his studio surrounded by sofa cushions, he raised his head to ask, "Natalie, have you seen the castle at *Les Baux?*"

"No."

"You must see it. And I want to be the one to show it to you." He reached over and kissed me, his arm pulling me close.

"Ouch! You haven't shaved for awhile." It was one thing to feel his soft moustache—his *balai d'amour*, he called it—and another to have his bristly cheek scrape mine.

He jumped up. *"Oui.* I will shave. And we will go."

We packed a few things, got in his Mercedes, and left. The road crossed sun-washed orchards, olive trees with silvery, trembling foliage, and the new green leaves of grape vines on either side. We drove through small villages and passed on the outskirts of large towns, my body pressed against Juan's, heedless of my seat belt for the entire journey. We drove through a deep, rock-strewn valley, climbing all the while, finally stopping for lunch at a parking area near a tall outcropping of rocks. We ate country paté, crackers, and *moussaka*, left over from the meal I'd prepared the night before in Juan's kitchen. And since there was no one around, we made love. It was more my idea than Juan's, who was ready to drive again after eating. But I pulled him behind some rocks and had my way with him. It was uncomfortable, gravel and dirt digging into our bodies, and I felt even more a ridiculous teenager than I had in any of our other venues of passion.

We got in the car, continuing to climb for miles into the Alpilles, or Baby Alps, passing hotels and fancy resorts. Juan said this was a busy tourist area, and he cursed the fact that we were traveling in July. "But if I don't show you now, I may never get to."

I didn't like the sound of that. I slumped beside him—hair disheveled, makeup worn off, clothes in disarray. I was gritty, sad and post-coital. I said, "Darling, perhaps we should spend the night at a hotel, and go to the castle tomorrow." He agreed, and amazingly we found a delightful little hotel; they'd had a cancellation. Juan went out and brought in food, and the next morning we got an early start.

We drove a few miles up to the parking area, then walked up, up, up through gathering crowds of tourists in the lower "living city," of Les Baux, making our way on cobbled streets that wound around the base of the hill. Gradually we left the crowds behind and began to make our way to the "dead city" above, where the lords of Provence had ruled for hundreds of years, ending their domination of that part of France in the fourteenth century. Finally we were atop the promontory, where I stood panting, my legs and knees aching. I stood on the edge of the crumbling ramparts and looked out at the dizzying vista—a landscape filled with craggy white hills, and below them, far, far away, a valley dotted with maquis, olive trees, and grapevines. The distances, far-flung, mist-filled, were astounding.

"That is the Val d'Enfer," he said. "You Americans call it the Valley of Hell. It is said to be what inspired Dante for his *Inferno*."

"I don't understand. It is magnificent, but nothing like I imagine Hell to be—not that I believe in Hell. "

"Perhaps Hell was inside the poet," said Juan. He put his arm around me and pointed. "*Voilà!* The Mediterranean—sixty-six kilometres away!"

"I can't believe any of this," I breathed. "In my whole life, it's the most incredible view I've ever seen!" I kissed him. "Bless you for bringing me here!"

Suddenly my thoughts were of Ben. For twenty-nine years we had shared everything. Could I ever come back to this magical place with him? It wasn't possible. This place should have belonged to Ben and me; instead, it was mine and Jaun's.

Guilt began to sit on my shoulders like a heavy black bird.

Compounding my culpability, we went to Arles and Aix-en-Provence, places Ben and I had always planned to visit together. We missed the bullfights in Arles that Picasso had frequented, and I said that was fine with me. Instead, Juan took me to the Roman amphitheater, built in the first or second century after Christ, and the *Réattu* museum, with Picasso's magnificent drawings, then he led me to the sites of some of Van Gogh's greatest works. I felt so privileged to have an artist of Juan's stature point out to me the places where the Master had painted.

While we dined that night, I tried to express this to him, but he scoffed at my gushing expressions of gratitude.

"Natalie, you are an artist too, a very good one—don't idolize me so much!" He took a long sip of wine. "In fact, don't revere me as an artist at all. That is not what I want from you!"

The lantern on the table cast light on Juan's high cheekbones, long black hair, and sensually curved mouth, which was turned down now in a fierce expression of warning. My throat closed, and I couldn't speak. He knew that I worshiped him as a man, and now I realized it was the only sort of adoration he wanted.

In Aix we visited Cézanne's birthplace and studio, and since the hotel named for him was occupied, we stayed nearby in a small rustic inn. It had a four-poster bed and earthenware jars filled with flowers. There was much to do and see in Aix, but we stayed in our room for most of two days.

On the third morning, I said we should return home. If Ben called, he wouldn't know where I was. Although Juan was impatient with my reason for returning, he agreed to go.

I wanted to reconnect with Sylvie before Ben came back, so I walked over to have coffee. I hadn't seen her for days, not since her show, and I made an awkward attempt to explain.

Walking over, I had tripped on uneven ground, and I was busy massaging my leg. *"D'accord,* Natalie," she said. "Word gets around. Did you enjoy it?" She smiled, but when she saw my expression, her smile faded. "Oh, my God. The thing with Juan, it's serious?"

I didn't answer, only continued rubbing my knee. Bent over, I was spared having to look her in the eye. We drank coffee, and I made many compliments about her show. I left quite soon.

When Ben came back, everything with Juan had to end.

I was in a heightened state of sexual awareness still, and Ben's renewed attentions, held back before he left but now reawakened (for reasons I didn't comprehend) produced a heated response. Rather than spurning his lovemaking out of loyalty to Juan, I fell into his arms with enthusiasm.

On his first morning back, I brought juice and coffee and we lay talking in bed for an hour. My verbal responses were automatic, since I was thinking of Juan the whole time.

Ben told me everything he'd done in California. He had checked our financial situation, and it wasn't good. He said that, very soon, he would have to go back to work. Our savings were dwindling and there weren't that many securities left to sell. I took the news calmly, probably too calmly. I didn't want to think about leaving, so I shoved the idea into a small mental drawer and locked it away.

"How did the roof turn out?" I asked.

"Fine. The new tenants moved in before I left. Everything inside the house is okay too, except for some minor repairs that need to be done in the kitchen."

"How were your buddies at The Trees?"

"Great. I saw Arnie, and all the members of my camp are in good shape, except for Bill Madison; he has to have a five-way bypass. Oh, and Percy Healy's daughter had triplets."

"Oh my God," I said. All those people seemed so far away, and I really wasn't interested.

"Vice-President Bush was a guest, gave a lakeside talk—he's going to get nominated for president. There was picketing outside the gates. Did you read about it?"

"No."

"Just some noisy leftists yelling that the camp's full of power-hungry capitalists plotting to rule the world. Local lawmen handled the whole thing."

He sat up on the side of the bed and slipped on a work shirt, and I stayed lounging against the pillows.

"Oh yeah, I saw Hana," he went on. "Took her out to dinner. She's doing very well, has a job, I can't remember doing what. And I saw Fia. She and Arnie are still having problems; from the way she talked, he may be out of a job. She invited me for lunch in Belvedere, but Arnie wasn't there. God, that's a wonderful area! The sailboats were out, and the sun was shining on the Bay—made me wonder why we ever left."

"What about Rosie? Did you see her?"

"Oh yeah, I almost forgot." He had turned away and was pulling on his jeans. "We went out to dinner one night. She's busier than ever with her miserably unhappy clients."

"Has she met a man yet?"

"Don't think so." He stood up and zipped, then sat down to tie his tennis shoes. "Oh yeah, she may come to France in a couple of months; says she has a conference somewhere over here."

"I hope she comes to see us."

As I said it, I realized it wasn't true. I only had time for two people in my life, Ben and Juan.

I had little news to tell Ben. I couldn't explain the fact that I had only finished one of the brown paintings I'd started after he left, but since I had worked with such prolific energy that first week, getting a start on six canvases, he didn't question my lack of productivity. As for his vegetable garden, six tomato plants had died, but I said there had been a scorching, week-long heat wave during his absence.

We dropped back into our old routine. Ben started remodeling another outbuilding, having decided it could be made into a workshop.

Gradually my sexual fever lessened, though occasionally I would waken in anguish and walk the floor in the living room, sinking down finally on the sofa where Juan and I had made love. Once or twice I cried until the early hours of the morning, and I began to smoke heavily. Ben never discovered me there; the manual work he did during the day—sawing, planing, nailing up timbers—helped him sink into the sleep of a child.

I began working on the landscape series again. I moved ahead quickly, because now I was preparing for a group show that I had been asked to participate in with Sylvie and some other local artists. The show was to be in December at the dockside gallery where Sylvie's show was held in Villefranche.

I was honored to be asked, and was sure it was Sylvie who had insisted that I be included.

I purchased the materials I needed in Vence, and buckled down to some serious work. I decided to use gypsum, polyvinyl glue, and sand to achieve the textures I wanted, mixing them with the earth colors I loved; ochers, browns, dusky pinks, sepias, Indian reds, and raw and burnt sienna. I wanted these paintings to say 'earth' if they said nothing else. I used no blues for the skies. Instead, I carried ecrus and sand colors into the upper portions of the paintings, lighter by several values than the earth tones below. I laid as much texture as I could onto the surface of the canvas, building until I achieved a third dimension.

After five unending days, I had to see Juan. Using the excuse of a grocery-buying expedition, I took the car and drove through Montcerny and up the winding road to his place. I found him in his studio, and we didn't talk until we'd made love.

Then, rising to get a towel, Juan stood over me.

"I hate it, for you to be with your husband. I have been unhappy."

"What about me? What do you think I'm feeling?"

"So, you love me then?" His voice barked out the question.

"I've told you I do, so many times!" I sat up, clutching at my clothing.

"Then you will leave him?"

It was the first time he asked me. A thousand times before I had wanted him to ask me to leave Ben, but now that he had, I was unsure. I dropped my head over my bundle of clothes and was silent.

"*Eh bien*. Please go."

"What?" I looked up, aghast.

"*Oui*. I ask you to go. There is nothing for us. I want you to be with me, live with me. If you don't wish to, I cannot continue this— this *petite liaison!*"

"I've never felt it was a small anything, Juan, and I don't now!"

"If you stay with him, it is nothing more. So go."

Sobbing, I got up and stumbled with my clothes into the bathroom. Like a robot, I began to dress and reassemble myself. I found a hairbrush and brushed out my hair, which was still short but not nearly as stylish as it had been. Graying, uneven strands stuck out in all directions around my flushed face. I remembered the day I'd had it cut, the day Juan and I first discovered each other's bodies.

I walked out of the bathroom, and when I left he had his back turned and was standing over his worktable, vigorously mixing his own special glue.

When I got home I suddenly remembered I'd said I was getting groceries. Ben was hammering away in his new workplace. Averting my swollen face, I made an excuse about the Renault having broken down. He believed me, I think, since I'd already told him it had been giving trouble.

I willed myself not to cry any more, put on fresh makeup and a clean pair of jeans, and drove back to the village to buy food.

Ben sawed planks of wood and pounded nails all through August, finally installing his lighting and worktables the first week of September. At one point he took a couple of days off to sell the old Renault and buy another used one. This one was battleship gray, an unpleasant color, but I was relieved to have a car we could rely on.

One day Ben got a letter from Claude Milford in Paris. Claude said British Motors was desperate for an American who spoke

French, someone to deal with all their new-found American contacts. Ben would not be required to learn about writing contracts, but he would have to learn about the automobiles—general information about their manufacture and all the different models and prices. There would be a lot of entertaining visiting American and English clients. This was what Claude did much of the time, he said, but he needed help. Would Ben be interested? Pamela and Claude offered to put Ben up until he could find a place to live. We thought the salary the firm offered was extremely generous, the equivalent of $75,000 a year. Of course this would all hinge on whether Claude's boss approved of Ben, but Claude seemed to think he would pass with flying colors.

Ben read his letter aloud:

> *Dear Benjamin,*
>
> *We desperately need someone as posh, intelligent and suave as you, mate—someone who knows how to order wine. Come up here and get me out of this nightly round, will you—I'm knackered! Oh yes, and Pamela seems to be preggers. The old bird wants me home more, complains all the time about being alone at night.*
> *—Best, Claude*

Sitting in the kitchen, Ben and I talked it over. He said he was anxious to put some money back into our bank account, since for fourteen years we'd been only withdrawing funds. "I never told you, but we lost quite a bit back in October of '87 when the stock market crashed. Worst day in history on Wall Street—$400 billion just wiped out!" He snapped his fingers.

"How much did we lose?" I asked, dreading to hear.

This wasn't the first time Ben had kept financial matters a secret from me, and I told myself I shouldn't be surprised. But I wasn't prepared when he said we had lost $70,000 on that one day.

"You can see how I might be getting worried. I think I'd better take this job."

I got up and walked over to the coffeepot. My stomach had dropped to my ankles. "I can't leave," I said, "I have this show coming up in December."

I turned and looked at him straight on. He gazed back at me, and suddenly I knew he knew about Juan.

We both were trying to decide whether I should confess.

But I didn't.

I couldn't. It would have been too painful for us both.

After an interminable pause he said, "Well, you stay here then. But this is a good chance for me to enter the job market again, and the Milfords being there will make it bearable."

"I can't think of any couple I'd rather have welcome you back to Paris," I said, and kissed him on the lips.

I was capable of such treachery and deceit then.

I'd always loathed Nikki's duplicity. Now I was just like her.

At first Ben came home on weekends; then his trips back became rarer.

I lived with Juan during the week, and went home when Ben came down. When he began staying in Paris permanently, saying that it was wearing him out to travel back and forth, I moved into Juan's place.

Our heat continued, my lust matching his, blending into one long, voluptuous mating.

When he would nag me to end my marriage, I would say, "For how long? How long before you tire of me, and want to be rid of me? I know you have had women before. Where are all of them now?"

He wouldn't answer.

I blurted out these questions when I'd had too much to drink, and his wrath would be awful. He would throw a glass across the room, or knock his canvas off the easel. Once he threw a tube of paint directly at my face and stormed out. I had a black eye for a week, but he was so contrite, so puppy-dog sweet, I forgave him. Why did I torture us both with these questions? Why was I so relentlessly meddlesome? Once, when I asked if he'd slept with Sylvie, then compounded my mistake by telling him she had called him a Casanova, he said, "That *brouteuse!* You know of course she is a lesbian. *Ça se voit, c'est une mal-baisée.*"

"Make up your mind," I said. "Is Sylvie a lesbian, or does she need to get laid?"

"She needs to get laid by anyone, man or woman! Probably she wants to get *you* into bed!"

I couldn't stand for this. There had never been the slightest hint of a pass from Sylvie. "She is not our problem, Juan. I wouldn't be surprised if she still loves you, so why are you saying such cruel things about her?"

That day I left and went home. I worked on my paintings, playing loud rock music and loud Beethoven for three days and nights. Then he came to me, and we went out to the courtyard and with tender passion, tasted one another again. He was slow and sweet in his lovemaking, and I was insatiable. This reunion was one of many we had during that autumn.

Once I wrote to Ben. I was thinking seriously now of leaving him.

It was what Juan wanted, and I thought I wanted it too.

> *Dearest Ben,* (I wrote)
>
> *I don't know how to start this letter. You know I love you, and will love you until the day I die.*
>
> *But now I love another man. It's Juan. Have you guessed? Once, I thought you had.*
>
> *I know I am hurting you, darling. How you must hate me! We have meant so much to each other all these years. Yet if life goes in other directions, what can one say? I have felt at times that you were involved with someone else. I don't mean to*

use that as an excuse for falling in love with Juan, because as far as I know you have always been faithful. But there have been times when you have been cold and distant—not the man who once held me so close to his heart. I blamed this on your worries about money, but whatever the cause, I had to look for happiness in another place, and I found it with him.

Please don't answer this letter right away. Think about what you want to do, and then we'll talk.
—Natalie

I never sent the letter. A few days after I'd written it, I burnt it in the fireplace.

Ben stayed away, and the mistral began to blow. But I had Juan to shelter with against the wind.

I had been doing all the cooking, and gradually, since Juan was getting ready to ship a dozen large paintings to a gallery in New York and working with great energy and fury, I began to take over some of the responsibilities of his studio. It started with my organizing all his mad jumble of slides, which I loved doing. I think I secretly wished some of his greatness would rub off on me. It took the greater part of two weeks to get them all listed by title, price, dimensions, year of creation, date of sale, and current ownership. I neatly entered all this information into a black leather notebook, and as for the slides, I carefully lettered each of them in ink—by title, size, and medium. Juan said his life had never had such order.

I began to be responsible for ordering his materials, too. By now I knew the owner of the art store in Vence very well. I could call with an order and say I was coming at a certain time to pick it up; canvases, paints, glues, whatever. Then either Juan or I, usually both, would drive the forty kilometers to pick everything up.

Once he had been working for a solid twenty-four hours—he wanted to ship everything at the end of the week—and became terribly angry because I forgot to pick up stretcher bars. When I came home without them, he slapped me.

I spent the rest of the day in bed, but I didn't return to my home. It was beginning to be a sickness.

The next day, a journalist from *Le Monde* came for an interview, having made an appointment through me the week before. She was young, blonde, delicate. She said she was writing a long article, and wanted to know everything. Their conversation was rapid-fire French, excluding me completely. I didn't mind that, but when I saw him light her cigarette and touch her shoulder in a certain way, I left and drove back to my house. My cheek still stung from his slap, metaphorically, and I was thinking that I didn't need this genius in my life, no matter how much he pleasured me.

I thought of Hana and how she'd been beaten by Bruce, how long she'd stood it because of her children. I didn't have children.

He called me later and asked, "Why did you leave so suddenly? I wanted you here! That girl is annoying. I don't want her around."

"That isn't the way it looked to me," I responded, cool as ice.

"Natalie, why must you be such a bitch! The woman is a mere acquaintance!"

"Is she gone?"

"Yes; well, at least I think so. She said she was meeting her boyfriend in St. Rémy, so I presume she is far far away."

I couldn't help myself. I began to sob over the phone. I hung up and drove back.

Our relationship went on, with its strenuous lovemaking and emotional battles.

Once I went to see Sylvie, saying that I wasn't sure I would be ready for the group show. I told her of some of Juan's and my problems, leaving out the fantastic sex.

"*Votre amour est un véritable mélo!*" she said.

"And I am too old for soap operas!"

"Don't say I didn't warn you."

In October I went on the train to visit Ben, staying only for the weekend. I still loved him, but he was not sustenance for me, as Juan was. He had moved to a small apartment in the Marais district. I felt sorry for him because the apartment was so bare, but I didn't have it in me to stay and decorate. We slept side by side, barely touching. He seemed to be enjoying the job, and told me the firm was happy with him, too, and he was being promised a raise.

It was pleasant seeing Pamela and Claude. We went to Aux Charpentiers one night, and another night Pamela cooked at home. She looked wonderful; rosy and plump, entering her seventh month. We laughed a lot, and it was the first time I'd had laughter in my life for a while.

I think Pamela sensed something was wrong, and when she asked, "Are you going to stay with Ben?" I changed the subject.

Ben said Rosie had come to Paris, and they had gotten together once or twice. When I asked why she didn't come to see me, he said she was in a hurry as always, on her way to a children's conference in Amsterdam. She was terribly sorry to miss me, he said, but she knew I was getting ready for a show and didn't want to get in the way. I thought that was a lot of hooey. I meant to sit down and write her some cross words, but I never did.

After the group show at the Art Moderne, Juan and I had another breakup.

There was a cold wind that Saturday on the streets of Villefranche—hard to believe, since the town was directly on the Mediterranean. But it was December, only two weeks before Christmas. People entered the gallery wind-blown and shivering, and the atmosphere was not nearly as welcoming and warm as it had been in July at Sylvie's show. Soon, though, as is the usual pattern at these events, everyone was talking and laughing, enjoying the wine and the paintings.

The show was a personal disappointment for me. I had been working hard, and had completed all six paintings of my Earth series, but when the time came to enter them, I was allowed to show only one, and could sense that there was some sort of background intrigue going on. I asked Sylvie point-blank if there was some animosity toward me from some of the other artists; I had noticed a cold response to my friendly overtures from two women painters. She admitted to me that yes, unfortunately there was a bad feeling about Americans who came to Provence to work and ended up competing with local artists for gallery space and sales. I could tell she was embarrassed about it, and sorry I'd only been allowed one piece.

I knew that some of this jealousy—what else could you call it?—was connected to my liaison with Juan. He was too famous to be in a local group show, and hadn't been asked to participate. As I stood with my arm linked to his, admiring the black-and-white geometrics of one artist and the splashing colors of another, I felt unreasonably happy. I loved to feel his body near me.

I remember thinking that I looked good. I was more slender than I'd ever been, and I'd had my hair cut and styled again by the gifted young Villefranche hairdresser. I was wearing a black pantsuit and white plunging neckline blouse that set off my tan. One could hold a tan for a long time in Provence.

Juan left my side to talk to a painter friend, and I walked over to Sylvie and began to chat about something or other. A few minutes later I watched Juan cross the room to talk to one of the women who had been so cold to me. She had five huge paintings hanging, canvases covered with small mosaic-like squares of color. From a distance they looked like magnificently painted quilts. *She was good, but why must he be so friendly with her!*

Twenty minutes and two glasses of wine later, I saw him talking to the blonde journalist who had interviewed him at his home. She was wearing a white satin miniskirt and a black bustier, and her legs were long and gorgeous. Her long article about him had come out the week before in Sunday's *Le Monde*, and now his fame was assured.

He'd told me he didn't want me to idolize him as an artist, but it seemed he did not mind having the world's veneration after all.

Suddenly all the blood rushed to my head. I felt dizzy, and as if I might actually fall to the floor. I found a chair in the gallery manager's office and sat there for a few minutes to regain my composure.

When I came out, Juan and the blonde were on the balcony. He was looking at her *d'une certaine manière* and she was laughing, excited. When I saw him pull her to him and kiss her on the mouth, I left and went outside. I found a cab and told the driver to take me all the way to Montcerny. It was a tremendous waste of money, but I couldn't stay another moment. The memory of our first sexual encounter at the same gallery was too potent.

Now he was starting over with someone else, and I knew I had to end the affair.

I was supposed to go to Paris to spend Christmas and attend the christening of Pamela and Claude's baby. Ben was to be godfather, and they were naming the child for him.

I didn't go. I stayed in the *mas* alone, with a fireplace fire and a bottle of Cabernet Sauvignon from the Napa Valley. I saw Juan only on Christmas morning. He said he was driving to his parents' home in le Muy. He didn't invite me to go with him, and I wouldn't have gone if he had. I didn't mention the girl, and we didn't talk about the art show. He brought me a gift, his pen-and-ink drawing of an old woman peeling apples, and I gave him a Louis Vuitton leather satchel. As I handed him the gift, I said, "It's over, Juan. Please don't call or come here. I need to be alone."

His face showed shock, even, I thought, pain.

"As you wish, my darling." He walked to the door, then turned to face me. "If you change your mind, or if you need me for anything . . ."

Now the blustering mistral came with a vengeance, pushing against the closed shutters. The olive trees near our house were whipped by fierce gales, and Ben's vegetable garden blew away. The wildflowers in the meadow disappeared, and it was as if they had never bloomed.

All creative drive gone, I spent my days leafing through magazines and crying. I practically stopped eating, and began to smoke even more.

I needed to work, but I didn't want to leave the house to sketch. Besides the winds, I was afraid of meeting another artist.

An idea gripped me one day as I gazed at my aging self in the bathroom mirror. I donned a long-sleeved gauze blouse I usually wore over a bra. This time I left off the bra and wore only the blouse and faded jeans. There were two very large mirrors facing each other in our bedroom, one on the back of the bedroom door, one on an old armoire. I moved my easel and paints into the bedroom, covered the floor with newspaper and the bed with an old sheet, and began a three-quarter-length self portrait, using the mirrors to reflect myself over and over.

This was not an easy task, and I failed in my attempt for days. Finally though, blessed by the forgiveness of oil paints and by beginning over numerous times, I began to get it right.

As the mirrors reflected my face and body ad infinitum, I painted the ages of Natalie, starting in the foreground with the middle-aged woman I was now, behind her a younger woman, then an even younger woman, and lastly, back to the girl I had been. I had brought no photo albums abroad, so I had no photographs of myself from the past. But the likeness wasn't as important as the overall effect. The first three or four figures had to be shown in detail, but the final ones, receding into the background, were so small they didn't require more than a few daubs of paint.

Ben called me once during this period. We exchanged pleasantries; I described the project I was working on, and he described the christening. He said that his namesake, baby Ben, was a handsome specimen, and I could sense that he was pleased at having the baby named for him.

The conversation broke down, and after a pause I said, "The thing with Juan. It's over."

"If that's true, I'm glad. But I'm not calling you again. I'll wait to hear from you."

The next day I went back to work. The painting, done in an intense three-week period, took every ounce of energy I had, and when I finished I had something different by light-years from anything I'd done before.

In the painting's foreground, my self-portrait showed a face with lines reflecting years of emotional pain. Nothing had been done to soften the creases and folds of this woman's skin. Here, too, were age lines created by decades of laughter: drinking coffee with Rosie, sharing food with Fia, laughing with Hana while we drank martinis at the bar in Mokelumne Hill, giggling at Ranie when she muffed her lines in rehearsals. The second figure showed an attractive woman who was no longer young, but younger than her predecessor. The third face was fresher, prettier, with a hint of a smile; the fourth showed a youthful exuberance, and so forth and so on. The features became more blurred as the woman changed back into a girl.

I kept the skin very pale, and used white to paint the translucent fabric of the blouse, using layers of glazing to emphasize its gossamer sheerness.

The day I finished the portrait, I drove to the local village for dinner, rewarding myself with a bottle of the local Burgundy and a mountainous serving of gigot de mouton à la Périgordine.

Now I was halfway over Juan. No, not halfway. Not *nearly* halfway. On the lowest of my low times—I remember I stayed in bed for most of the day, then forced myself to creep out to the mailbox— a letter arrived from Oliver. I clutched at it as a drowning man clutches at a lifeline.

January 20, 1989
Dear Natalie,

Comment allez-vous? By now you must be a confirmed Francophile—when you come back I won't know how to communicate! Just wanted to tell you there is a lot of new interest in your work. I sold one of your French landscapes to the managing editor at the Chronicle, and he wanted to know more about you, so I gave him some information and he had someone on the staff write an article. I enclose the clipping.

But here's the real reason I'm writing. What would you think about my giving you a retrospective show this year, say in April, May, or June? No landscapes, just portraits. You've done some important people in town, and you'd get a lot of publicity. I promise to give you a landscape show later on, if I last that long. Frankly, my darling, you'd be doing me a huge favor. The mid-'80s were fabulous, but things have gotten tougher, and I don't know how much longer I can stay open.

Let me know what you think.
My best wishes & fondest regards to Ben,
Oliver
P.S. I have a new assistant, and he's gorgeous!

I read the news clipping. It was full of inaccuracies and exaggeration, and I didn't like the picture Oliver had given them, but I sorely needed the boost of spirits. I called Ben that evening and told him about the letter, and he countered with some good news of his own. British Motors had offered him the dealership in San Francisco.

Another serendipitous quirk of fate! He said he'd been waiting to talk to me before he gave them an answer. His tone was unemotional, but my antennae picked up apprehension and insecurity.

I waited for a moment, and said I thought we should go home.

Ben wrote our realtor and told him to get rid of our tenants by April 1st, and I put the *mas* on the market for twice what we paid for it. It sold in eight days to a banker from Rouen.

I think Juan loved me, but I knew he never felt the passion I'd felt for him. Nevertheless, I went to him once more before we left.

Ben came home to sort out our things. One day, as I worked alongside him, all at once grief, regret, and an unfathomable sense of loss blew through me like a swirling, churning mistral.

I had to see Juan, and I left Ben and drove to him.

He was alone, painting, and we made love one last time. He kissed me over and over on my closed eyelids, and I cried all the time he was inside me—long, wrenching sobs of passion and sadness.

Part Three

SAN FRANCISCO
THE RETROSPECTIVE
TAOS
1989 – 1992

Chapter Thirteen

A Stab in the Back

My show had at last begun. I planted a confident smile on my face, and put out my hand to greet the socially elite Werners. Marlo and her husband had arrived at the gallery on the precise stroke of five o'clock, just as Oliver was greeting a few others.

I gave Marlo a hug. "Thanks for coming!"

"Sweetie, we wouldn't miss it," Marlo trilled. "I can't believe you're back after all these years. You look fantastic! I want to hear everything about France, but first, let's have a look."

She moved off with an eager stride. I was happy to see Marlo. Not only would she lend cachet to my opening, but she would really look at the work. Her portrait was here, and she was no doubt eager to see it hanging.

My heart was beating like a steam engine, and my palms were wet.

Oh! There was Fia, walking toward me with a large group. Where was Arnie? Instead, she was with Abner Rankin III. After greeting me with a kiss, she said, "Nat, I didn't want to tell you until I saw you, but Abner and I are married."

My brain went into playback mode. Fia had come to France in 1983, and right after that she'd gone to meet the Rankins and Healys at Giverny. Yes, that was how it would work, although Fia probably had had her eye on Abner long before that.

Fia and Abner were a white-haired, handsome couple.

"Remember Francine, Eric's wife?" she said, indicating the dark-haired woman at her side. I tried desperately to match this woman with the girl druggie I'd helped Fia move out of that big ramshackle mansion in the Haight. I couldn't do it.

"And this is my granddaughter, Amy." Her voice broke, and she whispered, "We lost Eric to AIDS. I'll tell you about it later."

Amy must be the child Francine was carrying when Fia dragged her out of there. She looked to be about seventeen or so, and she was a young Fia, the very image. Same dark hair, slate-blue eyes, and dimpled smile.

"How do you do, Mrs. Newbury. I love your portrait of Grandmummy!"

I heard a whoop, and turned. There was Hana coming through the door. She picked me up and whirled me around, then set me down and shook a finger in my face.

"How could you do this—go away for so long—it was *ridiculous!*"

"Well, I'm glad to be home!" I said, and kissed her on the cheek. This was an older, thinner Hana, but a woman who would forever stand out in a crowd. She wore dark pants and a leather jacket, and still had the same helmet hairdo.

I gestured toward the two young people with her. "These can't be your kids!"

Hans was six-foot-six and handsome, dressed in a sports jacket and turtleneck. Molly was tall too. Before I could reach out to hug her, she skittered by. Hana was with a man she introduced as Bill Delaney. I remembered him, the policeman who'd rescued her the night Rattler had thrown her off his motorcycle the way you'd dispose of a burnt match. Officer Delaney was blue-eyed and very Irish looking. What was it about Hana and Irishmen?

"I think we spoke on the phone a couple of times," I said.

He nodded, shaking his head imperceptibly. I got it; Molly and Hans, the 'kids', still didn't know what had happened that night.

"We'll talk to you later, okay?" Hana said. They walked farther into the room, where Ben gathered her in a smothering embrace.

People were crowding into the gallery now, and I greeted them effusively, as did Oliver. This was a big night for him as well as for me. He would make a strenuous effort to push my work; it was a night of business for him.

Another group came in, then the tall, distinguished-looking artist Austin Everhardt. "What a delicious surprise, Austin!" I was flattered he had come all the way up from Carmel.

"Very happy to be here, Natalie. Talk to you later." He moved on.

I greeted my architect friend Bert Leidecker and his wife, the girl he'd brought to my Berkeley show back in 1974. No longer the seedy grad student, Bert was dressed in a conservative gray suit.

"Can't wait to see your stuff, Nat. Remember Audrey? We're married now—got a kid!" He whipped out a snapshot of a little boy, and said, "Catch you later on."

The evening was an emotional roller coaster. In the beginning, my hands shook and my knees trembled. Then it got worse. This was not a simple case of nerves or stage fright. It was as if all my emotions were being exposed, with no protective covering for the endless range of feelings I was experiencing. For the first forty minutes I had to stand in one spot, when what I really wanted to do was follow everyone around and find out what had happened to them in the last decade and a half.

My druggist friend Charlie Sprague walked in, wearing his usual rumpled suit.

"I have your drawing of Lake Merritt hanging over my desk at home," he told me, holding onto my hand.

"Good. I'd rather hang in people's houses than anywhere else!"

This was an out-and-out lie. I'd much rather hang at the Met.

A very large woman was coming through the door. Not just heavy—obese.

My God! I realized it was Amanda. Seeing her was a tremendous shock. She was wearing a loose blue denim dress and flats, and she must have weighed two-hundred-and-fifty pounds. The last time I saw her, she was holding a flute of champagne and wearing a beautiful party outfit, and was slim as a model. Her hair was still that lovely auburn color, only a few gray strands showing, and her skin was smooth and without wrinkles. The Berkeley doctor was long gone, but what about the rich guy, the one I met at Pebble Beach? With her was a slightly younger man, her daughter Ashley, and a thirtyish woman with a spike haircut.

"Nat," said Amanda, "this is my husband Al—Al Bellach. Ashley told me she filled you in."

Al the roofer had the tanned, weathered look men get from working outdoors, and when we shook hands, I felt the calluses. He was dressed in a Hawaiian shirt plumped out by a swollen potbelly.

I watched Ben when he greeted Amanda, trying to see if he was as shocked as I.

He was. His mouth dropped open, but he quickly recovered, giving her a warm smile. She reached up and grabbed him, laughing, pulling his cheek to hers.

Her group moved farther into the room, and I stayed at my place by the door.

By now my body felt damp all over. I knew my clothes and hair must be suffering, with all the hugs I'd been giving and receiving.

Other strangers and portrait subjects I vaguely remembered walked in. Names of people I should know were beginning to desert me, but I tried not to worry about it. Best just to pretend I knew everyone—that they were my intimate friends. I made generic remarks like "How are you? Haven't seen you for so many years!" and "How wonderful that you could come!"

A beautiful black woman walked in, wearing a knockout magenta suit and a hairdo of intricate cornrows.

Ranie!

We embraced, shrieking each other's names.

I realized I'd better stop carrying on like a teenager; after all, I was The Personage tonight. I decided to try to temper the enthusiasm I felt for my old pals, try to maintain some semblance of decorum.

"Natalie," Ranie said, "do you remember my husband Carl Aldrich? He was in *Raisin* with me, remember? Played Joseph Asagai?"

I searched my brain, finally coming up with a scintilla of a fragment of a recollection. He had put on weight and was balding, but at last I recognized him. I took his hand and said, "It's so wonderful of you to come—such a long way from L.A.!"

His mouth widened with that broad grin. "Well, every now and then we have to get back to our roots. Ranie and I are both from Oakland, you know."

Every time I glanced over at Ben, he was chatting enthusiastically with someone. The jade scarf around his neck maddened me more each time I glimpsed it. Now I watched him become aware of Ranie. His face broke into a smile, and when he strode over to her, they threw their arms around one another.

Charlie Sprague appeared at my elbow with a glass of champagne. "You look like you might need this," he said, then disappeared.

"Darling—it's been too long!" Marian Morse trilled, as she and her husband entered the gallery. "When are we going to lunch at the Alta Mira again? Where's *my* picture?"

By now I'd had enough of standing in one spot by the door, and joined the crowd. I found Fia and Abner, who were standing near her portrait.

"Nat, you made me look so good!"

"You were lovely then, darling," said Abner, "but you're more beautiful now."

Abner looked happier than I'd ever seen him, and I said so, which pleased them both.

I asked about Eric. "I'm sorry—" I took both her hands in mine.

"He died six years ago, Nat, when Amy was only eleven. It's been very hard on her—on all of us." She said Francine worked now as an AIDS activist. I noticed that Francine never stood near Fia, but drifted about, and I thought it likely she didn't approve of Fia's lifestyle, her constant round of debutante balls and charity events. I wondered if Francine remembered me from that day we came to the Haight and took her away. I glanced over at Amy, who was chatting with Hans Kelly.

I wondered if I could ever tell Fia about Juan. Probably not, any more than I could confide in her about Ben's affair with—with who?

But maybe the note was from Fia . . . Once again, I put the painful matter out of my mind.

Fia started telling me some ridiculous anecdote about San Francisco society, but I was distracted just then by something else and didn't respond. Hana had walked up to Ben. They were almost the same height, and as I watched he took Hana's jacket collar in both hands and slowly turned it up around her face. It was the most loving gesture, as if she were standing in a driving snowstorm and he wanted to protect her from the cold.

Fia put her hand on my arm. I swiveled my head back, and she looked over at Ben and Hana, then again at me.

"What's the matter, Nat? It's just Hana."

"Yeah. S'cuse me, will you? I've gotta move around."

I walked over to Amanda. When I asked what happened to her rich husband, she took me by the arm and walked me a few steps away. "Do you know, Nat," she said in a low voice, "with all Grant's money, I was supposed to live in the same house he and his wife had lived in, and I couldn't redecorate, couldn't even buy new drapes! He wouldn't let me so much as move a figurine. And he was so possessive—wanted to own me. So different from Tom, remember? Always two-timing me!"

Her green eyes gazed out from her wide moon face. I couldn't help it; we were standing not far from her portrait, and my eyes slid over to the beautiful girl in my picture. Quickly, I looked back at the present day Amanda.

"I remember," I said.

Sylvie Montreau's words about Juan echoed in my head. *"Mais quelle gueule d'amour!"* What a Casanova! That described Tom Reichard, too.

We walked back to Al, Ashley, and her friend.

Just then a young woman wearing a long flowered skirt, tie-dye tunic, and waist-length hair walked in. They're probably not called hippies now, I thought; there's probably a new word I haven't heard. The girl walked toward us. "It's Lizzie!" cried Amanda, hurrying over to greet her. Was this the daughter who dropped out of college and moved to a commune?

"Does Lizzie live around here now?" I asked Ashley.

"Yes, she's at Green Gulch." At my baffled look, Ashley said, "It's a Zen center on the Shoreline Highway in Marin. They contribute tons of fresh produce to shelters and food banks, have a daily schedule of chanting, bowing and vegetable gardening. She loves it."

Amanda brought her daughter to me and said, "Nat, I've always wanted you to meet Lizzie."

"I've admired Mom's portrait for years. Sorry I never got to meet you before. Looks as if your style is very consistent. Do you prefer acrylic or oils?"

Dropout, hippie, chanting Zen Buddhist, fanatical vegetarian— whatever—the girl knew the right thing to say. I gave her my usual answer, that oil is more sensual, acrylic more quick-drying and practical, and said I liked both.

I moved away, joining Hana's group. She put her arm through mine and said, "This is such a wonderful party, Nat. I am so happy for us we could be here!"

How could I think this woman would stab me in the back!

"I'm delighted you came! I always wanted to get all my favorite subjects together, and now I have. Or almost all of them. Esther and Rosie couldn't make it, and I'm not sure about Nikki. I can't believe it's happening—you, Amanda, Ranie, and Fia all here!" I threw out my arms, embracing the room.

Hans walked over, putting one arm around his mother. "Hey, congratulations on your show, Mrs. Newbury," he said. He still looked like his mother, but now I could see Bruce in him too.

Hana said, "Bruce put Hans through law school, and Molly is an interior designer. I am so proud! When they became grown, Bruce realized he was a father, and provided them for their educations, but I still hate his guts—I am so bad!"

Hana was thinner and more muscular than I remembered her. She said she had taken up running, and even ran in marathons. She worked at a sporting goods store, and in winter organized ski trips for the public schools. "I ski as much as I can," she said. "Remember you and Ben took us skiing?"

I tilted my head in the direction of Bill Delaney, and she answered my unspoken question. "No, I am not going to get married. I do not lead my life now for any man; no more do I do that. And I am very content."

"I'm glad," I said.

"Don't you think Amanda is contented now, too? She seems to me—very *frölich!*"

"Indeed," I responded. Neither of us said what we were thinking. And she's so *fat!*

Ben walked over and put his arm around my waist. I didn't move away, but I didn't turn to look at him.

"So this is your family, Hana," he said. "They've turned out pretty well, I would say!"

"I remember you, Mrs. Newbury," said Molly, "you took care of us that time Mom had the automobile accident."

"Yes," said Hans. "And they took us skiing, and Mr. Newbury drove us up to Sutter Creek while Mom was gone."

"You didn't much want to go, as I recall," Ben said, slapping his shoulder. "You were my unwilling prisoner."

A few yards away, the gallery door opened and Esther rolled into the room in a wheelchair pushed by a stooped, elderly man. A young woman in a dark sweater and short leather skirt accompanied them.

I hurried toward her. "Dear Esther, you made it after all!"

The years since I'd seen her had taken their toll. Her face was more lined than ever, her body more shrunken, and her hair was now completely white. But time had sweetened her face, and her smile was warmer.

"Wouldn't miss it!" she said. "Nat, Ben, this is my friend Hubert, the one who shipped my picture. Arlene, remember Natalie? She was there when you first came." Esther's voice had a pronounced quaver, and her head wobbled a bit.

"Yes," said Arlene, "the artist!" She smiled and shook my hand, then Ben's, completely changed from the sullen girl I remembered. She had an abundance of curly hair; a few russet wisps coiled around her face.

"Esther, why are you in a wheelchair?" I asked, afraid to hear the answer.

She looked up at Hubert and patted his hand. "Parkinson's disease, my dear. Gets a lot of us older folks. Some young ones, too."

"Hans, Molly," I said, "Mrs. Phillips took care of you for a week when you were teenagers, remember?"

"I must have made a kajillion bowls and pots," said Molly. "You were such a good teacher, Mrs. P.!"

"What are you doing now, lovey?"

"I'm an interior designer in Soho, in New York. Have you heard of it?"

"Of course!"

"And you, Arlene?" I asked.

Esther answered for her. "Arlene graduated from college, and now she owns her own real-estate business. Gold Country land just keeps going up, up, up!"

I remembered how patient Esther had been with the difficult Arlene. What a happy ending!

Hana walked over, took Esther's hands in hers, and bent to kiss her, and Arlene walked away to look at the paintings. Esther said, "That girl has been wonderful to me—better than my own children."

A look of sadness passed over her face, fleeting as a magician's hand. "And Hubert has been a Rock of Gibraltar!" She reached back to touch his fingers. "It's time you took me around to look at Natalie's work."

I watched as they moved away. Here was someone who had overcome great sadness—a husband who abandoned her, and children who were less than attentive. Now she had poor health, but remained compassionate and gentle through it all. I remembered the Zen words I'd heard so long ago:

> *Don't fight the stream, or you'll drown*
> *Go with the flow*
> *Bend with the wind*

Three people I didn't know were standing near Rosie Rinaldi's portrait. I walked over and put out my hand. "Hi, I'm Natalie. So glad you could come tonight."

"She doesn't recognize us," said the yellow-haired woman. I looked from her to the others, then back again. "This isn't going to be a test, is it?" I moaned. Finally it dawned on me. The husband and wife psychologists I'd met at Esalen years ago!

"The Housemans!" I whooped. "But—" I peered again at the blonde. "Omigod—it's Rina the sea nymph!" Rina was dressed in a black business suit and wore thick, horn-rimmed glasses.

"I never knew you called me that," she said, unsmiling.

"Well, you had all that greenish hair . . . How did you hear about my show?"

"We saw it in the *Chronicle*."

The three made several flattering comments about the exhibit.

"Is Rosie coming tonight?" asked Hilda. "We liked her so much."

"I don't think so."

Rina said she worked as a secretary in an insurance office, and the Housemans said they were writing psychology books.

I couldn't get over the change in Rina. Our naked young nymph, transformed into an everyday, run-of-the-mill office worker! She'd had such a chip on her shoulder, and still seemed angry about something, so maybe it was life in general that pissed her off.

I found Ranie who, with Carl, was studying Esther's portrait. I asked, "Is Jason coming? I appreciated his delivering the painting. Where's he going to school?"

"UC Berkeley. He'll be here later, has a six o'clock class."

Bert and his wife were standing nearby. "You really came up with something there, Nat," he said, nodding his head at Esther's picture. "Reminds me of something, but I can't think what. Who's the woman?"

"Esther Graham. She's here, you should go introduce yourself. You remember Ranie, of course."

"Sure—Shaw's spoiled Bulgarian—our star!"

"Ranie's been filling us in on her life in L.A.," said Audrey.

"I was telling Bert I have no idea where Gloria is now," Ranie said.

Being reminded of his affair with the older actress in front of his wife must have been discomfiting, because Bert's face turned the color of the red stripe in his tie.

"I know what your painting reminds me of—that Gertrude Stein portrait!"

. "Yes, there's no question but that I was influenced by Picasso," I said, taking a few seconds to educate them about Picasso's debt to Ingres.

"And did Picasso ever owe a debt to those African masks!" said Ranie.

"How about Whistler, the way he was influenced by Japanese art!" enthused Audrey.

"Too right," I agreed. "I know someone who rips off Monet— big honking paintings just like him, the pond, the flowers, everything."

"How about the cave paintings in Europe—who influenced those artists?" Audrey asked.

Bert laughed. "Do you suppose the second cave painter visited the first cave painter's pad, and emerged with some great ideas to steal?"

We laughed, and Bert went on. "Hey, Natalie, guess what I'm working on? I'm doing plans for city hall, like you predicted. Only it's in Bakersfield."

"Well, nothing wrong with that," I said, touching his glass with mine. "Maybe I should take up fortune-telling."

Madame Lushenka and her tarot cards came to mind, and I felt a chill. Why would a memory of that day nag at me in such a troublesome way? Then I remembered, she had hinted dire things about my marriage. I shook off the feeling, slipped my arm through Ranie's, and asked if she was still acting.

"Yes, a bit. I love doing plays, but I don't get many parts. Carl's a TV director, he earns the living."

"Really, Carl? What kind of things do you direct?"

"Mostly sit-coms—have you heard of *The Washingtons?*"

I reminded them I'd been out of the country.

"It's just the highest-ranking black sit-com on TV, Nat. He's a multi-talent, this guy."

"If you're gonna talk about me, I'll go get more champagne," said Carl, and left.

"Wanna see pictures of our kids?" Ranie took out her wallet and showed me three handsome children. "I'm always after Carl to find some television work for me, but he wants me to stay home and cook."

"Did you and Jock make it, back in New York? I never heard from you, you traitor!"

"Nat, I'm so sorry. I was terrible about keeping in touch, even with Mama. It was just—we never got married. Jock was having a struggle, and I got some small parts off-Broadway, but it was tough.

There were a thousand other actresses just like me back there. After Jason was born things went from bad to worse."

"What's he doing now?" I asked. Not that I cared. I had never liked the man.

"Jock died of AIDS. I heard it from a friend of his who lives in Westwood."

"My God. There's another family here with someone who died, Fia's son Eric."

"It's claiming thousands of lives. Nat, I have to tell you—I admire your talent so much. The show is wonderful, *so* worth coming up for!"

"And you're more beautiful than ever!"

Ben tapped me on the shoulder. "I think you'd better come greet one of your old buddies."

I headed for the front of the gallery, but before I could get there, Nikki breezed in.

Whenever Nikki made an entrance anywhere, everything stopped, and tonight was no different. Talk ceased, glasses froze in midair, everyone became motionless. Her sister Ethel trailed behind her with a man I'd never seen before, and we met in the middle of the room.

"Nat—*sweetie!* We drove all the way up from Palm Springs just to see your show! You owe us gas money. This is my husband, Dr. Joel Moorstein. Joel, these are my friends, Ben and Nat Newbury. Nat, you remember my sister Ethel."

"Pleased to meet you," said Dr. Moorstein. "We had a helluva time finding this place. Where can I get a drink?"

Nikki looked fantastic. She was wearing a black suit with a nipped-in waist and wide shoulders, and was covered in jewels; a diamond-and-pearl lapel pin, a pearl necklace, and diamond-and-pearl drop earrings. Her jet black hair was cut short and draped over one eye. She'd had a facelift and had almost no laugh wrinkles. She looked wonderful, not as good as she'd looked fifteen years ago, but very, very good. She still hadn't had her nose done, thankfully. It was the same as in my painting.

Ethel had always been a pale imitation of her glamorous sister, with close-set eyes and thin lips. She *had* had nose surgery; now she had a turned-up button that didn't go with the rest of her face, and made her upper lip too long.

Nikki's new husband was a chunky fellow, and he and Nikki seemed to be a congenial couple. Of course, Nikki was always congenial with her husbands in the beginning.

I asked if her father were still alive.

"Yes, but he's got leukemia, and a new hip that won't heal. He's meaner'n hell. I don't know how Ethel stands him, she goes over there all the time."

Ben came over to chat with Nikki. I apologized and said that I had to keep moving. I went into the side gallery. Austin Everhardt had stayed longer than I'd expected, and he was standing with his head bent, conversing with Oliver's assistant. He said, "Natalie, you have a wonderful body of work here. It's helpful that Oliver dated everything, gives the viewer a good overview of your career."

"From you, my dear Austin, those are treasured words!"

I walked over to Esther and Hubert, who were in front of my self-portrait.

"What do you think?" I asked.

"Oh, Nat," Esther said, "I think it is the best thing you've ever done! What made you decide to do this? Where were you when you painted it?"

"I was in France, and going through a hard time. It's all smoke and mirrors."

My lips trembled as I spoke. I was about to crumble, and on the verge of weeping. Any reserve of poise and serenity was beginning to melt away, and I knew I couldn't keep up the pretense much longer. I had to make an effort to stand; a strange languor had overtaken me, and I felt my eyelids drooping with the onslaught of fatigue.

It must have been evident, because Hubert put out a hand to support me.

With some sort of uncanny sixth sense, Esther said, "Not you and Ben—"

I knew if anyone offered me sympathy, I would go to pieces.

I won't give in, I told myself. *Not yet.*

Ranie and Carl came into the room, and Carl tapped Oliver on the arm. They spoke, then Oliver escorted them to the back showroom. It looked as if Oliver might sell something.

I had been drinking champagne and socializing for an hour and a half, and I needed to be alone. As I walked toward the bathroom, I felt something rustle in my pocket, and my fingers found the note.

The hateful, damnable note. The note I had known about all evening, but had shoved into a back corner of my consciousness. I went in the bathroom, locked the door and read it again. At last I allowed myself to let go of my emotions, allowed myself to sob for several minutes like a little child. There were one or two knocks on the door, but I ignored them. Eventually, I put the note back in my pocket. I blotted my tears and tried to wash away my blurred mascara. I did the best I could at repairing my face, then returned to the show.

The crowd was circling around the edges of the front gallery, exchanging loud chitchat. I wandered into the empty space in the middle of the room and stood there alone, stilled and silent—like a tragic ballerina at center stage, with clusters of energetic dancers swirling and pirouetting around her.

I couldn't continue to ignore the thing Ben and one of my friends had done. I had to know who it was. I heard Hana's loud chuckle, and my eyes searched until I found her. It couldn't be Hana, could it? Hana was extremely intelligent, but the language of the note was too smooth, too confident. I shook my head violently from side to side, trying to shake away jumbled, incoherent thoughts.

Why did I have all that champagne—I needed to focus!

Hana was out of the question. I was positive her code of ethics wouldn't allow the slightest breach of our friendship.

That left Fia, Amanda, Ranie, Nikki and Rosie.

My eye was caught by Fia's white hair across the room. She looked old now, but once she had been young and desirable. It could be Fia; the words in the note could easily be hers. But she would never have betrayed me, would she? She had introduced me to Oliver, recommended me to her friends for portraits.

But Ben had always been so fond of her.

My eyes found Amanda. Al had his hand on her back, shoving her a little, trying to get her to stand in front of her portrait so he could take a picture, and she was laughing and shaking her head no. Probably didn't want anyone to see the contrast: the beautiful, slender Amanda and today's whopping jumbo version.

I hadn't seen Ben talking to Amanda all evening. That was nothing new—I remembered how he'd eluded her at the Pebble Beach party. Could it be guilt? Amanda—the young, gorgeous Amanda—had dropped me completely when she was divorcing Tom—it might have been a sign that she was bedding my husband. She'd been sleeping around a lot then—the young stockbroker, the young headmaster. Maybe she'd only liked young guys. I think there was a kitchen contractor mixed in there somewhere, too. And of all of them, could there be any doubt that Ben was the most desirable?

This was all so asinine!

Where was Ranie? I swiveled my head around, looking. Over there, with her son Jason. I hadn't talked with Jason since he'd arrived; hadn't had a chance to thank him.

Had Ranie slept with Ben?

Such ingratitude, such treachery! My enchanting model, my radiant actress! I had helped that girl; taken her to lunches and lectures, done all those frigging stage sets! And I had made her a gift of the portrait, the best one I'd ever done!

It *couldn't* be Ranie!

But if she'd lied . . . oh my God! She'd been carrying Jason when I did her portrait. Could he be *Ben's?*

I felt sobs start deep in my chest, heard small gurgling sounds erupt from my throat. Probably someone saw, or heard. But they couldn't hear the sound that came from deep inside, the sound of my psyche being cut in two and hanging, dangling and bloody, inside me.

Just then Jason walked over and told me he'd enjoyed the show, but he had to leave. I don't know how, but somehow I had the presence of mind to thank him for delivering the painting when only seconds before, I'd suspected my husband of being his father.

Out of the crowd noise, I heard Nikki's raucous laugh. I pivoted until I found her standing with her husband—was this her fourth, fifth?—and Ben. There she was, my prime candidate. Nikki always slept with whomever she pleased, but I was sure she wouldn't have done it. She loved me! She would never have been that disloyal! The three were standing in front of her portrait, and Joel and Ben were both grinning. No wonder Ben had wanted to make love to her, Nikki was so much fun!

To make me even crazier, now she and Ben were all over each other. Her hand was stroking his cheek, and he was patting her on the hip. Everyone was having a wonderful touchy-feely time.

I turned away, my thoughts returning to the rest of the suspects.

How about Rosie? Where was she? Oh yes, in Montana! My brain had temporarily switched off. But I knew it couldn't be Rosie—the most loyal and compassionate of friends. My bosom buddy.

I realized I had been standing in one spot for some time, the shadowy dancers in my imaginary ballet swirling around me. I forced myself to snap out of my gloomy reverie, and walked over to the refreshment table, downed another glass of champagne in three long gulps, and asked the bartender for another glass to carry with me. I had to get to the end of the evening without breaking down.

I began to mingle again, but was careful to stay away from Ben. As my movements became more spastic and my laughter more manic, he kept darting looks at me, and I knew that any minute he was going to come over and try to calm me down.

Fia approached, peered into my face, and asked, "Are you okay, Nat?"

"Oh, you mean my eyes! Well, like a boob, I stuck the mascara brush in one of them a few minutes ago. Guess I'm just nervous!"

I forced myself to converse with Marlo Werner and her husband. They had been the first to arrive and were still here. Marlo had a million questions. What had France been like? Was I still painting? Could I come for dinner?

Suddenly, standing with Marlo in front of her portrait, it occurred to me to wonder why I'd decided the note-writer was one of my seven beloved friends. I remembered the written words. *"Nat and I are so close, and I do love her."*

That was why. I didn't have the same relationship with Marlo or any female subject that I'd had with those seven.

The evening wore on. I looked at my watch; the show had been going for two hours.

I was standing near the door saying goodbye to the Werners when Rosie walked in. With her was a tall, teenaged boy wearing khaki pants and a windbreaker. She grabbed me and held me close. "I got back early, so I drove all the way home from the airport, picked up Paolo, and here we are!"

I was so glad to see her that I didn't even ask who Paolo was. She was lovelier than ever; her figure slimmer, her eyes more luminous. She didn't have the tired expression she'd worn in Montcerny.

Paolo looked familiar. I wondered if he was a relative, or possibly one of her young patients.

"Glad to meet you, Paolo." Giving her another hug, I said, "Do you realize how long it's been since we've seen each other?"

"Ages," she said.

Her tone was flat. She might have been talking to anyone—the dry cleaner lady, the drug store clerk. Was I wrong, or was she less excited at our reunion than I was?

"And who is this handsome youngster?" I asked, still smiling.

"This is my son." She waited for a beat, then said, "I wanted to surprise you."

Her son.

What kind of news was this? My body froze, and my mouth dropped open.

How could she have kept something like that from me all this time? In all the years, why wouldn't she have written, called, sent a telegram? More especially, why didn't she tell us when she was in France?

I was unable to think of anything to say. Finally I blurted out, "Well, you've surprised me, that's for damned sure!" I turned and walked a few steps away.

Good friends do not keep such secrets. Good friends may omit telling you what they owe on their credit cards, or that a pet died. They do not neglect telling you they've had a child!

I thought, *Wait until Ben hears this!*

I stepped back, trying to forgive. "Everyone's been here for hours. Look, here's Ranie!"

I walked her and Paolo over to Ranie. Rosie and Ranie seemed overjoyed to see one another, and the questions came thick and fast.

"Are you still in Berkeley?"

"Where are *you* now?"

"Still acting?"

"Still shrinking?"

"This is my husband."

"This is my son."

"Your *son!*"

I went to find the Housemans and Rina, all of whom were in the small gallery. I said, "You wanted to see Rosie—she's here."

They followed me, and after they'd had a few minutes of conversation, we went looking for Esther and found her in a quiet corner of the rear gallery. Esther and Rosie embraced, and we stood around the wheelchair and reminisced about Esalen.

I remembered that the Housemans had led one of the groups. "Remember that game you led, the one with the imaginary bags full of oranges and jewels?"

I noticed Ben showing Paolo around the gallery, gesturing and supposedly discussing my paintings.

It was unnerving how much Rosie's deceitfulness had upset me. I wasn't in a jovial mood, but the others were laughing about Felix Von Papen, the angry psychiatrist, and about the astronauts reaching the moon that weekend. Rina didn't say much. I think she'd had something going with Von Papen, maybe that was why she was quiet.

"We all got something positive out of that weekend, I'm sure of it," said Rosie.

I relented, joining the discussion. "Remember, Rosie, how you got your rocks off being stroked by peacock feathers in that Sensory Awakening seminar?"

"And how you finally took your clothes off in the hot tub!"

I saw Ben introducing Paolo to Fia. He seemed more animated at that moment than he'd been all evening.

Nikki was preparing to leave. I didn't want to say goodbye to her so soon, so I walked her to the door.

"Where we gonna eat?" Joel asked.

"I don't know," said Nikki. "Where do you wanta eat?"

"How about Trader Vic's?"

"That dump? It's probably not even open anymore."

"Well then, how about Ernie's?"

"You gotta be kidding—it's been closed since Kim Novak almost drowned in *Vertigo!*"

Ethel tried to get a word in. "There's a nice little place just down the—"

Nikki interrupted. "Nat, *you* tell us, where should we eat?"

"I don't know," I said. "I've been out of the country. Let's ask Fia." Fia and Abner were leaving too.

"Nat," Fia said, "is this the Nikki I used to hear you talk about so much? Great portrait, Nikki! And I love your hair!"

"Thanks! I should go grey like you—you're gorgeous. Nat says you'd know a good place to eat."

"Well, the restaurant at the Magnolia Hotel is good, but I can't think of the name. And Fleur de Lys is wonderful, but you need a reservation. How about Stars?"

"That's it!" Nikki threw her hands in the air. "Nat, can you and Ben join us? Come on, join us!"

I said, "We'll try, but there are a lot of people I have to talk to."

I didn't say, *I can't come because I'm getting a divorce right after the show, and you're the one responsible!*

"Oh sure," laughed Nikki, "Miss Diva! You're gonna stay here and milk this for all it's worth!"

Laughing in spite of myself I sputtered, "Get out of here!"

I walked through the thinning crowd, joining Rosie at the food table. Ben was standing with his back turned, immersed in a discussion with Oliver and Jake.

"Ben, come say hi to Rosie!" I called.

He turned and started to walk toward us. When I saw the way he walked, his head lowered, that was when I knew.

Suddenly the floor seemed to rush up at me, and I had to steady myself against a wall. I think I swayed slightly, and Ben reached out to catch me. Digging my fingernails deep into my palms in an effort to gain control, I gradually returned to normal.

No, not normal. I would never feel normal again.

Again, I was having to confront a loved one's treachery.

How could I have existed for so many years in a state of oblivion? It was only a few hours since I'd first discovered the note, and I'd spent an entire evening suspecting everyone but Rosie.

I turned and searched the room until I found Paolo. I let the realization dawn; he had Ben written all over him. He was tall and lean, with the same shock of black hair, the same slanted eyes.

"Doesn't Paolo look just like my dad?" asked Rosie. She wore an expression of such innocence, I wanted to slap her .

"What?"

"Paolo. Don't you think he looks like my father?"

I looked from her to Ben and back again. This, then, was my punishment for Juan. But these two had slept together way before Juan!

"No, I don't," I said. "I don't think he looks like your father. I think he looks just like Ben."

I heard Ben draw in his breath, and Rosie put her hand on his arm.

I left them and headed for the office in back, where Oliver and Jake were smoking. I bummed a cigarette from Oliver and lit up, sucking in all the poison I could. When Oliver said that Abner Rankin's sister had asked about commissioning a portrait, I had to pretend I cared.

I said something, I don't remember what. It was all bogus, because I was certain I would never do another portrait as long as I lived.

I barely remember how I got home that night; I think Hana and Bill took me.

Ben sneaked home later and slept on one of the couches in the living room, but the next morning I asked him to leave. Our last encounter was without words. Instead of speaking, I handed him a piece of paper which said: *Please move out.*

He looked at me and opened his mouth to say something, but didn't. I was glad to see that he looked as if he hadn't slept. God knows I hadn't.

By the end of the week, all his clothes and personal things were gone. Nothing was left but a few objects he'd accumulated in our years together.

Two days later, I called and asked Oliver if he and Jake would see that all the portraits were returned to their owners when the show came down next month. I couldn't face seeing my friends. I'm sure Oliver could tell from my voice that something was wrong, but I didn't want to burden him with my marital woes. He probably knew something had happened when the show ended and Ben and I left separately.

"We'll be glad to," he said. "The show is a great success, people are coming in droves!"

The shock of Ben and Rosie's treachery kept hitting me with incessant, stabbing blows. I went over the years of our marriage, every one of the twenty-eight years Ben and I had been together, and tried to think—what had I done to deserve this?

And what were my alternatives now? I considered forgiving him completely and making an effort to forgive Rosie, but every time I thought of them making love, the bile would rise in my throat, and kindness and mercy would go out the window.

That time I had come back from L.A. and the kitchen cabinets weren't finished, in fact barely started.

All those business trips to New York.

All his July weekends at The Trees.

It went on and on, new waves of brutal fact hitting me in the gut with sick-making comprehension.

Had I known? Perhaps I had, deep down. But loving him so much, not wanting to lose him, not daring to question the strength of my marriage, I had thrust all doubt aside. And not just once. I remembered my long-ago suspicions about Amanda and Ben— actually seeing them at lunch in San Francisco, the rumors Fia had brought to me. I would never know with certainty about Amanda, but the fact of Rosie and Paolo was inescapable. Like a fool, I had immersed myself in my painting, assured by Ben's supposedly unceasing affection. It wasn't until those last months in France that he'd dropped all subterfuge, and it was then that I reached out to Juan.

Solitude was again my refuge. I spent a lot of time in bed, tossing about in the covers. I threw Ben's pillow into the hall, then retrieved it and stuffed it into a closet. I drank glass after glass of wine, staring like a zombie into space. Sitting in the kitchen with the lights off, I obsessed about all the years they had deceived me.

Now I knew why he'd been so cold.

Now I knew everything.

As I drank, my mind was awash in experiences I'd shared with my husband—happy meals at home, dinners out, parties, picnics. We had shared the typical things—worries about his job, our finances, my portrait career. I had been so sure it was a normal marriage!

Who was to blame? I had been unfaithful, but Ben had shut me off long before that. I rationalized that my sins were comparatively trifling—*I* hadn't had a child and kept it a secret for fifteen years!

All those weeks in Juan's studio and our courtyard, all the deception I had so artfully contrived—had Ben known? Had he been humiliated too?

Probably.

My thoughts rolled around and around like a circus clown tumbling a ball. He had been so cold for so long, I defended myself, I couldn't be blamed for looking for love elsewhere.

Letters arrived from Ben every other day. I didn't open them.

The day after the show, Fia called, wanting to know what was up, but I said I couldn't talk. Whether I confided in anyone or not, though, I was sure the news of our breakup was spreading.

The curator at St. Adolphus College called, saying she wanted to start planning my children's portrait show, but I said my plans for the future may be changing.

After that call, I disconnected the phone.

The pile of letters from Ben collected in a tray on the hall table. I would pass them on my stumbling trips from the bedroom to the kitchen or bath and back again.

I only went to the grocery store when every last cracker crumb and shred of cheese had been eaten and every bottle of wine drained. I couldn't paint, couldn't draw; couldn't read. I would buy magazines when I went out at night for food, wine, or cigarettes, but I wasn't able to look at them without making a connection between every couple with Ben and me—our marriage, our love, his body, his smile. *Look at that young couple having drinks on their patio. Doesn't she know that he'll probably two-time her? Look at that happily married couple, showing off their new home. Don't they know what disillusion is ahead?*

Slowly, over the next two months, my sanity returned. I began to eat, and to take calls from friends. As soon as I plugged into the world again, Hana called. She knew something had happened, since she and Bill had driven me home that night, but she didn't know exactly what.

"I have called and called you, Natalie. Please tell me what is wrong! Remember how you helped me—you must let me help you!"

"I can't, not yet. I'll call soon."

Esther telephoned from Sutter Creek and said she'd been anxious to congratulate me on the show.

"Sorry, I had the phone disconnected."

"So, there is something wrong, isn't there, dear. You don't have to tell me. Keep in touch, dear Natalie. You know I love you."

Amanda wrote a long letter of congratulations about the show (no doubt she'd heard nothing up there in Yuba City) and Nikki wrote inviting me to Palm Springs. I heard from Ranie, too, who wanted advice on framing the painting she and Carl had bought. I didn't answer their letters. I couldn't face telling anyone. I wondered if everyone already knew about Ben's long liaison with Rosie, and about the boy. They had all been here while I'd been in Europe, and I thought probably Fia knew, if anyone did. She had so many connections, or maybe Ben had confided in her.

But none of my pals had acted differently that night. None of them behaved as if there was some secret they knew about and I didn't!

One late morning, still in my nightgown, I walked to the hall table, picked up the letters from Ben, and took them to my unmade bed, where I sat shuffling through them. I put them in order by date, took a deep breath, and opened the first one:

Dearest Natalie,

I know there is no way you can forgive me now. I can only hope that sometime in the future, you can. Why did I take you to Europe when I knew Rosie was going to have my child? For a simple reason—I was a coward!

I was escaping from something she chose, something I didn't want. I urged her many, many times to get an abortion. I said I would not be a father to her baby—that she shouldn't expect it. But she insisted she wanted the child; that her life would be fulfilled that way. She said she didn't want or need me to be around, and I couldn't persuade her.

I love you, Nat, and I always will. I want desperately for our marriage to continue. I won't say any more now, except please let me come back— don't throw away all our years because of this.
—Ben

I started to sob. Tears pouring down my cheeks. I picked up the latest one, mailed only two days ago.

Dearest Nat,

I can't believe you are still refusing to speak to me. I have done nothing but worry about our situation—and start my new job, which comes with plenty of worries, believe me!

Please, when I call next time, don't hang up.

I still love you. I still want to come back. I don't want to have a life with anyone else.

You are my love, always and forever.
—Ben

CHAPTER FOURTEEN

TAOS

I flew to New Mexico and cried for days on Mamaw's shoulder. Listening to my story, she couldn't have been more patient and kind. Then I woke up to the reality of my life, and began to realize that I needed to start over.

Even though she was three years past retirement age, my lively aunt still worked eight hours a day in Española's town library. She had no transportation, so when my spirits picked up a bit, I rented a car for a few solo trips into the countryside. One of the places I drove to, climbing up through the Sangre de Christo Mountains, was Taos.

Taos has a lofty reputation as an art center. Tourists travel here and to Santa Fe all year round just to buy art.

I parked and walked through the streets, looking in one gallery, then another. I soaked up the atmosphere, noting that the people were friendly, prices much more reasonable than in California, and the air fresh and invigorating. I spent another day driving around the Enchanted Circle, eighty-four miles filled with historic landmarks. The high alpine scenery was gorgeous, but I saw many signs of poverty. Roadside shacks with old cars going to rust, barefoot children along the road, waving at me for attention. I waved back, and drove on. I saw the exterior of the Taos Pueblo, the Rio Grande Gorge Bridge, an old ghost town, and much more. At the end of the day I was so intrigued by the area, I knew I could make a home here.

So I did it. I wrote Ben that I wanted a divorce, and told him that as soon as I'd established residence, I was starting proceedings in New Mexico. I said I would come back soon and clear out my things.

A week later I flew into Oakland, rented a car, and spent six days getting everything ready for the movers. I packed my tubes of oil paints, jars of paint medium, acrylics, acrylic medium, and brushes of every size and description. I packed my camping stool and toolbox, and all the equipment I used for outdoor sketching. My large blank canvases would be expensive to ship, but they'd be much more expensive to buy. After all my art supplies were organized, I packed my clothes and other necessities or near-necessities that I wanted to take. There was nothing I was emotionally attached to in the kitchen, save my coffee grinder and food processor, so I packed those.

Out of feelings of nostalgia for a vanished love, I left one of Esther's pots for Ben.

On the third day, thinking that I might see some papers that belonged to me, I rummaged through Ben's desk in the den. It was filled with bills, old check stubs and ledgers in which he kept track of money we had earned and spent. The drawers were chock full of mailers from art shows, newspaper clippings, old calendars—paper detritus from years of living in one place. In one drawer there was a pile of old photos, so I sifted through them to see if there was anything I wanted. Here were snapshots of the other artists and me on the day of our group art show in Berkeley, along with pictures of Hana and her kids. There were shots that Ben took of Hana after her accident; she was leaning on her crutches and waving at the camera.

And there was a picture of Ben with his arm around Rosie. It must have been taken years ago, because he was wearing the moustache he'd had in the seventies. Ben had only kept it for that one summer, when I was visiting Esther in Sutter Creek. He'd shaved it off soon afterwards, said he was tired of it. He and Rosie were standing in front of a famous inn in Mendocino. Rosie had her head thrown back, laughing, and Ben looked happy as a pig in shit.

It tore my heart out and I went into a funk, unable to think about packing any more that day.

The gall of it—the duplicity! My feelings of hatred for Rosie doubled, then tripled. Their affair had not been a few unplanned couplings, but a contrived intrigue, with me as dupe. *Me as fool, sucker, chump.*

I don't know who took that snapshot, but the good thing about finding it was that it strengthened my resolution to leave Ben. I no longer had any doubts.

I went into the living room, retrieved Esther's other pot, and packed it with its mate. If I had my way, he would never see it again. As for the snapshots of him with Rosie, I burnt them in the fireplace along with his letters to me.

My emotions teetered back and forth. On the one hand, there was my compulsion to torch Rosie's family vineyard, along with every building and shed on the property.

At the other extreme, I tried to visualize myself giving the pair my blessing.

I never did either. But one night, somewhere between sleeping and waking, I was visited by a memory. I saw that tall, mystical young man in the Haight, the one with blood on his white robe. His words were straight from the New Testament: *"Judge not, and you will not be judged—condemn not, and you will not be condemned; forgive, and you will be forgiven."*

I woke up, and the next image that flashed in front of my eyes was Juan and me, naked and sweaty, on the floor of his studio in France.

Eventually I decided that forgiveness was not possible, but you have guessed that already.

Before I left, I needed to give Ben some important papers I'd found when I was clearing things out: insurance documents, the deed to the house, etc. By now, I knew we would have to sell. There was also the pink slip to his car. There were too many documents to send through the mail, so I screwed up my courage and called Ben at his office. We set a breakfast date for the following day at Millie's Diner, and at 8:30 I was seated in a booth by a window, the briefcase bulging with papers next to me on the seat. I had thrown on a pair of jeans and a striped jersey top. A few minutes later, Ben walked in wearing khaki pants and a black cashmere sweater, looking like a Ralph Lauren model.

My insides tumbled around inside me like jellyfish, just like the old days. He sat down, looked into my eyes, and put his hand over mine. I withdrew my hand and picked up the battered menu. Neither of us spoke, and it was only when the waitress came that we broke our silence.

Ham and eggs for him, toast and coffee for me.

Finally we began to talk. We talked about the sale of the house, how much we would ask for it, which realtor to use. I asked about his job, and he said he'd finally settled in, had even made a few sales. Mostly they had him assisting the manager, which he seemed pleased about. He asked my plans, and I said that I had been to New Mexico and was going back soon. I told him I would stay with Mamaw, or live near her until I got my bearings, and that I was staying there permanently.

I didn't bring up Rosie's name, nor did he. Everything was very calm and civilized, but before the food came, I lost it. I felt blood rising in my face, and had to fight the impulse to reach out and hit him. I half-stood, leaning across the table.

"How could you treat me like that! Carry on with—with—*her*—my best friend—for so many years? *I hate you both!*"

Ben held out a hand to fend me off. "Natalie, calm down. Would you stop and think for a minute? Think about all the times you left, or were working on some art project, with hardly a thought for me and my needs!"

I sat down. Suddenly Ben didn't look like a young, confident man; he looked middle-aged, with a furrow between his eyes and deep lines framing his mouth.

"What do you mean? I was *always* there for you!"

"No, you weren't. You were off with one of your buddies doing one thing or another, having a high old time. Painting, or getting ready to paint. And when Rosie seemed interested in me, I admit it—

I was weak, I accepted the offer. But as I told you, I never wanted her to have Pao—the child."

I ignored everything he said, and began to sputter phrases about loyalty. Loyalty in marriage, loyalty in friendship! I wanted to shout out all the grudges and grievances I'd been brooding about for weeks. But customers were looking our way, and I realized I was making a fool of myself. I squirmed out of the booth, picked up the briefcase, and shoved it hard into Ben's chest. Then I strode out the door.

While I was in California, the only person I saw, other than Ben, was Hana. She was heartbroken that Ben's and my "ideal marriage" had failed, and she was almost as angry at Rosie as I was.

She was thunderstruck that Ben had a teenage son.

"Did you know?" I asked her one evening over Pad Thai.

"*No!* I swear I didn't!"

"Would you have told me if you had?" I persisted.

"Of course!" She put her fork down, and blinked. "At least I think I would. But maybe I would not have had the guts. Maybe instead I would try to protect you from Ben's sinfulness."

Tears welled in my eyes, and she reached across and squeezed my hand.

After that, I told her about Juan. I would have been a world-class shit-heel not to admit my own guilt.

"Thanks be to Gott!" she said. "I guess now you have settled the scales!"

Back in Taos, I fantasized about imitating Georgia O'Keeffe and settling on a vast spread in the desert, but not only could I not afford it, I didn't want to be shut off from the world—I'd been shut off long enough.

I found a small house to rent, stayed in it for six months, then bought a small adobe far enough outside of town for privacy, but close enough to jump into my used Honda and run out for groceries.

I found that my two best friends were solitude and quiet, and as each new day dawned, I felt reborn. Every morning I woke to the sounds and smells of the southwest. The sagebrush and mesquite aromas were powerful, the mountains splendid to see. There was woodland all around: piñon trees, juniper, ponderosa pines, fir and spruce. And the colors! Pale violets, sage greens, and soft browns tinted the surrounding hills with stunning artistry. Every sunset created brilliant hues, streaking the sky with dazzling ribbons of fire.

Making my little house into a home was a joy. The first thing I did was hang a few of my paintings, including my self-portrait. Oliver had shipped it to me when I gave him my new address. Suppressing all emotion, I gave Juan's drawing the place of honor over the fireplace. I didn't have any furniture except for a bed, mattress, and a cheap dinette set bought at a flea market, though Ben had written saying he would ship some furniture when I asked. For now, the paintings made the place look attractive and inviting.

The house had belonged to a dance instructor who gave lessons there for three decades, then grew to a ripe old age and died. Her practice room ran the length of the back of the house. It was huge, twenty by forty feet, and was easily converted into a studio. I removed all the flowered wallpaper, had more windows put in, and painted the walls white. The room had hardwood floors, which had to be refinished. I paid a local handyman to do it, and to install a wall of storage for canvases. Clarence, a Hopi with a dependence on chewing tobacco, did excellent work and didn't overcharge. I put my easel at one end of the room where the light was good, and at the other end I had Clarence build a large worktable like the one I'd had in Provence. This was where I would touch up drawings, work on frames, and cut mats.

Taos is full of artists of every genre—painters, sculptors, weavers, ceramists, glassblowers, printmakers. I decided to take some refresher courses in lithography and monotype in one of the local workshops. The teachers were outstanding, and I fell in love with printmaking. Six months later I purchased a second-hand press and several big metal cabinets for storing prints.

My prints began to pile up. Just as in painting, in my color lithographs I created abstract landscapes as well as totally abstract compositions. I tried to capture the sunsets of Taos in a series of prints that were fairly successful, but I didn't make any sales or try to get into any galleries. Nobody had ever heard of me, and I didn't try to come on too aggressively with the local artists; I had learned my lesson in Provence. I was meeting a lot of creative people, but because of what I'd been through I was more than a bit mistrustful.

After a year or so, even though Mamaw came every few weeks on the bus, I began to get a bit lonely. I finally met a few women artists I would have liked to know, but each was busy with her family, her lover, or other pursuits; none seemed eager to spend time with me. Maybe I gave off gloomy vibrations.

As for the men I met, they were mostly artists, and were either already involved, married, gay, or undesirable in some way. One attractive man whose work I admired turned out to be a born-again, prophesying Christian. Another artist and his ego reminded me too much of Juan.

And so it went. There was no one I wanted to spend time with. Then I discovered that, even though my husband and best friend had abandoned me, my old friend Serendipity hadn't.

On my second Thanksgiving, I invited Mamaw. She'd been traveling in Canada the previous November, and I spent the holiday alone. She arrived on the bus on Tuesday, and as soon as she unpacked, she asked if I would take her back to town the next day.

"There's a new biography of Robert Browning, but they don't have it in our bookstore yet. I could order it for the library, but the city fathers are getting tired of paying for my fixation." Bending down to untie her oxfords, she peered at me over her spectacles and asked, "You do have a bookstore in town, don't you?"

"Sure, and I have to go back anyway," I lied. "I forgot the cranberry sauce. I'll take you to Sofia's World of Books."

The next day I dropped her off at the bookstore and drove to the market, having thought of some things I really did need. I bought the groceries, then drove back, parked in front of the bookstore, and walked in. I was wearing a wrinkled pair of khaki pants and a T-shirt with a picture of a tapir labeled in gargantuan letters: PET OF THE WEEK.

Mamaw was chatting with a blonde man with eyes as blue as cornflowers, and I remember that when she introduced us, she wore a smug little smile.

He said, "Hi, I'm Matt Drexel. I hear you're new in town."

I must have looked thunderstruck, because they both laughed aloud. He called me after the weekend, and by the time Christmas arrived, we had gone out several times.

Matt is a writer. He's working on a series of short stories about New Mexico, and his publisher hopes to collect them in a book. They're set in a sort of southwestern Yoknapatawpha County, and are stories about local ranchers, farmers, Indians, and land men whose feuds have simmered for generations. Matt was becoming more and more nervous about the collection, sorely afraid he was no Faulkner. But he said that his editor had immense faith in him.

Even with Matt in my life, I still thought of Ben. I didn't think I would ever stop loving him, but the pain was easing, just as it finally did with Juan.

Ben and I occasionally corresponded about the divorce particulars, the property settlement, and my few investments, which he still handles. He married Rosie, and they moved to St. Helena. Rosie's parents are dead, and Ben helps Rosie run the winery. I never knew whether Flanders and Schuman's financial reversals affected the Rinaldi's investments, but with the surging growth of the California wine industry, I'd heard that he and Rosie had become quite wealthy.

Rosie and I would never be friends again, but gradually I attained a measure of forgiveness for my ex-husband. I didn't hate him anymore.

One Christmas he sent me a picture he'd taken of young Paolo. The boy was wearing a white shirt and dark pants, and had become remarkably handsome. He was a young Ben, though with a gold hoop in one ear and long hair. The photograph was well lit and sharply focused, so I did a small painting of it and sent it to Ben for his sixtieth birthday.

When he met me, Matt was acquainted with hardly anyone in the Taos artists' community, and I had met no writers, so we were fascinated with the newness of each others' lives. There was a strong sexual element too. The third time we went out he was driving us to lunch. I got turned on by all the golden hair on his forearms, and he could tell. He pulled over, but I said I was too old for necking by the side of the road, so he said, "Okay, we'll go to my place."

We began to be dependent on one another. He made a habit of bringing me coffee while I worked, and he would put his feet up and talk about his writing. He talked about his divorce, too; he said his wife was unfaithful, and more than once.

I told him some of my story, but not all of it, not yet . . . He admired my self-portrait and asked about its origins, but I wasn't ready to share that sad time in my life.

I never knew I could be attracted to a sandy-haired, freckled man—so different from the other two men I've loved. Matt has a wicked sense of humor, and he's kind and generous. Best of all, when I had the flu, he didn't seem to mind seeing me with no makeup, uncombed hair and a runny nose. That's what a woman wants in a man.

But one night in bed he made a reference to marriage, and I felt myself pulling away.

We continued to live apart.

One day I got a letter from Ben, and was astounded at its contents. He said that Rosie had liver cancer, and that she only had a few months to live. This was a complete shock, but when he added that his mother had come to live with them, I was stunned for a second time.

Ben had never had a relationship with his mother! He must be in truly dire straits to reach out to her. In the same letter, he mentioned that Paolo was going through a defiant period, rebelling against school, his dad, and anything else he could find. Ben's phrase was 'total mutiny'. No doubt Paolo was affected by Rosie's illness, but if what I had read about teenagers was true, his rebellion was nothing unusual.

When I wrote back, I tried for a tone of sympathy combined with reserve.

> *Dear Ben,*
>
> *I am so sorry about Rosie's illness. I'm sure you are seeing that she has the best of care, and with the remarkable strides medical science has taken in the last few years, I'm confident of her full recovery.*
>
> *I'm sorry, too, that you're having problems with Paolo. But isn't that typical—a teenager fighting his parents' every decision?*
>
> *I have faith in you, and feel sure you can weather the storm.*
> *—Sincerely, Natalie*

Refusing to be dragged into Ben's troubles was, I thought, completely justified. Things were quieting down, and I didn't want my calm disturbed.

One of the artists I met while taking classes at the Art Center was Sister Camille. A bright, outgoing woman, very talented, and with a lively sense of humor, she was a Dominican nun whose order allowed her to do artwork and sell it. (The profits helped pay for maintaining the convent.) We always took our breaks together on the sunny patio, enjoying coffee and the convent-baked pastries she brought. In turn, I shared my fresh fruit or bagels.

One day, when we were laughing about something, she surprised me with a request.

"Natalie, I wonder if you would ever consider teaching a drawing class, or any sort of art class, to a group of at-risk children. I teach English to them once a week, but I think an art class would be of even more benefit. You have that studio, and you would be a marvelous teacher!"

Curses! I never should have told her about my big studio! Why had I been such a braggy-pants?

I didn't reply right away. Not since Ranie's long ago request for a stage designer had anyone asked for my precious time. My life had always been about *me.*

Me and my art.

Me and my beautiful men.

"Who are these kids?" I asked, dipping a toe into dangerous waters.

"Most of them are minority children, either Native American or Hispanic, but some are white. There are twenty, and they're from families—or *no* family—where there's been some sort of abuse. Physical or sexual—you know." Sister Camille looked away, her scrubbed face a fusion of sadness and embarrassment. "Their names were given to me by Taos Social Services, who called the convent one day asking for help; that's how we got involved. They're all sweet children, except for maybe—uh—Chochmo. He's a bit of a challenge."

Curses again! At this point in my life, I didn't need or want a challenge.

I walked over to the trashcan, threw in my paper cup and napkin, then walked back to where she was sitting.

"Okay. But no more than eight kids."

Sister's face showed panic. "Oh dear! I don't know how I can cut the group down. Oh dear!"

But I was strong. I let a beat go by. "No more than eight."

She smiled. "All right. I think I can figure out how to choose which ones. I'll do it based on their emotional development."

"What are their ages?" I asked.

"Nine and ten. Thank you, thank you! When can you start?"

Two weeks later, I began teaching a drawing class of eight children twice a week. It eventually developed into two classes because later, when I felt more confident, I set up a class for the twelve who hadn't been included the first time. Sister Camille and her nun pals handled all the transportation to and from my house, so I never had to worry about any of that. I was shocked to discover that I liked teaching, so for the second six-week session I decided to teach the 'advanced' first eight how to do some simple printmaking, using my press.

Mostly we did monoprints, a method in which the artist makes only one print per plate, and the kids were delighted with this approach. We used small 12" x 18" plexiglass plates which I bought at the local plastics store; I also donated the printing inks and brayers. However, after the first printing session I decided this was sending the wrong message, so I asked the children to contribute $10 per class. Sister and her nun buddies helped the girls do money-raising projects like cookie and cake sales, and I helped the boys print up flyers to distribute in several neighborhoods, mine included, offering to do small cleaning or gardening chores. One of the boys, Ramon, suggested they offer pet walking and grooming as well, and I agreed that this was a fine idea. My heart melted when I saw the enthusiastic way the kids threw themselves into these jobs.

True to Sister's warning, Chochmo was a problem. He hopped around like a cricket, refusing to stay in one place, and was noisier and more disruptive than the other boys. When the class went outside to draw trees and flowers, he drew cars and fire hydrants, and when I set up a still life arrangement indoors of jars, vases and fruit, he drew the refrigerator, the table, or the printing press. Since he drew everything very well, I decided to give him free rein, and discovering that I was going to be lenient, he became more cooperative.

Most of the time.

Some children were surprisingly gifted, others not at all. Little Conchetta had a malformed hand, so I tried to teach her to draw with the other one, but that didn't work. She made up for her lack of productivity by becoming my chief helper, passing out and gathering materials, or scrubbing the floor if paint or water got spilled. She was an amazingly sweet child, with the biggest brown eyes I'd ever seen, and when Sister filled me in on her sordid background, my heart warmed to her even more.

After a few months, with Sister Camille's help we held an exhibit of the children's drawings and prints. Taos Pueblo Middle School offered their walls, and on the evening of the show, I think I was prouder of the work than the kids were. No parent showed up for Conchetta, but Chochmo's folks were there. His dad was a Vietnam Army veteran in a wheelchair who seemed distant and uninvolved. But the boy's mother's eyes filled with tears when Chochmo pointed to his wonderful drawing of the pueblo, and turned to me, saying brightly, "This is my teacher."

"I think you have a potential architect in the family," I said.

The 'artist's ego' I talked about to Rosie long ago was pretty much buried that evening.

Chapter Fifteen

Paolo

Rosie died only six months after I'd heard she was ill, and Ben called again. He was grieving, I could tell, and didn't stay on the phone long. Other than to tell me of Rosie's death, he wanted to ask a favor. He asked if I could take Paolo for a few weeks. He said the boy knew all about me and my career, and loved the painting I'd done of him. He added that Paolo was a very immature seventeen.

I wanted to stop him and ask, "How much does your son really know? Does he know about his parents' adulterous betrayal of me?"

Ben rushed on, saying that he was at his wit's end, that Paolo was smoking pot, and had made best friends with some of the worst teenage characters in Napa County. Some had police records.

Finally I exploded. "I don't know what you think I can do with a kid like that. I'm not a social worker!"

"I know, but if I can get him to talk to you on the phone, could you invite him to visit? Nat, I'm telling you, I'm at the end of my rope!"

"Let me think about it."

That night I called Mamaw and asked for advice. Should I relent, and take on Ben's son? A misbegotten son, one 'gotten' at my expense.

She said, "Natalie, you know I love Ben. The day you decided to divorce that man was one of the saddest days of my life." She had never said that before. "It seems to me that you could do this favor for him. Rosie is gone, and you needn't spend any more time hating her; it would be to your soul's detriment! But if it turns out badly, I'll get the blame. So do what you want to do."

I spent a sleepless night. I had taken on a bunch of troubled children—did I have to burden myself with a degenerate teenager as well?

I was brushing my teeth the next morning when Ben called. He said Paolo wanted to talk to me. I was beginning to resent the way Ben was stampeding me into this, but I said, "Okay."

A quiet voice came on. "Hi."

I waited for more, but nothing came from the other end.

I said, "Your dad was thinking that you could—I could—invite you here for a few weeks." More silence. "What do you think about that? Paolo, are you *there?*"

"I dunno." His voice was soft. He didn't sound like an angry rebel.

I let another few seconds pass. The last thing I wanted to do was encourage the boy to come here and freeload. I didn't owe him, didn't owe Ben, and to say that the boy was related to me would be ironic in the extreme.

Finally he spoke an entire sentence. "I heard you got a lotta Indians there, and a pueblo."

"Yes, that's right."

"And that British writer, he's buried there? I've read some of his stuff. We had a teacher who was hooked on the guy. We read "The Horse Dealer's Daughter" and "The Fox.""

"D. H. Lawrence, yes. His tomb is twenty miles from here."

I should stop him right now and say firmly, "You can't come unless you follow certain rules. No pot smoking! You have to be cooperative, and say please and thank you!"

Instead I said, "Really? That's great. Well, I could drive you around, show you the sights. But I'm teaching an art class; you'll have to help me with that."

Silence again.

I ventured on. "They're all little kids, nine to eleven."

A long, long pause before he said, "Okay. I could do that, I guess."

Ben got on the phone again, sounding relieved. Relieved wasn't the word. It was more like ecstatic.

Four days later, I met Paolo at the Santa Fe airport.

When he got off the plane, my heart lurched. Here was the son I should have had, the embodiment of Ben. Same graceful slouch, slanted eyes and prominent cheekbones. Even the Mohawk, pierced eyebrow, and black Nirvana Tee shirt couldn't disguise his good looks.

I walked up to him and said, "Hi, I'm Natalie."

"Hi," he replied. We shook hands.

"We've met before, at my art show."

He nodded, looking around. "Yeah, that was a great show."

We started walking, and he didn't volunteer anything else. I didn't offer more conversation, sensing his shyness. I had gathered from Ben's most recent call that this was to be an open-ended stay. In other words, if I chose, I could have Paolo until school started in the fall. Ben wanted him to attend the College of Marin, but said that Paolo refused to make any plans.

"No luggage?" I asked. He hoisted his carry-on into view, and we headed for my car. He didn't seem very happy to be here, but I decided to defer judgment. On the way home our conversation was pleasant, but minimal.

"Good flight?"

"Not bad."

We pulled into the driveway and went into the house. I had enjoyed outfitting the second bedroom with a few things I thought he might enjoy: a Navajo rug that Clarence procured for a minimum outlay of money; a couple of rock festival posters, and a Burro-Wearing-a-Sombrero lamp that I'd found at the flea market. There was room for only a single bed, but Paolo said that was fine. He threw his bag on the bed and treated me to his first smile. I guess he liked the room.

Slowly, we got used to one another. He slept until eleven the first two mornings, but when I let him know that I was an active person and would appreciate his being a bit more "present," he said, "Wake me up, Natalie. I'll get up when you do." Remembering all of Ben's complaints about the boy's behavior, I was shocked at his compliance.

I wanted to take Paolo on the Enchanted Highway, so on his first Saturday we started out early in the morning, raucous birds making an incredible racket as we packed our picnic lunch in the Honda. I didn't invite Matt because I wanted to forge a closer relationship with Ben's son. Up to now he had been rather unforthcoming, to put it mildly, and I hoped that on the drive some of his reserve and shyness would melt.

"We're not going to see everything," I said. "There are some Indian rock pictographs you might like to see another time. And I'm not a hiker, but maybe later on, Matt could take you on one of the hikes."

"Yeah, okay."

We headed north, driving east from Questa and traveling toward Red River, a town settled by miners in the late 1800s, and now a ski resort. We were surrounded by high alpine scenery with spectacular peaks, and the switchback roads made the drive seem like a roller coaster ride. The road we were on went up to more than nine thousand feet, then descended into a valley where there was a sign pointing to a lake.

"My handyman Clarence likes to come here to fish," I said. "He's caught some whoppers."

"You mean that Indian guy I saw yesterday at your place?"

"Yes, he's Hopi."

I was enjoying the drive. I rolled down the windows, breathing in the mountain air.

Gradually Paolo began to open up a little. He talked about his mother, and said that when Rosie became ill, he finally realized the seriousness of the situation. In her last months, he said he'd spent a lot of time with her.

"My dad helped me grow up," he said, his voice hoarse with emotion.

This was hard for me to listen to. I had once loved Rosie too, with all my heart. My eyes filled with tears, and the irony of the situation hit me full on. Here I was, listening to my ex-husband's son talk about his mother, whom I had come to hate. And I was bawling—bawling because her son had been good to her in her last days!

Paolo never once spoke a negative word about Ben, and I'm not sure if he was aware of his father's feelings of frustration. More likely he didn't want me to know about their conflicts. His only other reference to Ben was when he said, "Dad doesn't seem to get it; all my friends dress like this!"

I didn't comment. Kids were piercing themselves, shredding their jeans, and doing weird things to their hair in Santa Fe and Albuquerque too, but not yet in Taos.

I asked about Ben's mother. After his long estrangement from his mom during our marriage, I found it difficult to believe he had finally let her into his life. "Does your grandmother still live with you?"

"Yeah. She's eighty. Dad built her a cottage at the vineyard. I don't see her much, but sometimes she asks me to shop for groceries."

So after all those years, Agatha Newbury had adapted herself to a grandmotherly role. Would wonders never cease!

Paolo had mentioned on the phone that he was acquainted with D. H. Lawrence, so I drove to the ranch. We visited the chapel, a simple shrine for Lawrence's ashes, and signed the guest book together. I gave him a one-minute overview of the Frieda Lawrence/Mabel Dodge Luhan story, which I've always found to be a fascinating tale, then we drove on.

Paolo's most enthusiastic comments that day were about the gorgeous scenery, and the herds of elk and other wildlife we glimpsed. "I've never seen elk before! *Wow!*" and, "Look! Two golden eagles! Natalie, did you know they're the largest eagles of all?"

Angel Fire was another ski area, and where the Vietnam memorial is located. As we drove through the gate, Paolo surprised me by saying, "I've sorta got a girl back home, her name's Francesca. She's got another boyfriend, but she's given me reason to think, uh—I mean I'm pretty sure she likes me more than the other dude."

I turned to look at him. His face was a deep pink.

"But *fuck!*—s'cuse me—she's starting Stanford in the fall, so what chance will I have then!"

I said the only thing that I thought might comfort him. "Ask her, Paolo. When you get home, ask her to choose. If she doesn't pick you, then at least you'll know. You're a real handsome dude and a very nice guy, so why wouldn't she choose you?"

I turned to look at him again, and he was wearing an immense smile. I was dumbfounded. I had no idea that my words could have such power to inspire happiness.

We went inside the modern war memorial chapel. Paolo seemed interested, but made no comment. I didn't think his lack of response was surprising for a young man who had never been in any way involved with war. I spent some time looking at the pictures and statuary, and was as moved as ever by this tribute to Vietnam veterans.

All at once I remembered the night in Paris when the Milfords, Ben and I had celebrated the departure of the last American troops from Saigon. We had been so happy, had drunk our fill of champagne and sung all those American songs.

I opened my mouth to tell Paolo about it, then decided for my own sake not to dredge up an old memory.

We resumed our journey, and finally stopped at a roadside table to enjoy a late picnic lunch: chicken sandwiches, devilled eggs, and fruit punch. Paolo chuckled aloud at the antics of two chipmunks

311

who shared our table, and I realized it was the first time I'd heard him laugh.

It had been a full day, and as we drove back to Taos, I realized that I was exhausted. Good thing I had two days to recuperate before I had to teach. When we said goodnight, Paolo forgot to thank me. Maybe he'd think of it later.

Since it was summer, my classes were meeting three times a week instead of two, and for three hours instead of two. Paolo remembered that I'd asked him to pitch in, and he came into the studio as soon as class started. By the end of the day, I was amazed at how much he'd helped. Chochmo's eyes opened wide when Paolo appeared, and soon the little boy was hanging on his every word. As for the girls, I had never seen nine-year-old girls flirt before.

Were the children shocked at Paolo's piercings and shredded jeans? I saw no sign of it. They no doubt thought he was some poverty-stricken teenager I had taken in.

He sat quietly in one corner at first, then slowly began to make contact. While two or three children waited to use the press, he started entertaining them with scissors and paper, teaching them how to make cutout snowflakes. They were amazed when they each came up with an individual design!

"Time to collect paint tubes, Conchetta," I reminded my helper, as she stood leaning into Paolo's shoulder.

Everyone made snowflakes, and after they left, I Scotch-taped them to the windows.

One day Paolo taught a couple of kids how to do origami, the Japanese art of folding paper. Amazed at his skill, and impressed with his education—D. H. Lawrence! Origami! I asked if he would teach it to the entire class, so he took over for two days. His specialty was birds, and the class learned to create not only cranes, but ducks, herons, swans, penguins and a wonderful flapping bird with moveable wings. All Paolo's shyness had disappeared, and he literally basked in the limelight. I loved seeing his usually serious expression soften to a happy glow.

I called Ben one night after I thought Paolo was asleep. It was late for me, but only 9:30 in California.

"You should see your son. He's teaching my classes!"

"What do you mean? He's not doing that, surely."

"He's got them creating all sorts of winged creatures—herons, penguins and they're eating it up!"

I could hear the note of hopefulness in Ben's voice. His love for his son was evident in the uncertain quaver of his voice. We spoke for a few more minutes, and he said he was busy with the vineyard, that they had problems with some new bug attacking the vines.

Matt got into the act, acting as surrogate uncle. After the three of us had shared a few dinners, he asked Paolo if he would like to visit an Indian reservation.

"That would be rad!"

For some reason, Matt didn't want to take him to the Taos pueblo; he said it was too commercialized. "Every doorway has a sign on it advertising whatever the occupant is selling; art, pottery, baked goods, etc." Instead, he had a good friend, an educator who was 100% Apache, at the Jicarillo Apache reservation on Highway 64. This man had helped Matt with research for several of his stories, and when Matt called him, he said sure, he could take time to show Paolo around.

The question asked at my next class was "Where's Paolo?" I explained that my friend Matt wanted to show him more of New Mexico, and I told them where Paolo was going. They had never heard of the other tribe; I had barely heard of it myself. Paolo and Matt were away for three days; they slept near the reservation in a motel. When they returned, Paolo was bubbling over with enthusiasm, mixed with indignation. He had been captivated by the Little Beaver Pow-Wow, the rodeo, and the dancing, but was full of resentment at our government's treatment of Native Americans.

"After taking all their land, they just hide them out of sight!"

I had heard a lot of this dialogue before in discussions among liberal whites in my new state. The pros and cons of the argument were as old as the U.S. government's first broken treaties. In the case of the Jicarillo Apache reservation, as well as many others, the harvesting of fossil fuels has contributed greatly to the tribes' coffers, but Paolo could see no reason why Indian land should be used that way.

Matt played devil's advocate. "You mean you think the tribes should refuse all those millions of dollars, a lot of which contributes to their education?"

"I think they've been handed a pile of shit!"

Eventually the discussion wore down, and after dessert Paolo left the room. He came back carrying a large tissue-covered package, presenting it to me with a flourish. It was a beautiful tribal basket, with a diamond design incorporating images of horses and deer. I had never treated myself to any of the Indian baskets I'd seen since I lived here, even though I had coveted many.

"Paolo, you can't afford this!"

He sat ramrod straight in his chair, eyes downcast. "It's okay. Dad handed over a big stash of green when I left, and I haven't spent hardly any of it. That basket seemed like somethin' you'd like."

I stood up and hugged him. "You're a prince! Thank you!"

I carried the basket into the living room and put it on the floor next to the fireplace. It looked great there, balancing perfectly one of Esther's pots on the other side.

In mid-August, Paolo decided he wanted to go home; he said he missed his dad. His visit had lasted for three-and-a-half weeks, much longer than I'd expected him to stay. One evening after dinner, he called Ben to say when he'd be arriving in San Francisco. The phone was nearby, and I heard him tell Ben he'd decided he wanted to go to college, that he was thinking of studying anthropology.

"I've gotten kinda interested in all the different kinds of people in the world."

Matt was shamelessly eavesdropping along with me, and we grinned at each other across the dinner table. You'd think Paolo was *our* son.

The next day at the airport, Paolo asked, "Natalie, d'ya think maybe sometime I could come back for a visit?"

His carry-on hung from his shoulder, and he was wearing an unbuttoned blue denim shirt over a Darth Vader tee. His jeans had needed washing several days ago—w*hy hadn't I done that for him!*—and his Mohawk was growing out. Black, stubbly hair thrust out in all directions, and I had to restrain myself from reaching up to smooth it down.

"Of course!" I said. "Certainly!"

"I could bring Francesca. She likes to ski, maybe I could take her to Angel Fire."

"That would be lovely! We'll talk about it later on."

I didn't know if I meant what I was saying. I was beginning to care a lot about this kid, even though I didn't want to. *He wasn't my kid.* But sometimes life works out in dopey, disorderly ways.

We hugged and kissed, and Matt grabbed him in an exuberant embrace. We watched until he entered the boarding tunnel and walked out of sight.

We just kept standing there, getting in everyone's way.

"I thought you were so tough, kiddo," Matt said. "So what's that watery stuff running down your cheeks?"

I'm looking forward to some wonderful things in the future. For instance, a trip to Italy this fall with Matt. It was incredible that in the fifteen years Ben and I lived in Europe, we never traveled to Italy. What bountiful treasures of painting and sculpture are waiting for my eyes to feast upon!

There will be a visit from Hana and Esther next Easter; they've become fast friends, and Claude Milford wrote to ask if I could put them up for a few days, date to be announced, along with little Ben. Pamela is a D. H. Lawrence devotee and wants to visit his shrine.

Claude said that tombs of dead people give him the jim-jams, so he plans to, as he put it, "while away my time eating your food and criticizing your latest paintings."

I feel good about my life. I am blessed with good health—I finally quit smoking!—and blessed with Mamaw, and I was born with some innate talent.

And I have Matt. I may decide to make our relationship permanent. If I don't, I could lose him, but thank God he isn't rushing me. And I never thought I would say this, but now I'm so happy I have children. I only have them for a few hours each week, but somehow I feel like they're mine.

More good fortune—my paintings and prints have begun to sell. I'm represented in a gallery here in Taos, and last week was accepted into a gallery in Santa Fe. Oliver has managed to stay in business, so even though I no longer do portrait commissions, I still have representation in San Francisco.

I miss the Bay Area—the special ambience of the Berkeley hills, the streets of San Francisco, the sun sparkling on the bay. But I've found new challenges, a new lover, new friends.

I've even begun visualizing a new self-portrait. It will be of a woman who knows herself, and whose face mirrors an inner beauty.

A woman on the verge of a spirited old age.

ACKNOWLEDGMENTS

I would like to thank three women: Sofia Shafquat, the editor who first believed in this book; Christl Blumenthal, who generously helped me with the French and German languages; and Karen Mireau, editor and publisher, whose attention to detail in bringing out the novel has been both extraordinary and joyful.

NOTES

The description of Sonia Delauney's work and Passari's published prejudice against female artists are quoted from the catalogue "Women Artists Show; Los Angeles County Museum of Art/LACMA; 1559-1950" which opened in December, 1976.

The lines from *Raisin in the Sun* by Lorraine Hansberry are quoted with permission of Random House.

Lines from *Arms and the Man* by George Bernard Shaw are quoted with permission of Brill Publishers.

ABOUT THE AUTHOR

Marianne Gage is a San Francisco Bay Area artist, teacher, and writer.

Her first novel, *The Wind Came Running,* was a coming-of-age story set in her native Oklahoma. After that came *The Putneyville Fables,* with a plot revolving around a Colorado family's involvement with animals.

She has given readings at Bay Area book clubs, and has made appearances at Book Passage in Corte Madera as well as the Ferry Building in San Francisco.

Forthcoming books are: *Foolish Girls and Reckless Women* and a memoir, *How to Talk to Famous People.*

Gage is married to artist/illustrator Ed Diffenderfer.

To learn more
about the Author
please visit
MarianneGageBooks.blogspot.com

To contact the Publisher
please email
Karen Mireau
Azalea.Art.Press@gmail.com.

www.ingramcontent.com/pod-product-compliance
Lightning Source LLC
Chambersburg PA
CBHW022205010726
47493CB00002B/425